"A FICTION SPYMASTER. JOINS THE SE-
LECT COMPANY OF TOP THRILLER-SPIN-
NERS!"

—*Barkham Reviews*

"FASCINATING AND TOTALLY ABSORB-
ING!"

—*Houston Post*

"RIGHT UP THERE WITH THE BIG BOYS IN
THE SPY BUSINESS!"

—*Publishers Weekly*

TROIKA

DAVID GURR

BERKLEY BOOKS, NEW YORK

The author wishes to thank the following publishers for
permission to quote from the sources listed:

Random House for selection from *A Russian Songbook,*
   by Rose N. Rubin and Michael Stillman. Copyright © 1962
   by Rose N. Rubin and Michael Stillman.
   Copyright © 1962 by Miro Music Corp. Reprinted by permission of
   Random House, Inc.
W. W. Norton & Co., Inc., for selection as reprinted from
   The Complete Works of Gilbert and Sullivan,
   1941 Garden City Publishing Co., Inc. © 1976 by W. W. Norton &
   Co., Inc.

TROIKA

A Berkley Book / published by arrangement with
Methuen, Inc.

PRINTING HISTORY
Methuen edition published 1979
Berkley edition / October 1980

ISBN: 0-425-04662-1

A BERKLEY BOOK ® TM 757,375
Berkley Books are published by Berkley Publishing Corporation,
200 Madison Avenue, New York, New York 10016.
PRINTED IN THE UNITED STATES OF AMERICA

ACKNOWLEDGMENTS *Several people must be thanked for their help with this book.*

At the top of the list, Bill Hamilton: as ex-Moscow attaché and gifted linguist he is responsible for whatever sense of authenticity comes through the Russian scenes. For miscellaneous opinions of the Soviet Navy, I have to thank a very old friend and shipmate, Desmond Nugent. And for a child's guide to the gas turbine, another friend and a former term-mate, stoker Joe Cunningham. All these gentlemen have ranks and titles which I trust they'll excuse me for omitting.

For information on Portsmouth and its history, Mr. P. W. Hallett in the Port Admiral's Office.

For sheer hard work, my typist, Mrs. Betty Parkinson. Words are not enough.

And some bows for loose ends. To Anna Porter in Toronto, who stayed with a hunch, and Marion Wheeler in New York, who backed it up. To Peter Murray of the Victoria Times *for friendship, encouragement, advice, and first glimpses of the strange world of the literati. And to Ed and Gwen, the first to struggle with draft one.*

There's a final person I'd like to thank openly, but can't—*because after twenty years and ten thousand miles she still insists on anonymity. I call her my Latvian, and her fear brings home the difference between them and us.*

December 1978   *Prospect Lake*

For Judith and Pachinko

AUTHOR'S NOTE The newspaper accounts quoted in the postscript are verbatim extracts from official translations.

Russian denials notwithstanding, the event which they describe is fact. The rest is fiction. Any resemblance to persons, etc., . . .

TROIKA

PORTSMOUTH

CHAPTER

ONE

The lights are going down in the Briefing Room. Marshall standing, at his most blandly clerical, is about to speak. *"We are gathered together..."* For a christening. But Christ knows, not in the sight of God. Just myself and the godparents, two transatlantic civil servants with mundane manners for their macabre callings. The liturgy from tape transcripts not common prayer; cigarette smoke instead of incense; a kettle and a pot of tea for holy water. A jar of instant coffee as a gesture to our ally—compensation for the loudspeaker with the shot cone that drives an American mad at Whitehall's small-mindedness. Which is deliberate, of course.

And of course no squalling child. Because we're gathered together in no one's sight to name a year. Because for the spymasters, as for the Chinese, the years must *have* names: 1945 the Year of Gouzenko; 1951 the Year of Burgess and Maclean; '58 the Year of Abel, '63 the Year of Philby.

With any luck when the lights go on again we shall have pinned my name on this one.

Marshall, thy will be done. I shall sit through it, eating pills for the shoulder which numb both kinds of pain. Holding this black scrap in my pocket, thinking of happier times and places.

1

Of tomorrow in California where I shall walk with children on a beach of a cove where the surf falls against the cliffs with the cypress trees. . . .

"Not an inquisition, old boy."

Things have started. The machines are off and running, the first picture is on the screen. Christ! Was I so callow? So ready to salute all that glittered? He never told me they had that shot. Taken twenty years of names ago. Where it began: Portsmouth, on the day before the great arrival. The subject of this report, reporting, aboard HMS *Caliope*. Reporting in accordance with an Admiralty message and blind ignorance to that tall, passed-over, four-ring captain with the stoop, and the unlikely name himself, of Jackson.

"Lieutenant Dravin, sir, for special duties with the Russian visit."

"Oh, yes," he'd said, touching his cap with a cracked pipe stem as I waited rigid at attention. "Oh yes," in a slow English-Irish voice, "Young Dravin. Is your father well?"

Which was the last thing on God's earth I'd expected, and I'd blushed, and then blushed worse knowing I'd started.

"As far as I know, sir—I've been at sea for three months. Are you acquainted?"

Some flicker came and went in damned shrewd eyes. "You could say that"—courteously ignoring the redundancy of the question—"mention the name some time. Know why you're here?"

"Just guessing, sir—the language, I suppose?"

He nodded slightly and looked at me again with the searching eyes. "Same tall spare figure, same hair. You've a strong resemblance. I wonder if they'll notice."

"Sir?" I was hopelessly confused.

"Sovs, of course. Come and join me for a walk." He set off on the endless back-and-forth of the quarterdeck shuffle. I fell in beside him, matching his stride. "You were seven, I think, when you left?"

"Yes sir."

"Old enough for memory? Or is it just history now? What do you think of the Russians—any hard feelings?"

History, memory? My feelings? Too many questions by a

stranger, asked too soon. History was a father's parents and a mother's, all dead of starvation. History was a father purged, an uncle shot. History was blind luck and trouble on the Finnish border permitting an escape. History was hearsay to a seven-year-old.

Not memory. Memory was being dragged through snow, freezing dark. Memory was boots, terrifying overhead, and a dog snarling and a fur glove holding off the frost. Memory was a mother's gloveless hand amputated. A mother dreaming ever since of a St. Petersburg with the Romanovs returned—although in all her life she had only seen a tsar for one instant in a carriage in a square. "But his eyes were so blue and so kind." And his police had exiled her father. And his successors' police exiled her. . . .

Jackson had stopped for an answer.

"Yes sir. I suppose so. Certainly to the regime if not to the people. I think I feel that if my own parents had the guts not to knuckle under, then others could follow suit—and they haven't."

"A positive statement—although the camps never seem to empty, do they?" He let it sting for a minute and then changed the subject. "You got to Dartmouth on a scholarship, I understand. That must have pleased your father. To see tradition continue?"

Had it pleased him? So hard to tell what pleased that gaunt ramrod with the silver beard meticulously trimmed and pointed. Because he was already fifty-one when I was born, and scarcely seen by me either in Russia or out. My mother had lived with me in Leningrad for the years immediately before the purge while my father stayed in Moscow in some unknown capacity.

And after, in England, a place for me in a Good School, and from then on the School father and mother both—except briefly at holidays, when the silver beard would bend towards me and the angular figure would walk like a mantis through the garden asking questions in Russian or French—not a word of English. And never a word of himself and Russia later than the Great War. History and memory ended there apparently. But the day the telegram arrived saying that their Lordships were pleased to inform that Dravin was ripe for Dartmouth—that day, yes, I think there was a satisfaction, and he called me Pesha, which he never did because it embarrassed both of us.

"Yes sir," I said to Jackson. "I think he was pleased. But my expectations of tradition were a bit misplaced. When I first arrived at the college I was looking for Rimski-Korsakov, not Francis Drake."

"I can imagine. And what do you know of the modern Soviet Fleet?"

"Not more than the annual look at *Jane*'s, sir. With their past performance, I think most of us find it hard to take them seriously—although their sub fleet seems to be getting a little out of hand."

He got the pipe going again, looking absentmindedly for somewhere to throw the match. "Well, young Dravin, you ain't seen nothing yet."

He squashed the flame dead and dropped the burnt-out body into a pocket. "We'll be taking them seriously enough, and we should have started yesterday. Their building program will beat us and the Yanks combined within ten years."

Anything to keep the subject professional and not personal. "Have you been watching them long, sir?"

"Since twenty-five, in Vladivostok. The first time I met your father, as a matter of fact. Then off and on—Allied observer for combined ops in the Black Sea against Odessa. Archangel. Finally on the beach in Murmansk as a convoy coordinator."

"That must have been bleak, sir."

He looked contemplative. "One of the few times they were civil. That was our honeymoon period, when the common struggle against the fascist onslaught had been successful, and the docks were covered in American guns and butter up the yin-yang. It didn't last long!"

"Did you see much of them in action, sir?"

"They really didn't get a chance. The old cruisers stuck up the Dardanelles just lobbed bricks at the beach, and the newer construction in the Baltic ports couldn't spring loose. You probably know that half their hulls were ordered from German yards and never got delivered after the outbreak of war?" He looked hopefully at me.

"No sir."

His nod was resigned to ignorance. "Buggers hadn't learned much from experience—exactly the same thing before the first war—but they won't be caught a third time. All built at home now. Moving submarine hull sections in cardboard boxes on river barges . . . I'm wandering. What did you ask?"

"In action, sir."

"Some. Mainly Northern Fleet DE's full of piss and vinegar, but no patience. Out at thirty knots and ping for half an hour, and then bugger off home, leaving the rest of us to carry on for ten days without them. But balls enough—losses of submariners trying to run the Baltic minefields without benefit of sweepers were appalling."

We turned in unison on to another leg. "They've got a new C-in-C," he said, "but I don't suppose you know that either?"

I tried to earn a run for the name. "No longer Kuznetsov?"

"No." Another wicket flattened. "A man called Sergei Gorshkov. But it hasn't been widely promulgated. I met him too"—he broke off—"I seem to be giving the impression that I've done it all."

"No sir. Jolly interesting."

He gave me an amused look. "I'm afraid one becomes intolerant with age. It's the same with any ardent collector—we expect the world to share our passion." He studied his watch. "Christ! I have run on. I've got a meeting with the flag in ten minutes." He stopped where we'd started, beside the brow.

The interview was at an end. I paused. "Something else?" he asked.

"Well, yes sir. Just what will I be doing?"

"Of course. Stupid of me. Aide to Admiral Tredennick when he meets the Russians."

CHAPTER

TWO

Tredennick. Second Sea Lord. Admiral of the Fleet, Knight of the Garter. VC for beaching his destroyer to take troops off at Dunkirk. With the guns at Crete, Taranto, Dieppe, and D Day. The face present in the pictures as the flag came down and the sun set on Empire around the world. I felt physically ill. A need for drink was instant and acute and I headed for the staff officers' mess in the old Royal Naval Academy building. Holding up a corner of the bar was a former messmate, Jack Douglas, a horse-faced humorous man.

"Have a wet, Dravers," he said; and one thing led to four and then he suggested we go to a pub off Lion Street for dinner. "Hot pie and secretary—can't miss."

Ever the optimist. Under a mackerel sky we walked out through the Gate into Queen Street to watch the tax money being poured down the drain by dockyard mateys covering rust on triple time.

Douglas was repetitively unimpressed. "Bloody nonsense for bloody bolshies. Bloody town'd be like Versailles to the bastards even in its raw state. Bring on the birds!"

We arrived at the Shoveller's Arms, a small lopsided brick building glued to a stone foundation predating the birth of the modern dockyard in the late 1700s, and made our way into the dining room—a low alcove off the public bar with only four tables. The ceiling was curved and planked like the stern gallery of an old ship of the line and the bulkhead festooned with the mementos of two centuries of naval warfare. Douglas cracked a joke with the landlord and ordered up Guinness, and veal and ham on credit, and gazed around for business partners. A large-breasted bird had taken roost for the night beside the bar.

"Up five hundred, Dravers! Look at the lugs on that." He stood up for the charge, rocking the tankards. *"Bugger me!"*

"Now?" I asked.

But he was long gone—and in the opposite direction from the bird. He came to an emergency full astern alongside a solitary little male figure at a table in the darkest corner. The inevitable net of charm descended with a slap on the back.

"Come over."

"No, no. Can't butt in."

"Balls!"

A shrug of defeat. Douglas dragged home the catch. "Dravers—an authentic relic. Crabby.

"Crabby—Peter Dravin. One of the palace guard for B and K."

The relic extended a small hand with as much enthusiasm as an apparently violent attack of the trots allowed.

"Hi, Peter."

A lot of war types carried the American idiom as another medal—or in lieu of any. Why Douglas made such a fuss over five-three of bandy legs and flat feet was unfathomable. An old brown suit jacket hung like a chopped-off cassock from surprisingly wide drooping shoulders. The forehead sloped sharply backward from thick dark eyebrows in crumpled worried waves. A subdued beaten little bugger—the standard-issue unsuccessful salesman. With one exception. The leading edge of the palm and little finger of his right hand were like leather.

"Wingers in the Med," said Douglas. "Haven't seen each other for years. When, Crabby? Coronation Review, I suppose?"

The other nodded cautiously. Douglas leaned over to me in boozy conspiracy. "Crabby snapping feelthy pictures of Sverdlov's bottom."

Another flinch from internal pain. "In the press?" I asked him—he was the naval officer's image of the fourth estate.

Douglas guffawed. Droopy managed a slight grin.

"Pressed maybe, but not press."

I tried to digest the conundrum with the pie, but beer was blocking the nerve ends.

"Should have been more formal in the intro, Dravers," said Douglas. "Lionel Crabb—Buster to bill collectors, late of Her Majesty's Royal Naval Volunteer Reserve."

Impossible! That this threadbare flattened little figure could have ridden one-man subs into Taranto—tossing off limpet mines and underwater double Nelsons. A George Medal winner. Crabb was gracious about it but I felt a complete arsehole.

To cover embarrassment I got up and went over to the bar for another round. It wasn't my night. Turning back with the glasses I tripped over the rail at the corner, spilling the drink of the man standing there.

"Christ, I'm sorry." I made attempts to mop up the mess. "At least let me buy you another."

He shrugged me off stiffly. "It's okay." Crabb's Americanisms were infectious. "No sweat."

The rest of the meal passed well, although the water shallowed when I asked what Crabb was doing now. There was a noticeable pause while he looked for depth to maneuver. "Oh, not much, you know"—in his soft voice. "I'm just waiting to hear from a man in town about something quite good, actually—in yachting charters, which would be my cup of tea rather." And pigs might fly! Making the world safe for democracy has never paid much to the saviors.

The conversation fell back on the old days when the game could be played without rules and referees, and the ante could be a horse's neck or a pocket battleship. I should have found it exciting but instead I was turned off and depressed.

I made an excuse of my watch. "Midnight! Sorry, chaps, I've got to be on the floor by five-thirty."

Douglas offered the usual attempts to stoke the fire but Crabb made motions of departure as well.

"Sorry, Dougie"—waving apologetic hands like fins, "my own day promises to be a little involved."

We said our goodbyes, and I left them at the table, Crabb looking after me quizzically, head on one side, eyebrows pulled down, his face a mask of resigned sadness like a picture of the dying Christ.

An unforgettable face.

CHAPTER

THREE

Friday, the eighteenth of April, 1956, arrived in Portsmouth on the heels of my hangover and a cold southeaster.

The dentist's-waiting-room feeling of my approaching ordeal with the Second Sea Lord blocked out any intelligent grasp of the details covered at the meeting of the liaison team held in *Caliope* at 0600. After it was over Jackson took me aside.

"You'll stay with me until Sir Roger arrives this afternoon. Join me for breakfast."

"I haven't much appetite, sir."

He studied my wan appearance, "Well, get something down. You'll be sopping up gin like a sponge all day. And the Admiral's not an ogre. Keep track of the right spoons at dinner and who knows what vistas may open." He made a kind move to get my mind on happier things. "Where did we get to in our chat yesterday?"

"Admiral Gorshkov, sir."

"Of course. Gorshkov. In charge of the combined ops in the Crimea, which I think I mentioned." He lifted some sausages from a silver chafing dish onto his plate. "We found we were simpático—they've always had a sneaking admiration for an RN upbringing, you know—and I think, too, that the naval side was trying to compensate for the bloody-mindedness of the baggy pants. After Stalingrad the Red Army thought they could wipe themselves with barbed wire and enjoy it."

He took a mouthful and looked in some surprise at his fork. "These bangers are really not too bad—sure you won't try one?" The grease was coagulating on the end of the sausage. I shook my head.

"Wasn't he taking a bit of a chance, sir, palling up like that?"

"I suppose he was—but as they had the staggering total of half a million blue jackets in army trousers, and he bossed 'em, he carried quite a weight. He was valuable."

"That didn't stop them in the thirties!"

"No," he agreed quietly. "It didn't. But it nearly cost them the match." His voice quickened again. "You know, there's an interesting story—apocryphal I'm sure—that Gorshkov took a collection of fishing smacks and turned them into tank landing craft."

"How the hell could he do that, sir?"

"Magic wand, for all I know. Extraordinary man, though. Only thirty-two and an admiral—younger than Nelson." He shook his head, but whether at the promotion or the conversion, I couldn't tell.

The voice pipe shrilled behind him. The steward took out the plug and listened for a moment. "Officer of the Day, sir. Russian squadron in sight."

"Very good. Tell him I'm coming up to the bridge." Jackson put down his napkin and stood up. "Well, Gorshkov owns the whole lot now. Interesting to see what sort of an innings he makes of it."

Portsmouth was ready. The tugs waiting. The gap to hold *Ordzhonikidze* the cruiser, three football fields long ahead of us, open at the jetty. The massive bulk of the British flagship, the carrier *Bulwark,* lay beyond the gap, her ship's company mustered at Ceremonial Divisions—caps flat, chin stays down, collars lifting in the cold wind across the flight deck. Buglers perched high up on the island superstructure.

"Three minutes to salute!"

The firing broadcast speaker at the four-inch mounting forward of *Caliope*'s bridge crackled with the cautionary order. I heard the slamming of brass casings being set into the loading racks.

Behind us, the dull crumping of the guns of the Spithead battery were already rolling up the harbor carrying with them the shrilling of the bosun's calls from the ships out in the stream.

"The echo of wooden walls," said Jackson. "I wonder if she hears it?"

"Sir?"

He pointed. Across the jetty, HMS *Victory*, Nelson's flagship and heart of the navy, rested in her drydock cradle, dressed overall with bunting—flying again after a hundred and fifty years the immortal message that every man would do his duty.

"'*England Expects!*' Dravin, just look at that!" Jackson's face showed rare animation. "In the war, after the shore buildings were blitzed, she really was the flagship. An extraordinary sensation then, to report on board when our backs were to the wall and we were waiting for Hitler to try the Channel. One could imagine preparing for Trafalgar." He turned back out to the harbor and the Soviet squadron, now closed to a thousand yards.

"There's the difference between us. One signal like that's worth all the commissars and agitprop together. They just can't understand that tradition can't be sold like scotch in Piccadilly. You should see the slogans in Red Square!"

"Two minutes!"

And a sudden stir below us on the jetty, the spectators' heads all turning back to crane over the linked shoulders of the security troops. Led by a six-foot-four drum major swinging a silver mace, the marine and naval bands wheeled into view.

"They're late," I said.

Without music, only the quick-step rattle of the snares snapping them along, the white pith helmets, belts and gaiters seemed to move unaided in the shadow of the wooden hull.

Then in an instant, altogether they were out into the sun, scarlet, white and blue, the mace hurled arcing and flashing high above the major's head. With a spine-shocking thud the great bass drums under the tiger skins cut in. Answering the call of the guns, hammering the beat. And as the mace fell back the brass blared out in the march of the Royal Navy, "Hearts of Oak."

"One minute!"

"Well done—bang on," said Jackson. "I hope you're making notes—something for your grandchildren—present at history. The first state visit of a Russian since the tsar."

But I was watching the cruiser and her *Skoriy* class destroyer attendants through the glasses. "She's got nice lines, sir. Italian."

"Stole their architects." He waved an arm at the jetty and the flags flying from the dressing lines. "You're a bit of a cold fish, Dravin. Nothing conjured up? No hair on the neck from all this? No Russian feeling?"

But British schools and British ships had seen to that, had seen by the jibes and laughs that the Russian new boy played down any glad hand, any gee-whiz display. Self-defense knew now by instinct not to let the Russian through the carefully fitted British skin.

"Early days, sir," I said.

He looked briefly at me and then shrugged, raising his own glasses. After a moment he said, "Coincidence always surprises, doesn't it?"

"Coincidence, sir?"

"No sense of Russian fatalism either, eh? The name, Dravin—*Ordzhonikidze*—the death of Grigori Ordzhonikidze resulted in your being here. It put the purge in high gear—"

"*Fire!*"

The deck shook. Blue-white smoke and cordite fumes engulfed us, stinging and blinding, the blast drowning any speech.

"*Fire!*"

The surface of the harbor was hidden by the rolling smoke, the air filled with the concussion and the cutting note of the bugles calling and answering across the gap. I blinked. The wind, gusting, tore a sudden hole in the screen. For an instant that shook memory by the roots a vast red star banner appeared, dominating the morning.

"*Fire!*"

The star had vanished.

My eyes watered in the smoke. My neck twitched from the bite of the wind. Only from that—from wind and smoke. Not from the martial crashing of the Russian anthem played by British troops as an immense bow glides in total silence from the smoke.

"*Fire!*"

Force the eyes to stay unblinking as "God Save the Queen" echoes back across the water from a Russian band. Freeze the fingers steady at the cap peak as a Union Jack breaks from a

Russian masthead. Keep silent as the thousand pigtailed Russian sailors cheer.

"Cease firing."

And make a Russian hiding as an Englishman believe, if he can, that the throb in the throat was reflex. The swimming eyes just cordite. Not emotion.

The water boiled up around the cruiser's stern.

"She's stopped," said Jackson. "Very neat. Let's go and say good morning." The boiling eased, the surface calmed. *"Dravin!* Come along!"

"Sorry, sir. I was watching the destroyers."

"Yes," he said. "Of course."

The first encounter with my fellow countrymen was an anticlimax.

"Remember," said Jackson, "we want to hold some cards back. No lingo with them. Just watch and listen. It'll be a long game."

The meeting was held in *Bulwark*. Roughly a dozen Russians showed up, of whom three spoke some English. The rest showed a comprehension ranging from dim to blacked out. Foreigners. I felt nothing in common.

At the bar to get drinks, I found myself next to the carrier's first lieutenant, a bluff two and a half with a moldy beard. "Happy lot of sods," he said. "Look like stewards caught buggering each other in a locker. Half-guilty and half-ready for a punch-up." He sabotaged a coffee with a triple brandy and nodded at a particularly silent type in a corner. "Give this to that frozen bastard—a GRU lovely. Hundred to one."

"GRU, sir?"

"Military Cinderella of the KGB, boy."

Paranoia was therefore mutual, but with more drink we soldiered without problem through logistics to jollies for the troops.

Then, *"Nyet!"*

To all the dances and bitch lists of waiting girls. Only the soccer games received approval. For the rest the Russians demanded bus tours of any bombed slum relics of the war.

"Why?" I asked Jackson.

"Raise the level of social consciousness of the men. Show them how much better things are at home."

The first lieutenant grunted. "Only level of social bloody consciousness of any damned hairy arse I ever met reached crotch height."

Jackson nodded gently, "The efficacy of the persuasion, Number One, may well be doubtful." He wiped the grin off my face, "Oh yes, Dravin—Sir Roger will see you in forty minutes."

A slight smartening in the attitude of the gangway staff when I asked to be taken to the Admiral's cabin helped to preserve a fine balance between flaking out and throwing up until I was left between two huge and totally indifferent marines.

I rang the buzzer. A sharp-looking chief petty officer with a shock of red hair and steward's badges pulled back the curtain. "Lieutenant Dravin?"—and without waiting for confirmation, "Admiral will see you now, sir."

He led the way through a large formal outer cabin full of chintz and mahogany. We came to a halt in front of another door.

"Admiral's sleeping cabin sir"—saying it like a casket salesman in front of the solid bronze with velvet lining. He knocked on the sepulcher.

"Come in." At least the voice seemed human. I took a last deep breath and entered the portals of heaven.

There were two men in the cabin. One was Jackson, looking as though he visited every afternoon. The other sat facing me behind a severe metal writing desk, his jacket on a hook to one side between us. The weight of braid threatened to break it off. Above the gold was a square foot of medal ribbons and on the opposite lapel, by itself, the small purple ribbon of the Victoria Cross. In real life the photographic good looks had been pushed sideways by a wound and a long white trail of scar tissue over his left eye and cheek.

"Lieutenant Dravin, please sit down." A three-fingered hand indicated a chair next to Jackson. "Sorry for such short notice—my present flag lieutenant never got beyond 'my friend will pay' in anyone else's language. It must have been a bit of a problem for you to get organized so quickly." He raised an eyebrow and a slight smile. "I suppose that's what we expect, though?"

I wasn't ready for speech. He recognized the symptoms.

"Under normal circumstances I'd offer you a drink, but I understand you've already been entertaining and we must husband our resources. Perhaps you'd care for a cup of tea and some toast?"

Freedom of choice seemed absent. I accepted.

"Our first job," Tredennick went on, "is to make it appear that we've been together more than a dog watch, so don't jump out of your skin if I address you by your Christian name." He shook his head at Jackson. "Not that we're fooling the buggers, I'm sure. They'll know him right down to his drawers. *You think I'm joking, Dravin?*"

My smile had been a reflex—out before I could grab it back. His voice had chilled to an icy intensity.

"Let me assure you, I do not exaggerate. And you're a damn fool if you judge these people on the basis of half an hour at the bar. Understood?"

I could only nod.

"Good. Khrushchev in particular may look like something just off the midden—but believe me, there are no flies on him. As for his boozing, our attaché who was with them on the trip over is damned sure it's an act. I don't doubt it. If I had that bunch on the Kremlin wall behind me I sure as hell wouldn't take the chance of being pissed. We'll see. All you have to do is shut up, play dead to the language and sop it up like a blotter. Anything, whether you think it trivial or not. Captain Jackson will be the judge of that. Clear?"

"Yes sir."

"Good. Phillips!" The steward was back through the curtain like a magician's assistant. Tredennick stood up. "Monkey suit in ten minutes. And Dravin—Peter—we'll have our first drink with Messrs B and K in thirty." The bathroom door closed behind him.

Jackson's voice shook me gently back to life. "You'll manage. Don't take them on at vodka."

CHAPTER

FOUR

We were in Russia.

Not from the warship smells of paint and fuel, and not from the obvious badge of the new order—a scarlet carpet with gold sickles stretching ahead of us. But again—from memory. Carried by tobacco. Russian. Distinctly Russian.

The carpet covered the linoleumed deck of the main companionway leading into the superstructure. At the carpet's end, ahead of our guides—the Squadron Commander, Kotov, and the CO of the cruiser, Karisov—ahead of them a ship's watertight door veneered with mahogany panels waited.

At the precisely required moment, without a hand, without a word the door opened silently inward, and we were face to face with Lenin—that face known to me as Christ's to a Christian. Not in the flesh, but staring like a gilded wooden messiah on an ikon, from a four-foot-square portrait on the far bulkhead. Ranged on each side of the godhead, as acolytes, were the inheritors—B and K.

Like opening the bathroom door and finding the Queen, there are some things for which one cannot prepare. Thank God I had nothing to do but be pulled along like a dinghy in my Admiral's wake as he did his duty as his country expected: Pleasant, calm, correct—as hard as a marlinspike.

Bulganin was bowing—strangely enough, obsequious, almost groveling—fitting the first lieutenant's analogy.

Not Khrushchev.

Standing on the right hand of god the father, rocking slightly
from foot to foot, he was an egg in a jacket: bursting in the middle
and sagging at the ends. Nervous with first-night nerves. Twice
putting out a hand at the wrong spot—but not embarrassed. Obviously psyching himself up. A sumo wrestler pawing the mat in
his corner and watching his opponents with eyes swimming in fat
lids like pearls in an oyster—light gray pearls not missing a trick.
And then with a mental toss of salt over his shoulder he was
off—out of his corner and marching straight up to Tredennick.

"So, Admiral"—through the interpreter—"they tell me you
British admire our ship. Just like my admirals, all the same—all
in love with dinosaurs. Madness. One of our rockets—"

He had simply dropped his glass! Not hurled it—jush released
his fingers from it. Solid lead crystal. Onto a marble table top!

"Gone." No emphasis whatever, totally ignoring the exploded
shattered mess. "Just like that. So you take the toys, Admiral, and
we will keep our submarines and our missiles. What do you say?"

The trainers and hangers-on were left outside the circle. K
ranged deliberately alongside, shirt front to shirt front, deliberately
touching. Specks of spittle at the corners of his mouth.

"I don't know if she's a good ship, your Excellency," Tredennick the ex-gunner fired first, "she's sure as hell a long one."

K tipped his head to the interpreter.

The man was stuck and embarrassed. He explained awkwardly
in Russian. "The length of the ship, Excellency . . . two hundred
fifty meters? . . ." His voice trailed off. He seemed to be looking
directly at me for help.

"No." Like my smile with Tredennick, it was out without
thinking. "Our naval expression for nothing to drink."

"Nothing to drink?" The interpreter's eyebrows rolled over the
top of his head. A word of explanation to Nikita. The piggy eyes
narrowed, swiveled at me. Widened.

Sweat poured down my sides.

And then with an explosive roar of laughter that sprayed the
Admiral's jacket, K grabbed his arm, laughing in great heaves,
dragging him over to one of the bars. The pudgy hand waved
expansively across a hundred bottles, a thousand. *"Nothing to
drink!"* He grabbed a champagne glass off a silver tray, dashed

the contents into an ice bucket, shouting at a steward, "Vodka! Up, up!" He handed the brimming glass to Tredennick, eyes gleaming wickedly. "*Now* we drink. Toast. Royal Navy. Small fleet, big men." In one toss he downed a tumbler.

Tredennick matched him. The tension broke, the whole wardroom was drinking, following the leaders. Except for me, waiting for the earth to open for my faux pas with the interpreter.

"Our ship is too long for you also?"

Behind me I heard a deep voice, strongly accented, but trying hard in English.

I turned. A big man. Impressive. Two inches taller than my six-one and much broader. Hair shaved high up the sides like the rest of them. Uniform rather sloppy. Peasant shoes from a state store.

He was looking back at me with equal frankness. The blue-gray eyes were steady, the gaze direct. For the first time a Russian behaving as an equal. He laced some champagne with a splash of brandy and held it out. "I am Yanov. You are needing big guns for support."

He grinned.

And although I knew he was a hand-picked party man; knew that his brains were washed by a lifetime of Young Oktobrists, Pioneers, Komsomol, Dossaf and Christ knows what; knew that the clashing systems could never allow us to be friends—yet despite the charade which was the visit, despite all the games by the bosses, the grin was real, warm, impossible to resist.

"Dravin. Peter Dravin. Cheers!"

"As you say it. Cheers!"

New glasses replaced the old. "On Admiral Kotov's staff?" I asked.

"*Nyet*—with my cousin. What you call Flaggy, no?" Attached to one of the staff admirals, obviously. He grinned again. Took a drink. "Fighting fascists would be better than making small words at these meetings, eh?"

"Christ yes." Relief at finding a friendly spirit loosed caution. "My first show at this level."

"Show?" He was apologetic. "My English . . ."

"Is excellent. I mean that I'm just a sailor—this is the first time I have met such important people as their Excellencies."

He laughed, oblivious of the eyes our interaction was attracting. "Just a sailor. Good. Me also. Three months only since at sea. I miss old life too."

"Northern Fleet?"

"*Da—Kola* frigate. I hope for Baltic next time."

"A girl friend in Baltisk?"

"*Nyet*—a mother in Leningrad. My home."

"Leningrad!" Coincidence always surprises, Jackson had said just this morning. But it was hardly astonishing that out of a coastal city of millions Yanov should share my birthplace and profession.

"Ah—you have been to Russia?" The wide face was ingenuously interested. "You know it?"

I was saved from floundering for an answer by the languid intervention of one of the Whitehall people. "Flags, I'm about to suggest to our hosts that we should make a move. You might confirm transportation."

"I'll go aft—"

"No need, no need." Yanov held my arm. "You may see here." We were stopped beside the ornate cabinet of a 1930 radio Gramophone. It matched the rest of the place—more like a set from Uncle Vanya's dacha than a naval wardroom. Yanov opened a pair of shutters. A TV screen showed a clear picture of the gangway area.

"Useful," I said. "Perhaps you'll be able to reduce your regiment of guards on the jetty. We find that with television people stay at home."

He dropped an arm on my shoulder, heavily. I'd gone too far with the wisecrack. But then he laughed. "You are saying the price of freedom is eternal vigilance, I think?"

"Very good." For a moment I was impressed by the speed of repartee. But of course the bastards would have been run through a hundred dress rehearsals before they were allowed out to play.

Yanov pushed a button. Vignettes of shipboard life appeared in rapid succession. Cooks peeling spuds in the galley; a patient in sick bay; a seaman reading a barometer on the bridge. The last shot looked out over the fo'c'sle towards the carrier. She was hard to see in the dark.

"You are wanting light?" He pushed a second button. A powerful spot lamp flared across the gap between the ships.

"Most impressive." I reached past him and jabbed the channel selector. The screen went black. But not quite. A shadow in a shadow. I pushed the light switch.

We were looking at the mud of Portsmouth Harbor fifteen feet below the keel. A swirl of bubbles appeared at the top left-hand corner of the screen and then Yanov was blocking it with his body.

"I congratulate you on the clarity of the picture." Tredennick, B and K in tow, had come up behind us. "Perhaps, your Excellencies, we should proceed to dinner?"

With half a million iron curtain émigrés totting up old scores, the British Government wanted no repeat of Sarajevo in the home counties. We played musical cars on the jetty—stuffing dummy bosses into the Bentleys with flags on at the head of the parade, while the real things climbed into the unmarked units halfway down.

The decoys roared off in a flurry of blue lights and sounding brass from the police bells, leaving our half of the convoy to accelerate in anonymity along Ordinance Row. The Admiral's finger tapped in a pattern against the window, his nonchalance stripped off. "Bastards!"—savagely.

Was I to reply? The silence lengthened. He must want something. "They certainly knock it back, sir."

"What?"

He hadn't even known I was in the car. Now he did. His head turned, the long scar flashing on and off under the street lights passing in the rain. "Your knowledge of language was blatant, Dravin. And inexcusable."

Christ, let me die! I flushed until my eyes bled.

"Well, it's done." His voice was back to normal—incisive, cool. "Before you feed, get hold of Captain Jackson. Tell him that *on no account whatever* is there to be underwater surveillance of the Reds! And I want him to meet me immediately on my return. Got that?"

I repeated it back parrot fashion, unable to grasp the implications, oblivious of the nature of the play.

By the time we were out of our car, the Russians were already gathered in a threatened herd, facing outward at the crowd surging against the bobbies flanking the Guild Hall steps. From his face, Khrushchev's fuse was sputtering.

Behind the locked police elbows strange mixtures of fanatics intermingled. Ladies of the Primrose League in pearls passing out pamphlets on conservative principles to Docker shop stewards in red ties. Rough, haunted, Central European voices bellowing *"Butcher of the Ukraine go home,"* drowned out ragged cheers of *"Power to the Workers."* And weaving wildly through them all, a gangling black scarecrow in clerical collar and gold cross waved a six-foot wooden spoon and howled warnings in a high-pitched Oxbridge accent against supping with the devil.

"Hyde Park Corner gone mad," Tredennick said as we walked across to join the party. They turned to go up the steps, Yanov's bulk between Khrushchev and the loonies. Then Tredennick and myself. A mass of bodyguards walked backwards in front of us—hands on triggers, faces on the crowd.

The moment was unclear. One of the bodyguards just ahead of me tripped and fell. A policeman in the cordon reached to help him.

"Antichrist!"

A bleating shriek beside my shoulder. The mad vicar, eyes wild with a martyr's exaltation, spoon clutched in both hands high above his head to strike down the abomination, was lunging from the crowd at Khrushchev. But the blow was falling straight for Yanov.

Instinctively my arms went up to deflect it. I felt a sharp crack across the neck. The shaft snapped. I straightened up and the bowl of the spoon clattered onto the cobbles at Yanov's feet. His hat was knocked askew. He straightened it, gave me a slight nod. A disguised salute. Our eyes locked. The madman was dragged off chanting a psalm.

"Near thing. Well done." Tredennick wiped the slate clean.

The dinner couldn't match the first act and I've forgotten it—the speeches, the responses, the surface insults and the veiled threats.

Khrushchev remains, standing in his shoddy gray suit and cheap red ribbon in a sea of splendid uniforms and jeweled women, being eyed by them like a caged bear in a zoo.

But from the heart of the Russian masses—the black people to my father's generation—he'd clawed for a lifetime to stand there. And no amount of snobbery or democratic wishful thinking could disguise the central fact: the bear had the cage door open— and held the key.

The convoy formed in reverse order to pour the guests home to bed. Bulganin tripped at the top of the gangway and fell into the arms of the duty quartermaster. He waved beerily down to us on the jetty.

Khrushchev stood dead-faced beneath the guns and watched him. Then his head turned: Past Bulganin, past the gangway staff, past Tredennick. And stopped. Looking, inexplicably but unmistakably, at me.

CHAPTER

FIVE

"Your shake sir!"

I snapped on the light over the bunk.

The Players-package face of the duty quartermaster stared down at me.

"Thanks. What sort of day, P.O.?"

"Not bad, sir. Front's gone through and the glass is rising."

I was out of the bunk with a bound and with only the slightest twinge from last night. Head through the scuttle for a few breaths. Still good. A new sun shone on old hulls against the far shore, a light breeze dried the evening's puddles, some scattered cumulus scudded overhead. An English day to show Russians an English spring and London Town.

Briskly en route to *Bulwark* I felt just a touch less bright. *Victory,* with her traditions still in place, restored me. As Jackson said, the difference between them and us.

Phillips the steward was setting out plates. "Morning sir." He handed me the itinerary for the day. "Admiral would like you to give this to Mr. Yanov yourself, sir. He says to tell him there are some changes underlined in blue pencil—and when you come back he'd like you to join him for breakfast, sir."

"Thanks, Chief. What time does he sit down?"

"Seven, sir."

"Right. I'll be back in twenty minutes."

Not unless I got oxygen in one hell of a hurry. All the worst symptoms hit at once—legs shaking, something with large claws perched on my head biting me behind the ear. The distance between ships was too short for recovery. I set off for a once-around-the-flight-deck, gulping air and swinging arms excessively. The downstairs side of the navy was already hard at it. Blue boats making the first runs with the junior hands across the harbor, a destroyer squadron next to us getting underway for a day's exercising in the Channel, going astern with short blasts on the siren. Short blasts! *Dear God!* I grabbed for a handrail, my eyes squeezed shut with the pain.

I opened them to see a swirl in the water by the bow of the outboard *Skoriy*. The turn of the tide—or a cormorant getting breakfast.

But the bubbles were too large and too familiar after last night. I was staring into the broad, blank, flat glass face of a diver—for a second. Then he was gone. Not with a duck dive and flippers—just gone.

One of ours? It couldn't be. Not after the Admiral's night orders. I looked up at the Russian yards—no warning hoist. No tender alongside. They were taking a good chance at having their boy's head clipped by a blue boat. I half-turned back to tell our officer of the day. And didn't. The sortieing destroyers blew their top again and mine with them. And what the hell was one peasant more or less?

A platoon of them slung about with side arms was still clockwork strutting on the jetty to stop runaways as I went aboard the cruiser. A young Mladshiy lieutenant spattered with enameled tin medals met me.

"Sudar?"

I explained slowly in English what I was about.

"Dass! Yessir!" And he fell out of sight behind a hatch cover. Green as hell. The medals were probably for tying a granny knot twice in a row. I could hear him talking hurriedly over a telephone. He reemerged. We waved hands at our hats for a third time.

"Please to come, please." Scruffy little bastard. He turned and led the way forward along a route with no concessions to drunks or landlubbers. I fell in a pace or two behind the dandruff desert of his dark serge jacket. One of the guards took station behind me.

And with a neat, deft, sharply precise click of the latch removed the safety of his Kalashnikov automatic rifle.

And for the first time I realized the exact fact of what I was. An ex-Russian RN snob on exclusively Russian territory with a Russian gun barrel in the back.

I tried to keep my mind occupied by recording details of armament and equipment, but anything of interest had been covered under white canvas or gray plywood. The sense of claustrophobia intensified.

Out in the clear beside the AA batteries on the water side and level with the bows of the *Skoriys,* the tension lifted.

"*Battle stations . . . Battle stations. . . . All troops to quarters . . . All troops to quarters!*"

The shattering blare of an alarm klaxon ripped the morning open. A thousand screaming gulls exploded from the garbage scow alongside. Trained to react as quickly, my escorts half-wheeled, poised. Turned back. Indecision was slicing them in half. Go? Stay? Is he a friend? A foe? The eyes narrowed. The hands steadied. The decision was made.

Foe!

But still just speculation racing through my own mind. A tripped breaker? A game of Nikita's? An excuse for an incident? Was I the excuse? *Rational Dravin. Be rational.* But a 7.62-mm hole pointed at the stomach impedes reason, produces a unique sensation in the gut.

The alarm stopped. As suddenly as it had begun. The first gulls settled back. In the startling quiet, metallic heels clattered along the steel deck. I remember thinking how odd—because of the hazard from sparks or slipping at sea.

The guttural voice was back on the broadcast speakers. "Alarm concluded. Resume your duties. Resume your duties."

The muzzle drifted away from my solar plexus. I let out my breath, flexed my hands. The ensign smiled nervously. Shrugged. "Exercise, is all . . ."

But the clattering was louder. Upon us. Six armed men, doubling around the corner from the fo'c'sle skidded to a halt in a semicircle, weapons extended like spikes on a slave collar. I was the slave. A short tank of a man with a face dug out of a cliff about three thousand miles east of Moscow was the overseer. Warrant officer's rank—Michman.

"Back! back, back, *back!* Against the funnel. Around. Turn around! Arms out. *Out!*" The Neanderthal son of a bitch wasn't inhibited by protocol.

"Arms on the funnel!" His Asiatic Russian as poor as his manners.

The ensign, my escort, his titular superior, was arguing frantically. Not as frantic as I was. I could hear scraps.

"Hold him! He sees nothing."

"On whose order!"

"*Dermo!* Out of the way, arsehole!" Behind my back Russian voices shouting. More boots thumped on the deck. More muffled Russian anger. A smell of fish.

From the garbage scow?

Or from the past with the swearing and the clumping boots? From the black frozen foulness of the hold of a fishing boat stopped and rolling in the Baltic while the Russian questions fired overhead and an invisible stick of a man held a boy's face tight into a tobacco-stinking beard.

Now, nineteen years of British training later and I was still huddling from a bellowing Russian thug. But in the sight of Nelson's *Victory?* Not bloody fucking likely! A shaking anger blotted out even the thought of a bullet in the neck.

"*Yedlash.* MATCH!"

I bawled their own filth back at them, dropped to the deck, rolled out and up into a crouch to face the bastards from the front.

But face what?

Not this! The Michman frozen above me like a grotesque ballet dancer, his Nagant revolver clutched by the barrel. The young ensign, wan, pimples red against white, mouth hanging open. The troops looked from the raging warrant officer to my British uniform in utter confusion. And across the deck, twenty feet away, was Yanov. Between us, shuffling clumsily towards a door into the superstructure, three matrosi—half-carried, half-dragged an old bundle of oilskins.

I knew it wasn't. The bundle passed by my head, three feet off the deck, and I looked into the crumpled face, at the closed pinched eyes, the little wrinkled washerwoman's hands, the baggy green rubber skin, the hanging bandy legs. Our true frogman, Lionel, Buster, Crabby.

Crabb.

Then Yanov jerked his head. The cortege vanished into the hull of the ship; my assailant lowered his arm; his companion closed his mouth; the sailors pulled back. And I stood up.

"Yanov," I said, rude to use no rank, but better than driving a fist into the flat face of the Michman. "Yanov, they've ruined this suit."

He commiserated, appalled, insisted on helping, explaining. "Disgraceful . . . a diving accident . . . regrettable . . . the duty watch, untrained. A mistake to set the alarm. Peasants. And your uniform. I must get our valet, instantly." All the while looking straight at me. Not a hint that anything had teetered on the edge. Throwing it all onto the stupidity of some simple sailors.

"Your itinerary." I handed it to him, casually, hoping the hand was steady. "You will note that changes are underlined in blue. Please draw them to the attention of their Excellencies."

"I must show you to the gangway."

"Yes," I said, "it's too early for a drink."

He said goodbye at the brow. We saluted and I turned and started down to the jetty.

"Tovarish Leitenant!"

The Russian words made me look up automatically. "Congratulations on your vocabulary—like one of us." A trace of the grin appeared and vanished.

I'd been crude; no Soviet youth should be told to do things like that to his mother—and the expressions on the peasant faces had been gratifyingly surprised. So much so that I would have answered Yanov with smile of my own.

But all I could think of was poor bloody Crabb having his one last round at saving our world and being slung about like a dead fish as final payment.

The Admiral was cracking the top off an egg and not impressed by my appearance.

"Where the hell have you been?"

I began to beat about the bush.

"*Action alarm?* You mean circuit testing?"

"I think it was the real thing, sir. They had live clips when they held me up."

He put down the spoon. "Were you in a roughhouse?"

"Just a bit, sir."

"Sit down." He cranked the handle to the exchange phone at his elbow. "Officer of the Day . . . Captain Jackson in *Caliope*, right away." He turned to the steward. "Coffee with something in it. And take his kit. You've got thirty minutes."

I passed my jacket through the serving hatch. It slid shut, leaving us alone.

"Eat." The naval god across the table poked nursery fingers of toast into the egg until noises from the marines in the lobby announced Jackson.

"Sir?"

"Bad. Start again, Dravin."

We got back to the alarm. "How did you know it was Crabb?"

I explained about my dinner with Jack Douglas two nights earlier and about our meeting with the diver.

"Sweet Jesus, what a bloody mess!" Tredennick drummed his fingers on the tablecloth for a minute. "How sure are you that the Reds don't know that you recognized Crabb?"

"Not more than fifty-fifty, sir."

"Then we must assume that they do know. Bloody shithouse!" He stabbed the spoon through the bottom of the empty shell.

"Was he dead?"

"I think so, sir, but again I can't be sure."

"Any sign of injury—blood? Bruises?"

"No sir."

"Was he blue?"

"No."

"Suit ripped?"

"No."

He looked at Jackson. "You're my witch doctor. Was Crabb doing it for us?"

"No sir. Not naval."

"Quite sure?"

"Positive."

"Any ideas?"

Jackson gave a hush-hush glance that said shut up till the kids are clear. "Of course," said Tredennick. His eyes flicked across me briefly—once up, once down.

"He'll probably have to go. Make the necessary arrangements for a sudden absence."

"Aye aye, sir. Two years I think." Like colonials talking about a native servant in front of the poor bugger. Jackson left. The Admiral got up from the table and pushed through the curtain into his sleeping cabin.

"Come in here, Dravin."

There was only one chair at the desk. He waved me over to the bunk.

"Sit down. Can't stand people hovering." He paused for a moment, looking through me at the bulkhead behind. He reached a decision. "Right!" He picked up a green phone on his desk.

"Admiralty one zero, please," and over his shoulder at me, "Scrambler. I don't need to tell you that not one word to another soul."

"No sir."

"Sarah? Admiral Tredennick. Give me the First Sea Lord, please." There was a delay of about half a minute.

"Hello? Yes sir—Second here. Big problem. Yes—our guests."

The man on the other end didn't receive the news with equanimity. Naval curses rolled down the phone.

"Yes sir," Tredennick again. "I know. Their show. They were told expressly, as I said last night. They've overreached this time. Someone's going to have to get those bastards's balls. Yes, I'll wait. From the PM's office? Very good, and John—I'm sorry. R.P.C. for a brandy when it's over? Good."

He hung up the phone. "They'll be running for every head in Whitehall in ten minutes." He managed a smile. "I was slated for First's billet in August. I'll be in St. Helena by then. Well, let's finish breakfast."

He switched the subject to growing up on the China station before the war. I wondered how I was going to face the Russians again in half an hour. If they still wanted to play. Phillips returned with the jacket.

I was slipping it on as the phone rang. Tredennick gave me the victory sign—reversed. I heard him pick up the phone.

"Prime Minister?" Another repetition of the morning's events, but this time with no outburst from the other end. The conversation was dispassionate, dull, mundane. I listened to the bald facts as though they involved a stranger. A sudden phrase brought me down with a thud.

"No sir. He's only told me. And Jackson, of course. Yes.... More tricky because of his Russian background. They could be quite rough.... Yes. I've organized that—we can lose him in a hurry if we must.... Yes, I agree, it's their court.... No sir, there's simply no way of being sure if he was dead.... Well MI5 are going to have to tell us that."

There was a long gap in the conversation at our end and then Tredennick said, "Very good, sir, we'll play it by ear. As long as they proceed we'll proceed. Khrushchev'll give the sign soon enough. Yes, until then we can keep the thing going. Goodbye."

The curtain swung back and the Admiral came out. "As you probably heard, we forge on. You're to continue as though accept the fact that it was one of their own divers, and that the only untoward incident this morning was their bad manners to a junior officer—which we can obviously laugh off."

He put out his arms, "Help me with the jacket. Damn thing weighs a ton." I held it up. With medals on he must need a back harness. "Good. Thanks. If you have any questions you can ask Captain Jackson. Let's go and catch the train."

Questions! *Christ!*

CHAPTER

SIX

By 0915 we were all assembled in mutual good will beneath the wrought-iron Victorian horror of the Royal Railway Shelter.

Smiles all round as we embarked at opposite ends of the train—the dining car as a buffer between and B and K in it like a bomb in the luggage. Arrival at Victoria Station was a replay of events at the Guild Hall but the protesters made more sense.

Bulganin, as comic relief, was wrestling on the platform with the train's maître d' over an open bottle of Château Lafitte.

Tredennick's eyebrow moved up a notch, "Khrushchev'll be dropping that pilot before they clear the river."

The two of us left for the Royal Naval College at Greenwich. The Admiral succumbed to an attack of nostalgia and took me off to point out the famous men under the boys' faces on the walls. The afternoon passed quietly. I wandered around renewing acquaintances with Wren's architecture and the library, and then it was evening and starting again with the Bolsheviks arriving by barge up the Thames. Tredennick stood at the head of the flight of steps leading up from the river and played Wolsey.

The leaders were siphoned off for a private session. As Yanov's opposite number, I adopted him and headed for the bar in the billiard room, pointing out a few of the naval oddities en route—early logs of Drake, a primitive breechloader. He showed only polite interest. Inexplicably, it was the pictures that intrigued him.

"Like the Hermitage," he said. "Marvelous colors. Whose is-this work?"—pointing at a mural of cherubs doing odd things to each other.

"Sorry, I can't help you." To anyone growing up at Greenwich on sublieutenants' courses, they were just there, part of the place like the columns outside. "Vodka?"

"*Nyet*—one of your red gins, I think. More suitable, no?"

"Pink." I was jolted again by the unexpected sense of humor. He raised his glass, "*Za vashe zdoroyve*—and thank you."

"I don't have to pay for it."

"No—for the spoon." He shook his head, laughing at the incongruity of the memory. "Priests, all crazy, I think. A little."

I wanted to talk in Russian. There was so much we could have said, and he could have been so much more natural, without the childish feeling that comes with linguistic inferiority. "You mentioned the Hermitage Palace," I said. "Was that near your house?"

"A kilometer. Before the war. Irina Street." He looked at me and shrugged. "But these names are no sense for you, eh?"

"No sense at all." *Coincidence surprises*.

Irina Street backs on the Fifth Line, which fronts on one of the innumerable canals beside which, in a small house with a green tile roof, I lived with my mother for my first six years.

I asked him casually whether he could see something of London unofficially. "Tomorrow is possible perhaps, when their Excellencies go to Edinburgh. We see later."

Dinner in the Painted Hall was as dull as dinner in Portsmouth, enlivened briefly when K told a story of three nuns in an outhouse to a mesmerized Dean of St. Paul's. All part of the bird-and-snake act.

After interminable toasts we stood up for a last mixing over cigars and brandy. I was off by myself with no more pleasant things to say when I realized that Khrushchev, Yanov in tow, was heading unmistakably for me.

I braced for the ritual how d'you do's and handshakes.

The man said nothing. Just stood for a full minute and stared with his head rocked back on a butcher's thick creased neck to look up, and the gray eyes boring through and through me. And I felt myself blushing again and furious because of it. A fist with stubby fingers and a wart reached out and held my arm and tightened, pinching. Pinching bloody hard, even through the heavy doeskin of my mess jacket.

"So." The first word and a cloud of brandy. "So." The eyes had not blinked once. "Dravin—a Dravin of Leningrad. Yanov tells me you shocked our sailors this morning. He found it funny." He gave a short laugh without humor—a bark. "Well, life is a shock, isn't it, Tovarish? And full of funny surprises too, eh?" The hand of the ex-miner pinched harder, although I didn't think it could. "Like putting your hand under a chicken for the egg, and getting a handful of shit instead, eh, comrade?"

I had no reply. The interpreter was white and choking.

K released my arm and waved the official away. "No need of that. This gentleman speaks more Russian than you do, Sukhodrev." He talked now at Yanov but he still looked unswervingly at me. God—if I could rub my arm!

"Who knows Alexey Ilyich, if this Leningrad Dravin were still a loyal citizen of the Motherland he might wear your boots today and not those pansy pumps." He pointed at my Wellingtons. I tried to find a laugh, but the physical closeness was overwhelming—almost sexual. His hand was stroking now. The voice softened.

"Gospodin Dravin, there have been mistakes. We know that. Russia has been fighting herself and all the world for forty years. Some of her children were abandoned. Some deserted her—even when they were needed most. No matter. Times change." He smiled through stainless steel teeth. "Times *have* changed." I smiled back, hypnotized by his recognition even while scornful of the pitch.

"We don't beg, gospodin. What need? But we call on peace-loving men everywhere to work on behalf of the masses for the good of all mankind in our struggle against the militant forces of the imperialists." The crudity of the dialectic snapped the spell and I saw him for what he was. A thick peasant with the vocabulary of a bloody wall poster.

He knew instantly that he'd lost me. The left hand grabbed at a porcelain dish of chocolates on a side table. "We don't beg, gospodin"—restating the case he'd already lost. I waited for him to stuff the sweet into his mouth and keep talking, but it stayed in his hand. "The chance is there to be of service"—the right hand rose inexorably, the fingers curled and tightened—"but if not—if a man opposes the liberation of the masses"—the fist shook within inches of my face and we understood each other very clearly now. "If a man *opposes*—"

The fist drove smashing down on the left hand. I flinched, and would have given anything to have a second chance not to. The liquid center oozed redly out across the palm beneath the fist.

And then his head, which had been rocked back on its crease the whole time, snapped forward in a staccato bow.

"My regards to your father, comrade."

And he wheeled, scraped the visceral mess on his hands onto the flawless linen of the tablecloth, and left, ignoring Bulganin and the entourage, who flapped their way into a vee and followed him out to clump down the stairs to the water and the waiting barge.

I stood, feeling totally isolated, although there were crowds of people all around. I'd laughed. Ignored Tredennick's warning of their knowledge, but they knew all right. And remembered. From a sea of the butchered and lost, they knew.

"Cheer up." Behind me, the same deep voice from the first meeting the night before, but speaking quietly in Russian. Yanov was still with me. "A joke, comrade. My cousin jokes. We meet tomorrow. Call me at Claridge's. Ask for Alexey Ilyich."

And he gave me his irrepressible grin and doubled with surprising lightness for a heavy man down the steps into the boat.

Khrushchev's cousin.

Through a sleepless night of wide-eyed dreams and fears, words to the tune of "Onward Christian Soldiers" locked into my head.

Khrushchev knows my fa-a-a-ther. . . . Father knows Khrushchev. . . . Khrushchev knows my father. . . .

Yanov's cousin! I waited until seven to put a call through to Jackson in *Caliope* in Portsmouth.

"The Captain, please."

A banging clatter as the morning watchman dropped the receiver and it swung against the bulkhead. Muffled conversation among the gangway staff.

"Officer of the Day speaking. Sorry about the noise, sir."

"It's not sir, it's Dravin. I wanted to speak to the Old Man."

"Dravers?" The voice of a sublieutenant even more gung ho than myself. A good cricketer. "He's gone, old boy."

"Gone?"

"Sudden change of command. Old Jacko's flown off to the Admiralty. Number One's standing in until the new boy. Do you want the effective date he'll be reporting in? I think it was a couple of weeks."

"No. Thanks."

"All a bit of a rush. New man's from Singapore—rather exotic."

With the cut connection, I was utterly adrift. The slang world of Dravers' and Jacko's infinitely remote. Involved in business far beyond any that I was geared to handle. *"But I suppose that's what we expect?"* Tredennick's words.

Tredennick. But how could a Dravin find a Second Sea Lord on a Sunday morning? Did I walk through London knocking on the front doors of great houses, interrupting breakfasts, ordering butlers to call his Lordship from his omelet: "There seems to be a Russian sort of person here, milord . . ."

His Lordship's breakfast broken into so that I could say, "I'm scared shitless, sir. Khrushchev knows my father . . ."

My father, who was within five miles of me in Hampstead all this time with all the answers. I took a bus and got off beside the Pond. A May day in April, chestnuts almost blooming, sails and small boys playing sailor.

May day. May Day: call sign for international distress. But what help was I seeking? What could I be told by a father from whom, as the prayerbook says, no secrets are hid? Secrets so frightful that they stayed locked inside the mantis mind of a father for two decades. A father now a known associate of Khrushchev, Butcher of the Ukraine.

I stopped walking. Better to stay silent than to ask the wrong question. Better to leave a son's love for a father frozen than to know the answers.

I got back on the bus.

The cultural shock at Claridge's had been profound. The night before, a little do of Malik's—Ambassador of the boot-sole face— had cost six thousand quid just for the broken glass, and the resident population of dowagers and Indian army hands had taken refuge in their rooms with extra rations of tea and gin.

The bodies behind the palms in the lobby had never worn a skirt or seen Poona. Two of them followed me into the lift. The Russians had commandeered the top floor, and when we got out two more heavies looked us over. There were others scattered along the hall. Yanov was waiting against the opposite wall. For the first time he was wearing civilian clothes—a typical Russian suit of the forties-fifties, baggy pants, a sloppy double-breasted jacket, rotten material. A pair of circus flat feet and a custard pie would have finished it off. I tried to hide it, but he caught the glance, and he'd seen enough of Savile Row around him by this time to know the difference. "I would like to have one of your British suits if there could be time. You know a tailor?"

"Easy," I said, to fill the moral obligation.

He beamed. "Good, very very good." An arm like a boom smashed down again on my shoulder. "Now, something to wet whistles, eh?"

We walked by a room set up for a dinner party, and stopped in an anteroom in front of a table holding as much liquid as Portsmouth Harbor.

We knocked back the obligatory toasts. He came directly to the point. "Do we still play language games?"

"Not a game—I'm ashamed of my Russian."

"Of course, of course," with a broad wink, totally disbelieving.

I switched tongues, feeling genuinely self-conscious after the buildup. "What would you like to see in Mother London. The Crown Jewels?"

"The Windmill Theatre. I want to make the girls move. Can we find a mouse?"

We laughed. Had another drink. "Speaking of girls," I said, "I've made arrangements for dinner and dancing. They'll be overwhelmed by a live communist."

For a moment he was obviously keen, but then enthusiasm waned.

"That would be magnificent for me, but Sinyavsky not so much."

There was to be a watchdog. Three makes a crowd, and safety for the Party. "Married?" I asked.

"Not to a woman. You had better meet him. One moment."
He set down the glass and stepped out in the hall to bring in the missing link.

"Lieutenant Dravin—Lieutenant Sinyavsky."

The new arrival waited for an unnecessary minute before sticking out a perfunctory hand with long fastidious nails. Short, thin, with a sallow face and a mail-slot mouth—I never saw his teeth. The black eyes lurking behind a falling wing of black hair came out long enough to look bloody rude and then scuttled back to enjoy it. He was probably younger than Yanov and I but he already had an aged look about him—the sort who gets to fifty at twenty-five and then stays there.

"Vasily Georgeyvich is a political assistant to Captain Karisov in the *Ordzhonikidze*."

Yanov's voice was safely unexpressive.

I made the required effort. "Delighted to have you accompany us. Will you join us in a drink?"

He enjoyed the refusal with all the pleasure from pain of a Presbyterian in a brothel. "I shall wait in the other room." He shoved through between us, slopping the gin in my glass.

"A good friend?"

Yanov rolled his eyes. "You see what I mean? What woman could compete with that? The bastard would sew a snatch shut if he found it."

"Alexey Ilyich, let us ruin his political virginity." Hardly a showstopper, but he threw back his head and laughed till his eyes were wet. Russians are given to exaggerated gestures. He grabbed a bottle of vodka from the table and filled our glasses, still shaking with laughter. "To rape!" My stomach shriveled before the stuff hit the bottom.

We found Sinyavsky, after a quick change, perched like a molting blackbird in a cage, on a needlepoint chair in a small alcove. The cage was set up as a reading room, the floor littered with tracts and magazines for the education and delectation of the British masses. Packets of fading sepia photos like the stuff for sale on a Maltese jetty showed Lenin fondling little boys and girls. Demand seemed to have been light.

The rest of the evening was like any other naval officer's run ashore—with a five-hundred-pound Bible chained to the leg. Almost worth it to see the expression on Sinyavsky's Marxist face while Yanov was measured for his suit at Gieves'—surely the very heart of capitalist unction and class privilege.

At three in the morning we were in a squalid little place in Soho, not normally the haunt of officers and gentlemen. The whores spotting us as seamen from a tramp in the river zeroed in for a certain kill. I did the age-old, totally predictable act.

"My friend," I whispered, nodding at the commissar, "virgin!"

Her hand was still closing like a hawk's foot on the fiver as Yanov and I dashed for the cab.

CHAPTER

SEVEN

On Friday night before the sendoff, the *Bulwark*'s wardroom threw a bash for the Russians. About half showed up, Yanov among them. But not Sinyavsky.

"How is the commissar?" I asked.

Yanov had none of the ebullience of London. "Political virtue stronger than ever—damned politruks!"

He left after the second round, and I walked back with him along the jetty. We stopped at the foot of the gangway, to shake hands. "Thank you," he said, "for the suit, too."

"You won't need it after that report on the girls hits the fan."

The grin flashed across his face. He slapped me on the shoulder, "A virgin." Once again he roared with laughter, "You know, I'm sure the bastard is! Well—goodbye, my good friend. You must let me find you a Russian girl one day. When you come home."

"One day," I said, to be polite, and because it had been fun, "Goodbye."

But when the last of the Russian hulls dropped over the horizon beyond Spithead I felt only enormous relief, and after a debriefing conducted by a stodgy bastard weaned on the Official Secrets Act, I relaxed to excess with the liaison group.

It was midnight when we parted in the hall. My cabin door stuck. There were offers of assistance. Words of encouragement. A boarding party was organized to storm the door.

43

With a vicious crack from the frame, it flew open. Jackson was sitting on my bunk.

"Evening, Dravin. Sorry to intrude so late. Won't you sit down?"

I sat abruptly, without remembering that the chair was covered with gear waiting to be packed. The leather box with my only change of collars was squashed flat.

Jackson, dressed in plain clothes and sucking calmly on the pipe, seemed not to notice. "Tell me," he said, while I was sorting out the mess, "how you got on with the aide, Yanov—impressions and so on."

"A good type, sir—at least by comparison. I felt a bit of an idiot about the language. I don't think my excuses had any ring of truth."

"And did *he*?"

That stymied me. I thought about it. "God—I just don't know, sir. He certainly *seemed* genuine, although I had the impression he'd been primed pretty well. The Khrushchev's cousin thing seemed rather strong."

"I beg your pardon?" He was holding the pipe quite still. "Let me be clear—Yanov said that he was Khrushchev's cousin?"

"Yes sir. At Greenwich. I think to buck me up after K played his chocolate game. Do you think there's any truth in it?"

Any sign of interest was gone again. "Dunno. All's possible. The Russian extended family. Certainly Khrushchev has made a favorite of his son-in-law, Adzhubei. Put him in at *Izvestia*—and speaking of the old man, I understand that you held up well under a full broadside."

I remembered the sensation. "Raked to the waterline I'd say, sir."

"But still floating." Once again he became disconcertingly personal. "I gather also that it concerned your father—did that bother you?"

How did Jackson know? I hadn't mentioned the reference to my father, and that lack must have rung a bell, since he already knew. For a moment there was a sensation of invisible cords being drawn about me. "I certainly had a moment's curiosity, sir, but Admiral Tredennick had prepared me. I was surprised they still had the records of the prerevolutionary fleet."

"Your father's never spoken to you about the years between the wars?"

"I didn't realize there were any, sir. I thought he was out in 1917. He never gets past being at Tsushima in the *Souvaroff* under Rozhdestvenski when they got chewed up by the Japs in 1905."

"I see." He thought about my answer for some time. "I can't betray a confidence," he said eventually, "but in the light of what's happened I think that you must tackle him directly at your next meeting. Tell him that we've had this session." He eased himself about on the edge of the bunk. "Do you know anything about the intelligence world?"

"No sir. I read the end products in the digests. I suppose we all wonder where some of it comes from sometimes."

"From ordinary chaps," he said. "And some not quite so. Like you."

The pace of the conversation seemed to get very slow, as though it was part of the quiet smoke drifting in the room. And the slower the words the quicker the schoolboy images in the mind.

"Officers in regular jobs—attachés hearing a bit of this or that and passing it along. It can get more involved, of course, but not for most of us in uniform. Cumulatively the information's vital— but seldom individually dramatic. We leave any blood and guts to anonymous civilians." He stopped looking at the pipe to look at me.

"I always feel rather like the walrus and the carpenter at this part," he said. "You know—to the oyster. Will you won't you . . . ?"

"Join the dance?"

"That's about it."

On the tip of my tongue to correct him—you mean the Mock Turtle, sir—but I said, "Would it change my career pattern?" because I had to sound sensible. Adult. Discussing an implication of service like any other. To hide the secret voice of the schoolboy yelling from the side lines to play up, play up.

And Jackson—the headmaster who must have taken in so many boys—calm, serious, back to the sensible question.

"Doesn't have to. That really depends on you and the toss of the throw. Most people chug on as before, but with their eyes a bit wider. And some feel a little more useful."

The smoke wreathed up from the bowl and hung in the air between us, and in the smoke the spirits of Gordon and Lawrence and Mata Hari, because of course any schoolboy knew it had to be like that.

And I said, "Yes sir. I'll join."

"Oh good. Good." He stood up a little stiffly, tucking the pipe into his breast pocket. "Going back to your ship tonight?"

"Day after tomorrow, sir. She's out on fisheries patrol in the North Sea." It seemed irrelevant. "Sir—when would this intelligence stuff start?"

"Why, Dravin"—in that peculiarly slow, almost lilting voice— "it already has."

"Oh," I said, not brightly. "Crabb?"

Like Yanov's above the diver, his eyes could appear totally frank and yet reveal absolutely nothing. "If you like."

Some of the hypnotic effect of the smoke had floated off. "Well, sir, isn't that getting rather close to blood and guts?"

"Sometimes the line gets a little blurred," he said. "I must be off. You do realize that there's no word at all to be passed *about* Crabb—in or out of the service?"

"Yes sir. Do you know yet whether he was a . . ." It was difficult to put so harsh a word as traitor on a face with so much sadness.

"I don't know if the man's alive or dead," said Jackson, opening the door with no trouble whatsoever. "By the way, put in a claim to me for the entertainment of the commissar—that was a good touch with the whore. Good night."

He left me speechless.

The knocking intruded slowly into consciousness. The room was dark, although my shake was for six-thirty, after sunrise. The knocking continued, low but urgent, not stopping. My watch said five. I got out of the bunk, annoyed at the duty porter's idiocy. I opened the cabin door.

"Are you Lieutenant Dravin?"

Policeman—written in every manner possible. From the way he stood instinctively to block the door and yet be half inside; from the eyes registering me, my bunk, my suitcase packed and ready, my Wellingtons Khrushchev had sneered about. From his buckled raincoat—double cloth across the back, collar already turned up on issue with the job.

"I'm Dravin."

"Hyde. Special Branch." He produced a card.

"Yes, of course"—accepted, without reading. "What can I do for you?"

"Routine, sir. If you could get dressed."

"But I've got a hop arranged to Rosyth. I have to join my ship—"

"I think we'll be back in time, sir."

"But that's not quite good enough—I'd be absent without—"

"Captain Jackson will arrange for that, sir."

"Jackson!"

"If you don't mind. Quickly, please, sir. We have to catch the tide."

The car was a small Jag saloon, unmarked, with a driver dressed as Hyde's twin. The dampness of the morning chilled within a minute. Wisps of fog swirled around the lights at the main gate. I thought back to the ride with Tredennick which ended with the madman priest.

We turned south through old Portsmouth, coming out onto the Clarence Esplanade. Hard to tell direction, but the mournful bellow of the Blockhouse diaphone sounding now close, now far, as the fog changed thick or thin, seemed to stay on my right hand. We passed an open area which must be Southsea Common, then Lumps Fort and Eastney. We left the Esplanade, turning into streets smelling of tar and fish. We passed a tannery—the sauerkraut reek mixing unpleasantly with the others—and then a dilapidated pub, running down under brewery chain management. There were no more lights.

The decaying frame of a fishing boat appeared in front of us. The car stopped.

"It's a bit of a walk, sir," said Hyde. "Feet will get wet, I'm afraid." We went past the boat and down some steps slippery with weed. The ebb had left a hard-rippled, clay silt sand. Visibility still poor but now there was daylight in the mist, diffused and unreal. The boat vanished unnaturally soon. Our feet made slopping sounds and left sole shapes that filled with water.

"How the hell do you know where we're going?" I could see nothing now.

Hyde pointed at his feet at other sets of tracks. "Good thing it was reported early," he said, "or we'd have had a crowd and too many bloody questions."

"Reported what?"

"Only another couple of minutes, sir."

With the same abruptly sudden speed caused by the fog, a rock protruded from the sand. A third man in a raincoat stood shining a flashlight on it.

"It's a bit hard sir," said Hyde. "Take things easy."

A small crab scuttled away from the rock.

The gagging sound in the fog was mine.

"*Easy!*" A policeman's grip held my arm. "We've got to try for the ID, sir. Anything you recognize?"

The rock was a body, the body a man, the man a diver in a suit that I had seen before. A suit from the days before sponge rubber. A suit of wrinkled green neoprene with locking rings at openings, for wrists, ankles.

The crab had scuttled from the locking ring at the throat. But there was no throat. No head. No neck. Just an indescribable hole with something inside.

"The hands, sir. We can't get prints, but anything there, sir? Did he have on a ring?"

No prints. No fingertips, no nails. Some flesh on the palms. Hyde lifted them gently with a stick. There was no ring.

"I think he wore one," I said. "I can't be sure. I can't remember."

Once you accepted it as something of the sea's—like dead shellfish, it could be looked at, if you just didn't look in the hole at the top of the suit.

"It's his size," I said. "And the suit. But I don't think it's him."

"No sir?" Hyde put no inflection either way.

"No. I mean how can I tell like this, but I don't think that's his hand."

What flesh there was on the right palm was uniformly soft, yellow-white with ragged rips. But no sign of the leather callus on the edge.

We left the third man and walked back across the flats.

"Sorry, sir," said Hyde. "We have to get the first reaction without influence. Rough—I'm sorry. Will you call London, please, before we drive you back? There's a phone booth by the pub."

Already the ghouls were out. The watchers of the smashup on the road. The professional gawkers at fires, huddled, waiting for vicarious excitement. Two constables kept them from the steps. Half a dozen faces, growing one here, one there, asking the excited questions in the funereal voices. I trailed Hyde as he shoved through them to the phone booth.

"Hi."

Out of the fog.

"Hi there!" A ghost's voice using Crabb's little affectation—the American speech from Ike and the Sixth Army. But the accent was genuine, from the other side of the Atlantic, more genuine than the man waving the press card, trying to get past the police. I knew the man. I'd spilled a drink on him.

In the booth, with a connection made to London and a naval captain who came and went like fog or smoke, I tried to make my report concise, tried not to color it. "A diver, yes sir, with no head and no nails and perhaps no callus or ring and a man who watched him and we've met before . . ."

"Oh yes?" Even on the phone, Jackson's voice still softly Celtic in an English way. "And he's seen you?"

"Well, yes sir. He called to me—and I'm in a booth with the light on."

"Yes." Just the slightest pause this time. "Well then, Dravin, we must put out the light."

DISNEYLAND.

CHAPTER

EIGHT

The south wind which sweeps from the Pacific up and over the great horns of the capes that form the cove has cut the cypresses until their tops are flat as sailors' caps; but from the crescent of sand below them the wind is silent, invisible—shown only by the tree shapes and the constant rise and fall of sea birds. The birds watch the seals posted on the entrance rocks and hope for a free lunch. The seals in turn watch with affronted whiskers for intruders. Beyond the seals the surf rolls never-ending beneath the kelp beds to break against the capes with the thudding of far-off Portsmouth drums.

Three years, three oceans, after running from an American's questions on the dank tidal flats of Portsmouth, I lay under a noon sun on the American beach thinking of the past ten days and about to ask a question of my own.

The message which had finally arrived to bring me back into the light had found me in Suva. My CO had read me the tape.

1. Lieutenant Commander P.A. Dravin appointed on Staff Washington this date for temporary duties.

   2. Liase with British Consul San Francisco for arrival West Indies Squadron, Long Beach and San Fran, September.
   3. Re-establish contacts during visit K and Cousin Y to California if able.
   4. Report direct to this office as required.
   5. Don't forget the diver.

Ends. Jackson.

The CO had poured two gin and tonics. "The old music-hall line in Para five sounds a little ominous, Number One," he'd said. "Cheers!"

Paxton was the British consul. He threw a cocktail party for me on the evening of my second day. She arrived late, was spotted instantly by every male eye in the room, given a hug and a kiss by Paxton's wife, and brought over to me for mutual inspection. But the ring she wore was on the wrong finger for a man with little time in town. We endured the formalities.

"Nicola Ruarke—Peter Dravin."

Paxton dropped a pebble in the social pond. "Dravin was born in Russia."

The ripples widened. "Really. But you seem so English..."

A sensuously low voice for a girl in her early twenties. I explained a little of the purge and exile.

"That's fantastic! My own parents had to leave Italy just like that."

"Your father was a politician?"

"No, he's a scientist—"

"A Nobel Laureate—don't let her kid you." Paxton had a host's satisfaction in a job well done. "Get her to fill you in on Musso and the prize money."

"True?" I asked.

A lovely wide warming smile for the first time. "Yes, it's true. But I get kind of tired of telling it."

"Would you make the effort—please?"

"Okay, if you'll do a trade on Russia?"

"Done."

"Well"—she was slightly embarrassed at having to make the first move—"Mussolini wanted to make a really big show out of the award, you know, with all the marble columns and double-eagle banners—"

"For the new Rome of a thousand years."

"Right." She smiled again, more at ease. "So anyhow, he got it all lined up and they laid on this huge state dinner where my father was to be the guest of honor—orchestra and opera singers from Milan, cardinals from the Vatican—and it was a no show."

"I'm sorry?"

She laughed. "My father didn't show up. He had put us all on a boat for New York in the morning."

"And in a fit of pique the Duce pinched the cash?"

"He did."

"An expensive gesture," I said.

And it seemed to me that the fat man had got the last laugh. But perhaps scientists, like sailors, aren't worldly wise about money. Trying for some tact, I said, "But if your father wasn't political why leave the party early?"

"Early? By 1937 he almost left it too late. We're Jewish."

It shouldn't have made the slightest difference, and yet for a moment it did. Jews from Europe—Jews from Russia—who have escaped the tumbril carry too many implications for the rest of us.

Like the reaction to her appearance, she was used to the moment's lull, but it broke the stream of the conversation.

Paxton's wife materialized to take her off in tandem as women do on these occasions.

Paxton himself was looking at me thoughtfully. "Quite something, isn't she?" he said.

I had no funny remark for the reply. "Yes."

"She doesn't allude, but she's a new widow. Be a little careful."

"Oh Christ. What was the husband?"

"Naval air, I think. About six months ago."

I suspected the arrangements were deliberate. How else could something like that be accomplished gracefully?

She came back with a light red raincoat and long white boots.

"You're not leaving?"

"Oh. Hi—again. Yes I think so." Dravin had been tried and found wanting. Russian mystery was not enough.

"Could I get you a cab?"

"No, thanks anyway. I walk. It's only a few minutes."

"If I walked with you I could keep off the flies."

We both knew that I was desperate. "Okay," she said, after making me wait.

We went down to the street. A cable car clanged past us to switchback out of sight towards the wharf. I asked the usual tourist questions. She gave the usual responses and then said, "So why *did* your own father leave Russia?"

"I don't know."

"You don't? After all the buildup? Hey, come on!"

"No. I mean it. Like talking to an oyster, tackling my father. What's this building?"

"The Coit Tower." Not too pleased with the change of subject. "My place is just down there." She pointed towards the harbor. Below us, dead-end roads stopped on either side of a section of particularly precipitous grade, leaving it untouched, almost wild with trees and flowers. Three or four small cottages accessible only by a lengthy flight of steps, hung from the hill.

She decided to take another chance on me. "A drink—coffee? Something to eat?"

"Tea—or is that too much?"

She laughed. "We'll make a try."

Nasturtiums and flowering vines half-blocked the way. The steps creaked and swayed like a jungle bridge. "To absorb the shock when the quake hits," she said, smiling. "Don't worry"—reaching out to touch my arm—"it won't be this year, the pressures in the fault are too low."

"I'm glad to hear it."

"Not a woman's work to study geophysics?" She was laughing at me.

"Am I that transparent?"

"I'm conditioned. Okay, this is it."

"The quake?"

"Smart ass—home."

A birdcage of old bare wood, the house was as unique in appearance as its owner. Shutters with crescents cut in them; odd windows, some leaded, some colored; Victorian gingerbread scalloping down the eaves. Rounded fieldstones from the hill made a slope-sided chimney.

"Jesus! What a bloody monster!" A hatch in the wall by the chimney exploded outward. A Great Dane meeting me almost eye to eye held the bridge and blocked the last six steps.

"Largo, get down, you beast! He's really too gentle, but he makes enough noise to keep out the weirdos."

I agreed that he did. "I guess you're a nut about dogs," she said, "being British?"

"Not too much."

"Really? Were you bitten as a kid?"

"There were dogs during our getaway from Russia—it's a stupid thing. A witch doctor could sort it out for me."

She stopped at the landing. "You've really tried to find out about all that from your father and he won't tell you? What about your mother?"

"It's all very old-world. She won't talk out of respect for him. I sometimes think that I don't really want to find out." I laughed.

The front door opened off a flagstone patio on the down-hill side and matched the shutters. An enormous piece of glass beside it made a concession to the view. Inside, she searched for tea. One part of a single large room had been allocated galley duties. Other alcoves served other functions.

"Very, sort of open, isn't it?" I said.

"There's a door for the bathroom if that's what's worrying you. Okay—I've found the teabags. I guess you want a pot too?"

"I should have stayed with coffee."

"I'm kidding. I don't believe you, you know—about your father. I think it really bothers you." She plugged in the kettle and looked across. "It would sure as hell bother me."

"You may be right." I told her a bit about Khrushchev.

"You talked like that! My God, that's really something."

"It was at the time. Will you show me the town?"

She pondered, still looking at me. She had the most extraordinarily long lashes. I made the tea.

"Sure," she said finally. "What do you like to do?"

We both laughed. A first hint of intimacy. "No—I mean shows, tennis—this stuff?"—waving a hand around the house. Works of art covered the walls. Plants filled in any odd spaces. There must be money somewhere to support such a habit. The view through the ten-foot window was beyond price.

"I'm afraid I'm very dull. Sailors are, you know."

"Oh yeah! You're talking to a sailor's wife, boy..."

An awful gulf. Without thought I took her hand. Talked about anything, my sea time just over, shells on beaches, making copra, memory of Russian winter. Anything. Just to let time pass and heal. The fog rolled ice walls at the great red arc of the Golden Gate. She stared at it, finding her way back.

"And I've started to read a little," I said.

"Tolstoy, I guess," she said, with terrible effort.

"Christ, that's far too deep. Ian Fleming."

"Are you ever serious?"

"Always. To be honest, at the moment I'm reading something Paxton gave me—by a Californian, I think, I've only just started it. It seems to be about depression days and drunks in a fishing village."

"Steinbeck?"

"That's it."

"Neanderthal!" she said, but laughing again, thank God. "Well if it's Steinbeck then you've got to see Cannery Row. And maybe the butterflies. We'll go tomorrow."

I found Monterey run down, dull and ugly. Pacific Grove wasn't any better, and the gum trees were covered with dirt, not migrating insects. A few stragglers fluttered half-heartedly in one tree.

"Leftovers?" I asked.

"Some stay—I don't think anyone knows why they want to."

"Nor do I. Hardly an oasis."

She didn't respond. After the effort to be up at the party she was low this morning. We walked back to the car.

"Look at this," I said. Beside the door, a tiny gray cylinder attached to one of the gum branches with white silk made spasmodic jerks.

"Hey—he's trying to get out." She perked up with sudden interest. "Let's watch."

The movement stopped for perhaps a minute, then started again. The cylinder began to split. Hints of color were visible within the dull dirt-gray of the shell. The twitching stopped again. We waited. There was no sign of the show's resumption.

"We could catch the second act tomorrow," I said. "What about some lunch?"

"Sure"—rather half-heartedly. We drove to Carmel and a drive-in. I said something about the food that was meant to be funny and wasn't. After the meal she gave me a real estate salesman's tour. She asked me what I thought.

I was finding it an effort to keep things bright and beautiful. "Not what I'd call natural for the setting. Pretty, though."

"That's all?" There was a tenseness.

"Well it's all a bit Hollywood Tudor after living with the real thing." I made it worse. "I suppose that in California, Hollywood *is* the real thing."

More than I'd meant to say. The gorgeously full lips were compressed, a small line at the corner trembling. The thought of causing tears crucified me. I reached to touch her, say something conciliatory.

I was slammed back in the seat as the tires screamed and stripped black lines behind us. She dragged out on to the Coast highway. "What stodgy, stuck-up bastards you British can be!"

I studied the dashboard. Five minutes. Ten. The changeling act had floored me as well as the car. "You're almost out of petrol—gas, rather."

She didn't say anything but pulled into the next service station. The fumes and heat of the asphalt were unpleasant. The atmosphere inside was worse.

"Look," I said. "Please. I know I'm bloody hopeless, and I won't intrude again, but don't let me completely bugger your day. Back to town, whatever you want, just do it—and let me pay for the fuel."

She passed a credit card to the attendant. "You're rich?"

"A church mouse."

Part of the smile came back. I wanted to get out and dance around the pumps beside the road. She nodded, smiled again. "I know what we'll do. You don't mind getting the neat crease out of those pants?"

"Let them be ripped to shreds."

We left the highway to get closer to the sea. Half a mile down the side road she pulled off into a verge of dry, wheel-high grass.

"We have to walk the last part," she said. "That's what keeps it quiet."

Not quiet. Silent. Even the grass beside the narrow uphill path not rustling. Unmoving.

"Christ!"

A sea bird shot like a white bullet from the ground twenty feet ahead. The grass was gone. Cut to golf-green flatness by the wind tearing our breath away. I saw the cypresses for the first time. The surf three hundred feet below us.

The cove.

She was laughing into the wind. I realized that we were holding hands. I opened my mouth. She had her own against my ear. I felt her breath.

"You get your wish," she had to shout. "You're going to have to slide the last part on your gray flannel ass."

We walked along the sand towards the seals. She told me how she'd found it the first time, looking for somewhere to get away, to take the dog for walks. I climbed up on to one of the sentry rocks to view the surf outside. The large bull beside the wives and young moved with deceptive speed to repel invaders. I jumped back hurriedly. His head and neck reminded me of Yanov.

She laughed again, gave my arm a little squeeze. "He's okay if you bring him a herring." I felt the softness of her arm against me.

"You know," she said, "I can't really figure you out, I always thought Russians would be hopelessly extroverted. All emotion and intuition. Everything in life red or orange to compensate for winter."

"Not after five minutes in a British school. That was an artistic sort of turn of phrase—the orange and winter."

"But I guess it's not very smart to think of Russia as only cold and wintry?"

"I do."

"English Peter! Talk about cold, that name is it. What would you be in Russian?"

"Pyotr Andreyevich."

"God—that's worse."

"Petya perhaps—my mother uses that."

"You're embarrassed. I'm sorry." Again the impulsive squeeze of the arm. Worth any amount of embarrassment. "But I like it—Petya—the Russian butterfly inside the British chrysalis."

"I really am sorry about being so stupid this afternoon," I said. "Being such a snob."

"I was rough on you. We all have shells to break out of." She hunched, knees up, hands on ankles in the sand, staring out through the gap in the bluffs at the Pacific waiting in its immensity. "And stupid—I should talk! It must have nearly killed my father . . . Just like a country music song—nineteen and off to heartbreak hotel and a quickie marriage with a flyboy . . ."

The sun, like the random conversation, now past the point of no return, dropped with visible rapidity between the capes towards the sea.

"I went out in March to join him—"

"Out?"

"Vietnam. It wasn't like a war at all. I still don't know why we have guys there in uniform. I mean there were incidents. You know, a bomb in some politician's house, a flag in a village on the river bank in the morning. But to us it was just a honeymoon—in Saigon, Pearl of the Orient. We had an apartment with lizards on the wall that looked out at Diem's palace garden and the elephants snapping palm leaves by the fence—have you seen an elephant run, Petya?"

"In Ceylon—" But she hadn't heard, was away on the far side of a great ocean.

"They hardly seem to move, and yet they're across the garden—"

The day was going out with a vast red radiance spreading wide on the horizon. A pelican crash-dived for a final fish.

"He flew right into a hill—my folks saw it on TV."

The hands locked tight around the ankles, rocked her in tiny motions, grains of sand slipping from her feet. A tear fell like the sun, catching its light from the sea. Remembering death in a single blood-red drop. "I haven't even told my parents what it was like," she said.

Sitting in my flannels and blue blazer on the sand, I held her, and listened as the body rocked on, childlike, telling stories of a child's marriage ending as night falls on the Pacific.

"They sent a chaplain to tell me. He was worried about the soul of a Catholic married outside the church. That was my fault, too, of course, that he died in a state of mortal sin. And he just went over it and over it. The lizards watched him the whole time . . ."

As a man of God seeks solutions for points of fine doctrinal balance, and talks of grace and redemption of death for a noble cause and with eternity before us, it's never too late—if we can amend this form as next of kin. He addresses a girl, the cause of the problem, and the lizards listen with cold-blooded hearts and unmoving eyes.

"He was worried about the burial—it really mattered about the remains, he said . . . which part of the cemetery they went in. They'd showed me the plastic bag. It didn't matter . . . not the smallest bit . . ."

The surf beats against the capes, and beyond the cove, somewhere under a rising sun elephants outside a window walk in their garden, walk with footfalls of approaching thunder from the storms gathering beyond the palm trees by the fence in Saigon, Pearl of the Orient.

And in memory a girl in my arms remembers. Remembers waiting alone inside a window for a day measuring the priest's eternity, remembers waiting with lizards and a plastic bag for a journey home.

Ten days of San Francisco later, the cove at noon was shadowless, no bleak sunset thoughts getting past the seals and the dog.

"I've got to go to Long Beach tomorrow. The dinner for Khrushchev in Los Angeles is in the evening."

"Khrushchev—that will be unreal." She sat up on an elbow, the black hair falling around her throat. "No chance of me too with your Russians, I guess."

I reached up to stroke the hair. "I don't give a damn about the Russians. "They're coming to San Francisco. I'll try and set things up so that you'll get a chance to see one then. You'd like Yanov."

"Great."

The sun was eclipsed behind her head, haloing her hair, blocking out thought and comprehension. Our bodies warmed by it, pulsed with the mewling gulls. Our moment. Chosen by fate and free selection of the species.

"Niki..."—the sense of impetuosity, or a noon sun on a mad Englishman made my head pound. "When I get back to San Francisco tomorrow night, if I asked you to marry me would you say yes?"

She jumped up, laughing, brushing sand from the California legs. "That's the voice of the chrysalis, Petya. The butterfly would ask me now."

CHAPTER

NINE

Wearing my large plastic label I sat in the Ambassador Hotel waiting for N.S. Khrushchev to take on the mayor and citizens of the City of Los Angeles. I was blasé. The sense of watching another opening of the same old show was strong. For the citizens next to me, however, it was the thrill of opening night.

"Jesus Christ," said Harry the ex-sheriff of Stockton County to my left. "Jesus Christ!" We were on a first-name bsais from the labels.

Jack, on my right—numbing himself with double bourbons and stroking the Stars and Stripes pin on his lapel to ward off the evil eye—said nothing. Remembering the mad vicar I wondered whether we were about to witness another attack. I asked what he did. Stoned silence.

"Jack's real big in paper products, Pete," said Harry reverentially. "Would you just *look* at that guy Krooschoff."

But I was looking at Yanov two seats from him. Until the night before there had been no confirmation that he was traveling with the boss. Then a shot on the news of Dictator facing Emancipator at the Lincoln Memorial had panned back to show a group of officials, and there he was—in his Gieves suit. Writing a note to be left for him at the hotel I had felt a quite extraordinary sense of pleasure at the chance to meet again.

If the show wasn't canceled early.

It was vintage K. Fist waving, table thumping, threatening—

and not very funny. The society crowd were genuinely nervous, giving off a smell of collective tension like an electrical discharge—more than once imagining the rush of wind overhead from the Redstone birds leaving the pads out at Vandenburg.

There was applause at the end—surprisingly enthusiastic. Perhaps the listeners congratulating themselves for surviving.

"What the Christ do you *think* of that?" Harry the sheriff asked at large.

The tycoon finished the latest double, his fifth by my count. Set down the glass, prepared to speak for the first time. Harry waited breathless. "Praise the good Lord," said Jack, "they kept that commie bullshitting fucker out of Disneyland."

At this precise moment I received Yanov's note. In Russian.

Pyotr Andreyevich—you are almost as far from home as ourselves. We would welcome you for a little hospitality when all is over. The Presidential Suite. Bring this. A.I. Yanov.

The sight of the funny letters dropped the temperature at our table in Orange County, heart of Nixon country and the Cold War, to absolute zero.

It was hotter upstairs in the corridor outside the suite. The space was jammed: emissaries, couriers, arriving and departing guests. Black hats and snoops with battle scars from both sides monitored them. A Russian with lazy eyes and a cheek sucked in from a shotaway jaw let me through the final check point. There were two doors—one closed, one open. A group of delicate State Department creatures hovered around the former, wilting before the gusts of rage bellowed through it by a familiar voice.

"Imperialist bastards dropped in their own shit . . ." Change a word and the moderate language of the Chairman of the Council of Ministers would have put him on equal terms with Paper Products. "Who do these lickspittle sons of bitches and painted whores think they are? Get Lodge on the phone. *Nyet!* Get Eisenhower! Our trip is *off!*"

The diplomats collapsed. I did not. I felt tense, ready for a fight. But hell or high water before any Russian from Nikita down was going to do another bird and snake with me. I went into the reception.

The party had been transferred intact from Claridge's—bruisers, booze, pictures of Lenin and the kids, the whole lot.

And Yanov.

I might have seen him last the night before. Not a hair different. An extra ring on his sleeve—with the right cousin, going up like a rocket in his career. He saw me. And all the fears which had festered in three years of separation, my doubts of his sincerity, alarm at my own naiveté, were gone. Banished in an instant by that magnetic grin.

"Pyotr Andreyevich, Pyotr Andreyevich"—playing no language game, no hiding his affection. "*Wonderful* after so long to meet again. Didn't I tell you that we should? *Vodka!*" Slammed into my palm like a rifle butt.

"*Pod stolom!*"

Under the table. "A self-fulfilling prophecy, Alexey Ilyich."

"Eventually, eventually." He looked keenly at me. "Promoted too—and you look well. Brown. You've been at sea?"

"Three years in the South Seas."

"And now?" A friend's interest.

"On staff Washington. I'm arranging for the visit of our West Indies flagship here next week."

"Ah. How convenient—that we should be allowed a meeting. What pleasure. Fill your glass. Next time you'll be visiting us at home, just as I said. I'll have that girl for you yet."

"I've got one to show you. Can you get away tomorrow—in San Francisco?"

"For an hour or two; nothing will stop it for an old friend. Try the caviar, flown in this morning, nonstop in our great Tupolev."

The party was winding up for a flight of its own. The noise level from a group of musicians with balalaikas and button accordions in a corner reached the threshold of pain.

The music stopped. All heads turned toward the door. The apoplectic Premier of the USSR floated out, calm and smiling.

A puff adder, all for show. "I thought the boss was going home, Alexey."

"For the microphones." In a conspiratorial whisper, looking up at the ceiling.

"You could have fooled me."

"And Gromyko's wife. She brought him a nerve pill."

"He takes tranquil—?"

I stopped, sensing a movement. Behind my shoulder the guests had parted like papyrus reeds. Waddling up the middle through them, Nikita Sergeyevich, changed from adder to bull crocodile, jaws dripping sarcasm.

Again.

"Tovarish Dravin. From Portsmouth."

I bumped my head. "Your Excellency"—and held his gaze. But he still shook me rigid.

"What curious chance, eh?" He eyed my uniform with the disapproval of the ex-sheriff. "Not only a man without a country, but now without a ship. It's funny, no?"

Not to me. There was no chance in his memory and I was tired of question marks. But the crowd of suckholes found it as funny as the boss. Exactly as funny—at each level of hilarity and mirth: The first smile, the chuckle, the gut-heaving roar of laughter. *Was Yanov laughing?*

"Well, gospodin?" The noise died instantly. The eyes of the croc, hard and flat as river pebbles, looked at me unwinking. And sober! "What does one Russian say to another at such times? What excuses does he make?"

The eyes stared, and the eyes of the suckholes stared in parallel.

"I hoped, Excellency, that with my uniform I might get a free pass to Disneyland." In English, but the magic name needed no translation. The proverbial deathly hush. My bladder fluttered like a moth.

The message trickled through the interpreter. The pebbles stayed locked to my own eyes until it was complete, and then the crocodile laughed again. Laughed until the crocodile tears fell. His arms went around me in a tremendous hug. "Good boy—good boy!"

And we were off on the slippery slope of overproof. "Toast! *Toast!*" To Russia, my father, the crocodile, myself.

My father.

While consciousness remained I took Yanov aside.

"You're sure you can get loose in San Francisco?"

"Bloody right!" he said in English, dropping the now familiar arm around my neck. "We stay on the Top Mark."

"The Top Mark?" Asked in what I thought was a tone of calm reflection.

I must have misjudged the audio control. A room full of Russians, pissed as newts, turned to face me, clicked heels, raised glasses, roared in unison. "To Top Mark!"

CHAPTER

TEN

"It could be Russian," he said. "Anywhere on the cliffs south of Odessa."

In the light of another California sunset I stood with Yanov looking down the hill at the birdcage house. The bay, out of the shadow of the hill was still bright blue; a cruise liner leaving the Embarcadero with fireboats and sirens, brilliantly white.

"And you have this all to yourself?" He jabbed me in the ribs, and started down the steps. "Sly fox. Show me this woman."

There was a crash from the street. I turned back. An old green Dodge, its driver unfamiliar with San Francisco gradients, had failed to lock its wheels against the curb. "That was an expensive sound," I said, but Yanov, motionless beside the landing below me, wasn't listening.

She stood with her back to him, watering the flowers, green dress and dark hair part of the shadows of the leaves, skin glowing gold from sunlight off chrysanthemums.

"Christ's mother!" he said under his breath. "A beauty!"

"She keeps a beast—be careful."

The warning triggered the dog into baying bedlam.

"God," she said. "You scared me. Peter, you were going to phone!"

I made excuses. "Anyway, I've brought your red Russian. This is Alexey Yanov."

She held out her hand. *"Zdrastvuitya. Kak dela!"*

"You speak the language too!"—he was delighted.

She laughed. "Only a couple of words from Peter for effect—I'm sorry."

"I think I have heard that explanation before." His grin had an edge to it.

"For that matter," I said, "you seem to have made remarkable progress in your own already excellent English."

The hostess moderated, "Hey, no cold war tonight. I picked up some vodka for the occasion—imported Russian. How shall I mix it?"

"Just take the lid off," I said.

"Do you," Yanov said, with a disarming smile, "after so much trouble to get vodka, have what is in old-fashioneds? I have acquired a taste for them."

"I don't know. I've never mixed one, but I have a book."

"No no. I have made much trouble, we shall have the vodka."

"No way—it's a challenge. But first I have to find the instructions. Come in and help." We went into the house, the dog and I bringing up the rear. Yanov had to duck at the threshold. "Look for a book with a picture of a nude girl in a glass on the cover."

"An example of Western decadence for your report," I said to Yanov.

"An incentive to fulfill the norm. Where do we start?"

Finding the recipe required tables to be turned, book shelves and drawers to be ransacked. Yanov, like a child at its own birthday party, was allowed to make the find.

"I think I have it—under this pot."

Strange growths straggled over the edges looking for something to kill and eat. "My rabbit's-foot fern—right! I hope the water hasn't ruined it."

He helped her examine the index.

"After all that," she said, "the damn page is missing." They laughed in joint exasperation.

"I think," I said, "that whiskey, soda, angostura, sugar and a slice of orange is about it. Rather a brothel drink."

"That must be why I like it," said Yanov.

"And Petya"—she gave my arm the little squeeze burned into memory from the beach. "How would you know?"

I sliced the orange and watched them. Yanov, man of socialist realism, was now like a man on drugs, overwhelmed by the intensity of color of the pictures on the walls. Nicola, totally immersed as curator and owner, chattered about brush strokes and depths of background and types of bronze. She took the drink I offered, without noticing.

"That was excellent." Yanov approved the bartending. "A little exotic, but good for such a special occasion." He went back to examining the portrait of a woman with a skewed face the color of a Mexican sunrise—looking at it from the sides, tilting the frame.

"A bloody horror," I said as the critic, but for some reason he was caught by the picture.

Nicola came over and gave me a peck on the cheek. "Petya, I've neglected you. What about some food? Do you both like sukiyaki?"

"This is American?" asked Yanov.

"Japanese."

"Ah." His face was politely apprehensive.

"A couple of bottles of sake will numb the pain," I said. For both of us. Japanese food for a Russian by an Italian American in San Francisco seemed no more involved than my own feelings, watching them mix so easily together. They had reached in half an hour a friendship it had taken me two days to accomplish.

The timing of the food appeared critical. Bits and pieces were prepared to a precise schedule. Considerable sake was warmed and drunk. There were minor logistical problems. The dog ate the shrimp appetizers.

"Okay," she said finally. "We do the last part at the table. Are we going to be genuine and sit on the floor?"

Yanov's apprehension broke surface. We sat on chairs in relative silence broken by Nicola's laughter. Novices with chopsticks are amusing to watch but poor conversationalists. I found the meal delicious. Yanov tried hard.

"Well, Alexey Ilyich?" Realizing as I said it that we now slipped in and out of Russian without thinking.

"Interesting. The raw egg is perhaps an acquired taste."

Nicola produced coffee and an evaporated part bottle of a sugary liqueur. We moved away from the chopsticks towards the center of the room. Yanov pointed at the piano, talking to Nicola. "Shut. Do you not play?"

"Not well. It was a wedding present—"

I hadn't warned him. He continued, unaware of the black hole now invisible in the room. "Steinway. Very nice. May I check the tone."

She nodded. He flipped back the lid; ran a hand with apparent expertise.

"You're good?" she asked.

"Hardly a Rubinstein, but perhaps I can play for my supper. A little Tchaikovsky?"

He sat, looking ridiculously huge on the stool's spindled legs, his oversized square hands grotesque against the keys. He opened the top and set the brace, pushed back the stool, rocked size twelve shoes on the pedals, hunched his football shoulders in the Gieves jacket. The houndstooth race-course pattern accentuated the incongruity. He played.

The notes came forward softly, hesitantly, unwilling to believe that they were being freed by a master, but becoming louder as they met him, joined with him, became linked into chords, were swelled by the pedals, and went soaring and hammering in the room from this Russian playing a Russian's music.

And somewhere from my first days, other notes came out from memory to join them, and images of red and gold and a stiff figure in a splendid suit beside me and a night trip in white winter against spires with the figure humming, hand beating on a knee. Where and when? Where and when? Never in England.

It was leaving us, the music. Withdrawing. The chords dying, the last notes falling faintly back to wire and wood, waiting for perhaps a generation to be called out again like that.

"The B Flat Minor, Opus Twenty-Three, no? A 'showoff' piece, as you say in English, but pleasant."

"*Unbelievable*, you bastard!" I smashed him on the back, said inadequate things. He fielded them modestly, but obviously pleased as hell to be for once a Russian unequivocally superior. "Where, for the love of God, did you learn to play like that?"

"A long story—"

"You're bloody wasted in the navy. Niki, you know about this stuff; shouldn't he be doing it for a living?"

She wasn't with us. "She feels it too much," said Yanov. "She must have a moment."

"She lost a husband. Six months ago—a pilot."

"Ahh. I would not have played tonight." He got up from the stool and stood before the window, staring out across the Bay at the lights of Oakland. Behind them, the sky above the desert was a deep, deep violet. "I should not have played..."

"Truly, Alexey Ilyich, why waste such talent?"

He shrugged. "There are events... You remember the children's game 'The Gunner says'?"

The Queen, O'Grady, the Gunner, the State—a universal game—not just for children. I nodded.

"Well"—he spread his hands, again in English, "When Stalin said 'don't play'—besides, I think I enjoy the life of a sailor more than on stage." He flashed a grin wide enough to show a steel tooth, punched me on the arm. "Too many *zhopochnik*... what's the word?"

"Queers," I said, "or pansies. Take your pick."

"He could if you'd take him to Finnochio's."

"Ah. Good, our hostess—back with us." He stood between us, an arm impulsively around each shoulder. The life of the party.

"Did you mean that literally, Alexey Ilyich, about Stalin?"

"In front of a hundred thousand people, he asked what I wanted to be. The navy popped from nowhere into my head, God alone knows why. But how could I go back after that? Anyhow, a tale for another time. Too solemn. Is there dancing music, Nicolasha? You must be a dancer?"

Nicolasha. Taking her in a word from endless California summer to that frozen land of troikas, frosted furs and terror.

"Sure," she said. "What would you like? Old Vienna? I don't have anything with Cossacks on it."

"Something 'hot'—I must astonish them at home."

She put on a stack of records. Dinosaur noises of the rock age yammered with steel guitars. "Blue Suede Shoes—gotta let it all hang out, baby." She made the required writhings in front of him.

"Hot enough, Yanov?" I asked. His face was more of a study than it had been with the raw egg.

"She can't mean in Russian what she says, Pyotr Andreyevich?"

"I certainly hope not."

But he was game; after the moment's shock, up on his feet with the same surprising lightness from the steps of Greenwich—the spirit willing, but unable to overcome momentum of the torso. A bull dancing on two hoofs in the china shop. Ornaments were imperiled. Tables swayed. The dog howled outside the door. I laughed till tears poured.

"Not so easy off the hook, Petya." She grabbed my arm, pulling me up. "You've lost the beat," she said, "you were great at the Condor."

"In the clubs I was anonymous."

Her hips bumped suggestively, her head teased close to toss her hair across my face. "Chrysalis!"

The machine changed its mind and put on something slower. Yanov tactfully took a drink out to the dog.

"What a fantastic guy," she said. "No wonder you like him."

"They want to bury us."

"Professional jealousy. He's really Khrushchev's cousin?"

"So he says."

"You sound doubtful."

"Who knows? Let's join him for a breather."

He was lost in thought, sitting with the dog beside him, his hand rubbing its head. Man and dog staring together at a huge moon rising dead center through the catenary of the Bay bridge.

"A harvest moon in Russia," he said.

Or in prison. By moonlight Alcatraz could be Monte Cristo's island. I wondered what it would take to make him stay. Why should any man go back?

"What is the music?" he asked Nicola.

"*South Pacific*—you haven't heard it? I'm surprised." She explained the plot. "Almost too romantic."

"Like my Tchaikovsky."

The overture prepared us. Protagonists arrived, strangers saw each other for a first time. Pinza filled the night. Yanov listened carefully, having difficulty with the English. The first side ended. "Play that one song once more," he said. "Such a magnificent voice—particularly after that Shoes person."

"Pinza doesn't understand a word he's saying, you know," I said.

"Why does he need to? They meet, they know, they love. He sings it. Words are nothing."

"Christ, man, they're everything."

"The difference between us, my friend"—echoing Jackson. He was suddenly somber. "Words make politics—not music." He stood up. "Will you dance a last time, Nicolasha?"

The record and a world turned, the arm dropped, the music started. The singer in his ignorance sang. I sat with the dog as they danced behind me. I wondered what I was. I listened to the words.

"... A girl for one's dreams ... a partner for paradise ... a promise of paradise...."

"This nearly was mine!"

I organized a cab to end it. When I came back Yanov was staring out again at Oakland. *"Opposite sides of the sea*—where could one buy that record?"

Of course she gave it to him. "No. Really—I can get another any time. And you just must have a present"—writing on the album. "Send me a postcard or something from the Kremlin."

"I promise."

Not bloody likely, darling, when the hoods in the Moscow post office sort the mail, but reality was too rude an intruder for such a moment. The horn blared from the hillside. We went up the steps. Halfway he said, "My cap. One moment."

I went on to the top, stood waiting beside the cab, looked back down the hill. The towering silhouette of the Russian and the slim shadow of my American stood against a silver sea. I shivered. Felt a stab too mean and unnecessary to be jealousy. Remembered the old wives' tales of footsteps on a grave. He turned and climbed away from her.

I opened the cab door; he stood beside it for a moment holding his record. "An enchanted evening," he said. "In my heart, Pyotr Andreyevich—all my life." And in front of the damned driver, kissed me on both cheeks.

I watched the red lights receding down the hill. So many thoughts. So little time until I too was gone from California. I turned to recross the road, stepped off the curb. And the old green Dodge, racing without lights after the cab, almost hit me. Would have if the driver hadn't made a Grand Prix swerve with squealing tires across the line. Into the glare of a street lamp so that I saw his face. From behind a table in a hallway.

Shadowed. Shot away. Sucked in where the jaw was missing.

Without Yanov the cluttered house was bare. We sat looking at each other across a suddenly empty room and the ritual coffee, reverting for a moment to the stiff formality of strangers.

"After McCarthy," she said, "we think of them as one-eyed with three heads, not like..." She didn't finish the thought.

"Well, don't hold your breath waiting for a card." I stood up, unsure, feeling pale in his reflection. "His piano playing was a surprise—I knew he liked art. I don't know what he could have seen in this, though."

The painting of the skewed woman was in front of me, its frame, like the face, off square. I reached to straighten it, pushed it too far the other way. The wall behind was damaged, the plaster cracked. By Yanov's dancing, or a San Francisco earthquake?

But even Dravin, recruited spy who'd never seen anything more substantial of the trade than pipe smoke could recognize a microphone. And hide it.

I moved the frame.

"What do you think?" Nicola was behind my shoulder.

"Not my cup of tea, really." Shades of Crabb in "not my cup of tea."

"It's meant to create tension, anxiety."

"Remarkably well." I turned to her. "I must go."

"You don't have to."

Four words. Words that could be British in their understatement. Words offering what had been prayed for. Words already shared with some voyeuristic son of a bitch behind a picture.

She was waiting. The great brown eyes still offering. The pulse trembling under the golden locket between the breasts where a head could rest, hands could touch.

The eyes are closing as the lips are parted. And now there's no dog barking, Dravin, no strangers on the shore intruding. She stands with the wide hips in the green dress waiting for the schoolboy's chrysalis shell to give its final crack. For the man to tear Russian passion.

To forget that the walls have ears.

Which I could not do.

"I must go, Niki. A report to write that has to get away first thing."

"Tomorrow, Petya?" Her Latin frankness devastating in its honesty.

"Wild horses," I said. "I promise."

Alone in the Paxtons' flat I put in the call to the London number. My name and function were relayed through echelons of night staff in a panic.

"Marshall here. Spot of bother, old boy?" A plummy voice with ridiculous language.

"I think so."

"Say no more. Know all about you and Cousin Y. Where are you calling from?"

I explained.

"Go to a call box and call again. Toot sweet, as they say."

Seething at the thought of prizes sacrificed for this idiocy, I found another phone.

"Jolly good," said the already hated voice. "Now tell uncle all about the land of grand illusion. Who's been naughty?"

"That's what I haven't the faintest bloody idea. There was no time for anyone to know I'd take him to the house." The additional facts took ridiculously little time.

"And that's the lot, old boy?"

"Yes," I said. "Who the hell was after what?"

"*Who*? I'm not in San Francisco, how do I know? The what, of course, is you."

The conversation was too ridiculous to be occurring. "Me? Someone was after *me*?"

The voice dropped its trappings for a moment. "Get out."

"Out?"

"Come home."

"You mean to Britain?"

"Not to bloody Moscow, darling."

"When?"

The receiver sighed, "Just as soon as you can get the old bod in the air, and without saying ta-ta to your bit of stuff lying in the night flowers."

I would have killed him. Whitehall fucking pansy with its long legs crossed gracefully showing silken socks, stroking its hair in every window reflection, admiring its paisley ascot neck.

"You want me to take the first flight directly from San Francisco to London without informing Washington?"

"Precisely so, old boy. *Or anyone else*. And that is, of course, an order."

Which I obeyed as expected: Made no call, left no note, took a taxi to an airport for a first-class seat beside a window by a starboard wing for a lift-off at sunrise to return as suddenly as I had left the diver.

But as the aircraft accelerated and rose above the houses and the freight yards turning swiftly into tiny toys, as it banked out across the white lace border separating brown from blue, I drew down the curtain so that I might not see a cove with a crescent beach where a girl goes to stare alone at the Pacific beyond the capes ringed with cypress tops as flat as sailors' caps.

I was damned tired. And any woman who could drive a bloody car like that could look after herself until I had time to write or call or send some flowers. I settled back into the seat. I thought ahead to home. England. My father and my questions.

LONDON 1.

CHAPTER

ELEVEN

When I saw Jackson beyond the Gatwick counter I felt not an inkling. Surprise that a senior would take the trouble to meet the plane; pleasure at the compliment. Relief that transport into town was solved. Nothing more.

And yet Russians are supposed to sense these things. To know.

"Dravin! How very good to see you."

"You too, sir. This is most unexpected." Looking much the same as the last time on my bunk. Blue eyes and pipe. Hair full silver now. The hand just as steady.

But holding on too long. "A sad reason, I'm sorry to tell you," the slight Irish cadence coming through. "Your father's dying."

I could only repeat the word. "Dying?"

"A stroke, I think. This morning in his garden. He's at home now and I'll take you to him."

At eighty, death is in the garden every morning, watching quietly, waiting for a polite moment. Never intrusive or catastrophic as he is at thirty. But youth at thirty doesn't see him. Youth is always shocked.

And with every foot through London streets I was closer to youth, to the past, to a schoolboy rushing home in crackling leaves and gaslight. *But for a journey he should have completed long ago. While there was time.*

Beside the now boatless Pond on the Heath, under the chestnut trees of Boundary Road, swinging an iron gate through the dirty black-green privet of the hedge and up to the house and a door with the horseshoe knocker. And inside to a samovar that was not an embarrassing anachronism but an old and welcome friend. To a smell of toast on a toasting fork, to the gleam of a brass grate warming it. To a mother at the door.

"Mamuschka?" The house was warm and the samovar boiled, but no fire. No toast. And her hand so cold.

"Petya!" The gray head pressed into the brass-crowned buttons of my coat. "We were going to have tea."

But when were they not?

My father lay in the brass bed, eyes open, halfway to heaven, the snow-pointed beard across the sheet only separated from its whiteness by the yellow nicotine.

"Shouldn't he be in hospital?" I asked the calm figure of the doctor, known since the scraped knees of my boyhood.

"He knew it might happen—his blood pressure was much too high. But he kept his cigarettes and he asked not to leave this house if I could manage it. I would bow to your mother's wishes, of course."

"She would want what he wants," I said.

The room was crowded now with the attendants. My mother. Jackson. The black shadow of the priest from the orthodox church in Finsbury Park. Behind me I heard her knees complaining to the cracked gilt of the traveling ikon on the dresser, and then the droning of the catechism I could not have remembered but never forgot.

I held his rice-paper hand and wondered where he was bound.

"*Otetz*." Father. Even now not "Papa."

"He can't respond," said the doctor, but his lips were moving.

"*Pesha*..." in the faintest whisper.

And the eyes were already on their journey, beyond me and on to Jackson.

"*Mon vieux*"—the zephyr breath mixing the languages of the old Russia—"*Blagodaryu vas.*" Which is I thank you.

And his spirit left him.

The next day, at Highgate Hill within sight of Karl Marx's grave, he was buried—and any of his answers to my questions with him.

On the afternoon following the funeral I left my mother with a circle of White Russians all in black, and reported to the Admiralty to get away.

"Captain Jackson's office, please?"

"Second floor, sir." A good bust and a smile on the duty wren cheered me up.

"Thanks." I smiled back.

"And sir—"

"Yes?"

"*Admiral* Jackson."

The office didn't match the promotion. Standard Admiralty pattern, old cream paint with brown wainscot. Last done for the Coronation in 1937. He was out and I waited.

Pictures of ships' companies mustered for commissioning photographs charted a new admiral's career as the face aged, the braid grew up the arm, and the body moved closer to the center of the group. The Kisby ring of the lifebuoy in the last picture said *Caliope*.

The door opened and he came in carrying the broad stripe.

"Congratulations, sir."

He gave his humorous glint. "Not to impress you—uniform day for this floor. Give the tourists their money's worth. Come along into the sanctum."

The inner office was more of the outer plus a view of Admiralty Arch, and northeast across Trafalgar Square to St. Martin's and the Strand. The blue leather of the furniture had blackened and books hid the walls. A scrimshaw lamp on the desk had two large tusks as a base.

"Walrus, sir?"

"It would be appropriate—but baleen, I think. Very old. I forget where I picked it up. Sit down."

The interaction of his sitting and the pipe lighting was like watching one of those Victorian clockwork toys. "You talk first," he said. "Business or personal?"

"They seem pretty much entwined, sir—but personal if I may. My father."

"Short or long?"

"Short for now. I don't want to wallow."

"Very well. I was responsible for arranging your father's departure from the Soviet Union and setting him up here with a house and a pension."

"And Khrushchev?"

"Your father probably saved his life."

But that was too short—a hundred questions opened off his answer. I asked the obvious one first. "How?"

"In a nutshell, Stalin believed his wife, Nadezhda Sergeyevna, was being unfaithful with his lieutenant, Nikita."

"And was she?"

"Your father thought it possible, but not at the time of Stalin's accusation. Five years earlier—when Khrushchev was a student with her at the Moscow Industrial Academy. He was then a man in his mid-thirties. And she was a young political wife with all the usual problems of boredom and what have you. Sensitive, artistic. And caged—because Stalin wouldn't even let it out that he was married, let alone give his wife any scope for maneuver—"

"But with a thug like Khrushchev?"

He shrugged. "The gamekeeper syndrome—earthy animal vitality. I imagine that there isn't a combination possible that the Kremlin hasn't witnessed at some time in the last five centuries.

"And the fact *is* that one moment K was stuck immovably behind a log jam of men like Zinoviev, Bukharin and Rykov— and the next, after a word from Nadya in her husband's ear, he was through the jam and on top. And they were swept away."

"And one of them turned the word to a worm?"

"It's the usual course of events with jealous favorites."

"And my father's role?"

"To be the final witness for Khrushchev's prosecution—unwittingly. After a knock on the door and a summons to Stalin's private apartment in the Kremlin. If one can imagine what that must be like . . ."

Could one?

Sense the awful uncertainty of such a call? Imagine my father's stomach turning over? No. Because I couldn't see him ever knowing fear—or any other sense of feeling. And yet he must. He had called me Pesha.

Grant then, that he could feel. But what—walking alone on a December midnight across the squeaking crispness of the snow in the outer court? Wall shadows thrown by the moon hiding the arch and entrance to the inner yard beyond. Wondering what was through it. . . .

"The three of them," said Jackson. "Stalin, Nadya, Khrushchev. Alone after dinner. No servants—half-full dishes pushed aside and stacked on the sideboards, whole courses untouched. Joe at his most slit-eyed and amiable with a visitor. K with a face of death warmed over . . ."

Because if any man knew the rules they played by, Khrushchev did. The Jacobin laws—the special powers of the newly minted NKVD: powers of torture, the knock in the night, summary death—were on the books. The Terror worked. Seven million Russians were about to die.

"So there they were. Your father standing, facing Stalin's cat face, not a hint of anything amiss except for Nadya sitting like thin ice waiting for the hammer. For all your father knew, the victim was himself."

Stalin now asked the question. But phrased with an obliquity that any grudge-seeker in that Byzantine world would instantly appreciate—and make the most of. "Nikita Sergeyevich says that he was alone with you in your office on the evening before last?"

"Here," said Jackson, "you have to visualize the expression on Stalin's face, the smooth almost sleepy look, the eyes opaque, their thoughts hidden. High voice, 'I say he's mistaken on the date, Andrei Andreyevich.' Swirling a glass of red wine at the light, admiring the color, 'Who's right?'"

Setting the glass down gently on the tablecloth.

"Your father swore he could hear the thud of it. And your father was going to tell the truth as he knew it to be. But how could he tell which truth was wanted?"

I could not imagine. I just stared at Jackson.

"Your father said, 'Nikita Sergeyevich is right, Comrade'—Stalin prided himself on his egalitarianism at that stage. Before he made himself a generalissimo. And Khrushchev hung on to the table leg and nearly vomited."

"And as an end of it," I asked, "Khrushchev helped my father to escape?"

"Nothing so noble. And I omitted the fact that gives it its true irony. The purpose of the meeting with Khrushchev that provided the alibi had been to face your father with a charge by an informer that he had been involved in the Kirov assassination in Leningrad two years earlier. Khrushchev was in charge of that investigation and the military purge led straight from it. No, your father's name stayed on the list that went to the Procurator for Special Trials. And other arrangements which I had been concerned with took over and we made the escape. Buh perhaps you can see now why Khrushchev finds it interesting to see you."

"As the son of a traitor or savior?"

"Dravin, you have a Russian sense of the melodramatic. After so long, I think simple curiosity would suffice as motive."

Simple! A word without meaning in Russian politics. And begging the final question.

"Given all that, just what *was* my father?"

He got up and went over to a bookcase, brought out a heavy volume and placed it on the desk. "The Soviet Encyclopedia for 1938." Opening it with maddening deliberation, rifling the pages. "The purge moved too quickly for the presses." His fingers stopped at last, the book lay open, the left-hand page densely massed with childhood characters. The right was nothing. Blank, white, Siberian in implication.

"But in 1937, sir?" *Stop playing God, Jackson!*

"An admiral, responsible for all communications. Vice chief of their naval staff."

Traitor! As I had known, my simple answer. In my father's mind, in any mind locked in the labyrinth of Russian patriotism, quite simply, once and always: Traitor. To Russia. I knew it absolutely. With full knowledge of all that was inhumanly odious of Russian government I knew it. Because I heard it in my own mind.

"Give me this child," says the Church, says the Party, "for these first few years." I had been a Russian child for those necessary and sufficient years.

"No, Dravin," said Jackson, with that intuition which I seemed to lack. "Never a traitor. If Stalin had listened to him there would have been no Barbarossa. And by coming to us with what he did when he did, we won the war. He brought us our first Enigma. The machine that carried Hitler's code."

He put history in its place on the shelf. "Meet me in an hour at the Guards. We'll have lunch and tackle the present day and California."

We dined on turbot in a private room. Jackson was silent from start to finish. He drank some coffee and lit the pipe.

"The girl," he said, ignoring Khrushchev and the man in the green car, "any attraction there with Yanov?"

"Oh no."

"Yet he took her address?"

"But just as a natural exchange of politeness for the gift of the record."

"Which she gave him first."

"Certainly. But Americans are like that. Give you the house if you hint."

"Yes? I'm sure you're right. But it would be interesting if he sent the woman her card, don't you think? You'll be writing to her yourself, of course?"

I nodded. "The green car—"

"KGB nursing Yanov—like your commissar in London."

He stood up and thanked the steward. We walked down the steps.

"We'll tackle the mike business in my office," he said. "A little upsetting, I suppose, at the time."

"It scared the hell out of me."

The words seemed to make no impression. "A remarkable thing, this Yanov case—being let off the string to such a degree. Cousin or no cousin, he must leave something of considerable value at home. Any mention of wives and children?"

"A mother—but he doesn't give the impression of being tied to hearth and home."

"Well he's tied to something. We must find out what. If he ever cuts the bond he might drift in our direction."

"Do you think he really met Stalin for some sort of party laying-on of hands?"

Jackson allowed a very small smile. "By a Borgia pope, if ever there was one, but I don't see why he should need to lie about it." He stopped to look at a pigeon with buff plumage walk a neat circle around some crumbs. "D'you know that beggar always has the same spot. I've watched him for two years—"

"He sees the little sparrow fall—"

"Oh we do, Dravin"—still looking at the pigeon. "We do." His eyes were suddenly on me. "The sparrows and the whores."

We turned into the building and he returned to the funeral. "Who were the other mourners?"

"Emigré friends. My mother's part of a little group, the Anglo–White Russian Friendship Alliance. Formed in the twenties—"

"I know it. Fading spinster cousins of ex-dukes, and tea importers from St. Peterburg who got away." And all viewing old dreams instead of home movies on lonely evenings. I was surprised that he knew. More so that he was interested.

"That can be your initiation. All sorts of odds and sods get attached to the fringes. Take a filial interest—go to the occasional meeting, compile the names, talk in the language. Ex-dukes aren't much good, but a Balt with current links might prove useful."

This time there was a secretary in the outer office, a thin pen of a woman trained to write till the nib wore out and then go quietly. She looked up expectantly as Jackson spoke. "Miss Harris, find Mr. Marshall for me, please."

We sat down where we'd left history before lunch. "It's time, I think," he said, "for a short and frank child's guide to the underworld before you meet Marshall."

"We met on the phone, sir."

"Yes. He has that effect on first impression. But go slow with him." He settled back into the chair. "Now, to expand on what I said in Portsmouth, we are naval intelligence. Uniformed, providing our political masters with analysis based on info from various sources. We are normally passive, by and large staying out of harm's way. The active side—the people who have to operate in unpleasant places and dangerous ways—are civilian or pretending to be. Working for the Foreign Office through the

M.I.'s, military intelligence five and six. But there's a large body of water in between—"

"And sometimes it's muddied. Like Crabb?"

"Precisely."

"Any more about him, sir—did he ever show up?"

"No."

The tone said that any information needed would be given without asking.

He tipped his chair back and got the pipe going again. "I must tell you that there has been, undeniably, a certain increasing— let's say, reluctance—about following present lines of authority. Partly because of the Burgess and Maclean runaway to Moscow and partly, I suppose, because in the Service we've always thought of the backstage world as our show."

"RN, you mean, sir?"

"Yes. We began modern intelligence—or Captain Smith-Cumming did—before the first war. And we kept it after, with Admiral Hugh Sinclair who recruited me. By '39 it had become expected that we'd have a sailor at the top of the intelligence tree. A lot of people still think it was a better game then—tighter run. A higher class of man."

He stared at the plaster curls on the ceiling. "I'm biased that way myself—can't deny it. No one could, who served under Sinclair." His voice lost its softness with conviction. "If there was a single man besides Churchill who got us under the wire in time it was Hugh. We had *nothing*—a handful of people, no money. I can tell you it was hens' teeth to get the funds for your father . . ."

Even the headmaster had pipe dreams in the smoke.

"When Admiral Sinclair died the succession should have stayed with us—I've never doubted that he instructed the government to that end—but they picked a soldier diplomat. Fine man—no dispute. But not the same training or outlook. And too much liaison with the universities. Not enough control. And just look what we've got now. A few gifted all right—but the rest! Social-climbing bureaucrats with no loyalty, and unpleasant personal habits. We're in for a lot more trouble ahead. No wonder the Yanks don't trust us."

There was a flurry in the outer office. "Marshall," said Jackson. "Stay here—I'll only be a minute."

I stood up, ready to face the nemesis of my broken night in San Francisco. Realized with a sense of shock that three days had passed with death and no call to Nicola had been made. I didn't relish the thought of explanation.

The door reopened with a bang. The complete antithesis of my mental image of limp silk socks: Short and bald, with a weight problem held back by a vested suit and a watch chain. A man who bustled. He was followed by Jackson. "The dark face of our intelligence magic. Dravin—the contrast to our open simple sailoring."

"Balls, Jacko!" *Said to an admiral?* A broad smile of false teeth to me. "Already had the pleasure on the phone, old boy— glad to have a dekko."

Another warm smile with cold eyes from any boy's favorite rumpled uncle. "You've put the cowboys in an awful twist, old man, awful twist." The jolly adventure words remembered from the phone were bad enough. The giggling laugh clinched it.

"What the hell, may I ask, is a cowboy?"

"Our brothers-in-arms in the class struggle. The boys of the old OSS brigade riding out of the West to save it."

"The CIA?" The name snapped any pretense of a sport.

Not to Marshall. "In all its mechanical splendor, old man," he said, sinking with a fat man's *whoosh* into the cushions. "Your time in Disneyland—tell us all."

I went over the ground in California yet again. He was more interested in opening a bag of peppermints than in Nikita. "Humbug?"

I refused.

"Jacko?"

Jackson took one of the damned things and placed it solemnly beside his ash tray, in his glacial way amused, which annoyed me more. Marshall counted the remaining mints as I described the evening with Yanov and the finding of the mike.

"Rather pulled you off the nest at the old finale. Just as stars might shine and nightingales sing, what?"

I loathed him. "What the hell was going on? How could the Russians have known in time that I would take Yanov to the house?"

"Russians?" As though I'd said Greeks. "Russkis love you—

dinner and dancing and caviar brought in just for Dravers. It's the cowboys, old boy—thought I'd explained. Crying in their beer over your running on their track without permission. Don't trust you a bloody inch anyway. Viper in the bosom, Trojan horse. Just waiting for you to set the fire and fly away home to the Kremlin."

He offered the mints again in a generous mood and then twisted the top shut. "They already blame you for spoiling the Diver. Silly, of course—we all know—but then Crabbie *was* their play-mate."

"You're wandering," suid Jackson coldly. He turned to me like a judge instructing a jury. "Unproven hypothesis."

To be disregarded. Which, as every juryman knows, it never is. "Yes sir," I said. "But I *am* distrusted by Americans?"

"For the time being, Dravin, as I've already said, we are all distrusted—and a little of vice versa. Senator McCarthy cast a long shadow."

"And what about my girl?"

"I'll talk to them," said Jackson. "Soothe them down."

Marshall pushed himself up from the cushions. "Such a lot to learn. Well, send him around when he's free, Jacko, and we'll teach him hot from cold. Might even find old Face Hole in the mugs somewhere."

"*Wizard* show!" I said.

"Well, toodle-oo, then." But the light in the smile had shut off like a gas jet.

I looked at the closed door and then at Jackson. He stared at me gravely, weighing Marshall's peppermint in his palm.

"Head of his department, old man." The imitation was accurate but not explanatory. "As I said, he takes some wearing in." He threw the humbug in the gash bucket. "You'll manage."

I settled in at the Admiralty. Went back to school at a nursery level to learn a little of the Marshall world; hot from cold, as he put it. After that, by day I sat at a desk studying statistics of barge construction in the Volga basin. By night I met Latvian butchers and bakers to listen to accounts of escape and betrayal, and fan the flames of dissent in the Baltic states.

In any odd moments I dreamt about California.

Nicola, as an ex-navy wife, had been more understanding of

sudden orders than I had expected. She wrote regularly. The second letter was not a happy one:

"...Largo died. Some punks broke in. A couple of pictures were slashed and they punched some holes in the wall. I guess Largo tried to stop them—there was some blood. The vet says he probably had a heart attack....I think I'll move back near my parents at Orinda, close to the campus..."

No more stolen shrimp or staring at the moon for Largo. At the end, too gentle to keep out weirdos recovering a bug.

I tried to cheer her up by arranging a holiday to Britain after her college year was over, but it was constantly on and off. When the Admiralty switchboard put through a call from San Francisco in working hours, almost a year after our parting, I hoped for the best.

"Hi," she said, "you owe me a buck." To hear even the telephone voice brought overwhelming physical sensation.

"You've paid for the ticket?"

"What?" The transatlantic line was poor. "No, dummy. His card. You owe me a buck."

"You got a card from Yanov?"

"Ten. It's a packet of views of Moscow."

"Bugger me!"

I heard laughter at twelve dollars a minute. "And guess what, Petya!"

"You're going to marry me?"

"You never asked—no. He's going to be in New York. He thinks it would be great if we all met again."

"All?"

"He said if I told you, he thought you'd find a way of being there."

"Funny man." But it was difficult to keep things light with the implications buzzing in my head. "Would you go?"

"Sure. I can stay with a friend—she works at the UN, as a matter of fact, so she'll know all the tricks."

"Did he give a date?"

"Just around the end of the first week in September." East Side, West Side, all around the town. "He said to watch the papers. Will you make it, Petya?"

"With bells on."

"Even if he doesn't show?"

"Especially. I love you."

"Getting better," she said.

I went in to tell Jackson, expecting for once at least a small degree of surprise, but if anything he was cooler than ever. Just nodding to himself, almost expecting it. The only thing that intrigued him was the excuse, not the message.

"Strange that we haven't heard anything on the jungle drums about an outing."

They were beating the following week. "On the Baltika from Kaliningrad," said Jackson. "Khrushchev to join the circus at the Heads of State at the UN. I've made arrangements for you to go with the PM's party as an interpreter. Naval rank but plain clothes."

On the day of the flight I sat in his office waiting for a car to take me to Downing Street to meet the official party. He stood by the window looking out at Nelson and his pigeons. "I've tried to smooth the way this time," he said. "But with Castro and Khrushchev both in town, New York will be a hoods' holiday camp—be prudent."

"I will, sir." I felt a sudden need for some assurance. "Where do you think we're going with all this?"

"I don't know, Dravin. And I don't think the Sovs do either." He turned back from the window. "It's that uncertainty which upsets Dulles."

It upset me.

NEW YORK.

CHAPTER

TWELVE

All my carefully prepared opening remarks went down the drain when the wrong girl met me at the door of the apartment.

"Hi—I'm Chris Vorland. You must be Peter. Come along in."

"I wanted to propose to Nicola."

She laughed. "She told me you're a joker. She's in the shower. Let me get you a drink."

I made conventional noises about furnishings and location. Relatively sincerely. The carpets were as thick as the fleece on the sheep and the eleventh-floor view of Central Park across the street was as pleasant as the heart of a city can be.

"My folks' place," she said. "I caretake while they're in Washington."

"I gather you work at the UN?"

"Just a junior body on our ambassador's staff."

A blonde, charming and screwable one. But in the wrong place at the wrong time. Staring at the park, I wanted only to be alone with Nicola, tell her bluntly and straightaway my intentions.

"Boo!"

"Niki!" I jumped from the poke in the ribs.

"For scaring me last year." She held out both hands, reached

93

up and gave me a quick kiss on the cheek. I stood like a clod. No matter how desperately the mind hangs on, the picture fades in a year, loses the living touches that give it crispness, anchor it to reality. The green dress and the locket took me back as though she had spoken in San Francisco that very second.

"Counting wrinkles, Petya?"

"Checking the trim of the vessel. None of the cargo seems to have shifted."

"I warned Chris you had a silver tongue." She was laughing again. "If we're going to have a drink, I'll need my hands back."

I released her. We picked up the pieces, commiserated about the passing of my father and her dog, explaining enough to the other girl to make her part of it. But on my part willing her to leave us. She stayed. I asked if they wanted to go with me to meet the *Baltika* in the morning. "Wave at Yanov—throw ticker tape?"

There was a girlhood-chums look between them. "But he's already here, Petya. We met—it was the wildest thing. This morning at the UN while I was waiting for Chris. Talk about your Russian fate!"

Fate.

Fate didn't send postcards—or jump the gun by arriving early to meet another man's girl. This artificial fate was laid out in straight lines drawn in a Moscow office.

"I took him to the Guggenheim this afternoon," she said. "There was a special Picasso exhibit. You would have hated it."

"I'm sure I should. All melting watches with eyes in them."

"That's Dali, idiot. But see, Chris, you just can't tell when he's serious. Anyhow, Petya, we've got it all fixed for this evening. We're going to meet at a Hungarian place on 52nd for a meal and then come back here after."

"Wonderful," I said. "Horsehair and fiddle strings in the soup."

The blonde girl got us past security arrangements at the restaurant comparable to those at Khrushchev's suite in LA. "It's the in place for the beautiful people, right now," she explained. "They get a lot of gate-crashers."

"Do I qualify as a beauty?"

"To be truthful—no. But then neither is Aristotle Onassis. They know me through the job."

Inside, the decor was Transylvanian—fiddlers with kerchiefs and spaniel eyes sawing away under crimson hangings.

Yanov arrived promptly to the second at eight. He was towed over by the maître d', a tiny man hardly up to his chest. There was a lot of embracing. Alexey was looking natty in an American button-down shirt. I admired his tie.

He beamed. "From Paris—for special occasions." He asked me with a straight face what brought me to New York.

"An RAF Comet," I said. "And your good self?"

"Funny bugger, Petya. But in a way my reason also. Our Tupolev. It is to fly home nonstop to Moscow and I was to weigh the discomfort of the journey for the Chairman. I like this place—very rich. What are these people, Austrians?"

"Hungarian. They came over after the uprising." He didn't bat an eye—the reaction by an Englishman fifty years earlier to news of another Afghan war. He got up to dance with Nicola. I danced with the blonde and watched them. His use of "Petya" seemed another first.

The food arrived in front of a bloodsucking photographer with a drooping mustache.

"Your pictures? Ladies—gentlemens?"

For an almost unnoticeable fraction, Yanov hesitated: the inborn fear by a native that a camera might snatch the spirit, or send the image home.

"Why not, why not?" Smiles and toasts followed by the next act—Madame Irena stuffed into a cart more covered wagon than gypsy caravan. With the fortune teller's advantage of making statements which might be definite or interrogative as the personal preference of the listener determined, there were generalities for all.

I missed them.

Unless I was now as paranoid as I'd thought the Russians were, four years earlier, the man watching us from the table beyond the caravan, and holding a long glass of dark beer in his left hand, had never drunk it.

". . . white shadows and dark reflections . . ." Madame was sliding along with the patter. There was something about being united over water.

"A safe bet in the jet age," I said.

"Oh Petya, come off it." Nicola shoved my arm. "Anyway, that part's already happened. Our meeting, Alexey. The fountain at the Secretariat." She grasped my hand and held it firmly on the table in front of Madame. "Let's see what's in there."

"No. I'd rather not."

"You're being stupid—"

"Not for the first time. *I'd rather not!*"

"Okay, okay." She let go of the hand. The woman went on to the blonde, and kids with a handsome stranger. Total nonsense. I'd been a fool. *Then why the flush on my neck? Why the raised voice? Why this claustrophobic feeling of a moment's panic?*

The woman moved crystal ball and camp to another table. Chris diplomatically changed the subject.

"How about a drive tomorrow? My folks have a farm upstate near Albany."

"Wonderful," said Yanov. "I should love to see the country. I understand it is very much like home."

"How, Alexey Ilyich?"—in Russian, to keep things private. "The Yanks won't even give you visas to get to your embassy retreat on Long Island."

His voice froze into a Slavic protest meant, like Khrushchev's the year before, to be overheard. "The denial of the visas was an inexcusable humiliation to the Soviet Union. The Chairman has made this sufficiently clear and the United States recognizes the injustices of its actions. I shall join you with the greatest pleasure."

He reverted effortlessly to type, gave me the broadest of grins to show a second steel tooth—now one on each side, like Dracula. "Let's go for a landau ride in Central Park."

I paid off the taxi driver while the others crossed the street to the carriage rank.

On my side and on the corner of the block another cab stopped. Beer Mug got out. I walked towards him, feeling an absurd sensation of a cowboy showdown in a movie back-lot street.

He started to walk away. I increased my stride. So did he. I broke into a run, realizing that I was being a fool for the second time in one evening. He was in better trim and kept effortlessly ahead. Behind me, horseshoes clicked on pavement.

A whip cracked.

Across the street, with a gleam from a cabby's high top hat and the winking brass of coach lamps, the carriage, with only Nicola and Yanov in it, vanished into the New York night.

The blonde was waiting. "Do you want to hang around?" she asked.

"I want a drink."

We went up to the apartment, danced, exchanged anecdotes about the frailties of the famous. I watched the street. After half an hour the horse drew back up to the cab rank. Even at this height, her head was visible on Yanov's shoulder.

He was ingenuously grateful. "I stole her from you, Pyotr Andreyevich. Strike me for it, but you can fly here whenever you wish. I have only this moment." To make her high cheeks flush, her dark eyes shine.

"Fill your boots, old boy. What's in the bag?" He was clutching a parcel.

"A too small gift. For San Francisco."

She unwrapped the paper.

"Alyosha!"

Another first—her use of the endearment. After one bloody cab ride!

"Illegal to get them out of the country, isn't it, Alexey Ilyich?"

He laughed, "I know." Throwing his weight about in the gentlest manner imaginable. "Don't tell my cousin."

He had given her an ikon—a miniature: A saint's gold head on a turquoise background, small semiprecious stones around the frame. Worth a great deal.

"Another present?" She shook her head at him, "Alexey, it's too much!"

"No, this one is really nothing—records. One for you, one for Petya."

He gave me a great hug. "How could I ever have expected to find such affection outside my own country? Never. Never friends as you. Thank you. Thank you both."

In London, and later, Marshall might sneer with all the weight of the old school, but I was almost overcome.

Folksongs.

I looked at the names, heard the simple tunes already. Simple, but based on harmonies of a thousand years. Music and words of the *byliny*—the folk culture and soul of Russia. "Slender Mountain Ash," "Little Bell," "Troika Rushing." With things as they are in post-revolutionary Russia, the inevitable paeans to the army and war and factory quotas. But even around them, wonderful melodies.

"By your standards," he said, "the sound is not good. These are our very first slow revolution records—what you call the el pee."

Chris brought Irish coffee and we sat on the floor. Nicola put on my record. I traveled back a quarter of a century. "What's this song about?" she asked.

"I'm sorry, there are no English words," said Yanov. "Perhaps Petya will write them out for you."

"A girl watches a young boy stroll past the house each evening and wonders about him. The title is 'Who Knows Why?' I can't catch it all yet." Which was a lie. I got the words. I just couldn't recite them dead pan:

> "...Who knows what he's saying
> What game is he playing..."

Yanov stood up. "I would rather not this next one—"

"Too partisan, Alexey?"

"Difficult memories, Petya. Of the siege." He looked at me keenly. "You must often have thought of it—how close you came to being there?"

I felt the board jump as the game moved forward.

"What siege?" Nicola was interested at once. "I don't know a thing about Russian history."

"Leningrad versus Adolf," I said. "Every Russian west of Moscow claims to have been there for the big show. The much-clichéd 'nine hundred days.'"

"But Leningrad's where you were born, right, Petya?" Trying for the story I hadn't finished in San Francisco.

"Right," I said. "St. Petersburg before the Revolution. The place where Europe was once allowed to meet all the Russias."

The men stared eye to eye above the women. "I don't think about it at all," I said to Yanov.

"But *you* were there, Alexey?" Nicola asked him. "During this siege?"

He nodded.

"Can you tell us about it?—It's like reading medieval history. I just can't imagine anything like that. Can you describe it?"

"Try and stop him," I said. Lightly.

The show was off and running on schedule. "Talk, yes," he said. "But not describe—no one can adequately do that." He hadn't stopped the record after all. The tune that triggered memory played as background. I assumed intentionally.

"My mother always says that when the German armies came in August of 1941 and I was eleven, I was five feet tall and weighed fifty-two kilos, and that when they left I was fourteen and six feet but I still weighed those fifty-two kilos. So that's one measure of it. And luck—I was damned lucky." Not to be part of the six hundred thousand—like his brother, killed by a bomb, or his sister killed by a shell, or his father taken during a raid across the Obvodky Canal on the southern perimeter. "We never knew how he died."

Or his uncles, his cousins and his aunts. Where was his passion, his fire, his guts for Mother Russia? The act was stale from rehearsal. "You say these things rather matter-of-factly."

"Am I unique? There were twenty million dead—why should my people have survived? Where are your own Russian relatives?"

But he *knew* where. *Why?* was the question.

"Isn't this why we must be strong, Pyotr Andreyevich? Why we shall be stronger?"

The match was degenerating into dialectics. It seemed more interesting to ask about the piano.

"In our house—I think I mentioned once. On the Irina Ulitza, Number 64. A two-bedroom apartment—luxury by our standards. Before the Revolution . . ."

From one bourgeois and his oppressed servants to seventy-five lucky liberated families, to twelve by 1940—we couldn't avoid the statistics of building a new world. More to the point, after forty years the housing shortage hadn't eased. He described the home, one of a hundred put up for merchants with French tastes in the boom of the 1820s. Graceful buildings of yellow sandstone.

"And big rooms," said Yanov, "at least before they were sub-
divided for the people—"

"And the piano?" I said, for the second time of asking.

"In the ballroom. A huge room, and for some reason the only
one unaltered. The piano was there from my earliest memories . . ."
His voice slowed for a moment, jarred from the script. "The piano
was always there. You're quite right. That was the unique thing
in my life—not the war. No one had a piano." A small smile of
pure capitalist satisfaction came and went. We were back to the
universality of revolutionary suffering and existence.

"We had no kitchen or bathroom, of course. They were com-
munal on each floor. But at least the people in our building knew
how to use them—no one crapped on the deck—"

"And your parents?"

Nicola glared, but he didn't make the association.

"Both worked, naturally. My father was a naval draftsman in
the dockyard. I was looked after by an aunt—a funny old thing—"
*Again something had changed. The mechanical note of a repeating
record was gone.* "Too affectionate and protective, as we Russians
are with our children . . . She used to turn my music. . . .
take me on walks across the Neva to the Peter and Paul Fortress
and the Winter Palace.

"I remember every day when we went out, we would pass a
swan carved in stone and resting on a patch of grass behind a
chain beside the bridge. The chain to keep people off the grass,
but in winter it was hidden under the snow—and no one would
stop a child anyway. And I used to climb on the swan's back and
imagine I was flying up and across the ice of the river to Finland.
But holding tight to my aunt's hand."

*Somehow we were through the looking glass, because that was
MY swan—MY grass, my vision of ice floes tumbling. My mother's
hand. BEFORE THE FROST.*

"The last time I saw my aunt she was being rolled like a log
across the street for the death cart . . ."

Six million could die like autumn leaves and leave me free of
Russian pain—unmoved. But the thought of one old aunt was
suddenly obscene. "Why Finland?" I asked. "Why did the swan
fly you to Finland?"

"My grandparents on my mother's side lived there in a village.

My grandmother still does. My grandfather was the postmaster. They had goats, a horse, a garden, two small fields on the lake. Like paradise."

Surely paradise lost.

"I thought people couldn't go places after the Revolution?" Chris said it for me.

"Elsewhere, perhaps, but Finland has always been a part of the Russian family..."

"Try telling the Finns that."

He grinned at me, showing a hint of the conqueror. "There are arguments in most families, Pyotr Andreyevich. Let us say *almost* part of the Motherland—at least until the war—and both my grandparents were Russian. My mother saved for the train tickets all year. My father didn't go with us."

Jackson's, something of value left on deposit at home.

We got into old family history: Mother Russia moving in as mother-in-law on the reluctant Baltic states—the breaking up of the common law marriage between Berlin and Moscow. Fascist and communist suitors fighting for property that neither owned. There were no more family holidays.

The Yanovs' horizon shrank back from Finland to Russia, to the city limits of Leningrad, to the Neva, to Irina Street, Number 64. To Yanov and his mother.

Waiting to die.

"In February, nineteen forty-one..."

The month chosen by the Russian frost to arbitrate between the dead, the living, and the living dead.

"The cold was the worst in memory... and we had nothing..." No cover to repel it. No fuel to defeat it. "Only music from loudspeakers—this music..."

Music drifting through the empty iron streets and blasted buildings, drifting like icy strands of cobwebs into the garrets, the sewers of Leningrad—St. Petersburg before the Revolution. Playing, drifting, night and day. Through bombing, shelling, freezing.

Dying.

With words. Words from generations before commissar and party. Words calling from the soul of Russia to her people, words echoed by the speakers of a hi-fi in a New York room—words whispered by Yanov.

> *My Russia, my Russia, dearest Motherland,*
> *Whenever I go near to Moscow,*
> *Where mint is fragrant in the fields,*
> *There nature whispers to me gently—*
> *Her loving words to me reveals. . . ."*

"*Nothing,*" said Yanov. "No word. No music. . . . Only tick, tick, tick, tick . . ."

On the sixteenth day of February in that coldest Russian winter of a hundred years only the ticking of a giant metronome reveals that a Russian pulse still beats in Leningrad.

"*It stopped,*" he said. "The metronome stopped."

And in the utter silence the tenants of Irina Street, Number 64, found their last springs of admiration frozen shut, and they pulled Alexey Yanov from his piano and smashed it, chopped it, hacked it, to make fuel for a tiny point of fire in that dead-white land.

What did Alexey Yanov think as he watched in the arms of his mother? What were his thoughts as the flames took hold?

I didn't ask.

"*And then the metronome ticked,*" Yanov whispered. So that Leningrad lives. And music lives. Words live.

> *"And far away the leaves of autumn,*
> *Are all aflame so brilliantly . . ."*

Words, the difference between us, fired by the heat of a piano, spreading from the speakers and across a frozen world.

> *"And there my old familiar birch tree,*
> *So softly, softly, says to me . . ."*

To a Leningrad Dravin watched by wet-eyed girls

> *"My Russia, my Russia, my dearest Motherland . . ."*
> *Which had been mine.*

I walked out on the balcony and stared at Central Park. I almost wept.

For no clear reason, Yanov arranged that we should assemble to go about Jackson's business at the St. Andrews' golf club near Ardsley in Westchester County.

The parking lot was as empty as the weekend streets. Only a tow truck with a heavy, bearded black man cruised aimlessly, hoping for trouble and offenders in reserved spaces.

At five to ten a black car with New York plates and an official innocence about it rolled in. Yanov stepped out. A second car hid behind a hydrant. The official car left. Nicola and Chris got out to talk to Yanov. The driver of the second car got out to take pictures of an empty lot and a closed café with a lens that could catch a fly walking on one of the stale doughnuts in the counter behind the window. Yanov looked at the photographer. Russian or American? For that matter, what difference?

The girls brought Yanov over. He got in. The snoop, trying to withdraw without indecent haste, gave up and began to run as we gathered speed.

There was a loud clang. The tow truck had struck like a barracuda. Already the snoop's car's arse end was up in the air. There were furious gesticulations.

Yanov was mildy curious, "What is happening with the truck?"

"Free enterprise," I said.

The city left us. Across the river the rolling waves of color were stunning. Yanov used the rear mirror a lot.

Through small towns of decreasing population, Catskill, Ravenna, Rensselaerville, past clapboard houses and fall wood piles, just boys and girls together in New York. Without a chaperon. Over the crest of a final hill and down an avenue of arching maples, leaves carpeting the ground in scarlet. Vivid reminders of our first meeting in the cruiser.

At the farm the women prepared a late lunch. Yanov and I walked by a pond with a beaver lodge and ducks shoveling along the edge. An old church pew was set to take advantage of an aspect of the house up through the orchard. We sat. Yanov offered a Karavella.

I refused. "My father put me off. I can still smell the damn things."

He laughed. "I forget that you know all about us, my friend Petya."

"Your memory has seemed acute until now." He started to replace the cigarettes in his pocket. "Oh, for Christ's sake Alexey. Smoke!"

He lit up gratefully, sucking it in. The ducks dashed greedily to fight for the floating match, then disconsolately rejected it. As he replaced the packet I saw a chain around his neck. "A secret vice of religion?"

"Superstition"—reaching inside his shirt. "You'll be amused; my talisman." The chain was threaded through a dull black scrap of wood.

"The remains of the piano," he said. "You know, for a long time I thought I missed it more than my relatives—thought that they were equally irreplaceable. It took me years to realize that there were more pianos." He dropped the chain back down the throat of his shirt.

"You've never been back to Finland?"

"Oh yes—occasionally. I've been fortunate in my career."

"Which wasn't picked by choice. Tell me about meeting Uncle Joe."

"At the victory parade for Leningrad to be made a Hero city. My mother was to receive her medal as Hero of the Soviet Union at the same time—"

"She must have been a remarkable woman."

"Is." It shunted him onto a side track. "She's still very much alive, teaching in Leningrad. I used to wonder, through those worst days, how anyone so small could survive, when so many covered with Russian fat were dying like flies. it was because she never stopped long enough to think about herself and the cold. She was always helping others to find food or clothing, organizing orphans, nursing wounded. The cold froze inactive minds before inactive bodies. That was the secret..."

And as my mother held ME in the stinking dark, and the frost wrapped her bare hands in white crystals, was HER mind inactive?

Yanov's dream of Russian glory for a mother differed from mine. "When we stood on that platform and I saw her embraced by the Generalissimo in front of half a million people—well, there are no words for it."

"And Stalin?"

"I don't remember clearly, but he was quite pleasant. Not terrifying—certainly not to a young boy—Christ off the cross to us then. Not now, of course. It's funny, I'd thought he was a giant, but he was hardly bigger than my mother." He drew on his cigarette. "Well, I made my speech to him and the wheels were turned and I couldn't get off the cart. Not that I've really wanted to since. Perhaps on a few days at the Academy—but I don't need to tell you what things are like in a training ship."

"Which academy?"

An ironic smile. "With such friends? Only the best—the Frunze in Leningrad. Like the Admiral." *Like my father*.

But hardly a definite description of his boss. "At my last count," I said, "you had four hundred and thirty-two broad stripers."

"Only one with a capital A, my friend—the Fleet Commander."

"*Gorshkov!* You've met him?"

"Met him?" Punching my arm. "Come on, you know I work for the man. He's often said he'd be interested to meet you—his godson."

It had the effect of falling down the stairs. But I said *"Dermo."* Bullshit. Threw a twig at the ducks, not to let it show. Treated it as a joke—the last syllable of a charade. Walked with him casually to the house, chatted as the girls tried to make him stay. In a low-key way he was anxious to get back to the city and the lost watchdog, but once in town he allowed himself to hang on for a drink in the apartment.

"But only one—what do you call it—a night hat? While we play Nicolasha's record." He turned to her. "Nothing of war this time. Ladies love tenors. This song has a very strong tenor part and a good chorus."

"What's it about, Alyosha?"

"*Kalinka*—the snowball bush. The first to flower in spring and end our winter. Even in the Irina Street of 1942 there was still a kalinka by the Canal which survived and flowered. And the most beautiful smell—this is what made me bring you the record. You wear a scent that reminds me."

"And the words?"—she asked softly, smiling.

"Little nothings. Rustling pine trees—you know the sort of things in folk songs. I leave you with it. Au revoir, Nicolasha."

They exchanged no hugs and kisses. He held her hands and her eyes briefly, said, "Until the next occasion, Petya," and then he left. The tenor shrilled his untranslated final verse of little nothings.

> *In the garden grows a berry*
> *Like sweet sherry wine*
> *...Oh my lovely darling maiden*
> *Won't you promise to be mine...?*

Mine. Sick to death of a word which seemed to have lost all meaning, I snapped at her, "I suppose he belted this out on your jolly around the park?"

"No, Petya." In her voice of the highway drag race. "He didn't sing. He asked me to go to Finland."

FINLAND.

CHAPTER

THIRTEEN

"Granny lives!"

Marshall was expectant, waiting for applause. With only Jackson and myself in the room it was not forthcoming. Undeterred, he continued.

"As hoped for, Cousin Y stole a visit. My tame Finn had him nabbed start to finish—all here." He waved fat hands airily over a litter on the briefing table. "A triumph," he said modestly.

The expectations referred to had been raised the month before—February, 1961—when Marshall showed up in my office, clutching a message from our attaché in Helsinki and playing "I Spy."

"Finns have invited Goliath to a sports meet for cadets. Sovs have graciously accepted."

A presumably self-extended invitation. "For this you run a budget of millions?"

He dropped a smirk and the next hint. "There will be a chaperon for the flower of Soviet youth."

"Of course." The opposite might have been news.

"Beginning with Y."

I made the required guess. Marshall did a little jig on the

carpet. "And our first piece of solid info, our cousin's in at the old school as X.O."

"You've lost me."

"The subject of your last Boys Own chat with him, dear boy. The Frunze Academy. Yanov's been made exec. It'll keep him close to us for three years."

He danced away to feed the news to the files. Arrangements were made for surveillance. The present meeting was to dissect its results.

"Yanov left the capital on a Saturday morning," said Marshall. "Nothing hidden about it—even traveled in uniform. By the way, he's visited half a dozen times since the war—the visa records are too smashed up to check out before that." He started the slide projector. Pictures of Yanov stepping down on to a winter platform, heavy greatcoat, arms caught in mid-swing, puffs of breath. Yanov embracing a mound of coats and scarves.

"Granny?" I asked.

Marshall nodded. The pictures took us through increasing depths of snow on roads narrowing eventually to a lane. "Totally isolated," said Marshall. "Ideal for a snatch." The camera moved under an old pole gate with a counterweight of rocks and traversed a drive with ruts from sled runners. At the end of it Yanov and Granny sat in the sled.

"Straight out of a Krieghoff print." Jackson made his first comment. "This is home, I take it?"

A small log house with outbuildings was set starkly into a clearing in the trees. The light had faded in the picture, day must be ending.

"Now" —Marshall had the air of a man about to produce a nude from a cake—*"this*—this really is jolly good stuff. I admit that the pictures leave something to be desired, it's all low light and slow frame, but the sound is absolutely first class."

"What's the clicking noise?" I asked.

"Dog's claws. Our spook caught it from the barn." Marshall preened as though he'd done everything himself. "Membrane mikes on the windows."

Hinges squeaked. The dog exploded. There were voices, faint and hollow like a kid's tin-can phone on a string, not yet audible. "Pictures now," said Marshall. Flickering images from early days of black and white TV moved in slow motion. "This is the kitchen."

A dumpy shape with a slight limp puttered around—from the noises, setting out dishes. Yanov arrived, shadow filling the kitchen, dwarfing the woman.

"The next ten minutes is rather tedious," said Marshall. "Compliments on food, state of the roads. Asking about mother—"

"So there is one," I said. "Hero or not."

"Well, that hardly narrows the field, old boy." There was the clink of metal, liquid pouring. The shadows left the field of view. "Moving to the parlor to let the spider see the fly," said Marshall. "The light's a little better—there's a fire."

Creaks as they sat into chairs, a sudden flare as an oil lamp was turned up. A knock as Yanov set down a bottle after pouring spirits into the coffee. Dull. Aimless personal conversation. More from the old woman about food—not enough, a bad batch of jam. Yanov's shadow was nodding. In the briefing room I was nodding. Jackson was wreathed in smoke. I missed some frames.

"Milaya—can you read French?"

Out of context!

Marshall was bobbing beside the machine like a frog. "You got it, old boy; now you're going to be most surprised."

"Dear heavens—what a question." The old girl's voice was sturdy. Capable. "I haven't used that language in forty-five years. Not since my time in the customs house in Kotla. How did you know of it?"

"From Mamuschka—now can you? Read? Write in a letter?"

The grandmother's shadow was bending forward to look at something on her knee, her words were lost intermittently. "...strange requests, Alyosha...if I had a book..." The voice was clear again. "A letter from France?"

Yanov was evasive. "How is it with your leg? Is it the rheumatism?"

"The cow. The creature trod on my foot at Christmas feeding. Some thanks from her. What has that to do with French, dear boy?"

"Shrewd old duck, isn't she?" said Marshall.

But I was watching Yanov, back to the camera, looking at the old lady. Thinking? Making up his mind?

Then the object of the trip. "There is a foreign girl with whom I wish to correspond." Strangely formal.

Silence from the tape. I waited for the inevitable.

"What is her name, Alyosha? This girl?"

"Nicola."

Sounding in my ear like a bell ringing through Finland.

"Nicola—Nicolasha. Pretty. She must be special, this girl, Alyosha. A French girl?"

"American."

"But in France?"

"America."

"Ah!" An inrush of breath. More silence.

"She could write to you in French," Yanov said. "You translate and send it on to me as gossip. 'Marya says she is well—Tanya broke a leg—.'"

"One might do that." The smaller shadow nodded. "One might."

"And from me to her?"

"One can only try."

"I cannot ask more, Miloshka."

"No?" Gravely. "Where is the heartbeat in a letter, dear boy? And secondhand, yet?"

"I want to meet her here in the autumn if I can obtain leave."

"Of course"—as though he'd asked if it got dark at night. "I shall tell people that she is Darya's granddaughter—my sister who went to Montreal after the first uprising."

"Excellent woman!"—Yanov, frank in admiration.

"But Alyosha"—her voice tightened with anxiety—"you will take care. The agents of the Cheka are everywhere."

Her use of the old term for the secret police intrigued me.

"An exaggeration, Milaya," Yanov's voice was confident. "Things are much improved with Nikita Sergeyevich. The terror is long past."

A giggle from Marshall. "Tell that to the First Department and they'll have him for a lampshade! He's all ours now, old boy."

"Alyosha—" Voice slowed, thinking as she went. Now asking the obvious question. "If you go so far, why not farther?"

Yanov loud, instant, absolute. "Treason, Milaya? for a *girl*!"

"Stop the tape!" Jackson's voice cut through the room. Mar-

shall blinked owl-eyed in the sudden light. "Now," said Jackson, "why did he say that?"

"We've finally met a man who doesn't trust his own grandmother." Marshall laughed at his own wit.

Jackson had put down the pipe. "And where, Sammy, while this Chekhov scene was being enacted, were Shelepin's people? Where are the thugs?"

"None," said Marshall. "Not a trace."

"Exactly."

CHAPTER

FOURTEEN

The body of the dragonfly was the same brilliant iridescent blue as the ikon Yanov had given her in New York. I watched it hover before landing on the lily. It dropped. Done in high-test alloys at a cost of millions it would be a marvel.

"She's definitely going?"

"She is, sir. Next month." A year after New York.

Five months after the film viewing, I stood with Jackson in the garden of his country home in Dorset. An enclosing wall of Elizabethan brick threw late summer heat onto the espaliered fruit trees. We watched the dragonfly.

"I've finally got her to agree that at least she'll wait in London until I get word back that all's clear."

The lilies shook with ominous movement. "The civil side are getting anxious," said Jackson. "They don't feel you have the required training. Marshall will be here shortly to argue their case. I wanted to talk to you alone first. Where do you stand with the girl?"

"I want to marry her."

The water boiled. The marvelous mica wings fluttered for an instant outside a gobbling orange mouth. The pond was still.

"Shall we walk?" He set off along a herringbone path beside the wall. "They say Thomas More visited this garden; extraordinary to think of that, isn't it? Why haven't you asked her?"

Do I reply, well I have—not on my knees but in my fashion—

and she won't have me. "I think she's reluctant to take the plunge again. Fear of another mess-up. She admitted to me once that her husband's crash probably got her out of a bad show over the long haul. I gather he had the mind of a gnat when it came to the finer things."

And my own mind?

Jackson didn't say it in so many words. "She must find Yanov rather more to her liking then?"

"He's a pretty impressive chap, sir. Really is. There's something there—it can't all be an act."

"But you're not jealous. What do you think of these dahlias?"

"Remarkable." Two could be as casual as one.

But not jealous! When I stood at the top of the stairs? Saw her head on his shoulder?

"I don't honestly think he stands any more chance than I do at the moment, sir. And short of his coming over, it's physically impossible for her to get embroiled. In fact, I think that's half the fascination."

"And you'll catch her when she tires of waiting. That's damn cool of you, Dravin!" The blue ice eyes looked up and out past the thicket eyebrows. "But as coming over is exactly what we may achieve, aren't you preparing to be attendant at your own funeral?"

I couldn't answer. The mind lowers its own asbestos curtain sometimes to block the stage.

Marshall arrived, unbelievable in his plus fours for a day out of town. We went to the library. Banks of charts curled on sticks like ancient manuscripts from floor to ceiling. "A hobby," said Jackson. "Not for navigational exactitude of course, but fascinating historically. Well, Marshall?"

"Our Ministry"—said with pompous pride of ownership—"has concluded that your Yanov's a siren." He deflated with a little giggle laugh. "Oh yes, a siren. Singing all the old tunes of mother love and Motherland to drag you across the line and hang you up to show off your horns."

"I think that's Ministerial balls!" I said.

"Show off those too, dear boy. But if we're *thinking*, old man"—he pulled a smile back inside the round little carp mouth—

"what *I* bloody think is that they'll outwit you. Hang you, skin you, stuff you full of commie crap, and throw you back over the wall to play against us."

I denied him the pleasure of a spilt temper. In disappointment he dropped some affectation. "Look—God knows they've set it up. No one disputes that, surely?"

No one did. Dravin least of all.

"Well then. *K's cousin! Gorshkov's godson!* Talk about burrowing in bullshit—Jesus wept—it would turn the head of a plaster saint, let alone a young expatriate Sov with an inferiority complex—and now after all that, Cousin Y proposes to drag your girlie's baited parts within grabbing distance in a client state." I was livid. Marshall was quite exhausted. He took his mints out and ostentatiously turned pages of an old issue of the *Sphere*.

"Set it up for what purpose?"

Jackson, master of the quiet word, stopped Marshall in midpage. "I wish that you people would begin to appreciate that with Shelepin running the other side, we have matured from the blood-and-guts frontal assaults of Beria and Serov. Why should the Russians permit actions so transparently obvious as those of Yanov? The fact is, we *know* nothing. But let us take worst case—"

"My death?"

"My dear Dravin"—looking wryly past the pipe—"what harm could you do us dead? If we return to first principles: Marshall and the Ministry want Yanov physically at the first suitable moment—which is most certainly *not* Finland at the present time, Sammy, as the Foreign Secretary agrees . . ."

Marshall's face went gratifyingly red at this internal coup. Jackson continued without looking at him. "Let us concede, Dravin, that Moscow wants you spiritually, presumably on a long-term basis, and that Yanov has invited the girl. We assume further that they take her—and then as Marshall expresses it they ask you to play as the price for getting her back—"

"Finland's neutral in the armed struggle." It emerged on its own. Again the mind refused the actuality of Nicola in such circumstances.

"Oh for Christ's sake!" Marshall, disgusted, threw down the magazine. "*Neutral!* The granny's shack's only fifty miles west of the '39 border. The nasties could have her into a car and out of there and home for tea between the milk and the sugar. For that matter, they could do it in a bloody toboggan. Damn it"— directly to Jackson. "After Blake—to say nothing of Houghton and the Portland mess—haven't we got enough names on the wall for this year?"

It seemed a valid point. The latest round of Admiralty spy scandals and defections were dripping all over the *News of the World*. Jackson might not have heard.

"They take the girl, Dravin, then what?"

"Would you be asking this question if I were native born?"

"Good God, I wouldn't trust you an inch more. Marshall's side's riddled with Oxbridge queens of impeccable pedigree, and leaks like a sieve—it'll take years to close it up."

Marshall was looking plain bloody nasty now. "Lest we forget, *sir*—Burgess was Dartmouth. And as queer as last year's egg by the time he left it."

Real band-of-brothers' stuff. There was a sudden lull. I heard a clock ticking behind Jackson. He was still waiting for an answer. "I'll manage," I said.

"Good." He tapped his pipe out. "Marshall?"

"Manage? We all try to manage." He stalked to the door. "That's our job. Managing. Cleaning up, holding heads." He threw a scrap of paper on the table beside me. "Just bloody remember that Finland's no effing New York. Nanny can't always be watching."

The door slammed.

I picked up the scrap and turned it over. "Acme Towing— Ardsley, N.Y. Impoundment charge: $15.00."

Marked paid. October 1, 1960.

"You may go if you wish," said Jackson. "But he's quite right; you're crossing a line. Drinking with Russians at a party is one thing. Running close to the border in plain clothes and some other man's name is quite another."

"At least I feel a little better for the nursery training in throat-slitting."

"Don't try to be funny. You asked me a year ago where we're going." He stared out at the garden and a summer storm sweeping across the downs. Thunder—the pressure wave magnified by the heaviness of the air—crashed through the open doors. "This business is like cave crawling. You see a fissure in the rock face and you follow it in. Sometimes, very rarely, it opens on the treasure of Ali Baba. More often on a wide dead end. But on the bad runs the rock may simply squeeze and squeeze until you can't go on and you can't turn back . . ."

A brilliant flash of dragonfly electric blue illuminated his face. "No matter what Marshall says, we have not reached that stage with Yanov. You're not in a fissure yet." Enormous drops of rain smashed through the opening. He closed the doors and drew the curtains. "But in the dark you may not always notice when the walls begin to move. Give me your final decision in the morning."

CHAPTER

FIFTEEN

Helsinki basked in Indian summer. I booked into a tired Hotel Seurahuone under the name of Andrew Davis, sales rep for a Midlands firm.

Marshall's tame Finn had been to the same training school as Jackson and was waiting in my room. "May I introduce myself? Mika Kallas."

Short, thick, red-headed, with a sense of humor and an aversion to Russians. Or a strong acting ability. Marshall believed in him. "Solid as the rock, old boy. Used him for years. An excellent host."

We forewent social niceties.

"I gather, Andrew," he said, "that you have sent a telegram from London to the old lady at Takanen in which you announce arrival of the American girl for Saturday next?"

I nodded.

"And that we take station at the farm in advance of that arrival, that we may apprehend untoward intrusion by any other foreign power—principally, Ivan?"

His English was almost a minuet of speech, curiously genteel. I assured him that his assumptions were in all respects correct. "As I anticipate, Andrew, that it would be difficult for us to be upon a border-crossing train and remain unseen, may I therefore suggest that we travel by road?"

"You may. Is there a bus line?"

"There is, but with the further matter of the last ten kilometers to the village, perhaps the satisfactory thing might be for my taking you by car?"

"It might indeed."

"An early start will be required. May I suggest that I meet you outside the hotel at half-past seven? Would that be satisfactory?"

"Eminently."

"I am so glad." He really was.

With an empty road the long rows of drab postwar refugee apartments gave way quickly to board and batten houses, steep-roofed on postage-stamp lots perforated with picket fence. Marshall's disclaimer notwithstanding, the countryside reminded me strongly of the trip up the Hudson Valley the year before.

We went on two wheels round a curve. "A grand day for a drive," I said to Kallas.

He flashed a broad grin of nicotined teeth. "I enjoy the little challenge. You have observed that we are followed."

"No."

I could never tell when to put a question mark on the end of his statements. The road in 1961 still followed the coast and whipped accordingly, but between bends there was nothing in the mirror. Despite that, any joy in the day was being rapidly extinguished by fright mechanisms.

"Some actions will have to be initiated, will they not?"

"I suppose they will," I said.

"But after coffee. We shall stop first in Lovisa and confirm our watcher's movements."

"Good. Let me buy. How do you know about the snoop?"

"One develops a sense, Andrew." He spoiled the image of a black art by revealing trade secrets. "Also I have a second car following us some distance back. If we were alone he would have overtaken us. Now we shall proceed to Hanima to arrive at one-thirty. There is a hotel with an adequate dining room."

Not to judge from its gray block walls. But the *pitopoyta*, as the Finns call a smorgasbord, was excellent.

Kallas ordered bacon and eggs. "I cannot abide fish." Which seemed abnormal in a Finn.

"When is the Russian to arrive?" he asked.

"There's no certain date; any time after Sunday." I was more concerned for the immediate present. "What about my tail?"

"Tail?"

"I'm sorry. You believe I'm being followed—"

"Ah. Excellent. A tail—quite descriptive. Parked over there." He nodded at a Volvo, dimly black under a crust of salt. The driver was missing. "In the station house," said Kallas.

"What do we do about him?"

"Forgive me, Andrew. The question becomes *when*, perhaps, rather than *what*. We are not yet aware of the reason for his interest. It seems reasonably certain that he is Russian, but there may be no connection with our own concerns. He may simply have become attracted to you through the word 'electronics' on your visa. An unfortunate choice of profession."

I imagined strangling Marshall slowly. "I suggest," continued Kallas, "that we prevent the 'tail' from observing our departure and then see what transpires. Should he become an embarrassment we shall take corrective action. We must of course be prudent— we are in a sensitive position with Ivan."

"I understand."

"We shall wait for a train," Kallas said.

At three-ten, one arrived, a powerful green-painted diesel. Passengers stepped down. Baggage was loaded. Black Volvo ignored the platform scene. Kallas started our car. An answering white puff came from the Volvo as the driver snapped it into reverse.

"So it's me," I said. "What next?"

A hell of a crash.

A blue twin to our Saab had arrived from nowhere to be smashed by the Volvo full amidships on the empty passenger side.

Assorted witnesses converged. A policeman came to life. Kallas whistled "Cherry Ripe" and swung us out of the yard.

There was no cross reference for orientation from the pictures of the white winter landscape. We drove now through a pine-green and light brown land of granite grooved and scarred by the passage of glaciers; thin moss and grass burned by the sun. There were no houses visible. Kallas slowed, and pointed. "I think we have arrived." I recognized the old pole gate with its counterweight of rocks.

We backed into a space under the pines and switched off the engine. The air was redolent with sun-warmed resin. Kallas talked to someone on a radio.

We waited for the Friday night before Saturday morning.

With sundown it was suddenly chill. By an hour after, there was a feeling of frost. We set off. An owl shrilled a long haunting cry raising hair on the neck with imagined terrors. I counted paces. Four hundred to the clearing in the trees. Fifty more to the small log house. A wisp of smoke, gray against the night, came from the chimney. A lamp shone in the kitchen.

Kallas halted at the edge of the clearing. "I shall look quickly once around." He was gone before I could remind him about the dog. Frogs croaked. Somewhere a twig cracked. A leaf fell.

"Nothing." Kallas was back and whispering. "We wait in the barn."

We kept one to each side of the door. He touched it. No movement; pushed harder. It began to open. Slowly . . . creaking.

"Damn"—under my breath. We waited for the dog. Silence. He pushed again, abrupt, savage—like tearing off a bandage to get it over quickly.

A cow and some roosting hens ignored us. Kallas pointed overhead. We climbed the ladder to the loft. I arranged some hay in a heap against the gable end at a crack offering a view of the house. He took the other end to watch the drive. He reached inside his coat and passed me a pair of small, high-power Zeiss night glasses.

The chickens below us gave a last cluck and returned to sleep. "Thanks," I said. "By the way, your English is superb."

His yellow teeth lit up the loft. "From the BBC news." I hadn't the heart to tell him the accent was out of fashion.

Through the glasses I studied the house. The fire in the parlor illuminated the room in faint red light.

It might have been my mother's. Fat furniture with lace covers on the backs and a lace cloth on a round table. Family and needlepoint in round frames. Faded gravures of a tsar and tsarina frozen for eternity from a time before a Russian world turned upside down. A picture of a young man in a stiff collar, peaked cap and watch chain before a raw-brick building. Another face hidden by white beard stared from the wall above the fireplace. The same watch chain measured the passage of a life.

In the other window, the old woman repeated in color and real time the actions from the tape. She wore a print dress with flowers, wool stockings, a cardigan. Hair in a tight gray bun. Indistinguishable from the women on the station platform in the afternoon. A tiny mesh of light flickered from a stove damper onto the sleeping dog. She said something. He woke. They went through into the other room. She sat in a chair beside the fire, drinking from a mug.

The cold seeped through the walls. The yard outside turned from dim color to black and white, reversing the process with the old woman. The moon rose above the pines. I thought of San Francisco. Of Jackson. Far away in a Dorset garden he had seemed omnipotent. In a hayloft fifty miles from Russia his hold was tenuous as moonlight.

Out of the tiny night noises the sound was wrong, jarring. Kallas heard it at the same moment. A faint running of an engine from a quarter mile distant, approaching, pausing, going on.

Kallas's eyes were sewn to the opening in the boards in front of him. *"Visitor!"* —hissing the word. For a stocky man he moved like a wraith across to the ladder. "I shall wait below and cross to the far side, up-moon. Are you armed?"

"A knife."

"Try not to use it."

My heartfelt wish. He vanished down the ladder. The owl cried again in the night. I felt the unseen walls move gently, imperceptibly inwards. Inside the house the dog barked. The old woman bent to it.

I looked back up the drive towards the road. From the gap in the trees, five feet out from their greater blackness, etched in moonlight the owl floated on great wings sweeping a silent shadow across the ground. Grotesquely large. Distorted. The mingled shadow shape of a bird, and a second a human, shadow.

Across the yard in the other world a log fell, sending sparks leaping, streaming from the chimney, the shadows of trolls across the walls. She bent to the flame. Half-turned our way.

"Not yet, granny, not yet!"

The door protested on the hinge. A gentle whinny from the

horse. The figure walked softly, cautiously. Behind it, I sensed rather than saw Kallas springing blackly from the trees. I waited for his leather glove to chop through the night to the neck. Waited for a harsh animal scream to be cut short in the sick crunching snap of a corduroy knee against a chin.

The owl, still floating, shrilled directly over the intruder. A white disk of upturned face reflected for a moment the immaculate empty brilliance of the yard.

Kallas was out, cut crisp as cardboard, raised arm dropping like the owl. The disk face turned at me.

"*Kallas!*"

Screaming unremembered words, I jumped from the loft to stop his arm, and fell at Nicola's feet.

CHAPTER

SIXTEEN

"The horse with his hat—those ear holes. This place is a trip backward in time, Petya. It was like that with the train. That's why I arrived at such a crazy hour—"

"You weren't supposed to arrive at all."

"Oh, don't go through all that again. You exaggerate everything. In fact, except for the weird language, you and your clown are the only abnormal things about Finland. I'm sure the old lady thinks you're a nut. She's just too polite to say so. I'm amazed she didn't scream."

"I agree she showed remarkable restraint." Expecting you all, old boy, Marshall would no doubt insist.

"Well, she was sure good to you, considering."

"She was." The old girl had offered carte blanche with first aid. "'This house is given to any friend of Alyosha's, monsieur. We must bandage that foot.'"

Now I passed her the reins, wished her a safe journey to the village for supplies. "You speak Russian almost too well, monsieur."

"Since I was a child, madame."

She slapped the reins. Clucked. Nothing happened. She gave us an exasperated smile. The horse eventually looked around to check things out for himself and then ambled with his hat slowly up the drive. Except for Kallas still tearing strips off his assistant somewhere in the bush, we were alone. There was no Yanov.

"In spite of her bad eye and the limp, she doesn't miss much," Nicola said. "Can you walk okay this morning?"

"I'll manage. Tell me why a horse is like a diesel?"

"That's just the point"—she slipped her arm through mine—"the engine wasn't a diesel. It was straight out of *Dr. Zhivago*. As soon as I saw the picture in the folder at the airport I just knew I had to ride in it. But Europe's so complicated. The train left in the evening and only the first section was old-fashioned—and that was restricted to people crossing the border for Leningrad and Moscow."

"So nostalgia went ungratified after all?"

She laughed. "No way! I bought a ticket to Leningrad and got out early. There was some fuss about that!"

A breath of fresh American air blowing on European bureaucratic inertia. "I imagine there was!"

"Anyhow, it was worth the money. All old green velveteen upholstery with buttons and tufts and Russian music. I recognized Alexey's snowball bush. It kept time with the rails—*kalinka-kalinka-kalinka*. I expected Cossacks to swoop from the trees."

"Down on to a beautiful girl riding alone through the forest to Grandmother's house." Oblivious of red hoods in hiding.

"I wasn't alone; there was a guy from Sweden." She gave me a pinch. "Maybe one of your spies, Petya. Except that he was kind of out of shape."

Full of fat smiles and lust, anxious to fetch her pies and tea from the attendant listening for Shelepin on the wrong end of the intercom.

We came to a gate of woven wicker strips. I opened it. She stopped. "No wonder he dreamed of this as a kid."

A barley field cut out of the pines sloped silver and gold away below us. At its foot the lake of Takanen glittered in the sun.

"Should I say 'very pretty'?"

It took both of us back to California. "Two years," she said. "It seems longer. I really *am* sorry about your ankle—I shouldn't have laughed the other night." She gave me a quick kiss. "But it was like every third-rate western I ever saw: Zorro leaps! *And misses his horse!*" Swishing an imaginary sword, she began to laugh again.

"What if the real Zorro doesn't arrive, Niki?"

"You can give me that holiday in London that we missed last year. But he'll show. Watch your step."

She helped me across to a granite outcrop sloping into the deep end of the lake. A family of swans sailed in column. The adults frowned at us under black brows. "The Ugly Ducklings!" Nicola made sentimental noises over the cygnets.

"What else for Scandinavia? Ragged little buggers; the name suits them."

"But they're just waiting," she said, "for their second chance. Like the chrysalis."

I didn't respond. My ankle ached. I lay back on the rock. The sun still had an August warmth for this one hour of a September afternoon. She stopped talking and lay beside me. The last sounds of summer filled our silence: insects humming across the rock, the dabbling splatter of the swans, the slap of a beaver tail near the lodge in the shallows at the far end. A harsh *craanck-craanck* from two ravens riding air currents on spastic wings.

"A penny, Petya?"

I turned my head. Her face was nearly touching, eyes drowsing half-shut against the sun. "The cove..."

"I know." I felt the pressure of her hand, the slightness of her breath on my face. "I never really thanked you. For listening—"

—to Dravin bellowing.

"Holy Christ, my toe! *My bloody toe!*"

The old cob swan, neck stretched four feet ahead of him, all the feathers up like a hedgehog along the back, still scrabbled furiously at the rock to get out.

"My God!" Nicola in safety was holding her ribs. "What a secret agent!"

"Bugger off, I'm bleeding to death."

She looked at the wound. "Hardly. Does it hurt?"

"What the hell do you think?"

"Sorry." With a mercurial feminine change, she kissed me again. A proper kiss from long ago. The ravens croaked.

She shivered. "They're macabre, Petya. Like vultures."

"You've been reading too much Poe. In Russian folklore they're the matchmakers."

"Really! Like the Fiddler—'matchmaker, matchmaker...'"

Make me a match. A chrysalis's moment for a second chance.

"Marry me, Niki."

She looked at me, the brown eyes with the golden fleck not laughing now: appraising rational eyes of a Master of Science, weighing me in the balance. She almost spoke. The ravens watched and made their match. They croaked again.

"Hullo!"

Beneath the birds on their endless circle, Alexey Yanov waited at the wicker gate. They knew, as I did not, how long he might have been there.

But *I* knew now—before she spoke—what Nicola would say. Squeezed forward on a track by forces invisible in an open field, I knew before the words what the answer had to be.

"No, Petya."

"In your report," said Jackson, "you state that you asked Yanov directly to defect but that he refused. What was his exact reaction?"

"He slapped me on the back and roared with laughter."

And then he'd walked with me between the pine trees up the drive. "Don't worry," he'd said. "Grandmother Tarasinov will watch her like a hawk."

"If anything happens—"

"You believe I'd allow that while I live?" he'd asked.

Marshall tittered. "Let Kallas get a picture of them with their knickers around their ankles. Catch Yanov coming quietly then, old boy. So to speak."

"Sit down, Dravin!"

I subsided. Jackson sent Marshall a look that would have speared a fish. "We shall let things mature," he said. "Let it take time. His utility can only increase as he climbs higher in the tree. We shall let him climb, shaking gently, until his own weight of involvement brings him down into the basket."

"If they don't shake Dravin loose first." Marshall made bland amends by passing round the sweets. "Humbug, dear boy?"

DENMARK.

CHAPTER

SEVENTEEN

The telegram from the First Secretary at our Danish mission would not have brought me back in time to Copenhagen except that Erik Lindholm, the man I was visiting in Stockholm, was a Swedish wing commander with considerable flair, and access to his own fighter.

His efforts went unappreciated.

"You're going to be late, Naval Attaché." The Secretary was bobbing back and forth inside the hall like the White Rabbit as he spoke to me. "And it's a *personal* invitation—H. E. has not been asked. Damn poor form, but then, they are *the* most awful boors. Khrushchev *quite* ghastly, one gathers." The true import of events struck him. "You'll pass your report through channels, of course?"

"Of course. May I use your phone?"

"There's no *time*, N.A." He fluttered the engraved card. "Surely I have explained to the point of *exhaustion*, the dinner begins in half an hour."

I wondered where the hell Whitehall found them. And with more relevance, why a totally unexpected invitation for dinner with Nikita had come with no clearing word from London. I put through the call to the Admiralty. The duty operator made consultations.

"I'm sorry, sir. Admiral Jackson is unavailable."

"Try his London home."

"He's not there either, sir. Admiral Jackson left on retirement leave two weeks ago."

"Do *hurry*, N.A." The Rabbit poked his head through the door. My own head was whirling, throwing out useless thoughts. Did the Rabbit use initials to address his wife?

"Are you married, First?"

"*Married*?" His horror answered.

But Jackson out? And so abruptly? With no formal message, no grapevine buzz? Marshall would be ecstatic. The next in line was a bureaucratic delight. I couldn't stick him. I went to dinner.

The display of Sov goonery at the doors, although muted in comparison with shows past, was still enough to conjure up a strong sense of déjà vu and hold me at the wire for five minutes while two thugs checked me out. I was so occupied with my phone call's implications that Yanov was beside me before I saw him.

"Old friend! So pensive." We hugged. "Three years—too long, much too long. A pity that you couldn't have been with us when Nicolasha made her visit last year."

Her second, and carbon copy of the first, less Dravin and his midnight leap.

"Yes," I said. "It was too bad."

"But perhaps you *were* there, Pyotr Andreyevich?" He winked. "One way or another?"

The answer to that was no. If Marshall had made arrangements with Kallas to bug the bedrooms, Yanov had swept them. There had been no tapes to listen to. I thanked him for the invitation.

"Not me. The Chairman. He picked your name out of the embassy lists. Congratulations on your third stripe, by the way; now tell me what you have been doing."

As though they didn't know. I returned the congratulations. If my progress was a little more than adequate, his own was still meteoric: full captain. "I'm just finishing a two-year stint as attaché, thank God. I have to split myself in three between the Scandinavian capitals. An endless bloody shuffle."

"With wide eyes, I think."

"An enlarged liver."

We laughed it off. "And you're still at the Academy, Alexey?"

"Like yourself, just finishing. A new job after this trip. I'm not sure where yet. Ah, they are ready for dinner. Come. It should be better than most of these things—there are only a few people."

About thirty. As we sat down there was a lull around the center table. Nikita had dropped his opening mixed metaphor, that with no birds to sing, Gromyko's arse would be a nightingale. It was safely filtered by the interpreter. I waited for the rest of the performance, the breast-thumping and browbeating, the rocket-rattling. There was none. The conversation was stranger without it.

He spent most of his attention on Helen Krag, the actress wife of the Danish socialist PM; and although Red and Pink are usually oil and water, for some reason they seemed to hit it off. The only person I had ever seen laugh *at* him, not with. And he took it! A little surprised, but took it. And when she placed a hand on his arm, he patted it.

My father's story of the affair with Stalin's wife seemed for the first time plausible. Even in old age there was something in the coarse peasant body and skull that worked on you. I'd felt it that first time at the Portsmouth dinner. This woman felt it now.

Had it worked on a queen? He was talking about her—Elizabeth.

"In the park at Windsor she might have been any mother out on a sunny day." He waved off any dialectical objections. "Oh, granted that she must have an enormous supply of capital"—the first time I ever heard the Marxist use of the word—"but she is never alone. Always a young woman in a goldfish tank, no time with her children. Always trapped."

Which was untrue, and in any case how *could* a last bolshevik feel sorrow for a queen? Unless he remembered another young woman, in another fortress, shut away in gilded quarters behind triple walls and silence.

"And today, when I met your little princess"—talking directly to Helen Krag—"that is what I found so sad: this little girl who is to go to Greece, and be trapped too. And Greece is not England. She will know real troubles... real troubles."

It was extraordinary. The man was truly moved.

So the evening ended, changing all my preconceptions. I was

in front of him to say good night and thank you, the first words we'd exchanged. And what I should expect as a diplomatic dwarf, except for Yanov's statement of his interest at the start. And the distant past.

"*Blagodaryu vas,* Excellency."

He grasped my hands strongly between both his own, and gave me a funny little bow in the manner in which they applaud themselves on stage. I bowed back.

"Kapitan Dravin—from Portsmouth. We are now old friends. Known to each other for how long?"

And I looked him straight in the eye and said, "Perhaps since I was born, Excellency." The eyes as unwinking now as in Los Angeles, but not hostile, just looking very deep. "My father is dead, Excellency," I said, although he hadn't asked.

"I regret it. When was this?"

"Five years ago."

"At a great age, then. Was it easy for him?"

"Yes, Excellency."

"Good, good"—still holding my hand in both of his; "and did you talk as a father and a son?"

And I lied and said yes. For business reasons, so that he should know that I knew about him.

He jerked his head forward with the characteristic snap. "You shall make a visit with us. Andrei Andreyevich here"—nodding at Gromyko—"will arrange it. You will be a guest of the Soviet people, and Alexey Ilyich will show you Moscow and the Academy, and you will know your Motherland."

And the strange part was that for a moment I believed the old man. Not belief that I would be boarding a bus for Moscow, but that his sentiment was genuine.

"It would be a great honor, Excellency." And then he released me and Yanov saw me to the door. We shook hands in a more conventional manner.

"Pyotr Andreyevich, as we stand on neutral territory, let us see it together tomorrow."

"Delighted," I said. We agreed to meet at noon and I returned to my room at the Angleterre Hotel, to fall asleep and dream of an incredulous queen watching Gromyko drop his drawers in her garden.

And in the morning I found the bug on the phone. Beside it, actually, disguised as a brass ashtray. Two little wires sliding over the edge of the night table and into a hole the size of a wasp bore through the baseboard on the wall of the adjoining room.

How typically and infuriatingly Russian—the gift of trust and invitation offered with the one hand; solid old-fashioned paranoia with the other. I went down to breakfast—to find Beer Mug from New York watching from a corner. The bug was Cowboy.

Rage was sudden. And irrational, because while sticks and stones break heads, even chronic mistrust by allies should not. But it had gone on too long and there was a dead dog in San Francisco and a lost ride around the park in old New York to be paid for. I knew how. Marshall's man had shown me. "Makes fried eggs of the ear drums, mate."

Following me to my room, Beer Mug didn't even try to be discreet. He went into the wasps' nest next door. I picked up the phone and put through a call to a porno theater. A girl answered in good English. I asked for a complete description of the show, and as the most salacious and explicit nuances were being given and the ears of the wasps were glued most closely to the line, I ripped the wires from the mike and jabbed them straight into the female outlet plug carrying two hundred and twenty volts.

I heard the scream through the wall. A dark medical-looking man with a brown bag and a TWA sticker got out of the elevator on the double as I got in. "Third door down on the right," I said. "Tell them it was for Largo."

I found Yanov, dressed in a new suit apparently cut from a dark gray Russian sack, waiting on the steps.

"You've buried the Gieves number?"

He grinned ruefully. "After a long period of mourning."

"Come and have lunch at the Tivoli and cheer up."

We found a billet at a bread-and-sausage place just inside the north entrance and put in our order. An attractive pair of commercially packaged girls made overtures. Yanov fended them off with a smile.

"They remind me—an odd incident that I must tell you. Do you know the name Grishanov, our top *politruk*?"

Politruks, zampolits. Party arm of the forces. Combination padres, spies, and social workers. Directors of erring feet. Failures are heaved over to the inquisitorial hands of the KGB.

I shook my head.

"Grishanov's a pleasant bastard, a real man of the people. He called me up a few weeks back. 'Come in, Tovarish Kapitan, come in. Sit down. Cigar? How's your mother? In hospital last month, I hear? Better now, I hope.' To let you know they can be at the throat in two considerate words.

"I said she was better. 'Good: We're so proud of our Hero Citizens.' He was smooth as a buttered arsehole. You'll never believe what he brought up." Yanov looked at me over the beer. "*Fornicating deviationism!*"

Another first for Newspeak. We burst out laughing.

"'In London, comrade'"—Yanov imitated an earnest party voice—"'I understand that you visited places of bourgeois decadence in the company of an active counterrevolutionary, and that you behaved with discredit to the good name of the Motherland with common harlots.'"

"Sinyavsky?"

Yanov nodded.

"But why so long after?"

He threw up his hands. "With those bastards? Impossible to tell. They're like worms fucking in darkness. Who knows who's doing what at which end?"

I saved the expression for the verbal war against Marshall. "What did you do?"

"Sucked. Grishanov acted the father. 'You must believe me that the imperialist pariahs encourage this jackal behavior.' As though I'd never spent months in the West. He sent me away with a pat on the head: 'Good, good, off you go. Sorry to have to bother you for such a little thing. Our job is not easy, tovarish, not easy. But as important for the state as the barrel of your guns. Remember that when dealing with our people, particularly one like Sinyavsky, who has not had all our advantages.'"

"Advantages?"

"*Zhid,*" said Yanov. "Sinyavsky's a Jew. Like most good party men, Grishanov won't say it openly. They let their anti-Semitism hang around in the air like a ripe fart. Anyway, that was all—but I thought you'd be intrigued."

We strolled down to a kidney-shaped lake full of kids with toy boats and boats full of couples.

"It looks pleasant," said Yanov. "Shall we row?"

"Why not."

We hired the last dinghy and took to our sailors' natural element. A ferret-faced individual took a punt and managed to find himself close to us too damn often. I pointed him out to Yanov.

"Not ours," he said.

"They never are, old boy." I rested on the oars and watched the bikinis.

The small dart had drawn blood. "Petya," he said slowly. "Are we Russians really the villains? *Always?* Do we do nothing of benefit in your eyes?"

It was not polemical. I was a little embarrassed. "Well—of course. In many ways the masses are better for the Revolution—"

He waved impatiently. "Not that; around the world. Do you really believe that a Batista Cuba was worth dying for? Do you truly want to see Germany on the march as one nation?"

We agreed on the answers but the questions were too simple. "It isn't like that, Alexey. It's the constant westward-shoving. And not just under Stalin. There's Hungary. Admit frankly, you want *Lebensraum* for the first circle of nukes to land on. But don't say it's for mankind."

"You don't understand, Petya. Ten years after the war it really mattered that that buffer stayed. Even now. But there *are* differences. Nikita Sergeyevich at home is not the clown. The changes; the thaw is real, and our people know it. *I* know it."

"Well, if he sends me the bus ticket, I'll believe it myself."

"Match!" His neck was flushing. "Always so fucking funny! Nothing ever matters to you."

"Nicola matters, Yanov. Playing games like *that* matters. Don't tell me Nikita's thaw extends to a Russian captain screwing a Yanki bird in the bush in Finland."

We sat glaring at each other. I think I was shouting. "Every time she goes it could be dirty. You *know* bloody well! But bugger that. Slap and tickle and run to Mama."

He was white, holding an oar so tight that water dripped between his fingers.

"Not so. *Not so!*" He half-stood. The boat rocked perilously. "You son of a bitch, Dravin. Sitting there in your perfect clothes and your lapdog manners and thinking you have everything in life. Which you may—*everything but loyalty!*"

"To what, Yanov? Mistrust? Suspicion? A million secret police—fear for a lifetime?"

He almost struck me.

"No." He dropped to the thwart. Anger, any other emotion, gone.

"What then?"

"*Rodina.*" In the flat hopeless voice of the Russian damned, the voice of the archipelago. "You can never understand."

Understand? In my mind, in Jackson's office, had I not accused my *father* because I understood?

Any Russian child caught for those first few years understands *rodina,* knows that with cosmic irony the land of Pavlov which gave the world his frantic dogs gave itself this reflexive verbal bell. A bell ringing louder than the cries of serfs and wasted peoples. A bell summoning Russians to run through frost and famine for tsar and commissar. To tear their own flesh. To build their own cage.

Oh, I understood.

But like Yanov's siege, how can there be description of its force? Try. Take the emotion of Churchill and Lincoln, the Berlin Philharmonic and an Olympic Gold and motherhood and apple pie. Then prostitute it and degrade it and debase it for fifty years while you deny Russians God, monarch, freedom—even the right to hustle for a buck. And still, in Pavlov's walled-off land, ring the *rodina* bell and watch Russians run to the wall and die.

"It's only a word, Alyosha."

"I know."

"And words are politics, you said, not emotion."

"I know."

We were stopped by a gate which in the Boolean language of electronic logic was neither *and* nor *or* but in the middle: Catch 22.

"So what do you do, Alexey Ilyich?"

"I suffer."

In the face of that, what use Anglo-Saxon or computer logic?

I could have said what I'd thought a thousand times, that half your Russian suffering would vanish overnight if you weren't so bloody ready to put up with it? But what was the point?

"And nothing else?"

He shrugged, deep into a Slavic slough of despond. "What else is there?"

Beyond Nicola and freedom waiting in San Francisco?

"I don't know, Alexey. It's not a perfect world in the West, God knows. But it's closer, and we only make the journey once."

"Clichés." He gave a brutal uneven tug at the oars and spun the bow towards the shore. "Nothing but clichés."

"On both sides," I said.

We were in convoy at the boathouse, waiting in the backwater of the argument to give the line to the attendant and pay the bill. The place was busy with a summer rush of business. Girls climbing in and out of boats. We had forgotten all about the punt—all too easy to forget, lose track, dreaming of sex in a Danish afternoon. And there was no smell.

Not at first.

Only the sterling naval crowns on the gold-plated buttons of my blazer cuff turning a peculiar shade of greenish black to match the navy barathea of the sleeve. A piece of sleeve fell off into the bottom of the boat.

"That's bloody odd, Alexey, don't you think?"

He was standing again, his face contorted, horrified.

"Not round two, for God's sake," I said. "Sit down."

"*Petya*! Your arm. Your fucking *arm*!"

"It's the sleeve, old boy—"

Yanov was moving in slow motion, although later it seemed so fast, like the change in the sensation. A tingle—no, more a mild warmth like a heat lamp. Pleasant. Relaxing.

"Christ, Christ, Christ Christ *Christ!*"

The pain sliced through muscle and fat to bone, to head, ricocheting from arm to brain and back in uncomprehending agony.

Yanov lifted me bodily from the thwart, plunging me over the side. "Keep the arm under water! Take off the jacket." With the cold and the dilution of the acid the pain came off the boil briefly.

I saw the punter throw away a child's water pistol and scramble out onto the bank, leaving an unpaid bill.

Yanov was a charging bull, waste-deep, hurling the punt aside, lunging up onto the bank in a single movement, head down, arms flying out around an ankle. The punter crashed face first into the gravel of a carriage walk beside a car. Inside it, Beer Mug looked out at me under a bandaged head.

"*Alexey!*"

The dark medical man was out of the off-side door, a pointed foot aiming a kick at Yanov's face. Somehow I was on the bank. Now four of us were struggling on the grass. An unequal contest with my one arm and Yanov half-stunned. The hoods accelerated away, spitting gravel and teeth.

The pain came back to stay. Yanov was holding out a light-tan pigskin shoe.

"Please," I said.

He put it in my hand. "American—from your less than perfect world."

The nationality made not the slightest, smallest difference. I bit the leather until my teeth met through it. But the pain remained.

The holiday crowd stared. The ambulance arrived. I said, "Sorry, Yanov, sorry that my clothes upset you, sorry Yanov..."

He was still gripping my hand when the shock and the morphine blacked me out.

CHAPTER

EIGHTEEN

The head of the burn team at Yeovil said I was lucky. "If you'd been carrying the blazer rather than wearing it, or if the stuff had been a little bit higher or lower..." He shrugged.

Possible effects on either extremity were best left in the box. "How long?" I asked.

"The Danes made a first-class start but it's going to be several months. Acid's not run-of-the-mill. You've got a visitor, by the way. I'll send him in."

Jackson.

I expected to be withered. Instead he set down a gift. "Something to keep your mind occupied, Peter. I haven't read it—the new way of looking at our business, I gather. Extreme realism. Red-brick university types and Germans, all rather depressing I'm sure."

I thanked him. "I should have employed some realism myself."

He brought out the pipe. "May I?" I nodded. He flashed it up. "I warned, I believe, about false enthusiasm. In future, wear the cloak and leave the dagger to the psychopaths who enjoy it. There's no shortage of 'em. Do you feel able to talk?"

"If it gives a twinge I gobble pills. I understand that you've retired early, sir?"

He looked at the white hammock of bandage. "Twinge—I should think it does! As to retirement, there are loose ends. Tell me about Denmark—not your vendetta. I know altogether too much about that."

"I suppose it made a hell of a stink with the Yanks?"

"A partial description; go on with Copenhagen."

I told him about dinner and the boat ride. "I should never have fought with Yanov. It was inexcusable."

"But useful. Unless he's a truly phenomenal actor that was probably the first glimpse we've had beneath his skin." A nurse arrived to make some changes. He waited for her to finish before he continued. "Khrushchev's reflections on the past are curious."

"It was a weekend for reflection." I told him about Grishanov.

He agreed that the timing was odd. "Probably just the right hand keeping the left cut down to size. Mixing metaphors, even a cousin can get too big for party boots." He stood up. "I think you're having a twinge. I'll drop back; I'm staying down at Swyre for the next couple of weeks." He paused at the door. "By the way, since your mother died last year do you have anywhere to convalesce?"

"Not really. I've had the Hampstead house converted into flats. I keep one for myself."

"Rather public. Use Swyre if you like. It's off the beaten track. I shan't be around much myself, but the staff are laid on and they might as well be of use. My wife's sister's girl boards a horse and keeps an eye on things for us."

I was only too glad to accept. And yet after he left—and only because I knew him so well—I had the impression that I could not have refused, that I had been placed in a very loose but quite definite house arrest.

In any event, it was six weeks before I could take advantage of the invitation and twice as long before I could really move the arm. I kept the sleeve rolled down.

Jackson visited only twice, on each occasion driving down for a long weekend and avoiding any mention of service matters. I found other distractions in the country, among them Jackson's niece.

On the first Saturday in September I received a phone call from Marshall.

"I thought you were dead," I said.

"Wishful thinking, old boy." He made tender inquiries as to health. "Can you feel anything with the hand yet?"

"As long as it's wet, warm, and breathing."

A giggle. "Then you must be better. Come up to town tomorrow. Take the late train. I'll collect you."

I arrived at the dinner hour. Marshall bustled me along the platform, dropping gossip which continued in the car. We passed Admiralty Arch without stopping.

"We've missed the turn!" I knocked on the glass.

He patted my knee. "Changes, old man. Changes. C will explain all."

"What the hell are you talking about?"

"Lips sealed, old boy." Infuriating bugger.

We turned between the office warrens on Great George Street on to Birdcage Walk and Queen Anne's Gate, and finally reversed course into a tiny mews at the head of Dartmouth Street. A handsome Georgian house blocked the cul-de-sac. Inside, a major domo in a cutaway stuck his hand out wordlessly and I dropped my cap on it.

Marshall's little legs trudged ahead of me up a sweeping staircase. A clock rang seven. The butler type opened the door at the head of the stairs and left us in a large room with an Adams fireplace and an enormous Chippendale table. Through long windows there was a pleasant view across the walk to St. James's Park.

"Well, old boy?" Marshall wanted to keep playing. I looked instead at the books and pictures.

And then a section of a bookcase opened and there was Jackson, in a smoking jacket, smoking. "I couldn't resist the melodrama, Dravin. Come along in." The rest of his effects and the picture with the Kisby ring had followed him to the inner room. Small and intimate: three colored phones on the desk beside the whalebone lamp; maps with pin markers; a smaller fireplace with a fire burning. "You haven't told him?"—to Marshall.

"Of course not, sir." He'd never used sir to Jackson in his life except to be rude.

My ex-employer saw me looking at the bookcase door.

"Only one of the boys, Dravin. One's own secret stair as well— my business office is on Storey's Gate."

"Business . . . you've not retired?"

"Just slid sideways, you might say. H.M. government have seen fit to put a sailor back at the top." His mouth twitched. "I'm rather pleased. Now do sit down. Help yourself to coffee."

A sailor at the top. Grand Vizier of the Looking Glass World in Britain, the one appointment still requiring the sovereign's personal approval, given to this strange silent man with the slow movements and fierce eyes and slightly shabby clothes and dropped tobacco: Our spymaster.

"C." I said. "The Carpenter. Now you really are."

"But you think I'd make a better Mad Hatter." And for the first time ever he gave a full and proper smile.

Marshall looked at us as though we were both mad.

"The initial's not from Alice," said Jackson. "Just a small touch for tradition. Smith-Cumming and Hugh Sinclair both used C, whereas my military predecessor was J. Simpler than names and ranks and observes a certain anonymity. The job will not be common knowledge, by the way."

"And there's to be a full re-org, old boy, to a single intelligence service." Marshall's voice had an almost sexual excitement at the bureaucratic prospects.

Jackson closed them off. "Thank you for making the collection." The dismissal brought a look of anguish to the fish face. "Toodle-oo," I said as the bookcase closed on it.

Jackson eyed me. "Don't prod too hard. He's got the mandarin touch. If there's a change to Labour in next month's election, he'll end up in a minister's pocket."

"And me, sir?"

"Ah. You, Dravin. Well, as usual, you're a problem." A joke? Impossible to tell. "Your prolonged convalescence has served more than one purpose. Doubts about you which have been mentioned in the past have finally had to be resolved." My suspicions confirmed—and Marshall's Dorset absence. Trust the bastard to avoid the chance of anything catching while the body was in quarantine. "I've achieved that resolution." Jackson continued: "Copenhagen notwithstanding. Washington now has a better appreciation of your value. In fact, you seem to be wanted in all quarters." He slid a sheet of paper across the desk. "Read that."

From the First Deputy to the Minister of Defence for the Union of Soviet Socialist Republic.

To the Secretary of Foreign Affairs for Her Majesty's Britannic Government.

On behalf of the Soviet government and people, the Minister extends an invitation for cultural exchange to Commander P. A. Dravin R.N. to visit Moscow and Leningrad during the week of October 10, 1964. Liaison Officer for the visit, Kapitan Fourth Rank A. I. Yanov.

Signed J. J. Marashnikov
First Deputy

"God Almighty! The old bugger meant it."

"So it seems. I want you to go."

The arm gave a sharp stab of recoil.

"I realize what I'm asking—your background, and inside Russia—but let me say *why*." He leaned across the desk. "*Mortality*, Dravin! That's what we see from Copenhagen. An old man's mirror turning to the wall, killing the light on all his dreams." Holding the pipe in both hands, his intensity had physical impact. "No absolute despot lets that happen without making one hell of a play for the books."

"The old pope's last fling."

"*Exactly!* A man hiding in the rules for sixty years and still shattering the lot when he gets the chance. Well, K's motives may be different, but the view from the top's the same. Even to an atheist the opinion of the hereafter begins to make the mortal present look puny. And as he can't possibly outdo his predecessors at butchery—"

"He'll become the Father of his People, using Dravin as his instrument of fate."

"I agree I've put things in melodramatic terms. He's obviously making an overture through a side channel, as they did successfully with Cuba; no one damaged if nothing comes of it. But as to his mental state, I have many sources—and I'm *convinced*." The voice became casual again but none of the zeal had left the blue eyes burning through me as he asked the question. "Will you go?"

"Of course."

"Good!" He was immensely pleased. "We must have a drink

on it." He found whisky and glasses. "Another thing"—passing one to me—"when you come back, I need a salt eye kept on the lace-hanky world at the end of the tunnel, but it would mean your separation from the Service, so take your time with the decision." He raised the glass. "And congratulations. I understand you're marrying my niece?"

"Next week, sir. I thought it might help to get some roots down. Have something of value, as you put it."

"I think you're wise." He took a drink. "And California?"

"Chasing rainbows. It's been five years. One can't wait forever."

Marshall came with me to wave goodbye as I boarded BOAC for Warsaw and points east. "It's all rather dodgy, don't you think?" he said. "I'm sure my minister has regrets."

"Don't we all?"

"Of course *I* don't believe they'll try anything physical, not with the diplomatic net alerted, but you'll have to keep your hackles up. The aparat's incapable of resisting a knee-jerk try at an orgy."

"You've destroyed my last objection." For some foolish reason I shook his hand.

"Yes, well..." The little carp mouth tried to show human warmth. "Take your own arse wipe and don't diddle yourself in the hotel room, old man. You'll be the lead on the evening news."

MOSCOW.

CHAPTER

NINETEEN

The engines screamed resentment at the ground, invisible talons grabbed the runway; we were stopped. Fresh air flowed into the hull, but not the usual babbled relief that joins it. Shades of the wartime slogan: *Is your journey really necessary?*

Through the door, down the steps, and twenty-five years from childhood, I stood again in Russia. My Motherland.

A land of gray. Gray sky in the puddles and bleak glass of the terminal. Gray women lounging at the foot of the ramp they'd just rolled out, gray troops and police lounging with them. Gray faces of officials waiting to hate us. The only splash of color a bunch of flowers being presented by school children to some fraternal comrades from Bucharest.

"Produce your passes!" Russian voices all around. But for what?

"Not this door! That one."

All four doors seemingly the same, but our random trickle across the runway was funneled by the single entry and then dammed into a lake around the island of the immigration desk. The unspoken question offered with every passport: Will the bastards give it back? The moments pass, the wheel spins, the odds

145

move from simple red or black to the thirty-five to one of double zero.

"Produce your passes!"

And already the first fever of emotion was stamped on, crushed out by little things: by denials without reason, by boredom beyond caring.

"Produce your passes!" For the door, for the ticket counter, for the tea urn.

"No more tea." In a land that floated on it. And the woman, pleased to bring equal frustration to all, not making more. No one fought it. A Kafka's customs bureau with no power of appeal.

"Pyotr Andreyevich, welcome to the Soviet Union!" An impressive Yanov, resplendent in dripping braid, materialized from the masses to kiss cheeks and stop the roulette.

"Allow me to introduce you to Alexandre Alexandrevich Yulinovsky, who will be your guide when I am unavailable."

Marshall's opposite number, a happy bubbling little man, grasped my hand, and made a bow. "An honor, Kapitan. Welcome to your homeland. This way please," and he set off to teach the first great truth about the totalitarian state: It can do what it bloody well pleases. In my case it was pleased to see me at the head of the passport line, book stamped and returned, smiles all around at my infuriated fellow passengers, and out into a limousine as quickly as Yulinovsky could wave a hand—and waive all the rules.

"Allow me, Kapitan?" he stowed my case lovingly in the trunk. "It will be placed in the room reserved at the Hotel National. I hope all has been well prepared."

"I'm sure of it." But he had a duck's back to sarcasm and hopped cheerily in beside the driver, a dour bastard with the smell of Security on him.

Our twenty-minute drive along roads miraculously cleared for official progress was a eulogy to the glories of Russia according to the gospel of Intourist. The first stop was just north of the airport, thirty miles south of the city. We disembarked.

"This is as far as they got." Yanov pointed at the crossed massifs of the tank barriers beside the highway. A single rusting gutted panzer stayed behind as mute testimony of the onslaught. Scattered poplars clutched at a last few yellow leaves.

It was cold. Snow had been and gone a little. Winter, the only absolute ruler of Russia, had reminded his subjects that their year's third was over and his two thirds due. Cold. A light wind moaned at the tank, the sun hung pale behind the gray sky and low on the horizon.

And if we could have stood alone on the vastness of the plain, stood with just the weeping steel, I would have felt it. Because, assumed indifference notwithstanding, I was ready—eager even, to feel, *to know* that the blood of twenty million of my people had drenched the soil to drown that tank.

But we weren't alone. Half as many as the dead were with us now, pouring from a constant succession of tour buses. Starting and stopping cameras never-endingly. Laughing and chatting. Spitting. Stinking of garlic and tobacco and smells of poor hygiene forgotten in the West. A jolly. A day off at the State's expense. Like Armistice Day for us.

"Impressive," I murmured as expected, but the missile-tracking radar on the rise above the monument was more so.

En route again and now Moscow beckoned. Moscow, too low and gray to be impressive from a speeding car, and yet I found it hard to talk, to keep up a sophisticated veneer. Moscow, the world's largest town-planned spider's web: the streets following the old lines of the city walls forming the concentric circles, the great road arteries providing the supporting and connecting threads.

And in the very center of the web, its own red-gray walls forming the first and inner circle, by some humorous quirk of the universe, squats the body of the Kremlin, with the Lenin Mausoleum as its head.

The head eats a million people a day as they come in a never-ending black string of humanity to view the wax stiff in the glass box.

The string stared dumbly as we roared, tires drumming, across the cobbles beside it.

"You will want to pay your respects," said Yulinovsky in the voice of a vicar burying a duchess. "We shall go this afternoon."

"Should I take a chair?"

"A chair? Ah—a joke." Laughing enough to indicate that faith was not a funny business. "No, we shall enter through an official door. It will take about ten minutes." To achieve salvation.

Under a canopy designed for the Railway Shelter on the Battleship jetty, we walked into a lobby full of ragged ferns and ragged maids in once-white caps and black dresses, and sagging chairs with carved feet.

An undertaker's assistant behind the desk began the passport routine. Yulinovsky didn't squander his happy nature on a clerk. "Number 100!" The questions stopped instantly. An ornate key slid across the counter beside an abacus.

"I wish I could spend the afternoon with you," said Yanov, the hypocritical bastard. "I know you will find it rewarding."

"You're quite sure you can't make a change and remain?"

"Alas, no. But tonight we are booked for the Bolshoi and a dinner after, and tomorrow we shall meet some interesting people. On the next day, the thirteenth, we go to Leningrad."

The picture frames in my room were nailed to the walls to hide the mikes. After fifteen minutes Al arrived with the prodigal suitcase. "A mixup in the lobby," he said sadly.

I opened the bag. "They've been very neat," I said. He looked relieved.

In the afternoon we went hand in hand to see The Leader, St. Basil's, the Arsenal Tower, the Gum store around the corner from Kuibyshev Street, and the Glory to the Partisans mural in the Izmailovskaya Metro station. I felt my level of social consciousness being worked on and pleaded jet lag.

At seven-thirty we made the next spontaneous leap to the ballet. After the first act Yanov asked for an impression. "No wonder you wanted the Windmill and a little honest lust."

"A pity it's 'Coppelia.' With something like 'Swan Lake' you could not have failed to be moved."

"Perhaps it's an acquired taste."

"Like sukiyaki!" We both laughed. The first small chink in smothering formality. He asked me about the arm.

"Good as new." Which was not quite fact.

"Yes? Well one hopes so—a terrible business. That's the filthy side of things." I agreed.

"You hear from Nicolasha?" he asked, being elaborately casual.

"No—but I've been rather involved romantically in other directions." I explained my marriage. He was suitably astonished and then congratulatory.

"You should try it yourself, Alyosha."

"Perhaps I shall," he said lightly. "I hope for a leave after the New Year. You might tell her."

Without giving us a chance to talk further he excused himself, and when he got back he had Yulinovsky with him and the second act started. We sat through the rest until the last of the plasticized bouquets had been tossed on stage and then we went for dinner at the Aragvi restaurant. And under a torrent of vodka things got blurred.

I remember endless toasts and the group unaccountably thinning as we moved from place to place, until there seemed to be only Dravin and a dancer called Gisela, and the music of Rachmaninoff in a tsar's apartment of bed and mirror. Legs all the way up to the cheeks of her arse, and a mouth as wide and questing for a worm as a young sparrow. Sitting like one of those French paintings of a ballet dancer on a stool, examining a foot crossed over the opposite knee—all frilly tutu and Nikita's pansy pumps.

The pose was right, cross-legged. But on the edge of the bed and nothing frilly—in fact, under a sheer wisp of slip nothing at all. Eyes unwaveringly on mine, watching the effect of the pose; knowing the effect. Unbearably erotic, provocative, flagrant.

"Petya"—the mouth made for the word, pouting, lush—"Petya..." a throaty whispered essence of sex, "give me your hand." I gave it mindlessly, watching it about to drown in darkness and pull me in with it, felt her other fingers sliding up my leg.

A tiny sliver of frontal lobe escaped from the animal center and shrilled, *"Evening news"* at the hand. It stopped. *"Evening news, old man,"* and dragged it from the lip of the pit, as the girl fell backward on the bed....

In the hall, Al the friendly guide was planning the campaign with a burly chap of no fixed address. Al smiled his warm true smile.

I nodded at Burly. "The outraged husband?"

Husband! Guilt sliced off the fog of liquor. I had been held back by Marshall, old school tie, drummed-in security since Dartmouth. Not once by marriage. I felt thoroughly ashamed, then hostile. Why had they tried? Why now? A little insurance if mother love failed? But what blackmail effect was there on a bachelor officer in normal sex? None.

Yet only Yanov knew I was no longer single.

"Kapitan?" Yulinovsky's smile was crushed. Hurt of course by the implications of a setup. Too many setups. And they could have read about my marriage in the *Times*. I gave up. Booze beat out concentration.

"I understood," said Al, "that you would require a ride to the hotel after your entertainment." He sent across his all-men-of-the-world wink.

"Ta," I said. "Let me off at the Kremlin."

He took me seriously. In the very center of Red Square the car was stopped. "You will wish to be alone, comrade." The door slammed, cynicism fell away. The impact hit.

I was dwarfed by the proportions. A light snow fell through spotlights, dusting ledges and raking bottomless joints in the face of the walls. Between the lights. I walked soundless in spaces tunnel-dark. Two guards passed me, jackboots barely thumping. A bell sounded in a steeple. For church or time?

For time.

Because time, with winter, was the meaning of this country. My country, my father's country. To the land and the walls the age of the new masters had the span of an infant. Would be, and be gone, and the bell would toll, the snow fall on the ledge. England Expects. Russia Endures.

I set my stride to match the guards' and to keep my feet dry in light shoes. A Christmas card come early, "In his master's steps he trod . . ."

My father.

At this gate beside me? Standing here? Stalin there—through that inner arch—cat face waiting?

A Zil limousine roared out through the gate, not pausing, not looking. I jumped back, turned to watch its lights dwindle in the hugeness of the square. Above us all the basilica of St. Basil, gloriously beautiful, shining golden in the night. "My Russia, my Russia . . ."

But not beautiful enough for party eyes. From Portsmouth, the huge red star of the regime was tacked on top, and on the lower walls, neon ads: MARXISM LENINISM GLORIOUS FU . . . the tubes burnt out, not replaced.

I was suddenly half-frozen. I looked back for my car. It crept with me at fifty feet.

"What now of the Motherland, comrade?" Al in his vicar's voice.

I pointed at the sign. "You need a new bulb, gospodin. Your 'future's' shot."

The dining room offered a breakfast of thin pancakes over a copy of *Izvestia;* instant constipation for body and soul. Feeling like a ball in play at Wimbledon in front of all the swiveling heads, I wandered out to the lobby to avoid it.

A small television screen showed a picture of Nikita chatting to an astronaut whizzing around in the current space spectacular. The announcer said the Chairman was holidaying at his Black Sea villa.

"We shall beat you to the moon yet," said the familiar voice of the Chairman's cousin.

"I can't even see the bloody sun. My tongue feels like death on the half shell."

A loud Russian laugh slammed it shut on my ear. "You need a proper breakfast."

"Not those damned pancakes."

"Proper. Come." I followed him out and around the corner to the Metropole.

"You haven't raised my hopes, Yanov." A mirror image of my own hotel. The same bricks already falling off the new wing into the safety nets. Being watched by the same two idle workers in sexless quilting. The same Victorian lobby overheated and smelling of last night's drinking.

He wheeled into a small dining room which was almost empty. A waitress dragged over with a menu. Yanov grunted "Tea," and began to look unwell.

"I'm glad to see that your head's catching up—" I stopped. Something about the group at the end of the room . . . three men, all middle-aged, dowdy. But not Russian—the tailoring was wrong. My own was equally observed, the uniform undoubtedly a conversation piece. The closest man watching: that thin effeminate nose, sardonic upper lip. . . .

"*Philby!*" Number one of Marshall's Oxbridge queens.

He bent forward to talk to the man across the table who turned—half-turned. A single flashing glance. From eyes turned down like commas and inexpressibly sad. *Don't forget the Diver!*

How could I ever in my life? *It must be Crabb.*

I stood. So did he, keeping his back to me, but a back with pearlike shoulders hanging above bandy legs. I took one step, and he was gone through a service door. A crude-looking waiter was coming out.

I walked by reflex to the table. It was the damnedest thing. Like the scene in the space film, *2001*—of the replica of earth set up at infinity, in Moscow a copy of breakfast in a refectory off the Quad at Oxon. A kipper on Philby's plate; toast in a silver rack; Dundee marmalade in an earthen pot. Even a week-old copy of the *Guardian*.

"Good morning, Commander." Philby at the table sat with one cheek off his chair. "Recently out from home?"

The unspeakable filth had written off a hundred names when he flew. Unbearable to see him here, unabashed, at ease, with that chronic bloody smirk. I walked behind him and he changed cheeks gingerly to follow me around. There was no name for him. And while I would have liked to do anything slow and revolting, the thug waiter was hoping for the excuse.

"Was that Crabb?"

"Who, Commander?" A mince of smile filleting the fish.

Turning away, I gave an "accidental" jab of the knee hard into his arse. A brief agony gashed his mouth. It was less than nothing for the hundred names.

"Mind the kipper, dear," I said. "The bones are bad for the piles."

Yanov, waiting with ham and eggs, was as uncomfortable as Philby. "I'm not hungry," I said.

"Nor I." He stood up. "Let's walk."

We went out past the queues already forming at the shops. "You knew about all that, Alexey. What the hell's the point?"

"Orders." In the freedom of the street, he was bluntly frank. "As I put it to you in Denmark, we're not barbarians. We recognize international service, and for it we grant a good life—families are welcome." He wasn't even trying with the pitch, but the association of my role with Philby's stung.

"You'd bring Nicola? Introduce her to that *thing* back there?"

"Don't play your goddammed Danish games again, Pyotr Andreyevich." His voice had a sudden shared bitterness. "You know the bloody answer. It's so easy for you—right or wrong, your parents made the decisions. But if you stood in my shoes—well, just think of that sometimes."

"I do. And more than sometimes! But just don't mess her up. If you won't come west, for Christ's sake let her go."

"*Let her go!* Twelve thousand miles apart, meeting twice, you think I hold her? I only wish to God I did."

We had turned into the Frunze Ulitza. He stopped in front of a three-story building of artificial stone painted an unpleasant soot-streaked yellow. It was distinguished from a row of others by TV cameras on the corners and a complicated antenna structure on the steep black roof. The basement windows were incongruously pasted over with newspapers.

"What is this place—do you keep the bomb in the cellar?"

He smiled, shrugged, welcoming the relief. "You know Security . . ."

The inmates had cut holes in the screen to look at girls' passing legs. And been allowed to! No outsider can understand the asylum's rules. He hadn't named the institution.

Now there was too much to see and we moved too quickly for anything but impression. A crippled veteran from the *Aurora* taking coats, grandeur of a marble lobby gone to seed, banks of ancient elevators hiding in cages of wrought iron, rocking in their shafts and missing floors. Filigreed brass leaves and flowers on the gates. A long, long corridor. Chestnut paneling, chestnut parquet floors and doors without names. Faded threadbare Asian carpets. Original oils of battles and leaders from Borodino to Nikita. Novelty-store plaques with exhortations from the Master hanging tattily between the masterpieces. Red eyes of closed TV watching the faithful.

The passage ended at a switchboard installed with the elevators: hand-plugged wires and chest sets. A man with a shaved head monitored it for the party and passed us with a nod.

Yanov showed me into a room with a lot of brass-tacked, cracking leather on heavy mahogany. "I'll be a moment."

He knocked on a connecting door, went through it.

To what?

I was alone with a racing pulse to wonder. Or was I a kid left unattended in a sweet shop for a crude loyalty test? Because I wasn't quite alone—Red Eye was here too.

It must be Yanov's office—all around the memorabilia of a Russian naval officer: Obligatory faces of Lenin and Khrushchev; a group portrait of officers passing out from a course, Yanov in the center, receiving an award from an admiral. The inspecting officer's back to the camera in a PR snafu. An engraved sword, presumably the prize, hung on the wall beside the portrait: "On guard for the glory of the Motherland—V. I. Lenin."

As many quotes as fragments of the true cross.

The overriding picture sat beside me on the desk, in a heavy rococo frame. A tiny woman with Yanov's eyes, standing between him and Joseph Stalin. Wearing her Hero's star.

"Am I less a liar now, Pyotr Andreyevich?" Yanov was back to read my mind. "You must need tea—you're a true Russian in that."

"An Englishman," I said, just to keep the record straight for Red Eye.

He grinned and held open the door.

The face from my files, the face of the enemy, sat with his back to the Kremlin and looked at me.

CHAPTER

TWENTY

Sergei Gorshkov, Admiral. In full, *Admirale Flota Sovietskova Soyuza:* Master of all the Russian Fleets.

For a moment, standing in his doorway, I felt frozen, pressed to the floor with a gravitational force. Why? Any of Portsmouth's delayed adolescent reaction to braid and ribbons was long gone; in fact quite the reverse: This excess of golden oak leaves, anchors, lapel embroidery and shoulder boards was Third Reich. Goering not Tredennick. Yet buried under it there was something—some psychological third dimension—setting the man apart from his peacetime-committee-world Western opponents.

Power.

Power in the absolute: biblical power. *The Lord of Hosts is with thee and shall smite the valley of thine enemies.* Smite with a signal from this extended hand to a thousand captains created literally in his own image.

The creator came around the desk. "Andrei Andreyev's boy. Welcome to Moscow. How is Admiral Jackson—in a new position, I hear?" So much for schoolboy playing with initials.

A quick strong handshake. "Thank you, sir. He's well. I'm sure he would have wanted to send his regards." Keeping it light, but rattled by the casual dropping of the names, and by the fierce intensity of the eyes—unblinking hooded hawk's eyes over a flattened hawk-beak nose, far more predatory in the flesh than on film. The eyes were eased a little by a sensual mouth with fine lips. But any sense of an aesthete was smashed by a jaw projecting all the outward thrust of his expanding fleet.

Releasing me, he indicated a chess set of red and white carved ivory set up on the desk. "You play, of course?" A pair of gold-rimmed glasses, evidently put down in haste, lay beside the board. Marks from their recent wearing abridge the beak nose indicated a possible Gaullist touch of vanity.

"Only the simplest moves, sir."

"You surprise me. Yanov is excellent—he beats me too often. Please sit. Tea, Alexey Ilyich." An order from a man already twenty years an admiral.

He went back to the window and sat down heavily into his own chair, an elaborate Scandinavian design with a dental mass of knobs and levers: Other than the gold rims, the only sign in the room of self-indulgence.

Yanov poured a third of a cup of black liquid from a silver teapot into three glasses in silver holders, then filled them with water bubbling over charcoal in a battered antique of a samovar.

Gorshkov saw me looking at it. "My Aladdin's lamp—it came to me in 1942 and has been with me since."

"And what spirit does it release, sir?"

"Memory, Commander. The power of recall and association. The strongest of spirits."

Too strong. I searched for something less. "You really turned fishing smacks into landing craft?"

A blank stare.

And then a wide smile cracking the marble face for a first time. "Not quite, boy. One on each side of a raft between. Not much as a ship, but what you call in the West good advertising, eh?"

I agreed.

"From Peter the Great. A man much to be admired despite aristocratic faults." His hand toyed unconsciously with a red chess-man in the form of a Genghis Khan spear carrier on horseback. "He built his first ship at sixteen."

And chopped the heads off half the mutinous Moscow garrison with his own hands a few years later.

His admirer offered me a thin sugar-coated biscuit with his next move, a quick switch to the personal address. "I heard of

your father's death with great regret, Pyotr Andreyevich." "'I
weep for you,' the Walrus said: 'I deeply sympathize....'"

I accepted at face value.

"A historic man. A protégé of Kolchak, our greatest admiral
until his insanity." A euphemism for running a White army in
1919 and getting shot for it by the Reds. "I counted it a privilege
to be close to him. And your mother."

"Yes sir."

The eyes dilated for an instant. "But you doubt it!" From a
drawer of the desk he brought out a battered scrapbook. Another
admiral making another run at lost family history. Filling in the
encyclopedia's blanks with words?

With a picture. Gorshkov young, thin, sepia-toned—like Yanov in New York, looking unhappy with the camera. Standing in
uniform beside a priest outside a church door in the Russia of
1930, he had better reason.

"The Fortress chapel at Leningrad. I was his aide."

Aide to the stick figure when the beard was dark.

Standing on his other side. Between them, my mother, holding
the object of the occasion with his new names. Another picture
in a room of uniforms, gruff faces looking down, glasses raised.
To baby Dravin's future? To their own? If so, a bleak one. The
purge got the lot.

Except my host.

"Not a good time for admirals," I said.

"Or for Russia. There were acknowledged excesses. Some at
great personal cost—like your father." The hawk eyes blinked
once, slowly, as though the hood had just come off. "But this
country is being moved from the Middle Ages in one generation.
During events of such historic scale what are twelve gold sleeves
in a picture? Or a hundred? Or a thousand?" He flicked a single
pawn across the board. A Khrushchev gesture. But no trick. I had
the absolute certainty that he could have kept counting. That he
would.

I went back to the picture world. Two or three years later—
the fo'c'sle of a battleship in drydock. My father pointing with
a gloved hand at a barrel. Young Dravin being lifted by young
Gorshkov to sit astride it. Both men laughing. My father *laughing*.

"Did he laugh often?"

"What?"

"My father—"

"Not often, but he enjoyed humor. Practical jokes in particular."

I could not believe it. Nor religion in an atheist Russia. But the pictures showed him laughing.

"May I ask you about the christening: How it was possible—why there was no fuss?"

"No fuss!" Gorshkov laughed himself for the first time. "My God, boy, it was the most frightening experience of my life. The Party was certainly against it." He winked. "But there are ways in any organization—like papal dispensations. We're not what the West wants to believe—certainly not now. I hope that at least to a small degree you're beginning to see that for yourself. It's quite wrong that we should be set as adversaries—our two countries, with so much linking us from the past."

The opening bars of an overture through a side channel. "The Entente?" I asked.

He waved a hand, "Much closer; the anthem..."

"God Save the Queen?"

"Of course. The tune. Almost the same words. Until eighteen thirty, forty—somewhere there. And so much more. The English church in Riga, our training systems—free of caste, I have to say; a long, long list. Don't you agree?"

"I—"

The door opened abruptly. A broad striper gave me an astonished look and stopped in his tracks.

"Fleet Admiral, your pardon. A matter I must bother you with..."

"Very well. Commander, you will excuse us." It was a definite statement. He softened it slightly with a hint of the earlier smile. "Take your tea. Alexey Ilyich, go too." I'd forgotten Yanov was in the room.

The door closed. "Full marks for surprise," I said.

He was vastly self-satisfied. "Was I right about interesting—"

"Yanov!" The voice on the intercom had the stridency of an action gong. I was alone again. Wondering the truth about my

father, trying to lock in words and meanings for reports, sort out sense from nonsense.

The door opened. A Yanov that I hadn't seen since the morning when we faced each other across the body of the diver re-entered.

"There has been an unavoidable change to your schedule."

The scar tissue on my arm began to crackle. Marshall's words: *"Hang you up on the wall, old boy. Skin you, and throw you back."*

"The Admiral's joining us for dinner?"

He ignored the chance to make it easy. "I will see you down to your car. Comrade Yulinovsky will make the required arrangements." In the passage, the switchboard at overload blinked like a punch-drunk Univac. I turned towards the filigreed gates.

"Nyet!" Yanov grabbed my jacket. "This way!" Abandoning any charade of antique obsolescence, we were through a door into a stark hall, white paint, green tile, bulbs overhead. A small modern elevator, "Ministerial Use Only." Inside, for the first time there was no Red Eye. The doors hissed shut. Yanov leaned against the wall and passed a hand over his face.

"What is it?" I found myself speaking in a church whisper.

"The earth's moving. A change of politicals."

The elevator, dropping, took my stomach with it.

"Will you be affected?" *Having had a cousin for a friend?*

"Naturally one wonders." He straightened up. "But things may not happen. There's to be a meeting of the full committee, a vote." Democracy in action. The elevator stopped. He kept his finger on the button to hold the door.

"Petya—Nicholasha. I won't be able to write. I'm sure no leave. Will you explain . . . give her my love . . . ?"

Hold her hand again, Dravin. Sing her the old songs though we may never meet again over the rainbow as time goes by.

"Of course," I said as he embraced me. And locked in a man's arms in an elevator in Red Defense Headquarters I thought, *Jesus Christ, if I had only waited three months more!* And felt an absolute shit. To my wife as well. The door began to open. I held it with my own finger on the button. Dravin's pound of flesh.

"There's a price, Alexey." He knew. "Do I tell her that with another chance you'll take it—and come West?"

"I have to answer *now*—like *this?*"

A fist was pounding on the door. Yanov's world was shaking.

"Now."

"Yes."

"A flight control radar is affecting departures," said smiling Al, "and there may be some delay. You will probably wish to rest in your room."

Under guard by goons in the hall. Sleep was out of the question. There was no television and the Gideons stop at the wall in Berlin. What passed for radio—a one-station wired-in extension speaker—played party Musak.

Mantovani syrup fiddles. "One day as Ivan Ivanov guides his new tractor from the Irkutsk plant, a wheel drops in the ditch. Pledging his life to the eternal memory of our beloved Vladimir Ilyich . . ." He lies under the wheels? No, thirty women come from the commune and the norm of dung removal is exceeded. "Glory to our dear Communist party, inspiration to us all." Birth to death.

Every minute, every hour, every day. *Through nine hundred days?* Probably. More probable than folk tales. Nine hundred days. The days of our years. I lay on the bed and watched my life pass for inspection from the roots to the present, forcing back the waves of fear contracting in the gut. Would an Englishman, a Jackson, feel it? No. Because these bastards could only claw a Russian who believed, only a kid from once upon a time.

From as long ago and far away as Dickens's London. I knew that now. Knew that Russia in all its dreamed-of Tolstoy images was truly memory. History, whether as the party boasts, or as Gorshkov flatly stated, had won this smothering gray, mind-grabbing, bullying mass outside my room: The Union of Soviet Socialist Republics. The ultimate in Pyrrhic victory!

I got up. I might not be British—perhaps I could have been Russian. I would never be Lenin's. I yanked the plug on him.

Seven o'clock. A knock on the door. A *special sound in the U S S R.* Yulinovsky's smiling face lit up the hall and the miscellaneous bodies in it.

"Good news." Billy Graham saving sinners. "There is an Air France Departure for Vienna at ten. Please come."

The extras came too, flat feet scuffing the carpet to explain the threadbare look. The hotel staff, cattle-spooked by foreshock tremors of a major quake, ignored our departure.

The driver came around to be attentive, to help me into the back seat. One hand opened the door. The other touched my left arm, above the elbow where the burn had been deepest. Memories in the muscle cells screamed.

He looked in to tuck me up. "Apologies, comrade," in a hard flat voice. "One would think the arm was healed." He slammed the door. With only intimation the bastards could make one's guts run like water.

He pulled us out into the traffic and turned on to Manyezhnaya Ulitza, the main road running beside the northwest side of the Kremlin into Red Square. The snow had changed to rain and the fortress walls were now a dungeon: Moscow a garrison under siege. There seemed to be troops by thousands.

The patrol stopped us at the entrance to Kuibyshev Street. Hostile peasant faces from the past glared at my uniform over a wooden barrier.

Beyond it, a bizarre cortege of official hearselike limousines deposited without flowers or a body outside Number 4. Gray, drab, two pillars flanked an unassuming entry. Capped with a sign: "Central Committee of the Communist Party of the Soviet Union."

Yulinovsky gave up the effort of conversation. The driver ignored me in the mirror. I imagined the departure of the final flight from Moscow before the borders closed for repairs.

My host from the tea party quick-stepped into the building beside Malinovsky, the Defense Minister. The barrier came down. We started forward. My head slammed against the glass.

A last hearse cut across our bow. The doors opened, the chauffeur and the man beside him jumped out. Then, from the back, straightening up rather slowly, stiffly, the familiar dumpy figure emerged. I looked at the heavy, pugnacious, white-fringed head, the stumping feet and the short thick legs. He was wearing his Red Ribbon.

He tripped at the curb. Angrily shook off his companion's arm, put out a stubby hand with age spots, on our car for support. The old gray eyes freed of metaphor looked at me. Perhaps he *had* tried before his mirror turned. Perhaps his thaw was real. I saluted. He nodded, paused, almost spoke. Looked up at the scarlet sign with golden letters—the colors of the carpet—nodded a last time and walked out of my life to meet his makers.

Speeding now, out along the ring road through a Moscow hunkered down in Lyndon Johnson's phrase. Devoid of people. *"Nearly there, nearly there,"* playing endlessly behind closed eyes.

"Halt!"

Once more at the tank memorial. But not this time for rusting steel, tour buses, cameras, garlic, laughing drunks.

The old panzer was at the front again. With shouted orders, smells of oil and paint, exhaust. Clanking metal grinding from the half-tracks on the concrete. Personnel carriers in khaki, twenty millimeter batteries in loading drill. Searchlights sweeping the bellies of the clouds, faces, the wartime blood-drenched soil. Trees.

"And far away the leaves of autumn are all aflame so brilliantly . . . my Russia . . ."

Yanov's.

This unhappy country waiting with the weeping iron panzer for another fire from a piano to release its frozen heart.

Through the last cordon and into the building. The newsstand closed. A lettered sign in pencil, "No issue of *Izvestia* today."

Two thousand frightened people trapped in a fog of tobacco smoke for five year-long hours. Yulinovsky sat beside me chainsmoking my father's cigarettes. A fund of funny stories. I can't remember one. Troops elbow to elbow around the walls of the waiting room.

"Kapitan"—Yulinovsky had risen. "This way please." But not to the main boarding gate. A small door at the side. "More convenient." *For what, for the love of God?*

A small bulb above the door shone thinly in the rain. In the blackness beyond the light a car squealed across the tarmac. A door slammed. Footsteps ran towards us and a man came out of the darkness so that I could see his face. Again, under a light. Shadowed. Sucked in where the jaw was missing.

His hand bulged in a pocket of the coat.

"Commander Dravin." A tinge of American in a warm voice. A trace of an impediment. Christ! Why should I worry about that? The hand was coming out of the pocket.

"This was apparently left in your room." Looking at me with steady eyes. Glad to grant a favor of the planted incrimination. Photos? Electronics? *Life imprisonment for treason.* "May one hope that you will come again to your homeland?"

"One never knows," I said, gripping the small brown paper package and knowing with every fiber in me.

"Well then, *au revoir,* Commander." A pleasant short smile. "Not goodbye."

Al smiled me to the plane before all the others, still breaking all the rules—and then the false advertising of the giant star above St. Basil's passed below the wing and the squalid slogans of Moscow were rained out.

Double zero. Free of the web twice in a lifetime.

The plane banked suddenly to port, the pilot, passengers, dazzled, blinded by the searchlight beam. The cabin in daylight showed the package on my knee. I tore the wrapping.

A note in Russian. "From a godfather—" The beam already falling off the paper. "In friendship."

The light on its way out picked up a last reflection from the engraving of the characters on the silver of the tea glass holder.

GORSHKOV.

TAKANEN.

CHAPTER

TWENTY-ONE

"The machines have scored a hat trick." From his expression, Marshall was taking any credit personally.

"We're at war?"

He waved a printout triumphantly. "Cousin Y's been found at Viborg and Face Hole has a name!"

Nineteen sixty-seven, and Jackson had been right all the way. Labour in; an idiot minister who found Marshall refreshingly jolly for a civil servant; a new empire of personnel analysis and computers to be built. Marshall loved them, especially the program labels: Face Hole, Baker, Cousin Y. He played happily for hours— dissidence and bloody-mindedness at the push of a button.

"At Viborg?" Their naval infantry school on the shores of Lake Ladoga. Just a jump away from Finland. "How recently?"

"Within the month. As CO—"

"He must be back in their good books."

"Perhaps." Coyly, "But, that's the hat trick. Guess who's mother's little helper?"

I didn't try.

"Virgin!"

Sinyavsky. I felt for Yanov. But as a blood relation of the fallen idol he was lucky to be received at all in party circles.

Marshall had the same thought. "I would have sworn he was one bird flown forever. Talking of which, I suppose you're going to tell the Quail?" Nicola. "I think we should, old boy. Rev her up before she goes off the rails again."

There had been a near marriage to an engineer at Southern Cal. Triggered initially by my brutal letter about my own marital status and Yanov's doubtful prospects. Brutal to be kind, I'd thought. We had not made contact since. Now presumably we would.

"They wouldn't have hung the Virgin round his neck if all was sweetness and light, would they, old man?" Marshall was daydreaming again, exposing his fetish that through rot in the ranks we'd see another Potemkin: A coup brought up to date with a nuke lobbed at the Kremlin's golden balls by an independent mind at sea. "It's not a bad spot for trouble to start—Viborg. Nicely tucked away. Get up a good head of steam."

Frozen muskeg seemed an unlikely place for an infection which prefers warm darkness. "You said the program's nailed Face Hole?"

"Travinov, a major in the nasties when you were in the States. A colonel now for his unpleasantness."

"He wasn't. That was the most disturbing thing about him. Too damned considerate by half."

"Couldn't see the scorpion's tail in the dark, old boy. Get in a closed box with the bastard and you'll feel it all right." He returned to his first love. "We could ask Bakersman if there've been any noises at Viborg. Why don't you visit Finsbury Road?"

The home of the Baker, one of my Latvian émigrés. Bakersman was his brother, a petty officer with hurt feelings working his way through the submarine repair yards in Leningrad.

"Next time I buy a sausage roll I'll ask."

"You scoff, Dravin, I know you scoff." He pushed himself away from the edge of my desk. "But one day—well, I'm off. You'll pass the good news to C? We'll watch for a note to the Quail."

Yanov sent it and she went. For three weeks. And on the fourteenth day, in accordance with our elevator understanding, I went myself to reclaim Faust.

He wasn't with her in the farmhouse kitchen.

"Petya! My God. You said next week. We weren't expecting you."

Nor I her.

After six years, the last meeting—in this very place—could have been this morning. At thirty, the face seemed longer, a little more triangulated, touches of fullness chiseled off. Stunning. She wore her hair pulled back into a bun. It suited her but made her more practical. It went with the air of increased confidence. "From running my own field office," she said. And extensive travels to South America and the Cordillera to study earthquakes' aftereffects—the practical ones. Not emotional like ourselves.

"And you, Petya? Alexey tells me you were made a captain. Congratulations!"

"The KGB's behind the times; it was a retirement rank. I'm a civilian. Where is he, by the way?"

"Down by the lake—out of the Service? No more Heart of Oak—you *have* made changes." She was looking for them in my face.

"May I have some of that coffee?"

"Sure." She stood by the stove, pouring but still looking. "And how's marriage? Any kids?"

"Not yet. We're going to start thinking seriously one of these days. My wife's hoping to make the Olympic team with her riding next year—thanks." I took the mug. "How is it, Niki—with him?"

Our eyes met.

"Hopeless," she said. The little laugh undercut by the pain in the eyes. "He wants more time. *More goddamned time!* Can you believe!" The buoyancy left her. She slumped into one of the old cane chairs.

I found myself taking her hand. "I was afraid of that. Why—?"

"Did I agree to stir it up?"

When the fires were banked. When new lives could have been made. History changed. Which isn't possible, of course. Like asking the fortune teller to make things different by revealing the bad news in the tea leaves.

"Call it the last bid at an auction," she said. "I know, I know—you told me. They don't transplant, Russians. Not even as kids—"

"It's a fact, love. Look at me. And with Yanov—if you pull the roots of his country and his navy, what's left of the man?"

"His wasted side. The music—he paints, too, did he ever tell you that?"

"No."

"He brought a picture with him this time. He could be really good . . ." She looked away, fell silent. I drank my coffee. "I just want him, Petya . . ."

I patted the hand. "I'll go and do some talking. Is the old lady around?"

"She took off to a friend's place in Virolahti, wherever that is." She made the effort to get back to normal. "Don't just talk, Peter. Make him an offer. Kidnap the bastard—isn't that what you guys do?" The laugh was right on the edge.

"Talk first, kidnap afterwards. I'll be back."

She didn't know it, but a grab had been discussed, and totally rejected by ministerial fiat. Too high a provocation, too risky for the Finns. But under the counter, Kallas was ready: drugs, passport, ambulance to flight connections. At this very minute.

If I blew the whistle.

I walked down to the lake through the barley field. The grain was cut and a flock of wood pigeons ate leftovers. Yanov was standing with his back to me, watching the swans.

He was strained at the eyes, but looking well. And not surprised to see me. I had a sense that he'd been waiting. We talked around the subject by discussing the aftermath of Moscow.

"The vote of the Committee was damned close. Almost a tie. Funny, I didn't grasp that he'd really gone until we went back to headquarters and there was just a square of lighter paint where his picture had been hanging."

"I liked the old man," I said, "Genuinely—for all his shit disturbing."

The old grin came out. "The chocolate—the expression on your face! He loved that trick." The grin faded. "We miss him. We'd grown used to things becoming more relaxed, and now it's tense again."

"The bad old days?"

"Nothing like Stalin. But unhappy. Perhaps just until we get used to the new men."

"Working with Sinyavsky doesn't help, I'm sure."

"You know?" He was briefly intrigued. "But you're right. A

strange son of a bitch, that one. Came from nowhere after the war—an orphan, but who wasn't? Worked like a fanatic, top of all his courses. Brilliant naturally at toadying to party arseholes. Although I'll give him this: he cares about the troops, not just the political angle. But even now, when there's no cousin at the top and dinner with the Admiral, the atmosphere between us stinks. I don't know why; I don't hold *Zhid* over him." He nodded up the hill, "How could I?"

"About her . . . we've been talking." I waited. He was silent. "I haven't told her yet that we had a bargain."

"I can't keep it—"

"So I understand. More time. *Rodina*, no doubt?"

"That sarcastic fucking wit." But he hadn't even raised his voice. "And spare me all your logical analysis." I felt the whistle in my pocket. The Kallas solution would be concrete, not analytical.

"Do you know where I was two weeks ago?" asked Yanov.

"Sinyavsky aside, I'm not clairvoyant."

"In Dzerzhinski Square."

The opposition's headquarters. Rather than Lenin's tomb, the real and actual head of the spider. I remembered the hand on my arm, the knock at the door. I thought I began to understand.

"The day before, I'd been told to report to Moscow for my visa rather than collecting it from Leningrad—special instructions, they said. A meeting with the Finns, they said. I should have guessed! He met me at the station. *Polite?* Shit—you'll never know. . . . 'Good morning, *Tovarish Kapitan*—how's Ilena Petrova?' "

His mother.

"It took about ten minutes . . ."

For a guided tourists' tour through the Lubyanka Prison. Rather dry at first—facts, statistics. Names of former royal patrons, builders, famous literary prisoners and revolutionary heroes. And then in the same dispassionate guiding voice pointing out the human interest, the little bits and pieces. A stain; gouges in stone from clawing fingers. . . .

"We were in the oldest wing. Wet, cold. Very deep—at least two flights down. There was a passage of cells with the doors open . . ."

For a ceremonial parade of the faces hidden behind the Bolshoi, and Dialectic History, and scrapbooks of young admirals, and young lieutenants watching cheering troops in Portsmouth.

"Men of all ages. A young woman..."

An old one.

"Someone's mother, Comrade." The tour was over. "A pleasant leave..."

The swans drifted immaculate reflections across the lake. The sun shone as always at Takanen.

The guide had suffered too. "The whoremonger had only half a face." Yanov was unnaturally casual. "You've got all the answers, Petya. What do I do?"

"Publicity on our side—"

"Would stop them from announcing heart failure? With three specialists in attendance?" Voice hardening, just a touch. "But go on, tell me"—voice rising—"only no more of the future." Louder. "You think I don't *dream* of future?" Shouting. *"That I haven't worn out that fucking San Francisco record with eight years of fucking dreaming?"*

Calm again. Flat. Like a prisoner's guide. "Just tell me, Pyotr Andreyevich. Make the choice for me."

By blowing a whistle for Kallas. And ensuring a ticket for the death cart that a Leningrad mother missed in that coldest month in a hundred years almost that long ago.

"Want to wash your hands?" He pointed contemptuously at the lake.

I almost lost control. Which perhaps was what he wanted. "I won't choose, Alexey. But I'll change the rules. After today it's ended with Nicola. "No more 'on my honor next time.' There won't be one. She'll get no letters, in or out. They'll be water-damaged, delayed, lost in transit. Phone lines will be cut. If there are holidays planned they'll be wasted; visas will arrive too late. Health regulations won't be met. Customs investigations will miss flight connections."

"Bureaucratic death." He threw a crust at the swans. "A Russian Tuonela."

"Whatever that means. Look, I think you underrate publicity. Artists and writers and dancers with relatives behind them leave every day. And from our side—house, money, protection—"

"I don't doubt your generosity, Petya." He patted me gently on the back. "You've given me the girl."

He meant it. With the old warmth back, I *must* try harder. "Alyosha, I've been through it. Not the same, I know, and it doesn't help—but about your mother; if it was mine she'd have wanted me to take this chance." Instinctively I grasped his arms. "And I think, Alyosha, that I would—that's all."

"You think you would." He tried to turn his head away.

He wasn't listening. *But he must.* "There's a last reason. The real difference between us—for Christ's sake don't shrug me off"—I shook him—"There *is* a difference, Yanov. If positions *were* reversed—if it *was* my mother—your side would make the choice for me and put a bullet in her."

He had heard. He nodded.

I held out my hand. "I didn't use my bullet, Alexey."

I threw the whistle out across the lake and it fell flashing like the drum major's mace scattering the swans.

"I'm sorry," I said.

"That's okay," and she kissed my cheek. "Free will or not at all."

"It's a second siege, Niki. You'll need a miracle to lift it."

She gave me a small sad smile. "I've tried, sweetheart. If there's a God, I'm pregnant."

"And if there's a bun in the old oven," said Marshall with his usual delicacy, "I hope she doesn't drop it before it's cooked. This is our last chance at a winner."

Alone with Jackson, thoughts ran deeper. "How did Yanov receive the news?"

"It hammered him."

"But he must still say goodbye to mother?"

"Yes. I left at that point. Frankly, I don't believe it. Even if he's allowed another chance to run, I think the glow will wear off."

"Marshall's phrase was 'lover's nuts,' I believe. Is the pregnancy confirmed?"

"Whatever rabbits do under the circumstances has been done. I haven't had that experience myself."

He threw me a long look. "Being tied to children lasts a long time, my boy. Your wife'll come round. There's nothing physical—?"

"Oh no."

"Good. As to Yanov, who knows? The metaphysical may do it—fate pointing, that sort of thing. He obviously broods. His reference to Tuonela—"

"What was that about?"

He was surprised. "The Finnish version of the Styx, Dravin. The Swan takes the role of Boatman and sings the names of those called to cross the black river of death."

"Bloody morbid."

He agreed. "But it's three in a row. I'm surprised Marshall's toys haven't sniffed it out."

"I'm sorry, I don't follow."

"Superstition." He ticked his fingers. "The stone swan as a child; the charm around the neck; the classic concern with swans and death."

"I didn't realize it was."

"Swan song, Dravin. The birds stay mute until they sense their demise, whereon they pick a private place to sing a special song for the occasion, and then proceed to the hereafter. Not a shred of truth biologically, but its roots go very deep—the Norse legend's only one facet. You haven't heard the Sibelius composition on the theme?"

"No."

"Extraordinarily evocative—long winding horns. I'd like to meet your Yanov." He brought out his tobacco. "You haven't lost sight of the other aspect: Why they let him out at all?"

"Mother Church is still fishing for men?"

He nodded. "Until the day you die, Peter. Never forget it. They won't." On my way out he said, casually, "I'm glad you didn't blow the whistle."

I hadn't told him.

CHAPTER

TWENTY-TWO

On the evening of the first of June—the Glorious First in British naval history—the phone rang in my Hempstead flat.

"Petya?"

Only the most conventional remarks seem to serve momentous personal occasions. "You sound fine; are you?"

"Just great."

"And the baby—what is it?"

"It's not an it, it's a both."

"Twins?"

"One of each."

One or two—what difference? Yet for a moment I couldn't speak; the gesture of commitment on her part seemed enormous. She filled the gap.

"Last night—and I really am fine. We all are. Listen, would you do something?"

"The world; name it."

She paused, "Well—it's telling him. I guess it sounds stupid but I'd just like to know that he really *gets* told, I don't know how, but something more than just a postcard to Grandmother Tarasinov, you know?"

Such a tiny thing.

I felt an overwhelming hostility for Yanov. Not envy or jealousy—just rage. Because every day I read about the others, the ones who swim and crawl and bleed and hang on the wire and die in broad daylight, only to get away. Not for a fraction of what he was offered at no risk and had refused.

As I had in San Francisco. For an idiot's game of Marshall Says, not my mother's life. The feeling turned against myself.

"I'll see that the old lady's told in person, Niki. With Alexey— I'll try. . . . It's not very likely, I'm afraid."

Another silence.

"I guess—and I'm sorry to bug you. It's just there's no one else who knows him. It's kind of a funny feeling. I mean I have friends here and my parents are being marvelous"—she got side-tracked—"my mother's never forgiven me for not taking you, you know that?"

"I was on her side for a long time. *You* know *that*."

"Yes. . . . Are you alone there?"

"Do I sound sorry for myself? My wife made the team—she's moved into the stable for the duration."

"That sounds ambiguous."

"A joke; look, this is costing you a fortune. I'll do what I can. Is there anything else? Money?"

The so well-remembered laugh. "Petya, honey, that's the *last* thing. But you're sweet. And it won't be long—" But there was a first momentary weakness. "Just till August. Will you come and meet the train this time?"

"Try and stop me. What about names, by the way?"

"Like you said, di Sica for now." Which Marshall, tapping his egg head, had thought a waste of time. "Get it through the old bean—the nasties know. Probably the minute he slipped it in; no offense, old man." Lying swine.

"I meant the kids—but that must be a bit tough, deciding on your own."

"I'd sort of done that ahead of time. We had a long session on that last day. I haven't told you much about that, I guess."

She hadn't.

"Alexey wanted Peter for a boy, and his mother's name, Ilena. I didn't like the sound too much so we settled on Lenya. . ."

Peter for a boy. Would I have made the gesture in return? I could see the grin now if I asked. . . .

"Do I call him baby Petya?" she asked.

"Pesha. It would be Pesha. A pity we can't drink to them. If we were closer—"

"That would be nice..."

A crackling break in transmission from too much emotional voltage on the line.

"Listen, I've got to go. Nurses. I like Pesha. You'll be an honorary godfather."

"The right man to keep them from the lusts of the flesh." She laughed again. "But just until August, Niki."

Not in 1968. Wherever else the country which Yanov was pledged to defend sent its armed forces in that Czechoslovakian month, it wasn't on leave.

I used a papal dispensation of my own to get the news to Russia. Went to Jackson and got approval to go through Bakersman direct to Yanov's mother. Marshall never knew. An acknowledgment came back, once removed, in a stiff little note from the granny. There was nothing to read even between the lines. Through the winter a trickle of news continued from Takanen: The cow had calved, the dog ate a hen; Yanov's mother was ailing, was on the mend. Leave might be in August, one year late. Could be. Would be. The twenty-fifth by train.

I met her in London this time, to fly on to Helsinki.

"You don't need to, Petya; I was feeling vulnerable on the phone."

"Just to see the smiling faces, love." And to be like glue until it was done and safe. This time with no delays: Into the station and out of Finland in a day.

Old friend Kallas and a young assistant came with us to ward off anyone else's body snatchers and drive us the two hundred kilometers east to the border crossing point at Vainikkala. We arrived late on the afternoon of the twenty-fourth to sleep the night in a small hotel with all the other tourists. To stay. Who could sleep? I sat with her until midnight and I can't remember what was said.

My room was on one side of hers, Kallas's on the other. The assistant was too young to need rest and prowled all night. I became a psychopath for a day and wore my Browning in a shoulder holster.

The morning was bright and clear, but not too hot. She came down to breakfast in a slim white sheath of dress, shoulders bare and tanned, hair out of the tight bun and ten years younger.

"How do I look, Petya—about to fly apart?"

"Just bloody marvelous."

"That silver tongue again," she said, laughing.

Caviar and champagne for breakfast. Kallas with his ham and eggs. We walked to the station, a pleasant trio lightly chatting: Nice day, lots of tourists. . . .

Keeping the lid on for fifteen minutes of eternity. Looking at a native land from the outside, in front of us stretching away forever to the east, and no nirvana to a prodigal returning.

Nor escaping.

For ten miles a land scalped, flattened, strung with watchposts, minefields, men, men with dogs. Men wearing the green patches and cap bands of the KGB border divisions.

Waiting.

Imagining the appalling tension for Yanov if he had to stand calmly in Leningrad while the ancient engine and its antique retinue pulled in from Moscow and the tourist surge rushed forward around him to be held by the barriers. Watching tourists panic as the train with baffling Russian illogic appeared to leave the station empty. Hearing the audible relief as it returned with engine back to front, and the passengers for the West were grudgingly embarked.

At last! A casual parrot's screech of whistle, first tentative puffs bellying up at filthy glass. The lurching grabbing of old metal claws at rails. Then out of the station, out past the palaces, out across the Neva, past iron railings. Railings shaped as griffons, stars and pikes. Railings scraped by boys running beside them with their sticks.

A man must look through them, back to the granite and yellow sandstone. Back to buildings melting, blending into purple shadow. Seeing the last of them, of carvings and columns, of circular cobble patterns in squares with tsarist castings on the manhole covers that boys jumped over. Seeing the last of a stone swan watching our river.

The last of his mother.

"Petya—listen! The whistle!" Nicola grabbed my arm, jumping childlike herself, snapping maudlin reverie.

Yanov probably boarded unemotionally at Viborg—if anything, glad to see the back of Sinyavaky and barren rock on the edge of gray water. Settling into the splendid isolation of his reserved compartment, ignoring tourists glaring in at him from the crowded corridors. The intercom with ubiquitous balalaikas playing, and more ubiquitous microphone ears listening. The attendant, owner of the ears, bringing tea from his *kipyatok*—the samovar built in at the end of the coach.

The first KGB patrol also boarded at Viborg.

The internal check. A Green Cap knocking at the door, heels clicking to the rank but eyes looking with the same derisive mistrust reserved for every loyal citizen.

"*Spasibo,* Comrade Kapitan." A stamp, another click, withdraw. In just an instant, halfway through the fence.

Others, in the compartment next ahead, treated less kindly. An American banker? Bags slammed to the deck, tipped open—harassed voices through the partition.

"Petya, I can see it—look there!"

Funny old Zhivago engine and gingerbread cars, chuffing from the past to form a future, rocking to itself in satisfaction.

Slowing now for the external search. Dogs barked. Balalaikas played faintly, *Kalinka, Kalinka, Kalinka, My Love,* with the scarcely rolling wheels.

The train stopped a mile away. A group of personnel disembarked and moved off into some sheds. Another group of twenty-five or thirty took their place for the exterior inspection of the six old coaches. Heavily armed, they inspected every inch of roof and sides and wheels with sticks and barking dogs.

Dogs barking.

From thirty years ago with the marching tramp of boots above my head, the tap-tap-tap of blind men's canes outside my door. Fifty miles from the sea, a smell of fish.

From crates of herring on the platform. The men and dogs moved back to the sheds.

Waiting.

The train jerked once. Nicola not breathing. "If there's a God—"

Be on our side!

The train jerked twice, anticipated by the puff of smoke, moved forward. *Kalinka, Kalinka, Kalinka, My Love*. Five hundred yards away, and slowing, wheezing with exhaustion after sixty years of trying, of coping with Russian routine.

Routine that must be followed wherever Russian rails meet and don't match the outside world.

Waiting.

For the men to come along with cranks, and operate the jacks built into the road bed; to lift each coach, and move the axles into their new position to take the narrower gauge; and then to lower the coaches down again onto the second set of rails, lying between the first.

Ka-lin-ka, Ka-lin-ka. . . . And at two hundred yards, stopped. Heads poked from the train, peering in our direction. One above the rest.

But no men with jacks.

A car pulled swiftly alongside. And I held her and said *"Oh Jesus!"* Because of course there were no jacks. The gauge in Finland? *"Just part of the Russian family, Comrade."*

The car stopped, two men got out, the door in the coach adjacent to them was unlocked; they climbed the two steps. And then they came out with Yanov.

"Don't wave!"

Pinning her arms between my own. Sensing her face on the rack of my shoulder being torn apart. Hearing words from a record of slow revolution:

> *Who know's why he's sighing*
> *He's practically crying—*
> *Perhaps his heart's broken. . . .*

So we saw each other, but made no sign for the men and dogs. The trio got into the car, backed up, turned around, drove away. The train started again for the third time, and lumbered casually to freedom, with balalaikas playing, *Kalinka, Kalinka, Kalinka, My Love*.

ALAMO.

CHAPTER

TWENTY-THREE

The polar flight from London to Los Angeles was uncannily the same duration as the hours spent waiting in my Moscow hotel prison. Similar, too, in its sense of being a watershed in my life.

Because I had asked to get out. Six months after Jackson had left the house with the secret doors for Dorset, and the Labour government had replaced Tradition with a civilian of their own and then found bugs in Number Ten and bitched about it, the job had become intolerable. And last month the reality of my marriage had been faced and separation in name as well as fact, accomplished. The name-calling through all the years, so politely British, ended.

Names and years. Nineteen from Portsmouth, sixteen from the summer of the cove, eleven from Moscow and marriage, six from the station: So many, and all with bills. Bills that had been rendered and must now be paid; in just one week of a year which, starting from the moment I left to fly for this meeting—against Marshall's expressly stated order—would, if I failed, be known as my year. Dravin's Year: 1975.

Marshall. Even though now a deputy enjoying refurbished splendor, still playing—even still pretending that his game had

179

rules and sidelines. Even still wearing the same expression of silly satisfaction for his last card, as when he'd dropped the gen sheet from the reading service on my desk after the train, and said in the voice getting plummier with age and booze. "That's why the bastards slammed the gate, old boy—pity the old girl couldn't have hung on an extra day."

And I had looked at an abstract from Leningrad *Pravda,* September 6, 1969:

> Comrade Ilena Petrova Yanov, a Hero Mother of the Soviet Union . . . of heart failure . . . with glory and honor in the Garden of Heroes . . .

And had wondered whether she'd been buried with a certificate signed by three specialists. Then, as now, not knowing—because Yanov, even to the extra senses of the machines, had been buried with her. No mention from a signal, a paper, a sighting. No letter. No visit to granny still alive at eighty-six. For six years, gone.

Until Marshall's last play on the evening before the polar flight, seven days after my visit to the Baker.

Five in the morning—the beginning of a Baker's day. The smell already hung out over the pavement as a sign for the blind. A late October dew—almost a frost—covered the ground. A bobby's helmet turned the corner. The street was empty. I entered the shop.

The Baker and his wife, dressed for surgery but sweating like stokers, stood by racks of pallid mushroom shapes growing out of black greased pans. "Sandwich, then buns!" the Baker shouted at a teenaged boy and an older man staring balefully at the mushrooms.

I nodded towards the man. "To help instead of eldest boy," said the Baker, "who wants to fixing cars, not bake." Given the working conditions, it seemed an understandable decision. The younger lad grinned. We knew each other well. Flowers for his arrival had been my first émigré duty.

The Baker sat us down clear of the heat between the ovens and the shop counter. "Katerina—for Mr. Peter, tea." Baker's Wife, as Marshall called her, set out three mugs and some irresistibly fresh rolls.

"I got your note, Mr. Milgravis," I said. He never used the phone, having the absolute conviction that the KGB heard every call made in Greater London. Perhaps they did. "What do we talk of?"

He pulled off his white hat. An owl's-ear tuft of hair stood up quizzically on each side of a gleaming dome of scalp. He mopped at it with a towel and preened the tufts carefully with a thumb and two fingers. "Katerina will tell." He looked at me earnestly. "Is not joking, Mr. Peter."

Baker's Wife had never seemed a fanciful woman.

"You know, four times since war I stay with my sister in Riga who is married to Henri's brother." Henri was the Baker. "Never with children except young boy. Red Army grabs them if they are older." A favorite sidetrack. I brought her round gently.

"And this trip, Mrs. Milgravis?"

"We are back yesterday." She rested forearms the size of Yanov's on the table. "Mr. Dravin, Henri's brother, Jans, and my sister, wish to come out—and with them many others."

Who didn't?

"They must have help," she said definitely.

"Mrs. Milgravis, we can't. People have to make their own way, as you did."

"When we come, after Reds are invading, Germans help us to Austria. Is not possible now."

Nazis in retreat, helping conquered subjects to escape, was not the least of Baltic ironies. "That's what I'm trying to say. They are too far inside, too far from the West. If they wish to emigrate they must try through the government."

Baker's Wife regarded me as a recalcitrant lump of dough. Her fists made little oscillations on the table.

"Katerina!" Milgravis stepped in as referee. "Mr. Peter, this business will be different—there are so many."

"How many? What business?" With his English and my Latvian, syntax often suffered.

He went across and turned up the speed of the fans. The noise of the pans being slung about became inaudible. He cast a glance at the helpers and said in a low voice, face to face, "Fifty. A hundred?"

"If they're intending to hijack a plane—"

"No plane, no plane. Is boat."

"Fishing boats?" I took a bite from another roll.

"Mr. Peter, what is it we talk of always from Jans's friend you call Spider?"

I put down the bun. The introduction of the category-four informant, our highest in the Baltisk Naval District, was as the Baker said, no joke. "Spider's in on this? *Himself?*" Both fat faces nodding. "You're talking about a warship?"

"Two"—happily.

"How?"

"They escape to West—to Sweden."

"I understand that. But *how*?"

"A letter coming's," said Baker's Wife. "If they are told is help for outside in Baltic. Russkis do nothing if Royal Navy is."

Fifty years ago, dearie—the child's faith would have made Tredennick weep—today, just a bomb down the funnel and a note afterwards if they feel magnanimous in victory.

"What ship and where from?"

"New, from Baltic."

Which left us a hundred options. And unlimited buyers if it came off—the bidding grew hysterical for a single jet pancaked across the line. In my present circumstances, and with no chance whatever of a helping British hand, concern was academic, but a residual professional interest lingered. I asked for anything else. Reasons?

Were unclear. Perhaps general unhappiness? But then the whole idea of men shut up for years in a floating steel box was inconceivable to landlubbers. "I think is going to Africa, reason," the Baker said finally with a shrug.

Possible. Off to free Angola. Gunboat diplomacy with a bigger bang.

A bang. A for Atomic? Still possible, because certain classes drew a complement of special weapons for foreign service.

But in hands with nothing to lose?

"A *Bounty* up for grabs with nukes on!" Marshall was having himself. "Don't waste time with Leningrad, Dravin. Look from Baltisk, south."

I cross-checked the satellite status sheets against the ground reports from merchant ships and tourists. "Three mixed cruisers, all getting on. A nuke attack boat with a damaged rudder, a few DE's for training. Ventspils is waiting for the ice season; Liepaja has a few OSA class chasers. Nothing that'll make Lenin roll over."

"Try Riga itself."

"Riffraff for repairs, I think. Anything else will have cleared—"

But not quite.

"Well?" Quite literally, panting.

"The Fourteenth Baltic Destroyer Squadron seems to be still in from the summer—"

"Krivaks!" Marshall's face shone like the sun on a bowl of cornflakes. *"And a Squadron Command.* CB's, ciphers, crypto. Their machines, the rotors, the on-line computer stuff. *And nukes!* Oh sweet Jesu!" He fell back in his chair in a post-orgasmic collapse.

"The first swallow of spring for your uprising."

He sat up a little. "I often wonder," he said coldly, "where your sympathies lie. Can you recall anything even remotely like this before?"

I could not. Nor the probable reaction by the Russians.

"This letter," he asked, "when does Baker expect it?"

"Following confirmation of assistance via Songbird"—an underground rock station beamed at the Baltic States—"I've explained it's not on."

"Not on?" His hands beat a rapid little patter of annoyance on the desk. "You had no right—"

"To answer for your gutless wonder at the top?"

Huffily: "There are, naturally, political considerations—treasury approval."

"I think you'd better look farther than Whitehall for that, old bean."

He missed the intent.

"Dravin—of course! How sound you always are." He would have bounded from his chair. If he could. "We shall seek a sugar Cowboy."

A day later, his tone on the line was arch. "Could you drop in? I've got a chap who might be able to arrange our loan."

Nixon's mortgage broker in a neutral vested suit and a neutral face. Marshall was anxious that we should be friends. "Peter Dravin, old boy. Peter—Jack Selbach. From the Director's Office."

"Mr. Dravin, a pleasure. I missed you in Washington in '73." The voice was neutral too—a Midwest TV news neutrality. "This is an interesting case, and I would think we would be prepared to assist." More barrister than broker. "*If*—certain terms and conditions are met." On second thought, definitely a man used to making a gift of loans.

"Conditions?"

"An observer"—briefly plebeian—"some guy who speaks white—on the ship. To assure absolute confirmation that things would go as planned."

Marshall was suddenly engrossed in drawing an elephant on his blotter. Doodling had replaced the mints in a vain attempt to regain the mere corpulence of youth. Directions were transparently clear.

"You've been drinking too much at lunch, gents," I said to head them off. "My letter's in and I'm out. For a kamikaze run like this you need someone solid. Why not Baker's Wife?"

Selbach was used to a certain unpleasantness when matters of earning capacity and repayment limits had to be laid bare. "You seem uniquely qualified for such a function, Mr. Dravin. Even a year in command of a gas turbine ship before your transfer to the civil side." Trying to draw me in: "As an expert, what manpower input would be required for this venture?"

"In our new construction—one man. They'd need at least a dozen. And not some half-pissed hairy ass with a grievance. Good day."

Selbach wasn't going to let an inmate certify himself sane. He referred inquiringly to Marshall for a second opinion.

"Let's wait for the letter, old man."

"You transmitted?" I said. "Without your minister's cuddle? Someone's stuck a bayonet up your backbone."

Marshall squirmed as though it had gone in arse first. "Early days, old boy—nothing really lost." Only some Latvian wogs. "And this *is* Joint, our allies—"

"Will put up the investment," said Selbach smoothly. But under his corporate calm he was in a feeding frenzy.

CHAPTER

TWENTY-FOUR

The Baker's son, swinging a horsechestnut on a string by the gate through the privet hedge on Boundary Road, cast shadows of a schoolboy.

"Sorry," I said. "I'm late tonight. Been waiting long?"

"Beats workin', guv." Bow Bells had claimed him at birth. "Me dad says to tell you it's come, like. The letter."

"I'll get the car."

We drove via Hampstead Lane and Highgate High Street, past my father and Karl Marx, through Holloway and Seven Sisters Road to Finsbury Park and Finsbury Road. Fog, a pale shadow of its former yellow sulfur self, wound around the street lamps. Stronger memories of youth, New York. The old lamplighter of long ago. My father's death.

Baker and Wife, wound up for the occasion, met me at the door. The air in the shop was sharply redolent of yeast.

"This afternoon, Mr. Peter, from only three days. Very quick." Special delivery perhaps. "I have locked up."

We formed a small procession, Baker leading. Past the counter and the waiting white corpse loaves, the dough at this hour lying flat, inert. Past the massive iron fronts of the ovens cast in 1902. We stopped beside a door and a stoneware jar marked "Honey." The Baker removed the lid and brought out a key. The lock clicked. The door opened with a slight squeak. A single bulb on a string lit a small room, eight feet square, lined with sacks of flour, sugar, raisins. Beneath a small dirty window, high up on one wall, was a safe older than the ovens.

The Baker's replacement helper sat beside it reading the letter. And going to make a run for it.

The pale blue sheet dropped, a hand went to a pocket. His eyes shifted, rapidly flicking left to right. I braced myself in the doorway to take his weight. The Baker was gasping something in Latvian behind me. The helper came up on his toes, lunged forward.

The dough hit him across the face with a vicious slapping *splat*.

In the moment's shock I had him against the wall, my thumbs behind his ears. He blacked out. I picked up the letter. Baker's Wife wiped her hands on her hips with grim satisfaction. Her son was open-mouthed.

"Got any rope?" I asked. The Baker shook his head. "Lock him in then."

I looked at the cause of all the fuss. Riga written at the top. The date. "Dear Henri." Three lines of characters printed in Latvian:

> As we haven't heard from our friend in the East and we can't arrange a suitable time because of the holiday, our trip must be canceled. Goodbye.

"Show me the phone."

Dialing the number and waiting while it rang, I looked quickly for the easy breaks in the code: Geometric progressions; every second letter plus two; adding one to the position of the vowels. Nothing—perhaps because of the language. The scramblers would have to tackle it.

His wife's voice answered. "Oh, it's you."

"Is he at home?"

"Temporarily engaged. I can relay a message."

I gave the address. "Sorry out of working hours, but it's urgent."

"It's been urgent for twenty-five years, Mr. Dravin," she said. But she had learned somehow to accept it.

"If he would—as quick as—"

The unmistakable crash of breaking glass from the storeroom.

I dropped the phone. Outside the front door the fog was thicker. In the lane at the side the helper was already getting to his feet, blood streaming from his forearms. He began to run. I knew I couldn't get him. I started the car. The blank walls of the Victorian brick buildings closed us in.

The head turned in the headlights, blood showing black on the scared white face as his arm came up suddenly, realizing. I tried to make the blow a glancing one. The body crashed into a group of cans. I stopped the car. I felt a sudden wave of shock.

He was conscious but at least one leg was broken. The Baker's son had run behind me. The back door to the bakery was fifty yards away. Beside us was a warehouse loading platform, a pair of heavy planks against it. "Give me a hand."

We got the helper onto one of the boards. A steady stream of curses—Russian and Latvian mixed. Baker and Wife were waiting inside the door. "Stop the bleeding on his arms," I said.

"A doctor—"

"Shortly. The letter. What's the code?"

"Code?" The owl tufts tilted.

"What it means. The message. How can I understand it?"

"The corners," he said.

"Corners?"

"Are cut." I looked. Rounded, with scissors obviously.

"So?"

"Is backwards."

Too simple. Simply the reverse of what was openly stated. "We have your message. The trip is on. Hullo." And the date as well, by implication.

Implications. Fatal. If they were really going to try they didn't stand a chance. Not least because of the implication of the moaning figure in front of me.

The shop bell rang. "I'll go," I said.

The familiar figure, still in the issue raincoat but a size larger, looking even more menacing with added weight. Only a fringe of hair left. We had worked together many times since Portsmouth. Hyde, now Chief Superintendent with domestic SIS. The policeman's eyes with nineteen years more practice took in the scene and asked the minimum questions.

"Lose him for two weeks," I said. "And if there's anything inside him I need it by Friday."

"Yes sir." He looked at the Baker's family, "And them."

"No visitors."

Appetites in the office were ravenous.

"If you believe a word of it," I said, "the mutineers are going. With a *Krivak* from Riga at two A.M., November eighth, relying on the national piss-up for cover. That's a guess, by the way."

"But I would think the right one, Mr. Dravin." Selbach was trying to flatter.

"Mutineers is rather strong, old boy," said Marshall. "For brothers-in-arms. Rather Bligh-ish."

"The act of taking a vessel by force—what do you want: 'Misappropriation'? Don't be so bloody stunned. The sole relevant question's whether, once these thugs own nuclear warheads for the SSN 10 system, the Kremlin will be inhibited from blasting the shit out of them."

"We would think so," Selbach said. "At least for the first critical hours that they need to clear the Gulf. But I think we all agree with your sentiment"—slipping in a little masculine vernacular of his own—"it flies on the leadership's reading of the guy with his finger up the missiles, if they figure he has the nerve to blow one off at the homeland."

"Or incinerate some Swedes on Gotland."

"Which is why, Mr. Dravin, we must be there. To encourage prudence all around."

"*We?*"

Marshall tittered. Selbach reverted to the role of accountant. "Perhaps, Mr. Dravin, there are personal considerations of a material nature?"

"Money?"

He pretended embarrassment at the word stripped naked. "We would recognize any obligations—"

"A form of life insurance?"

Grabbing the bait, he dropped all roles. "Eighty thousand."

"Dollars?"

"Done!"

I looked at Marshall. "Pounds, Sammy?"

A squirm. "It's difficult, old boy, with appropriations as they are. . . . An absolutely dentproof cover, though." New eagerness. "Make you a bang-on, pusser colonel in the nasties. Good for right into the Lubyanka."

Even Selbach saw the joke in that.

"I hope Ford will think it's funny too," I said. "When it cracks the nuts off détente."

"We recognize it's high profile, Mr. Dravin," talking around the question. "Both the Secretary and the Director have their necks out a mile with this one." ·

"No!"· It had to be stopped.

A look—the flash of a blade—between them, but no feeling yet from the wound. Marshall cleared his throat, pushed a file across the desk.

"Yesterday, old man. *Red Star*."

I flipped the cover:

> More Co-operation Required of Authorities in the Four-
> teenth (Riga) Squadron:
> Complaints received by the editors from many sailors as
> to tenets of Marxism-Leninism, not followed . . . glorious her-
> itage of the Motherland's fighting units earned in blood, ig-
> nored . . ."

"The usual driveling bilge."

Marshall pointed with a finger.

"After the last letter from the boys, old man."

From Maladshi Matros, J. E. Vladvidov, who writes:

> . . . the extra duty for many days now leaves no time for
> our studies of the labours of V. I. Lenin for the workers and
> peasants. Also there have been no food parcels—

"The first word that sounds like Jolly Jack—"

"Read on, Mr. Dravin." Selbach, dead flat.

> . . . with thoughts for the safety of loved ones ever in our
> minds it is the duty of us as Soviet sailors to report these
> matters.

"This letter," said Red Star, "is typical of complaints made to the Squadron Commander, Kapitan Fourth Rank, A.I. Yanov . . ."

"Oh you bastard, Marshall!"
Silence.
Thoughts for the safety of loved ones. I reached across the fat hand doodling on his desk. Pressed the intercom. "Give me, Mr. Weeks—Reading Service."
"We should like to urge commanders," said Red Star . . .
"Weeks here."
"Dravin. Bring me the original of the latest *RS* and *Morskiy Flotte*."
Silent, each to his own: my thoughts, Marshall's elephant, Selbach's coffee. He sipped, eyes watching over the rim. Weeks entered, a thin seedy little man supporting spectacles and in on the plot. "Second page, sir, green-lined."
In both papers. Not a fake. At least on our side.
I felt dizzy—just for a second—from breath too long held in. I put my hand on Marshall's desk for a moment of support, felt something under it. A tortoise-shell-handled paper knife I had given him once, from Fiji—before that first trip to California.
California.
"I'm going to tell her, Marshall."
The fat face was half-defiant, half-frightened. "You bloody well don't, Dravin."
"I fucking well do!"
The blade stabbed down into the blotted body of his elephant and quivered between his pudgy fingers.
Selbach sipped.
"Two days," I said.
He nodded. He was unconcerned.

CHAPTER

TWENTY-FIVE

Released by the bell, a flash flood of noise washed along the halls, broke through the doors, spilled with a mass of color into the school yard.

"Uncle Petya, Uncle Petya!" Young eyes found me first.

Two small figures separated from the herd with frantic waves. Into a race across the grass, a slip—a trip? Lunch pails falling, spewing tinkling thermos flasks. Sheets vital to seven-year-old scholastic progress away on the wind. Insane barking from the collie in the car behind me. Front runner losing ground; gasps, laughs.

"Dead heat!" I bent down for a quick wet kiss with tiny arms from the girl. The boy held back. "Too old for mushy stuff, Pesha?" I put out my hand. Having to return the shake was almost as difficult for him as a kiss, but the gesture was appreciated. A grin. *Christ, he was Yanov!* Except for the haircut.

Some delay now while we made up the losses. I accepted full responsibility for damage. We looked at the pictures recovered from the trap of the fence. Vivid grease colors with eleventh-century perspectives. To my eye not much talent, but any faces looked happy.

"It's a picnic." The boy looked doubtfully at his own work. "Maybe dumb for trees to be pink?"

"Perhaps it's autumn, Pesha. The fall. I've seen trees that color."

"Yeah?" Great relief.

"Not Christmas trees." His sister hopped adroitly out of range.

"Artist's privilege," I said. "May I keep it?"

"Sure. That's me, Mom—"

We went round the broken family circle. Now everyone wanted to sit beside the driver. Compromise was achieved with the collie in the middle. "We didn't know you were coming," said the girl accusingly. "We could have got out early."

"It was very quick, Lenya—I only knew, myself, last night." And had heard the same note from her mother when I'd called on landing at Los Angeles this morning. "You're crazy—I might have been anywhere."

"Oh—ve haff vays."

"Don't I know it! But I can't get away till four today—a goddamn conference." Pausing—"I guess if you want to come out early you could go get the kids for me, with Marie." The Mexican housekeeper. "You know the way?"

"I think by now."

"It's great to hear you, Petya. There's nothing . . . ?"

"Just business," I'd said. Completing a routine gone through how many times since the station? Because of my two-year stint in Washington and innumerable inspection trips, a dozen visits—perhaps fifteen? Enough to complete the metamorphosis back from onlooker to participant. To a favorite uncle fallen in water over his head.

"You want to see my fish, Uncle Petya?"

"He's still mine," said the boy. "We only traded for a day."

"Is not!"

The dispute and arbitration saw us home, fifteen miles past her parents at Orinda, on the edge of Mount Diablo Park. I was dragged down to the little creek with the famous name to see the crux of the argument, a domestic goldfish kept from the wider world by a net. Briefly, one suspected. Thoughts flashed back to the dragonfly in Jackson's garden. The ominous shaking of the lilies. Thunder. Warnings of fissures that could lead to Arabian nights. Or to California and Dravin playing in the long grass under the eucalyptus trees with Alexey Yanov's children.

"Hi!"

Vividly, extraordinarily, with her call from behind me up a hill by a house, I had a sense of history repeating: that she was walking down to join me on the rock by the lake at Takanen.

"I like the smile," she said with a kiss.

"The swan and my toe—do you remember?"

"Are you kidding! You look ready for a drink."

"We've been frisbeeing. Not well."

"You were okay." Loyalty from my namesake. "Mom, can we swim before supper?"

"Only for ten minutes—it's getting too cold."

"Tropical, by my British school standards," I said. We watched them run up to the white mock Spanish of the bungalow behind its flowers blooming in Californian disregard for season. "I don't know how you pick these spots, Niki."

"Better than the men in my life"—with a rueful smile. "Will you watch the kids while I change?"

Kids swimming, kids eating, kids clamoring for stories left little room for an adult to feel sorry for himself. Until he stood beside the small beds looking down, and had to be like Marshall, falsely bluff and hearty, and kiss good night. And laugh when he's asked, "Do you have visiting rights?"

"No. No rights, Pesha. None at all."

"Well, that's what Don says, at school. And that you aren't a really uncle."

"He's quite right. I'm not." I tucked them in.

"He says you're probably the father."

"Who cares?" from the girl. "Have you checked the closet?"

Who cares....

"No ghost," I said. "Good night."

"The frisbee was neat," said the boy. "Will you come back soon?"

"I'll try."

"Real hard?"

"You'd better believe it. Now, good night!"

"Good night," from the two small voices. "And leave the light on . . . and bring us a present . . ."

Alone together in the kitchen.

"Petya, tonight—you really have to go back? So soon?"

Back to the Baltic and a rocking boat and that gray flat land waiting.

After bedtime there could be no doubt. "Yes, love. I'm afraid I do."

"I'm sorry about that, upstairs," she said; "the role of derelict parent."

"It does leave a certain sense of inadequacy. Bringing them up single must have been grim at times?"

"At first maybe"—a small tight smile—"when some friends—"

"Weren't?"

A nod.

"But you wouldn't—"

"*Not have them?* The sanest thing I ever did. I was an old lady, Petya. A few years and the options were closed. Career only. At least this way . . ."

What? A limbo of uncertainty? I remembered the terrible scene just after my arrival in Washington, when I made my first trip to the West Coast. I had sensed the ice instantly. Gradually worked out the cause, a visit by a nameless friend in pointed cowboy boots from Langley. And I'd said something meant to soothe, defuse. Instead, triggered an explosion pent up for years.

"*You bastard!* Nixon's taking a swap list of names to Moscow. A *second* list!" The words had poured almost incoherently. "And we could have had Alexey on the first one *two years ago, for Christ's sake,* but they've got some kind of cooperation thing with you guys and they can't horn in well damn you damn you *damn you,*" as tears had streamed, "how *could* you make me part of a deal when you promised—you *promised!*"

"No, no"—having been almost speechless myself by the intensity, "no deals, Niki. Not like that, not about Yanov, no deals." And the Mexican face of the housekeeper left standing by the door had been ready to put a cleaver in me while I had said inadequate things. I imagined knifing the owner of the boots in a Hong Kong alley, waited for the storm to blow itself out. And when she could listen I'd said, "It isn't like that. . . . Nixon's names are Jewish longhairs, tailors, troublemakers. Not naval captains sitting on the right hand. . . . But If you want to take the chance—*do it!* Put him on the list . . ." And pick up the pieces of your life, because they'll just stuff him at the back of the cupboard and smile with the stone face of Asia and say, *Who?*"

She hadn't tried. Had recovered, apologized. On the next visit announced she'd named me executor for her children in her will. And here we were. With only one option left open.

"Petya?"

"Sorry, love. Just daydreaming."

"It didn't look happy."

I stood up to get a drink. "It's not much of a record, is it? Job, marriage up the spout. Us—"

"Stop that!" She reached up and held my arm. "Stop always making it one-nothing against yourself, Petya. Because it isn't—it's always fractions."

"Even our first summer?"

"*Especially!* Hon, I didn't have to make you play last-minute word games; I could have said yes on the beach. And I could easily have made it over for the first Christmas. I wanted to."

Why must I hear this now? Why, in God's name, had I ever come?

She misread my questions. "So why Alexey? Looking for Daddy, my shrink always said—"

"You had a bloody witch doctor?" She nodded. "For how long?"

"Was I with him? Years. Right up through Finland—1967." She gave a little smile. "When I took on old Mother Russia I guess he figured I really *was* crazy. But, you know, he was mostly right. About the-escape-from-the-child-marriage bit and being given my life back. He said I'd always go for the apple safely out of reach."

"Not unreasonably."

"*Reason?* My God, since when did that have anything to do with it? Alexey *moved*. He made things happen—out of the blue. Life didn't just sit there—"

"As it did with me."

"I didn't mean it to sound like that." She squeezed my hand.

"It's true, though. But at the time it didn't seem an equal contest—heart of oak against Slavic hugs and kisses."

"But you wouldn't *try*, Petya. God, how I willed you to smash out of that old-school shell. If you'd made just one good grab in

New York, it would have been game over. I was scared to death about all that Russian stuff. Even now. If we were back at square one. . . ."

And if ifs and ands?

"Niki—with the kids, and Alexey—do they even know?"

"That he exists? Sure. Can it have any meaning for them? I don't know, but we talk." She stood up. "I've got to show you something. I put it together since your last visit."

Another album.

Dravin's ripped flannels on the seal rocks at the cove. Dravin beside Yanov at the piano. Yanov glaring, next to a crystal ball. Dravin clowning in the horse's hat. Both of us sharing the same girl. Yanov and granny in the cart. Dravin with the twins at Disneyland: Reality reversed. None of a father with his children.

A paper fell from the back of the album. I picked it up. "What's this?"

"He wrote it out for me that last day at the lake. It's from my record. Schmaltz, but I listen to it sometimes. . ."

Sometimes? The folds were brown, transparent. *How many times?* Opened, closed, committed to the heart? "Wait for me":

> . . . *And I'll come back.* . . .
> *Wait! Have faith and wait*
> *Wait when gloomy autumn rains*
> *Sadness, sorrow, mate.*
> *Wait when snows will fiercely blow*
> *Wait through summer's blaze*
> *Wait though some will not come back*
> *Like all our bygone days.*
> *Wait though I am far away*
> *Though letters don't appear,*
> *Wait though others wait no more,*
> *Wait. Be of good cheer.*
> *Wait for me, I'm coming back—*
> *Death won't win me from your hand.*
> *Those who have not had to wait*
> *Will never ever understand*
> *How through battle, how through hell*
> *By your steadfast waiting*

> *Dear my life you held.*
> *How this happened, just we two*
> *Know the secret great.*
> *And the secret simply is . . .*
> *You knew how to wait.*

Waiting. Russia's single, unequaled skill. I re-formed the folds, slipped the paper back into the album. "May I keep a snap of the kids?"

"I never gave you one? I must have. Here, how about this?" Our fingers touched across the picture.

"Come outside for a minute, Niki."

We went into a conspirators' night without a moon, a night holding a black and silver star blanket above a creek that chatters across rocks and drowns out speech.

"If," I said, and I held her hands, "*if*—we could get him out. And if the price was rather steep and the chances a bit slim, and if we know from the computers that the magic figure for the POW families is five years and after that it never works, and if there are other wives and kids who can get hurt..."

Silent in starlight. I don't know for how long.

Then just a pressure from her fingers. And my acknowledgment.

"That's why the picture?"

"Yes."

"Could he have a letter, in case..."

A letter.

Because years ago, when I was just a sailor and unable to tell pipe smoke from reality, I read the mail coming to the prison for Lonsdale—the Russian who'd run the crooks in the Admiralty scandals—and couldn't understand that a master spy could get letters saying darling daddy and love from Trofim and Tria and Liza.

"No, love. Not a letter—but I'll tell him."

One small slip. Totally irretrievable.

"You'll *tell* him?" Her hands were making small frantic movements to get out. *"Hey, come on!"* Her voice rising, carrying the panic for me. *"That's too much.* I didn't agree for *that*. No Petya, not inside that terrible place again." The hands had broken free, were holding my face, stroking it. Anything to read it in the dark. *"Not if it means both of you, Petya."* Now slapping, sobbing, her body pressing with a trapped animal desperation. Scratching. Nails down my face. Blood. *"Not to lose both of you . . ."*

A chrysalis shell snapped and fell and was left beside a creek chattering under starlight by the Pacific. And who can sort out now the dreams and feelings of two people in a house on the banks of the Alamo as her arms were round his neck—and would it matter? If her thoughts were away in Russia? Or here with him?

And on his part, as he found himself accepting what was offered once in San Francisco, as he refused to fight against it one more second, was he wrong? Or was it as he told himself, that in some strange directed way, on this one occasion, he did have rights. That what was offered and accepted was in trust. On loan. Just in case. So that if wait-for-me should be forever, there would be something, a moment's heat and warmth, for memory to carry into the camps, and into the nights and stars that hide them.

We were at the airport.

"No—stay in the car." I gave her the note. "A chap in Sweden—"

"The fat guy in the train?"—smiling under huge hollowed eyes.

"Not Erik. Skinny as a rail, but better than Washington in case you need it from the horse's mouth."

I kissed the pale face and tasted salt. "Sailors' wives, Niki darling. No tears for a departure."

"Okay."

"But on landfall—"

"I can fill my boots, Petya?"

And still smiling as I turned away.

"It's confirmed Angola." Marshall was briskly business. "The *Krivaks* sailing date is Tuesday week following the holiday—hull numbers 504 and 507."

"They're put up and down like a whore's drawers. What about the missiles?"

"Embarkation's been confirmed. And through our Allies"—a regal nod to Selbach—"we have a boat, *Sailfin*—holding on patrol in Bohus Bay and cleared for a courtesy visit to Copenhagen.

Landing will be across the beach at a point of your choosing south of the Gulf. For the return rendezvous the defecting vessels must be twelve miles clear of a line drawn from the western tip of Saarema, south to the hook of Gdynia—west of Kaliningrad. After rendezvous, *Sailfin* will accompany the defecting vessels to Gotland for transfer of dependents."

"You believe what you're saying?"

"No worse than '71"—airily—"getting Vazhenko out."

"A slight difference in bloody degree, between one egg-spilling professor in a trawler and half of bloody Riga mixing it with a nuke. Whose bright idea was that?"

"Our best value judgment"—Selbach slipped jargon smoothly into the conversation—"is that insertion of a nuclear boat in the equity package will induce a Soviet reluctance to escalate."

Equity package! "You mean the bastards won't crap their own nest with hot waste." I turned to Marshall. "And Hyde?"

"He's had Baker *'en famille'* hidden in a hotel in Woking. Wife has been making rather a fuss. All seems clear, however, on the helper front. Hyde's certain that he passed nothing back, and seems satisfied that he had no recent instructions from the other side."

Certain at least that the policeman would have been thorough.

"Your nasty's papers, old boy." Marshall handed over the cards. Unless the fingerprint tripped some computer's memory, they looked adequate. "All right," I said. "Joining instructions?"

"By chopper," said Selbach. "Tonight in the North Sea. This is the good word for the captain." He passed me a heavy manila envelope.

The seals and stamps were straight from the top.

"Cosmic," I said. "Rather a rich diet."

A throat cleared. "Old boy"—Marshall shifted nervously in his chair, hands cautiously just on the edge of the desk.

"I see you've hidden the paper knife."

Falsetto laugh. "Jolly good. . . . Um, if you could see your way clear . . ." He had another envelope with him. I recognized my own handwriting. "It might look a bit odd, old boy. To be over there and not still in the club, what?"

"You want me to withdraw it?"

"Just for the duration, so to speak."

I tore it up. "I'll dateline the next one Riga." But he wasn't laughing. "Christ, man, you don't want a signed confession in advance as well?"

He had run out of funny words. He pushed a small pillbox across the desk. "They have to be bitten, or else—"

"Like shit through a goose, Sammy?" I pocketed the box.

"That's it"—brightening up at once. "Well, good show all round what? Our friends"—a warm beam of appreciation to Selbach—"provide the ticket. Cousin Y recruited to do the driving. And all the accounting at the end, through us."

"Oh." Selbach leaned in the chair, fingers forming a banker's pyramid. "Oh, I wouldn't think we could agree to that. Not with all the front end investment put up by us, and having to give the Sovs back the hardware—after a suitable turn-around, of course. Which only leaves us software—" The chair tipped forward to four legs. "And wetware—people. And I would think it only prudent that we would want to retain our fifty-one percent in that area." A pursed smile at his moneyman's joke.

"*What?*" said Marshall bleakly.

I patted his head. "You've been finessed, dear." I turned to Selbach. "What with?"

One of the pyramid hands slipped inside the waist coat to palm a winning card. "Your Spider, Mr. Dravin." Marshall's carp mouth was gobbling air. "We know your Spider. And right now, up front, *before we fly*—well, you just agree to give us the boys in the web." Nodding at the innate fairness of it all. "And we split the software down the middle and you keep Cousin Y."

"You *know*, Spider?" croaked Marshall.

"Oh, not to talk to Sam"—the hand came out of the vest pocket—"not to talk to. Just as a face in the crowd."

The photograph landed right side up.

The sour, self-righteous, and unmistakable kisser of Vasily Sinyavsky.

SAILFIN.

CHAPTER

TWENTY-SIX

The Control Room was a jungle darkness broken by red and green cats' eyes hanging on the bulkheads: Jaring, the *Sailfin*'s captain, perched on his stool, was a wizard in a clearing, studying entrails on the radar plot.

"The Skaw," he said, tapping a long curving hook of land stretched beside our indicated track. "Control, take her up. Stand by to surface."

The Skaw, northern tip of Denmark and entrance to the Kattegat—key to the Baltic and boyhood memory.

I went up to the open bridge. The long-short-long of the Fornaes Light on the Eastern tip of Jutland jumped abruptly over the starboard horizon. A swarm of pinprick lights spread across the Aalborg Bight ahead of us.

"Baltic fishing fleet," said Jaring. "Crews and boats both half-lit. A goddamn menace."

"Not always, Captain." I watched the last of the twilight leaving early. Time 1700, November 5, 1975. Thirty-two hours to landing—perhaps to life. "Not always."

"Captain, sir," the intercom intruded, "Exec here. Chow's up. You want a relief?"

"Affirmative. Come up and take over."

Naval routine. Unchanging. Comforting.

The cropped skull of the Executive Officer emerged from the hatch. He stood for a moment making the transition to the darkness. "Fleet news came in, Captain."

"Usual gloom and doom?"

"Change of quarterbacks at Defense and CIA. Gerry's taken out the hawks and put in Rumsfeld and Bush. Made the substitution on his own, he says. Like any good coach."

"Harry Truman," I said, "in a football helmet."

Jaring gave a short snorting laugh. "Well, Mr. Dravin, with the team on the field and the clock running they won't wreck the game now; let's eat."

Wrecks and wreckers. Jackson's last warning to me.

Our meeting had been the center of the sandwiched hours between return from California and departure. I had phoned Dorset.

"I can save you the trip," he'd said. "I'm coming up to town for a theater evening—a G and S Centenary revival, *Utopia Limited*. Haven't heard it since I was a boy. Let me take you, and a supper at the club to follow."

I found it typical D'Oyly Carte. All masculine women and vice versa, doing funny dances for no reason, although the words, when I could make them out, not inappropriate for the Britain a hundred years after writing.

And one of the jingles was my life.

> *Joke beginning, never ceases,*
> *'Til your inning, time releases,*
> *On your way you blindly stray,*
> *And day by day the joke increases.*

The entrance to his club was on a side street off St. James's. He was a little stiff going up the steps, but at nearly eighty better than I expected for myself. "I'm glad to see pillars of Empire still extant," I said.

"Only a handful left, and the Arabs'll have them in five years. I've ordered a mixed grill. They still do it well."

We talked in generalities through the meal—prematurely Arabian with a flavor of mutton fat. The wine was good. After it he said, "I've reserved a card room. I thought we might take coffee there."

The chairs were made to hold bodies for hours at a stretch. We relaxed into them. Jackson hauled out the pipe. Looked at me.

"Some of the Baker's naval friends and relations," I said, "are going to try and pinch a *Krivak* from Riga and run away with it."

"Yes?"—almost idly, waving out the match.

"Marshall's made an under-the-table deal with Washington to lend support if they clear the Straits."

"Ah."

Polite, but bored. Finding the idiocy from outside glaring: Raising dahlias and catching what was left of the sun before the mirror turned were now the only things of true importance. "There's an added nastiness—the ship almost certainly has special weapons."

Only a nod. And although I tried to fight it, I felt annoyance rising. Because the implications would hit old men in their gardens just as surely as their grandchildren. "I would like your opinion of the Leadership's response to such a threat."

"I see." He stood up, walked slowly across to the fireplace to throw in the match, at the last minute pocketing it instinctively instead. And with the action and the relativity of time we were back at our first meeting—Dravin less than a novice, looking up at the thatch of white hair, the piercing eyes, listening to the slow voice saying, "California must have been difficult for you."

And I realized that this old eagle of a man was still my master. Realized that the talons grown to reach dark pockets all around the globe must still be reaching, still be bringing all the scraps back to the beak brain in the center for comparison, acceptance: Rejection!

"Brandy, Dravin? You look as though you could use it. Besides"—the almost invisible smile—"the door to this room is locked. Now—the Leadership's response? That's all?"

Hardly all. But a start. "What'll they do?"

"Go into a flap, the politicals wondering if the naval side's about to blow. The military wondering if this might be the moment for it. A tight show." He looked at me again. "Too blasé? You haven't changed, Peter. Not when it comes to suffering old fools. Which takes us logically back to the leadership. Define it for me."

"The Politburo, Brezhnev—"

"Won't touch it. Your 'godfather' made the monster. He'll be told to destroy it."

"Gorshkov—"

"Alone."

"How?"

"I don't know. But you were given a glimpse, and there's been another full decade of superior-subordinate bond built up since then. When he reads the first message he won't see a Fletcher Christian in his mind; he'll be looking as you once said—"

"At his own image."

He nodded slowly. "Forced to make a decision between the missiles and mutiny, I think he'll react like a man with a knife in his hand and one foot caught in a railway switch as the express approaches: Hack first—"

"And worry about blood later."

"Yes. It will be an indelible example, and totally Russian. In the image of his own masters—your namesake, Ivan, Stalin? God knows, there's no shortage."

He set down the pipe with a sharp click. "Well, that's Gorshkov. Now what about Dravin? *Your* motives for setting the world on fire?"

I made no answer.

I don't think he expected one. "We'll toss out the political right away—Marshall's mad. The regime's solid if ten squadrons mutiny. So it must be personal—fighting your father's battles?"

"A little, I suppose."

"He more than won his own."

"An admiral hiding for his life in a fishing boat?"

"Ah"—slowly. "We go to prove that Leningrad Dravins aren't yellow. To expunge the white feather with blood. Beau Geste in the Baltic."

"Obviously not—"

"Obviously?"

Although it was a side issue, I felt myself coloring, heating up. "You must admit they always win. We *never* stand. In *thirty years* we've never made a stand. We peel the bodies off the wire and the elected second-raters on our side bleat, or foam a bit . . ."

"And Dravin, alone against the monolith, will make the gesture that cracks it, brings it down? No?"

"Yanov—"

"Who could have made his jump at any time, as your father did." My own childish words thrown back at me. "So it's Armageddon for Yanov?"

"You're reducing it. Nothing becomes worth anything if the price is always put that high. In this case, I don't believe the Kremlin *will* take the risk—and neither do our governments or they wouldn't be letting us play. I think we can get away with it. May I pour another brandy?" He inclined his head.

Setting the decanter back on the sideboard, I looked at the English essence of the room. The furniture, the Constable above the hearth. A picture of England where the village never dies and the trees are always green, the yeoman always ready.

I passed Jackson his glass. "Ever since the business with Yanov started, I've traded on my father's strength of character—or inversely, the lack of it. And without risking an inch of my own skin I've expected Yanov to throw not only himself and his mother on the wire, but now the kids and Nicola. It's got to be redressed, that's all. I don't give a damn about the bloody ship, or the unfortunates in her—they would never have stood a chance, anyway. As a matter of fact, with Yanov and myself they just might make it."

"Peter, it isn't that I don't think you'll give it a hell of a try." The blue eyes had calmed and rested on me gently. "Nor whether this time you really believe Yanov will come; do you, by the way?"

I looked for a long while into the flames, watching the patterns form dreams old and new and take them up the chimney's twisted flues and over London and down the river to the sea.

"No," I said. "I don't. But I'll bring him."

"Back through the looking glass?"

"Something like that."

"But that's it, you see"—in the softly Celtic lilt—"you may find it impossible to know which side of the glass you're on." He stood, for the first time rather tired. "From the beginning, Peter, with your little Alice joke—"

"The walrus and the carpenter and the oysters hand in hand?"

"The latter rather stringy and long in the tooth by now—but what I'm getting at is that there may have been only one walrus: Moscow. But since the war there have been twin carpenters. And one at least has always found that one too many. Haven't you wondered why they'd chance the investment in your head?"

"Simple greed."

"Not simple. Double-twisted. Because if it blows a gale and you're wrecked, and the wreckers take you, the world will say another Philby. Dead or alive, just another rotten apple. That once hung right at the top of our tree."

"Next to you." Now it was his turn for silence. "Are you asking me not to go?"

"The first rule of command, isn't it?—never give an order which won't be obeyed?" He walked with me to the door and unlocked it and gave me his hand.

I suddenly saw the logical gap in the truth table.

"But you don't have to ask. You could have simply stopped it."

"Yes," he said. "I could. And nothing becomes worth anything."

"I'm sorry—"

"No, don't. It's purely selfish on my part. Because if the dissidents are going to be allowed the run—and if they're only half-successful—well then, the genie may get out. And in that case, Peter, my dear boy"—and he meant it in its fullest sense—"I'd like to know there's someone there who, under all his cynicism, will do his duty."

In the tiny space of the captain's cabin, the Exec made it a crowd for the final briefing.

"I want to be ashore one mile south of the village of Palanga at 0100," I said. "That keeps us ten miles north of Klaipeda—Memel when the Germans controlled the Lithuanian coast."

Jaring was examining depths. "Coming up from the southwest gives us thirty fathoms in to eight miles. Twenty within five—

maybe to four if we're lucky. Cut your boat ride down if we can. What's the beach?"

"Shingle into sand dunes, wooded at Palanga, which is why we've picked it."

"Wide open to any kind of wind," said the Exec. "Could be messy even for an inflatable."

Jaring looked up from the chart. "If difficulty was a consideration, Sandy, they'd have bought the guy an airline ticket." He turned to me. "Met your boat driver yet?"

"Briefly. A solid citizen?"

"Should be. He's just come off the Miami to Cuba mail run. I guess he'll find this one a snap."

"Why?"

"No sharks—okay, Sandy, set launch for 0300."

Jaring waited for the door. "Now," he said, "let's cover the hairy part: going home."

Passing him Selbach's second letter, I wondered if he'd comment on the signatures, now rendered obsolete. I doubt he saw them.

"A *loaded DDL*—" His stoic veneer was finally shattered. "Sweet Christ!"

"When could you hear us coming?"

"Balls out—maybe sixty miles."

"If it'll help, Captain, I'll dance on the fo'c'sle."

His eyes leveled with mine. "I guess I would too, Mr. Dravin. And then some. You better get some sleep."

With the sickening, gut-wrenching, unreasoning fear that comes with thoughts of debt and death at five in the morning, I was suddenly awake.

Ten minutes to midnight. Not morning yet. But an hour before landing, time enough—and reason—to feel fear. Below the clock, I saw a loaded tape deck . . . pressed the key.

And shivered. Shivered as I had when I first saw them against the moon above the bridge. The music of memory, the Tchaikovsky piano music of Yanov's playing in San Francisco, filled the cabin.

"United over water." Words of a fortune teller jumbled with the Russian omen of the music, mixing crazily with Marshall howling in my head at the effect of a machine. *"Fortune tellers!* Old boy—I mean. *I say!"*

I stood up, trembling, blindly slamming the button to kill it all, to get back to shipboard noise. Back to life.

The piano and the voices died.

But my limbo time on board was over. The vibration from the screws was gone. The hull was silent. The ship was stopped.

RIGA.

CHAPTER

TWENTY-SEVEN

Dark and cold and wet in the Baltic. And frightened. History full circle.

I tried to eye the tiny light from the *Sailfin* through the lurching transit sight of a hand-held magnetic compass. "More to starboard." The sea was running directly astern, surfing us in to the coast at twenty knots—exhilarating, this low on the water. Twin Mercury outboards alternately whined and gurgled as the waves moved around them. Jacowzki, the cox'n lent by Selbach, was a tense shape under an invisible face in the stern.

We skimmed on for another mile. "Take the way off," I said. The bow dropped. "Listen for surf."

Only the hollow drumming of waves on canvas. Another splashed onto my soaking feet.

I swung the binoculars through the forward arc, searching for the white line of the breakers.

Nothing.

"Start her up."

The bow began to lift. I turned my back half into it, still looking. A spark flashed and went out. *"Stop!"* The spark flickered again, ten degrees to starboard.

"You want the Aldis?"

"No. Get closer—keep her at half throttle."

Time 0048. Thirteen minutes, about three and a half miles, allowing for the halt. *Sailfin* had been lying off just outside the four-mile line. "Fifteen hundred yards, Cox'n—starboard again."

Lying up in the point of the bow, glasses fixed ahead, I felt my stomach contract in waves of nausea to a cold steel ball bearing. The pulse in my temple throbbed against the eyepieces.

The will-o'-the-wisp was dancing across the frothy top of a giant beer.

"Surf's up," Jacowzki said laconically.

The engines softened. Traveling at the same speed as the wave motion, we seemed to float in one spot. A low rattling noise shivered under the splash of the waves—shingle moving on a beach: the only patch of shingle in fifty miles of sand. Bull's-eye! An irregular line of greater darkness—trees against a night sky. The wisp blinked three times quickly, dead ahead. Try not to think that in bogs it danced for death.

Jacowzki tilted an engine clear of the water—something to get home with.

Slower than the seas now, the waves hissed past us, eager for landfall.

The light flashed again and moved towards us, disembodied, a beckoning Circe.

I felt the 45-caliber grease gun tight in the vee beside me. Smacked the magazine for a final check. The light hovered, flittered into Morse—three shorts, short long long short, two shorts:
Spider!

The water torture dripping since the photograph: Sinyavsky—true or false?

> *"It seems a shame," the Walrus said,*
> *"To play them such a trick,*
> *After we've brought them out so far,*
> *And made them trot so quick!"*

The quick and the dead.

I set the trigger response to light.

The beam tilted down, showing the gray pebbles of Baltic

Russia, and ahead into the sucking foam of the backwash. Back to the pebbles.

"Take us in!"

Stern high on a seventh wave, motor roaring for a brief eternity we fell through the sea curtain to the shore.

Feet crunched.

A clear *click* from a cocking lever. I remembered the cruiser. My own fingers afraid to touch the trigger, pressure so delicate.

"Who goes?" I asked in Latvian to the beach.

"Baker's Man."

Perhaps. "Your sister bakes five loaves?"

"Yes. Three of black—"

Wrong!

"Wrong, Cox'n, *wrong!*" Jacowzki was already gunning the motor. The grease gun barrel jumped left on its own ready to scythe back through the waists from left to right. The light went out.

"No!" Anguish in the rising voice. "No! *Two,* two of black— *for God's sake!"*

I touched Jacowzki's knee. The engine died. I called to the unseen beach: "When?"

"On Wednesday"—babbling—"Wednesday and three of white on Fridays."

The waves broke and sucked and broke again. The light shone for an instant on a face without features at this distance, but still a target, a gesture of trust.

"All right, Cox'n, let's try again."

A soft bump and a feel of pebbles through the canvas bottom underfoot, hands grasped the line loops. I was in Russia. For the third time—and without nostalgia.

One of the hands reached for me. "I am Jans Henrijs."

"Good. Is all well?"

"We are ready. This is Laenaris—still shaking. His memory sticks."

"At the most awkward moments." I clasped hands with a heavy shadow, turned back to the boat, passed Jacowzki the gun and my weather jacket. "You did bloody well. Thanks."

"Twenty-four-hour service—holler when you want to go home."

"I'll wake the dead—your bearing out's 187 magnetic. Good luck."

"You too," he said.

The Latvians waded into the water and turned the Zodiac to wait for the wave. The first motor coughed, then gunned, and the boat climbed up into the sea and was gone.

"Come!" said Henrijs, urgently.

"A minute, please." And another. *Start!* The second roar woke up and faded quickly.

The Latvians were already running up the beach into the trees. I followed, feet slipping in the loose gravel. A hundred yards along a narrow track a small car waited beside a shed. "In the front," said Henrijs. "What do we call you?"

"Bursinov. My papers." I flipped the identity pass for the first time. "How are they?"

A soft whistle. "Group three, State Security—you'll be well received."

We squeezed into the tiny Moskvitch. With the courtesy of the front seat I was bent double. Henrijs, in the back, was a contortionist. The car lurched along on bottoming shocks.

The other man, Laenaris, spoke for the first time: "It gets better, once we are away from Palanga. We cross country for half an hour and then the main road from Klaipeda to Riga, straight through except for detours at the police posts."

"We could get onto it sooner," said Henrijs, "but this way we avoid a lot of authority. Close to the ports is always tight."

"These police posts," I asked, "are they fixed?"

"Every thirty or forty kilometers. They usually ignore local traffic but we won't take the chance."

"Amen to that." The shock absorbers got the promised breather as we came out of the track through the woods. A large building loomed in front of us. "Palanga Church," said Henrijs. "Very fine in daylight. A pity you can't see our Latvia; the country between here and the river is the most beautiful—"

"Forget it, Jans," said Laenaris tersely, "we won't be seeing any more of it, ourselves."

An awkward pause. "How long into Riga?"

"Four hours, God willing. The meeting with Spider is arranged for five-thirty."

There was little traffic, and few lights. The noise of the engine, and the complete darkness, helped me to doze fitfully between the small towns. At the halfway point the Latvians changed places and we drove on. I slept.

"Comrade!"

Stopped at an intersection. *"Oh Christ!"*

"It's all right! All right."

With half the Red Army jamming the road in all directions? The ground shook under the weight of the tanks—T54's and 60's.

"No—really." Henrijs laid a hand on my arm. "Units for the parade. But we must wait for them to pass. We may be late."

The missile launchers rode half-unseen on the broad backs of the carrier transports like mobile sphinxes. A traffic MP on a motorcycle beside them pulled in ahead of us and lifted his goggles. He looked at the car. Laenaris swore under his breath.

The MP climbed off the bike and came across to us, swaggering with the self-assurance of motorcycle cops worldwide. Panic scrabbled up my throat. I gripped the ID in my pocket. He wandered slowly along beside the car, stared casually in at us. Henrijs nodded politely. He walked behind us.

Half a minute passed. Laenaris began to laugh quietly.

"Stop it!" hissed Henrijs. "What the hell's wrong with you?"

"Look in the mirror."

Both laughing now. "For God's sake, tell me what's going on!"

I stuck my head out of the window. The cop shook off the last drops and swaggered bowlegged back to the road. A final bevy of personnel carriers crossed the intersection and then the road ahead was clear.

"We've lost fifteen minutes," said Laenaris. "I've known time pass quicker. Come on, Jans, goose the little bastard."

"How far now?"

"The Iron Bridge in a mile."

The tires took up a quick impatient thrumming on the bridge approaches. Beyond it, the lights of Riga, girdled in black velvet.

The River Daugava.

Illuminated steeples of ancient churches stabbed the sky. St. Jacob, St. Peter, St. Ann—Gorshkov's Anglican Cathedral. Lying at their feet along the Komsomol Embankment—etched against them like an abstract sculpture—the floodlit modern rigging of a *Krivak* DDL.

Hopeless. All for nothing. Lying head upstream, trapped between two bridges and twelve miles from the river mouth, she'd never get clear. And no way now to turn back.

"We didn't know the ship would have to sail from the city."

"Oh yes"—the Latvian voice was casual. "She is up here to be open for visitors."

"With a full crew?" It couldn't get worse.

"Except for a lucky few with families in the city."

"Stop the car! We were told that only a skeleton crew would be aboard. What the hell is going on?"

The light from a street lamp shone on Laenaris's face in the back. A very long, thin face, with bad teeth, and green eyes looking at me in perplexity.

"There is no confusion. It will be as we said."

"Crap! We're twelve miles up river with all hands on board."

"My friend"—Henrijs was calm at the wheel, his face still hidden—"she must be here. It is all planned. How else will our people be embarked?"

"This ship takes the civilian dependents?"

"Of course. This is 507, the *Dostoyny*. The one which leaves first is 504—down in the basin."

"I'm sorry." In the aftermath of too much tension my legs were jelly. "Please drive on."

"I understand your concern." He patted my arm and shifted gears. We came down off the bridge and onto the broad deserted expanse of a divided boulevard lined with bare trees and red banners. "Lenin Street—almost there." The car slowed and turned into a narrow lane between half-seen Hanseatic buildings.

A stone gateway with masonry posts set in cobbles under the arch stopped us in a dead end.

"The old Swedish Gate," said Henrijs, tourist guide. "Famous for lovers. Meet under a new moon and they lead a long and happy life."

Academic; there was no moon.

We uncurled from the car. My shoulder ached and my feet were asleep. A clock in one of the steeples rang the half hour. Laenaris knocked in a pattern on a studded door of the house beside us. It swung back silently. We went down three steps into a room full of hides and lasts—an illegal cobbler's shop. An old man in rimless glasses and timeworn leather apron gummed a smile.

Henrijs closed the door. "Here yet?" The cobbler shook his head and led us through another door into an inner room. Small, low, comfortable. A fire burning in an iron grate.

"Relax," said Henrijs. "Get warm; you have already been through much. I shall bring food and coffee."

I took off the shoes and socks, draped them beside the fire, held my feet to the flames, welcoming the pain of returning circulation. The door opened again behind me. "By God, I could use that coffee, Jans."

"A tiring journey, Comrade Dravin?"

The voice was deeper than I remembered, yet sharper; turned by the years into the voice of a professional accuser. But the eyes were the same. The black eyes of a black bird from a perch in Claridge's. And from the lift of the lip he remembered the whores.

CHAPTER

TWENTY-EIGHT

He looked fifty years old—but then he always had. And now he almost was. Recovering quickly from any surprise. *Or not surprised at all?*

"Sit down." No more shifty insecurity as in London; after a lifetime, he was used to party power and wore it easily. "There's much to discuss. We begin at once."

I stayed upright long enough to cut the apron strings and put on the sock. "You were expecting me?" The single most important question.

"No names were given. My job requires quick recall of unpleasant behavior."

Henrijs disturbed the camaraderie with food. "You've met. Good."

"Old friends," I said. The soup had a dash of liquor and the rolls were hot and stuffed with bacon and onion. Sinyavsky held an untouched mug of coffee and the party understanding of the word "discuss."

"It begins at 2300. The rendezvous—"

"How many will be aboard?"

"Something less than a hundred. The rendezv—"

"The remainder?"

"Billeted ashore. The—"

"Why?"

"Comrade!"—sharply, out of patience. "Later—Henrijs can tell you."

"No, now!" Things had to be made plain at the beginning. "Our friends across the sea, Tovarish—who are paying half the fare, don't trust your ability to pull this off. To be painfully blunt, they don't trust *you*." His cool was warming, a finger began a nervous drumming on the table. "Your ticket out will stay on the bottom of the Baltic until I send the signal to put up the cash. Am I clear?"

A grudging tip of the head.

"Good. Now, why are the crew ashore?"

"Painting ship prior to her departure."

"That's confirmed, then?"

"Yes."

"Africa?"

He tipped his head again.

"Were her nuclear warheads loaded?"

"Three days ago."

"And you plan to bargain with them?"

"Possibly." But a first note of surprised reappraisal.

"And the dependents?"

"About thirty."

"That's all?"

"I wish we were taking more. If you're going to hang for a loaf—but there's fear. It's understandable."

"Then what?"

"When clear, we send a message demanding that our people be embarked in *Dostoyny*; transportation to the Embankment in our own cars is all arranged. The assembly will be here this afternoon under cover of the parade."

"Who drives the ship?"

The finger was drumming faster. For the first time the set of the lips drooped slightly. "If I'm successful in persuading the duty officer or the second in command—"

"Is that likely?"

"No." Frank, anyway. "Probably myself with the help of the bosun—and God Almighty."

"That's shooting a little high. What about your squadron commander?"

"Not voluntarily."

"You don't sound shocked at the suggestion."

A shrug. "After twenty years as a political? There's an offer for anyone—but I can't think what it would be for Yanov. Despite some recent criticism, he's always been rock solid—"

"Try an American wife." The finger stopped. "And kids. Twins; a boy and a girl." I pushed across the picture.

"Shit!" The bitterness of the oath was a revelation. "Another of the supermen, caught by the cock."

"Some of us lack your purity, Comrade. What's his schedule?"

Grudgingly: "He leaves to review the parade just before twelve. That'll take most of the afternoon. Then he'll go to the shore mess."

"Which will write off the rest of the day?"

"The weekend, we hope."

"I want you to arrange his return to the ship—and before he's too pissed to read a gyro."

He stared at me. The finger had started up again.

"It won't jeopardize things," I said. "If he won't come voluntarily he can be kept in a sack. Just as long as he comes."

The silence lengthened and deepened.

"The wife's Jewish, Sinyavsky. Italy. She left just one step ahead of the ovens."

He nodded. I caught a brief flash of feeling in the black eyes as he turned away.

Glory Day for the Union of Soviet Socialist Republics. But not in Riga, capital of Latvia, a thousand years old.

Henrijs and I stood watching the conquerors disgorging six abreast from the Padomjo Boulevard into the Pioneru Luaukums, the square beneath our window. The square was lined by a ring of schoolgirls in red and white, laughing and chattering with cheeks to match. Banners and slogans swirled around them. Behind the banners, watching from other old houses with their vivid colors and white-crossed windows, the faces were hostile. Implacable. Cold as the November day.

"Bastards." Henrijs reached for the sash. "If you must watch this crap, Comrade"—sarcastically—"do it in comfort with a beer and television. Join our party."

"Soon," I said. "A few minutes."

He left me. Across the square the reviewers in great coats to the ankles stood like massive tea cosies. One showed a flash of shoulder boards: Kosov, the Baltic Fleet's Chief of Staff, according to Sinyavsky, who was there himself, almost hidden by another figure. The one I wanted. Next to Yanov, a nasty with plain clothes and a camera ignored spectacle for spies with random shots of the watching faces. I ducked instinctively behind a curtain.

The man turned away. There was a sudden tautness in the crowd, a new crispness from the band. Yanov stiffened, straightened. Saluted.

Sailors. The men of his squadron. Wheeling onto the five-hundred-year-old cobbles of the square, the scarlet ensigns of the Red Banner Fleet cracking overhead, boots goosestepping: *Crash, crash, crash*.

And as Yanov stands carved like the griffon on the corner of the palace, what images would go with the passing of the squad—what thoughts—if he could know that this was his last command? His last parade?

The boots crash across the stones, across the years—crashing with the beat of a metronome in Leningrad. . . .

A shout! Immediately below me, on a single string, a hundred heads snap right. A hundred throats cry out:

"STOROZHEVOY!"

"STOROZHEVOY!"

"STOROZHEVOY!"

The microphones amplify it, magnify it; take it from a word to a shout to a roar of meaning from a thousand voices. "We are your *Sentinels*, your *Watchmen*, your *Wardens*." From the crenellated walls the sound fell back. Smashed back. Blasted back. Through my window.

Storozhevoy Storozhevoy Storozhevoy!

I closed the glass and they were gone.

The stink of booze met me with the sound of the drunks singing at the bottom of the stairs. Five men in the outer room of the cobbler's shop were arguing the subject of flat beer. Bets were being taken on the number of bottles found wanting. Rejects were being smashed into a bucket. Laenaris, the chief celebrant, waved a happy hand. "A drink, Comrade! For the sake of Revolution!"

As I came by him he said, cold sober, "We wait for Valda. The others have arrived."

"How many?"

"Thirty-one plus ourselves." He nodded through the door. "Inside."

The small room with the fireplace was jammed to bursting. Women and children. Babies crying or being fed. Young kids of four or five staring with enormous eyes from behind mothers. An old, old woman rocking alone in a corner with a kerchiefed bundle from a strafing scene in 1940 France.

I hated it!

Hated Europe and its genocides, religious and political. How many millions like this, stuffed into garrets and cellars—herded into camps?

A sudden hush. For the second time, Sinyavsky stood behind me in the door. "Please!" A baby kept crying. Laenaris's long face took up a position at the window to watch the street. I watched him, only half-hearing the words of the leader.

"It will be two-thirty or three before you are able to move to the embankment.... Try to rest... Laenaris will arrange an extra room... sleeping pills for the children..."

All heard before. The other cheek—twelve million cheeks? Twenty million?

"Do not be provoked by the security people... be polite... Laenaris and Henrijs will do all the talking... we shall be with you on the radio... the world will be watching..."

After ignoring kulaks and Jews—watching a couple of dozen mixed bag? Jesus Christ!

"You will not be harmed... tomorrow—" *I shall be with my father in paradise?*

"...We shall be in Sweden. Go with God."

With God! Who helps those who help themselves, as Sinyavsky scuttles round, shaking hands. Giving blessings. *God help us!*

"Valda!"

Laenaris's voice ripped out in an instant any pretense of normality my mind had built since landing. "*Here*, to the window!"

Sinyavsky was already at the curtain. "Well?"

"Gone. But there was a watcher. I'm positive. Henrijs thinks he followed from the square."

"Has there been another hint?"

"Nothing."

"Show no movement of any kind. Leave through the passage. Jans"—to Henrijs—"you'll be the spokesman on the radio aboard the *Dostoyny*. We shall ask you to confirm that your treatment is correct. Remember, if there is coercion, use the words, *'This is Jans Kristin Henrijs'* when you begin. If all's well say, 'This is Henrijs.' Is it clear?"

"Clear. Have luck, Valda." A long hug; a handshake to me. "You too, Comrade. We appreciate what you do."

"It's nothing." *The only absolute truth spoken in that room.*

I moved to the door.

"No, this way." Sinyavsky pushed a spot beside the fireplace. A door swung open to a tunnel. For an instant I had an absurd looking-glass illusion that the other end would bring me under London to Jackson's office at Storey's Gate. Instead, after skipping two houses and a block, we came out into Teatra Street, deserted now in heavy rain.

"Stay!" Sinyavsky ran across the pavement to a dark olive Zil parked at the curb. The door stuck. I waited for the cars of police to whip around the corner. Rain ran down my neck. I felt the box in my pocket.

He waved. The door opened. I joined him in the car. He turned the key in the ignition. Twice; again. Four times. The starter bitching and moaning in the cold. At last the engine caught. Sinyavsky made light conversation. "The best part of Riga. The streets are named for crafts. This is Skarnu. All butchers before collectivization." Butchers! "We'll go out across the Pontoon Bridge."

"What pontoons?"

"Until the war this was a floating structure. A small thing for Latvian pride, keeping the old names."

The quarterdeck of *Dostoyny* was directly below us. "She's going to have a hell of a time turning at night in here."

Sinyavsky laughed, a harsh sound like a heron. "Pray for it, Comrade, we need the time."

Downriver in the dusk I could see log booms moored out in

the stream, a few merchantmen at jetties. We came down off the bridge and turned north again into a belt of apartment blocks ringing the city like playing cards set on end.

I asked Sinyavsky if he'd left relatives in the room.

"The last time I parted from a relative, Comrade, was in 1940. At the deportation."

Another statistic. June 18th. Forty thousand from the Baltic states. "Five in the morning—I was separated from my parents on the train to the camp at Khanty—Mansiyki. By the time we arrived, separated from my name as well. I was three years old."

Why the hell had I asked?

"Sinyavsky's the state's name. I was christened Valda Harijs Cimmermanis. You can't get much more Latvian than that, eh?"

He expected a reply.

"But you were Jewish?"

"Certainly; but my father wasn't picked up for being zealous about it. He was a schoolteacher—languages and history. Not Stalin's favorites. In the camp I was adopted by an old grandfather. So impressed by the fact that we escaped the soap vats, that we were on the right side of Stalingrad, that he felt it his duty to pass on the word through me. He died disappointed. I ignored my race for twenty years of party loyalty."

"What changed?"

But now he didn't answer. And wasn't going to. Just another of a million Russian reasons. He looked continuously in the mirror.

"How bad was that business at the window?"

"Probably nothing." He shrugged. "Efficiency's the least of Russian attributes, they won't think anyone's going far tonight. Probably nothing."

Say it again, Sam! The windshield wipers squeaked and clicked for another mile. The river came back beside us. Black, nearly dead, winding sluggishly through flat fenlands, past power poles set on tripods like enormous leading marks to escape flood waters, and shoddy barracks of asbestos siding lifted on posts above the ground beside them. A set for a prisoner-of-war film. But outside the prison walls. They came next. Double rows of chain link, ten feet apart, with an eight-foot wooden screen between. Gun towers. A brick guardhouse covered the entry. Lights were set to shine in horizontally through car windows.

"Be ready—they may wish to inspect the car."

I took a pill from the box.

Two guards on each side stepped forward for the check. "Papers, Kapitan"—recognizing Sinyavsky. "Comrade?" I passed my own. The ball bearing was back in my stomach. They stiffened. *I was going to be sick.* Examining the card minutely, comparing it to my face. *Stare straight ahead. Play the colonel.* Heels clicked sharply. "Spasibo—forgive the delay. Proceed."

But as with Yanov at the station, we were only halfway through the fence. A hundred yards ahead was a second inspection post: Behind every watcher, a watcher. There had to be an end. Like pyramid selling, the system was logically impossible.

The new guard was listening on the intercom. He half-rose from his stool, shrugged, sat again and waved us through.

"The party's started," I said.

Sinyavsky unleashed his warped smile. We drove across the center of a parade square, beside red brick ordnance buildings and between rows of four- and six-inch barrels mothballed on blocks. Past black loops of magnetic mine-sweeper cables, down on to a long U-shaped jetty forming the enclosure of the Bolderaya 'gavan.

Past four *Komars* secured abreast, and their supply ship, and two sets of *Skoriyis* and six minehunters, into the shadow of a sweeping soaring silhouette.

Second full circle. From memory and Portsmouth: familiar guards marched and crashed and presented arms. The last dog watchmen, sloppy, waiting for supper and relief, jumped to their feet after lounging on bollards and ventilators. Squared off their jumpers and white plastic belts with one hand, saluted awkwardly with the other.

Sinyavsky paused at the top of the brow. The lights backlit his face theatrically, casting deep lines of black about the mouth, a tragic hero from Kabuki theater. A young blond officer fell over himself handing back my card. Sinyavsky turned and walked forward, his shadow cutting off the lights shining on the sign beside the gangway; on its insignia of red star and anchor; on its name. Then he was past, and the light jumped out again, and the sign was clear and stark.

Storozhevoy.

The meaning from the square. Yanov's ship. Not a warden but a watchman after all. A watchman watching us to freedom.

We walked along the flush deck, past boats, rafts, intakes and antennae. Sinyavsky stopped briefly and pointed to the deck above our heads, aft of the split funnel, at the gaunt angularity of an SSN launcher. Our Aladdin's lamp?

We paused. I flicked the pill over the side. We stepped through a door into the superstructure below the bridge. The passageway was lit by dim red night lights, the cabin doors were closed, the deck rising quickly now to match the upward sweep of the bow. Sinyavsky stopped outside the last door set at the head of the passage.

"It's 1930," he said. "I've asked him to be back in half an hour. You can wait inside. I'll keep an eye on things."

I stepped into the cabin. Drab-colorless with pale yellow enamel. Tubular metal furniture with white canvas covers set about on gray linoleum. No attempt at decor, naval or otherwise. No life. I saw the sword hanging on the bulkhead. The photograph of Mother and Leader on the desk. Another of Lenin in a gilt frame serving as a stand for miniature metal ensigns—the scarlet hammer and sickle, and the blue and white with the red star of the fleet. Tacky. I looked for "Welcome to Blackpool" on the base.

There was only one other touch of color: On top of a locker on the starboard side, matching the schoolgirls in the square, the red and white of a chess set like the one in Gorshkov's office.

Everything was happening in pairs as I sat again in Yanov's chair at Yanov's desk, waiting for him to come back. Thinking that the getting on was so damned easy. Trying not to think about the getting off.

CHAPTER

TWENTY-NINE

The sounds of a ship at rest: Air sighing from the ventilators, slight rhythms of distant machinery, thuds felt rather than heard as hatches are opened and closed. A word exchanged between night watchmen. Footsteps. Approaching the captain's cabin.

I put my hand on the gun in my pocket. Stood to one side for the swaying of a curtain, the clatter of rings, the click of the door sliding shut behind him.

I held out the picture of his children.

Which was not what I had intended. Because for days I had rehearsed this scene. Had imagined myself saying, "Bursinov, State Security, my card . . ." Or slipping him a note: "Peter Dravin requests the pleasure of your company."

Anything for a joke, to keep it light and easy with a handshake, or hugs and kisses from the old days. Not to produce this moment of stunned nothing, of silence, of listening to the ship noises. This moment of no reaction.

But that was not quite true—there was something. A shudder. Once through the neck and shoulders as though a knife had severed the backbone of a fish. And then a twitch at the corner of his mouth.

He was being funny. Beating Dravin at his own game of old school tie. Sinyavsky had told him. A wave of relief swept through me. I turned up the bulkhead speaker. The cabin filled with the noise of the birthday party still under way in Red Square. "Dravin—double agent," I said. "I'm sorry if you were expecting Lenin."

"No. From Security. The officer of the day told me." Expressions were passing in a ribbon behind the eyes. I thought I guessed them and slapped him on the back. "Yanov, we're going out!"

"Out?" Too flat. Much too flat. But then the wait had been too long. It was only understandable that reversing would take time.

The speaker was rerunning highlights of the day. An invisible parade marshal bellowed invisible divisions into line. I passed across the crumpled picture with the pink trees and the happy faces eating new moon slices of melon at the picnic. "Drawn by Pesha."

He glanced at it.

"You see the extra plate, Alyosha? They always set one for you."

A nod. A burst of static on the speaker drowned out something he was going to say. *He wasn't looking at the pictures*. "What is it?" I asked.

"Aren't you afraid?"

And I realized he hadn't said my name. But perhaps we were still playing. "Petrified, old boy." I showed him the pillbox. "I've wasted one already."

Was there a tiny trace of the grin? Or just one of the new lines on the face? Because eight years had made a difference. Still with a full head of hair, and in uniform, things were under control—but the skin had aged, pouched, wrinkled on the neck. Not a lot, but there would be no going back.

Still not looking at his children. And even as it was sinking in that if it wasn't going to be voluntary, it wasn't worth it, I became desperate. Tried to force him with fatuity.

"Your mother must have been pleased, Alyosha. About the kids. Being born before she died?"

"Of course." But without a trace of feeling.

And standing idiotically with a gun in one hand and a child's scribblings in the other, I wanted to drop both. Grab him by the neck, kick him in the crotch. Pound it into him. Scream, not "of course," you bastard. Russian grannies don't "of course" about

grandchildren. They go off their nut, soppy, ecstatic—even sack-
cloth and ashes with *Zhid* in the family. Not "of course."

Instead, I said, "Yanov, snap out of it. For Christ sake, these
are *yours*. Look at that bloody boy." Losing my control, *"Look
at him!"* shoving the picture right in his face. "If your mother
could see *that,* wouldn't she say forget your bloody hero politics,
go to them, be a father. Make *some* effort. *Wouldn't she?* I don't
care if you don't lift a finger against the goddamn state—I'll drag
you. But for Christ sake, man—wink, nod, close your eyes—do
something to say YES!"

"An effort?" There it was. At last, thank God, some juice
beginning to bubble through the crust. "The day of the station was
an effort."

"I can imagine."

"Oh no." A look now that I couldn't comprehend. "She knew,
Petya."

My name. But if it was to be used like this I didn't want it.
"Knew?"

"Dying, *Petya.* Knew she was dying. We both knew." Now
I wanted only to turn him off, block my ears, turn up the birthday
party even louder not to hear the secret between mother and son.

Because it has to *be* a secret or they'll spoil it, she says. They
won't think it Soviet morality to let a son stock a hero mother up
on cans of milk and tea and bugger off to the station and the
grandchildren for whom Dravin wants an effort. Won't think it
meet and right that he walks out and locks the door and leaves
her there behind it to catch the cart that missed her by the snowball
bush in Irina Street in 1942. Not even if she begs him to go. *Not
even if she buys the cans herself.*

"Dear God."

"The apartment *upravdom* found her and informed." His face
and voice were flat again. "It was all wasted."

Something for the bodies on the wire, I'd told Jackson. Dravin
wants Commitment. Against Yanov's, my gesture with the pill
box was as hollow and banal as the counterpoint of music from
the speaker.

"Alyosha, make your own decision."

I gave him my gun.

And accepted it as force of habit that he should check the

magazine. Snap it in with a slap of the palm. But not that he would throw me roughly in a chair. Point the damn thing at my face, hiss, *"Stay very still, Dravin!"*

All wasted. Just as he said. Wasted on a game that should have stopped with children. In his case, a mother on the wire was the limit: in mine? The faces in the picture. He was crossing to the door.

"Yanov!"

He was turning. But would he listen? "The extra places in the pictures, Alyosha—I've encouraged it, but it was *their* idea. Those kids *believe*—"

"Believe?"

"In *you*, man. Like Santa Claus—Father Frost. To them it's the same damn thing—and why not? If milk and cookies by the chimney get presents, why shouldn't they think that with a plate and a chair and enough faith in bloody fairy stories they'll get a father? Stupid little bastards—"

"Shut up!" The speaker had suddenly gone dead. "Whatever was done in California was your life. Not mine."

Whatever was done. An eye for an eye. My life for a moment of starlight.

He yanked the door, ripped at the curtain. My looking glass turned to the wall.

The bulb of the night light shone down across the head so that the face was shadowed, jawless: half a face.

"Captain Dravin, please stay seated."

The rock closes, said Jackson, as in a clownish jingle you blindly stray. Into Utopia.

Travinov walked into the cabin. Quiet, polite. Flawless English; no trace of an American accent now. Well dressed for a Russian. A French or Italian silk tie showing his privileged position. Placing a cigarette in a long holder to filter Russian Gutrot. No gun.

It was in the hand of an assistant with Hirohito glasses and beaver teeth coming through the door. Kicking it shut. Wearing a tie of thin black official issue. An obscenely hairless head.

Pointless to make even the least excuse; even go willingly if I could have Sinyavsky first. It must *be* Sinyavsky.

"Mister Dravin, thank you—Colonel Travinov."

"Of course. General Travinov—just for the record, Mr. Dravin. A cigarette? Ah, but you don't. Your father."

And again Marshall's words as in Gorshkov's office, echoing, echoing, "Hang you, skin you... throw you back. Old boy." And realizing that when the moment comes, it's never willingly.

"Spasibo, Kapitan." Travinov spoke for the first time in Russian to Yanov. "Excellent. In one piece and undamaged, as I wished. If you would stand behind, we shall begin."

Looming above me, once again Yanov was hidden behind impassive eyes—the eyes over the diver! But *Christ Jesus,* how could they stare unblinking after our twenty years?

He placed the Browning in his pocket, moved behind my shoulder. The door clicked. And this was how things ended.

Travinov picked up the thought. "Pyotr Andreyevich"—any pretense of my British citizenship discarded with the Russian name—"some of these affairs take an extraordinary time to run, do they not? We have been awaiting your decision for what— fifteen years?"

My decision? Puffing filthy smoke deliberately. Calmly pausing for reflection.

"I felt, after discussion with Alexey Ilyich during your visit to Moscow that you might make it then, but events rendered it an inappropriate moment, and your utility to us"—a Russian mirror image of Jackson, for Christ's sweet sake—"was not sufficiently of value. You have picked a more auspicious time."

I scarcely heard him. Simply looked at Yanov. *Incredible!* But why feel that? Just Dravin reversed.

Russia Expects... Dravin must endure.

But a woman and two children were drowning invisible in the backwash. "Comrade"—Travinov again—"in the house by the Swedish Gate, who was your contact? Sinyavsky?" He passed across color photographs of Laenaris walking. Henrijs entering the door. Dravin mesmerized in a window watching a parade. But if they knew, why not Sinyavsky's picture?

"Good quality," I said.

"Polaroid—one of the blessings of détente." A general genuinely appreciative. "The cell was known to us—we shall collect it tomorrow, after the holiday; but until this moment, not your association. Such are the laws of chance. Comrade?" Inviting my answer.

Hirohito had moved beside his colleague—the gun sticking out between them like a snake's tongue. He was silent. And singularly ugly.

"Comrade?" Travinov tapped a finger on the desk. The first tiny hint of impatience. Hirohito licked his teeth in anticipation of the animal part. Travinov walked across to the chess set on the locker. "Comrade," his eyes were concerned for me, "you know the way of it. Our talk will end as it ends whether we stay here or walk ashore."

> *"O Oysters, come and walk with us!"*
> *The Walrus did beseech.*
> *"A pleasant walk, a pleasant talk,*
> *Along the briny beach"* . . .

With the end, as he said, inevitable. The run was off. But with time, if Sinyavsky was genuinely ours, if he was even now getting word to the huddled cellar? Could I give them time?

"Have you read *Alice in Wonderland*, General?" English seemed my privilege and it annoyed Hirohito.

Travinov shook his head patiently and stuck with Russian. "No riddles, Tovarish." He moved a piece on the chessboard. "The cell—who do you work with?"

Keep both language and topic at cross purposes. "A departmental exchange will be initiated," I said. But our cupboard was bare, we had no Lonsdales left for a swap.

"Ah." Travinov made another move. "You see, Kapitan Yanov—no longer a stalemate." He set a rook to one side with satisfaction and turned his full attention back to me. I knew it had never flickered for an instant.

"No, Comrade, no." He knew our larder. "If your old master was still driving your ship?" A shrug. "Well, perhaps someone might have made a move for you. But not now—we both know that. Damaged goods, shop soiled. They don't want you back. Marshall is at this moment, one would imagine, busily covering tracks."

Tredennick had said, "They'll know you right down to your drawers . . ."

"Accept it, eh?" He sat back again behind the desk, his damaged face between the Blackpool Lenin frame and the lamp, as I always remembered it. "So what will the file show?" he asked.

"What file?"

"Why, Tovarish, our file for the *Times.*" Musing: "We have a choice there—London, New York, Los Angeles. Los Angeles, I think—a suitable rounding-off spot. Or perhaps a scoop for one of the flesh-feeding tabloid rags. But in any event starting with the contacts, drop points. London, San Francisco, New York, Finland, Copenhagen. Photographs at each of information changing hands."

"Crap," I said. "All legal and ordered."

"Your perspective is still distorted." A firm but fair schoolmaster, gently correcting. "You see things from the viewpoint of a safe return, not as a runaway. So . . ." Brisk now, ticking off a list. "We have the initial contacts—and with Philby and the expatriate community. To the jackal press of course, that will seem to be the final link—Crabb. Once it's known that you were there from the beginning. Then film of your liaison with the girl, Gisela—"

"Nothing to show," I said. "I regret it."

"Suitably edited in parts—"

"You wouldn't need many parts," I said, nodding at Hirohito. "His head would do for most of it."

"Ah. The flippancy"—looking at me thoughtfully. "Your most dominant characteristic. Excessive cynicism. So often a mask for idealism—or affection—denied or disappointed. On the night you walked through Moscow, Yulinovsky was astounded by your response." His voice toughened abruptly. "And more parts than you might imagine, my friend, because you would be surprised how often the girl's dance troupe was in the same place at the same time as yourself. At least your wife's lawyer will be surprised. Pleasantly, I'm sure. No joke, Comrade?"

No joke.

For already the faces in my head were passing by and haunting. Kids—too young to really know, thank God! Marshall? Travinov only too right—already coping happily. All justifications ready in the bin before I left. "I always knew."

Jackson? *Jackson*—at last, a sailor back at the top to clean the stables. And now let down stinking, face rubbed. How the new wave would love that.

And worst, the faceless faces. How many wiped from the paysheet in Whitehall: Services Concluded? How many nameless gold stars on the marble slab in Langley? No joke, Comrade.

But time, for the other faces—in the cellar—was passing.

Travinov was still running down his list: "... funds paid into an account in Berne—"

"With the deposit dates all matching my trips abroad—I know."

"Of course you do. Didn't I say it at the start?" He lit another cigarette. "And you worry about loved ones, children. *Automatically* Soviet citizens, Comrade, with full rights and privileges"— *saying it with a straight face.* "Sacrifice is recognized. Your friend Yanov has made an enormous sacrifice, we know. That his dependents are prevented by the Americans from leaving—"

"I've heard the line: You're not barbarians. What do you want?"

The damaged face leaned forward, the eyes making one ignore the scars, piercing blue eyes—bluer even than Jackson's. *"Talk to us!* Rejoin your homeland. Be welcomed, honored. You are not a traitor, nor was your father. This is recognized now; his name is in the Hall of Columns as a builder of the new State— you shall see it. As a Russian!"

"Or?"

The face receded back behind the lamp, the eyes again as dark as the missing cheek. He took a deep breath on the cigarette, the holder upside down in his hand just like my father. He stabbed it out. Exhaled.

"You talk."

The smoke from a cigarette was thinner than a pipe, not full enough for a schoolboy's daydreams, and the harsh scent of the tobacco closed out the third and final circle—with my father, leaving Russia. I tipped my head, looked for a moment up at Yanov, impassive as the Kremlin wall, hands in pockets, waiting. Silent after twenty years of wait for me. So be it.

"Fuck the lot of you!"

Travinov nodded. Satisfied with the response. And now time was not mine to give. But perhaps silence. My fingers touched the pillbox. Gently, gently, sliding under the palm.

The gun butt crashed into the back of my hand. I retched. Hirohito smiled. Travinov placed the little pillbox next to Lenin. "Later, Mr. Dravin"—almost kindly. "Place your arm on the desk, please." The voice harsher—a memory of fingers squeezing the newly healed flesh ten years earlier. "On the desk." The snake-tongue barrel flicked sideways. The shadow of Yanov almost filling the room from the light behind him. I put out the arm.

"The sleeve!" I rolled it up.

He checked the hypodermic with a medical deftness. The serum gave a phallic spurt from the tip. He dispensed with any antiseptic swab. No risk of future infection. *"Your future's shot, Comrade."* Still funny.

As the needle came towards me I wanted to make some gesture. Not just go out like a lamp in a slogan. *Gorshkov's phrase, "My Aladdin's lamp." Dravin awed, "And what spirit does it release, sir?" Gorshkov again, "The spirit of recall and association, the strongest of spirits."*

The serum would release every scrap. Yanov must have felt like this at the border as the train stopped. Stupid Dravin—it was all a game! A joke. The needle slid through the skin. *Yanov!* The thumb began its journey to float away my will. Utopia.

> *Comes at last the final stroke—*
> *Time has had his little joke!*

The last laugh. The missing face. Nicola, given away for absolutely nothing.

Travinov looking calmly at my eyes, waiting for the dilation. Hirohito casting a professional glance at the acid scars around the needle. There was no gesture that I could make.

> *Then—and then*
> *The joke is over!*

This is the way my world ends.
With a bang! A deafening crack in my ear. Two cracks.

And General Travinov, Star of Lenin, KGB—Face Hole to Marshall and his machines—at last in death lived up to his description.

CHAPTER

THIRTY

The acrid smell of powder was sharp in the nostrils, the cabin silent, surreal: Hirohito's body subsided like a hand puppet without the hand, Travinov's back in his chair like a sunbather. An outflung arm had smashed down the chessmen. No sense of time. The incident might have taken a second or a year. I looked at the gaping tear of scorched cloth at Yanov's pocket, the needle hanging from my arm.

"Let's get rid of that, for a start." Yanov's voice was firm, unshaken. "The plunger barely started—has it affected you?"

But I had nothing to say.

"No joke, Comrade?" The wry, dead mouth on Travinov's shattered face seemed pleased.

"I'm all right. Alyosha—"

Now what? Thanks, sorry for the doubts, but I win, I was right all along. You lose—Russia loses? The scattered pieces on the chessboard threw back the question. The kings had fallen with Travinov. The only men left standing were the red Genghis Khan horseman beside his castle, facing the white queen and two white pawns. *"No longer a stalemate, Kapitan."* No. Two scorpions in a box. Marshall had said something about that. I couldn't remember. I had to thank Yanov.

"Alyosha—"

But Yanov, the whole Russian, who kissed men in San Francisco, embraced in public, showed emotion constantly—just dropped the boom arm on my shoulder. "No need for words, Petya."

"I—"

The buzzer rang. Yanov grabbed Hirohito's gun and tossed me the Browning. *"Da?"*

"Sinyavsky."

"Wait?"

"It should be all right," I said. "What did they tell you about him?"

"They've been watching for two months—I thought the attention in *Red Star* was for me."

"And the people in Riga?"

"They only made that connection this morning. Some word came in last night. They visited me after the parade. I said Sinyavsky'd asked me back to discuss a serious matter of party discipline. I thought they came along to pick him up." He kicked Travinov's body. "This bastard was a hell of a poker player. He showed me your picture as I was opening the door."

"And left you to it—Christ! Alexey, I'm sorry."

"No time. Enter!"

Sinyavsky had picked up a Commissioned Gunner and a Chief Bosun's Mate—and an arsenal. They were stopped by the bodies.

"They know?" Sinyavsky's voice was up an octave. "Our people ashore—"

"They're not interested in the small stuff tonight. There should still be time."

"We must go sooner. Not wait till one. We can be away by midnight. I've already had the shore phone let go—except for a line to this cabin. The OD's been told it's a readiness exercise." Pointing at me: "For a suspected fifth columnist."

"My ship?" Yanov had connected. And was appalled.

"After that?" Sinyavsky indicated the bodies. "Does it make much difference?"

"Mutiny?" Yanov looked at him almost pityingly. "All the fucking difference in the world, Commissar." He turned to me. *"This* is your way out?"

"All or nothing, Alyosha. If you can get us clear—"

"Insane." Back to Sinyavsky: "How many in the cadre with you?"

"About a dozen."

"Not enough. Officers on board?"

"Three. The OD, Brodsky. Ensigns Turchin and Marchenko."

"Are they in on it?"

"No."

"Start with them."

Decision! And commitment.

"Bosun, tell Brodsky you've found drinking in the forward magazine. Deal with him there. Ensigns in their cabins. Then the mess decks. Just seal the bastards in. Padlocks—no warnings, no choices. They can make those at sea. Gunner, take personal control of all keys. Ditch the duplicates. I want every compartment locked—end to end, top to bottom." To Sinyavsky again, "What technicians are with you?"

"Harijs and Bogoraz, engineers. Jacobson for electrics."

"That's something. They're sharp. Get the electrician to kill all power to transmitters and alarms before you start. Galich"—to the bosun—"someone who really keeps his head at the gangway. No one leaves. *No one!* Returnees will be drunk; sort them out as you have to. Any officers to me. And I want constant reports. Dump this filth in my shower before you go."

He waited for them to remove the bodies. "Now tell me the rest, Petya."

Halfway, he cut me off abruptly. "*Broadcasting?* Demands? Women and kids? Rubbing noses in the warheads? Petya, he knows me like his *own hand*—"

"But it's a first time, Alexey. Things will be unexpected, confused. And we only need five hours. Just until the linkup."

"Linkup?"

"Outside the straits. An attack boat—USN."

"*My God*—"

The curtain pushed inward without warning. A short fat steward with a tray. "Soup, Kapitan. Something hot after the parade." He saw the guns. And the blood. I grabbed the tray in time.

Sinyavsky arrived breathless. "The main hatch was locked . . ."

I watched the steward being led away. Yanov was watching the politician. "What do you make of him?"

"More than I did."

"Will he crack when the heat comes on his people?"

"I'm cracking myself. I keep hearing tanks on the jetty."

He grinned. The buzzer rang again. "Who is it?"

"Harijs, sir." A PO with a red plastic propeller on his sleeve and an engineer's fear of leaving grease on the carpet waited in the passage. "The fuel report, sir. Eighty percent."

Yanov took the sheet. "Good. How do we stand otherwise?"

"We can have full electrical generation now, sir. All diesels are on line, and all gearing and lube oil pumps idling."

"Bogoraz is only just promoted—can he handle a flash up on his own in Number Two?"

"Yes sir. I shall be monitoring both engine room spaces by remote from my control cab. There is only one problem. Full power. We can't deliver safely until the lube oil temperature gets up to 100. We need at least fifteen minutes."

Yanov nodded. "You'll have that while I'm maneuvering in the basin. There's no doubt that we'll have air pressure for turnover on all eight engines?"

"No sir."

"Very good, then. Flash at one-minute intervals."

"Das!"

The man left. The intercom squawked harshly for the first time. "Damage Control—" Yanov tossed me a red crayon. "Be a working passenger. Answer the phone."

A frantic hour gone. Thirty deadly but almost idle minutes left. The red crosses marking the locked compartments on the state-board waited with ominous fatality, like ambulances behind the lines.

Sinyavsky entered first. There should have been a camera, an old one with magnesium flare, for a daguerreotype of the faces filing in. An archive for the counterrevolution: Where Marshall's second coming came from. To go with the list staring back at me with its random facts: Young, old; Jew, gentile; officer and man; Russian-born and Russian bastard.

Sinyavsky, Latvian Jew, Commander, Political Assistant.

Maximov, Latvian, Warrant Officer, Gunner—(father Latvian, killed).

Harijs, Latvian, Petty Officer first class, engineer.

Andrijs, Latvian, Petty Officer second class,—fire control man.

Chalidze, Russian, Able Seaman, engineer—(brother arrested, died in hospital).

Ginzberg, Russian Jew, Petty Officer Supply—(family in Israel).

Chukovskaya, Latvian (mother) Able Seaman, radioman.

Jacobson, Latvian, Petty Officer second class, electrician.

Bogoraz, Russian, Petty Officer third class, engineer.

Galich, Latvian Jew, Warrant Officer, Boatswain.

What would he say? What would *I* say? Tell them, as they do at the camps, that this is a place where you're already dead? That the consequence of mutiny must be irrevocable? That you haven't got a chance and no one cares? Just fight and die?

Or treat them—as in fact he did—as they expected: as a Russian Little Father calming his children with a wornout joke.

"As I see what you've given me to work with, you remind me of the woman in the West who wanted to adopt a baby, and the girl left the carriage beside an organ grinder and the organ grinder's monkey jumped in?" Could there be a face on the list that hadn't heard it? And yet the grins were coming, the group unity was forming with the nudges and the winks. "The woman picks up the monkey," and on Yanov's face the look of every doting, besotted babuschka they'd ever seen, "You may be an ugly hairy little bastard—but you're *mine!* and I love you."

I thought of the bodies in the shower.

Of others undoubtedly to come. In the face of death his Russian children laughed like Russians. Roared, slapped thighs, punched backs. Coughed, wiped eyes.

He held up a hand. "You're worrying about dependents. I understand." But only polite attention now for mechanics, for conventions of discipline. Was the junior man at the end already having second thoughts? Yanov was holding up the picture. "My wife and children in the West."

A shock wave through the group. *"I understand."*

He put it down. "Security. Any man attempting to enter the command position or the engine control cab without clearance will be shot."

Letting it sink in. "Good. Until you're detailed off by the gunner, wait in the cabin next door." He slapped the nervous AB on the back. "And let go of your cock, Chukovskaya—you'll need it in Sweden." He saw them out on another smaller wave of laughter, a vicar shaking hands on Sunday morning.

"You wanted me to stay, sir?"

Maximov, the Gunner. The foreigner's Russian: Thick black hair shaved up the sides, flat face, Slav cheeks, oriental eyes. A G.I.'s chin, and a body like the proverbial brick.

"Get Jacobson," said Yanov. "The upper deck speakers and lighting must be off."

A terse nod. "Do we chop the lines?"

"No. Take them off the bollards inboard and let them slip—watch the stern line doesn't foul the screws. The same for the gangway—we'll ask the Swedes for a new one. *But no noise and no light.* Got it?"

Another nod. But the man was waiting.

"There's something else?"

"Will they really let our people go?"

Tell me another funny story, Captain.

"Yes, Maximov. Just hope *Dostoyny*'s crew aren't too pissed to get them down the river."

Two men alone in the cabin of a warship looking again at children's pictures, talking of children's games, describing children's bedtimes.

"Petya—Christ, how much I've missed."

"Not the best part, Alyosha. They only start to get interesting once they can argue back."

His hand was tracing constant circles around the picnic table of the drawing. "I almost shot myself," he said, "after my mother's funeral—so much for nothing. And then I thought that's what the bastards want, and if I'm going to do it I'll save it for a moment when it might be useful. But of course they never let me near the edge again. No one runs from Poliarnyi."

"But in the ship?"

"I hoped so to—but we haven't been anywhere. Did Sinyavsky tell you I was to be transferred next week?"

"*Jesus!*"

He nodded. "That close, Petya."

I altered the subject. "The chess set looks familiar."

"A gift on parting. That's what I mean—he knows me. All my moves, how I think under pressure. We met a year ago—he hadn't changed to me." A pause. "It makes things difficult."

"I trust he'll feel a similar constraint."

We both knew the answer to that.

He took some paper from his desk. I sat on the settee and watched him scratch across the sheet in the light of the writing lamp. Stopping to look at the pictures, thinking. Going on. I dozed. Slept.

Woke.

Another knock on the door. Yanov was answering it. The mass of the bosun blocked the other side.

"What is it?" I asked.

"A log boom. Two miles out; if we don't go now the channel will be blocked." He fired rapid instructions. The bosun disappeared on the run. Yanov came back to the desk and picked up an oiled silk pouch beside the lamp. He held it out. "For Nicolasha—a copy, and some personal things. Better not to have—"

"All the eggs in one basket."

I slipped the package inside my suitcoat. He passed me a weather jacket of heavy navy blue quilting and a set of white cotton antiflash gear with a tin hat. "One for cold, one for hot"— with the old grin.

Hot and cold. God, how far back that went. And in the same instant how many other questions to be asked. Things to be said. But Yanov was already stepping through the door. "Bring the coffee." The steward had left a thermos and two mugs. I picked them up. "Okay, Comrade," in his New York voice. "Let's go."

Up three ladders. Three locked doors to open and relock behind. A compartment with the *Sailfin*'s complexity: Console after console to be checked, range scales, volumes, brightness to be set. A last three steps to be taken to the pitch black of the control bridge. The time on the clock: 2353.

Out on the exposed wings, eyes widened to the night. He checked the ship's sides. A hundred feet forward, three hundred aft. Port, then starboard. From the height of the bridge, the jetty lay at the bottom of a mine shaft—silent, deserted, a light drizzle falling, no wind.

No tanks either. Not even a commissionaire.

He showed me a bank of small bulbs in a panel. "Engine response lights. Red for ignition, amber preparatory, green—"

"For go?"

"For go. A set for each engine, four aside. Read them off. I'll stay out here on the throttles. Can you take the helm? That joystick half wheel there."

"I'll manage." Jackson would like that.

"The ship's head indicator's over it." He walked back through the hatch to the wing. "And call out the time."

I checked the bridge by force of unsuspected habit. Waiting for the first small light to burn in the darkness.

"Red on One. Time 2355."

Red turned to amber.

A shudder, barely detectable, passed through the deck into the feet and up the spine. The hair prickled on my neck. I zipped up the weather jacket.

"Red on Two. On Three—on Four." Window wipers rotating.

"Amber on Two, on Three. Red on Seven. On Eight." All radars operating.

"Green on One, on Two. On Three." Depth recorder ticking.

"Amber on Eight." In the mirror on the wing, the stern lines falling.

Green on Five, on Six, on Seven.

"Time 2359."

Yanov crossed back from the starboard wing. The whole ship now throbbing, whirring, purring—but unheard through the whistling rush of air sucking into the massive intakes on the funnels behind us.

The helm and the control consoles vibrating gently, Yanov's hand poised above the pitch and throttle levers. Every needle, every dial waiting, trembling. Russia boozing, snoring.

"Thirty seconds."

Incongruous images of my wife walking like Thomas More in Jackson's garden.

"Green on Eight!"

His right hand pushed forward, left pulling back. Fifty-eight thousand horsepower eased the bow inward to the jetty. A quick look aft again, out at the black mass of the river.

Right hand back to the center—pull to the rear. And the bow slowing, stopping, steadying.

Holding.

And then the ornamental stand on the jetty, with its decorated life ring, and its star and anchor, and its lantern shining down, moved two feet forward—ten feet forward—sixty. Faster, faster— and the name plate was fading, was faded, and now was left behind: all that was left of *Storozhevoy*, a sentinel, on the soil of Russia.

STOROZHEVOY.

CHAPTER

THIRTY-ONE

"Bridge quarterdeck"—Maximov's voice on the headset. "Forty meters, sir."

I relayed the message. From the bridge the buoy looked a goner already. Yanov ignored it, knowing relative speed and distance intuitively. All his attention was fixed on the swing of the ship's head as she came around onto the exit bearing. His ship handling was superb, he might have been playing with a launch in daylight—not jockeying four thousand tons in the dark with only a third of her length to spare at either end, perhaps a fathom under the screws.

"Bridge—opening a little, sir."

Great clouds of silt swirled up in the intermittent light of the gunner's torch. Still nothing moved ashore. The jetties and the naval basin were sepulchral in shrouds of mist hanging from the few lights on the crane gantries and life ring stations. I crossed to the other wing. A tributary with the Baker's name, Milgravis, joined on the east bank two hundred yards up channel.

"*Yanov!*" The lights were crawling along the top of a shed.

"Freighter! Call him up—Christ, we can't."

"Bridge, Captain. Ship astern, sir—very close."

He slammed both throttles. The turbines gave a vast gulp for air through the intakes. The Daugava boiled up level with the quarterdeck.

"*Too shallow*—we're going to touch!"

"Bridge—half a cable, sir."

Uncontrollable shuddering. The antennae mast whipped in epileptic spasm overhead. A needle fragment smashed into the deck.

"Echo's gone on radar," I said.

"Pray."

The slab side of the merchantman was a moving cliff above our quarterdeck.

"The gunner's still back there."

"Maximov—get the hell out!"

The freighter's fo'c'sle anchor watch were paralyzed, staring down. The gunner hadn't moved.

"Bridge—she's holding sir."

The starboard fairway buoy was now racing back in the opposite direction. *"We'll be into the bank!"* He hauled back on the throttles. Again the vicious shuddering. Then a rattling roar and a colossal splash from astern.

"She's let go both anchors, sir."

Silence.

Yanov blew his nose. We looked at each other. He picked up the phone. "Gunner—a case of booze for you in Sweden. Now get forward and clear away the missile mountings—all arms loaded. How long will that take?"

"Twenty minutes."

"Good." He looked at me. "Log reading?"

"Six."

"I'll come up a couple."

Hardly a sense of motion now. Dead quiet on the bridge. The lights at the ends of the moles slipped behind us: The world was invisible. The famous beaches of Riga, fifty miles of sand the color and texture of white pepper, stretched away unseen and wasted.

Their desertion was illusion.

"Unidentified naval vessel—this is the Pilot Station. Over."

"Bugger! Petya, set the auto helm at 320 to take us out."

The voice in the darkness repeated itself more urgently.

"Unidentified naval vessel this is the Pilot Station. Come in, please. Over."

"I hear you, Pilot Station. Pass your traffic. Over."

"This is the Pilot Station. What ship? We have no harbor movements. Over."

"Pilot Station, this is hull number 507, non-reporting. Over." Aside he said, "It's standard for us to sortie without civilian liaison."

"Lucky you!"

The static of the carrier wave filled the bridge. "Trying to put a face on us," Yanov said.

"Giving *Dostoyny*'s number won't help."

"Just so."

Fate has Marshall's sense of humor.

"Hull number 507, this is the Pilot Station. Reduce speed to five. I say again, reduce speed to five. Incoming log raft, I say again, incoming log raft. Over."

"Well?"

"We can't alert them yet. I'll have to slow."

The rev counter steadied at 56. "Lights in line—dead ahead. I can't see the boom."

"I can." Yanov had magnified the radar range scale to a mile. Intermittent blotches straggled off to the northeast. "The whole fucking channel—the little bastard hasn't allowed for tide."

"I've got the oil lamps on the rafts—five in all. There's still a gap to starboard."

"Come to 325."

I turned the dial. The lanterns crept closer. *One Komar sent out to go rat catching now....*

A man could jump from the fo'c'sle onto the logs of raft three. Yanov flinched. "Nothing more to starboard—we'll ground!"

Raft four disappeared under the flare of the bow. Figures hopped frenetically on the towing platform of the tug.

There was an almost imperceptible bump.

"The chain. We've had it if the little prick swings that light on our number."

The tug's searchlight was sweeping in agitation back and forth across a widening mass of logs joyfully liberated in the current.

Yanov pushed a button. Dense clouds of smoke roiled from nozzles on the stern. "Poor little buggers," I said. "They'll never find them now."

"Weep later. What depth."

"Twelve meters—trace dropping sharply. Eighteen . . . twenty-two. Twenty-five, twenty-five." I looked to port. "And the whistle buoy abeam. Yanov, you bloody bastard. You've done it! We're off. *We're off!*"

A huge grin. "A start, Pyotr Andreyevich, a start. I'm coming to a full speed. Set the auto pilot to 316."

For the Irben Straits, sixty miles dead ahead.

Elation wasn't shared all around.

"Hull number 507, this is the Pilot Station. Tug reports that you have cut the tow. Over."

"Five oh seven, acknowledged. Will check and file report on return. Closing down this net. Out."

"Are you?" I asked.

"No. We'll need it to hear *Dostoyny*. But it'll keep the bastards out of our hair while we deal with the home front." He pushed the intercom. "DCHQ, this is the captain. How is it with you?"

"Damage Control—all's well." Sinyavsky's voice sounded calm.

"Good. I'm going to kick them out of bed."

For a second time in my life I heard the clangor of an alarm in a Russian ship. Words of caution. Words of warning.

"Attention all hands. Attention all hands . . . we're going to Sweden . . . help if you wish or we'll send you home . . . don't rock the boat and no one gets hurt . . ."

Useless.

"*Captain!* Brodsky's locked himself in Radio Central."

The chatter of the Ratt in the Operations Room behind us made Sinyavsky's distress superfluous.

"I know; get him out."

"Is he to be shot?"

"Not after the fox has had the hen. How—?"

"The emergency panels on the doors—kicked out. I have sentries on the two ensigns. Forty-one men are coming with us."

"Very good. Send the bosun to the bridge." Yanov stretched.

"Brodsky, poor bastard. If he doesn't come too, he's dead anyway; he's been exposed to the infection." He glanced at the clock. "And we'd have been transmitting in ten minutes. When the bosun gets here, I'll draft the message."

But ten minutes was six miles. And six miles . . . ?

I stepped out on the wing for some air. The sky was still overcast but the drizzle had stopped. I leaned out past the bridge coaming. Without protection of the baffles the wind across the deck beat and screamed with gale force. At thirty-seven knots her stem sliced like a flensing knife through blubber, great white curls peeling away to merge with the boiling arc of the wake.

Yanov had joined me. I pulled my head back. "Magnificent."

"At a price. We're throwing out a hundred thousand BTU's with every belch. An airborne Hot Box heat seeker could home in on us from Moscow." He walked back to the Command. "And probably will. Galich's at the door."

I went to let in the bosun. There wasn't room for both of us in the passage. "How are things below?"

He rumbled a laugh through the black bush on his face. "All lambs, Comrade." For the slaughter?

Yanov talked while the bosun got his night vision. "When I'm in Ops, keep her straight and level on automatic. The radar scan's at a hundred miles. That's Kolkasrags on the port bow." He jabbed a grease pencil at a spot twenty miles farther to the northwest. "The turning point. Keep your eyes peeled—and shout if you need me. We'll have company soon."

I stared at the stark words on the printer.

"Storozhevoy at sea mutiny."

Brodsky's message. The fulfillment of a prophecy. Marshall listening in the cellar at the end of the Swedes' satellite relay must be breathing hard.

Yanov sat at the keyboard.

The machine waited.

Waited to receive the characters and encode them and sort them into groups and send them to the world. Yanov switched off the encryption line. Secrecy was the last thing we now required. He began to peck at the machine with two fingers.

"Your piano playing hasn't helped your typing."

"No." But he couldn't manage a smile. With his name hanging out there I couldn't blame him.

To: Fleet headquarters, Baltisk
From: *Storozhevoy*. Time: 0243
1. At sea, proceeding independently to Gotland, A.I. Yanov in command.
2. SSN system operational, armed with Mark Nine (N) warheads. Designated targets one through nine, Baltic Grid, Southwest.
3. If attacked, after receipt of this message, weapon will be activated.
4. Civilian dependents now enroute to board *Dostoyny* in Riga are to be embarked and to confirm by voice on Primary Tactical net.
5. Dependents are to be transferred when ships in Swedish waters.
6. Acknowledge.

Message Ends.

We looked at each other wordlessly. What was there to say? The Ratt was chattering back to us.

To: *Storozhevoy*.
From: Fleet Headquarters Baltisk. Time: 0248
Your 0243 acknowledged. Duty Officer urges you allow time for relays to appropriate authorities. Stop.

"Good boy," said Yanov. "One small cog using his head. Let's hope he's not alone."

CHAPTER

THIRTY-TWO

On the main display plot the land stood still: *Storozhevoy* appeared to move. Looking down, her plotting symbol with its outward sweeping circle of the radar was a storm viewed from a great height—a hurricane, moving, like our destinies, from unobserved beginnings along an immutable track. In the early stages, straight, predictable, feeding only on itself and empty spaces. Waiting for the unknown mixture of forces and effects which would make it turn, become suddenly capricious, veering, violent—smashing out at trade routes, islands, men and women.

And as it must be, the eye of the storm where I sat with Yanov was tranquil, motionless, waiting for the turn. Waiting for an old man with hawk's eyes to think of his example.

"Petya, does she know?"

Alexey was looking at the photograph. "She knows we're trying. I felt I should—"

He sensed the hesitation. "No, don't worry about it. That's good, I'm glad you did. Meeting will be difficult enough. How in God's name do I begin?"

"Take them all to a Japanese restaurant."

"You think I don't know that at seven it's only hamburgers in America?"

I laughed with him. "You won't have trouble understanding, Alyosha. Fitting in."

"Not for want of imagination, certainly. You should have seen me"—an embarrassed smile—"I could have been arrested. So much time looking at kids in the parks. Wondering are they that big now? Having a birthday like that group at the swings? Do they like music; can they swim?"

"What do they look like?"

He shook his head. "One just assumes they'll be miniature versions of ourselves. Such egotism. Of course they're not. The eyes perhaps, in Lenya—but look at the hair on that boy!"

"I thought you'd—"

"Captain. It's Galich. *Dostoyny*'s transmitting."

The click of a switch shattered the calm.

"Riga Tower, this is 507. Radio check. Over."

"This is Riga Tower; 507, your signal strength one, clarity one."

The Ratt threw up a sudden gush of characters. The message traffic was building too quickly for Primary to handle. The second machine cut in to assist. Sortie information from Riga Tower, mobilization of the patrol squadron at Ventspils, requests for clarification from Baltisk. Nothing to us.

"Pontoon Bridge Control, this is 507."

Silence.

"Bridge Control, Bridge Control, this is 507, 507."

Yanov grinned tightly. "Ledvidev's going to have to swing the span himself."

"Riga Tower, this is 507. Have shore authority contact. Pontoon Bridge Control directly. We are ready to proceed—"

"That bridge operator's headed for a mine holiday," I said.

"He won't be alone by morning."

"Are you going to raise *Dostoyny* directly to confirm the embarkation?"

He shook his head. "I'm just going to run like hell—"

"Riga Tower, this is *Dostoyny*—" An embarrassed pause for the error of the name; "Correction. This is 507. Send tug. In collision with center abutment. Damage minor. We cannot turn in the current. Over."

"Hopeless bastard." Yanov was disgusted. "Ledvidev's forgotten what settings he's applied to the variable pitch—" He stopped, looked at the teletype.

"What is it?"

"The next step. Fleet H.Q."

Personal from Baltic Fleet Commander:
To: A.I. Yanov. Time: 0317.
Halt while there is still time, and before any injuries to personnel.
Civilians embarked. Higher authority will negotiate.

[Signed] V.V. Mikhalin
Admiral.

"You know him?" I asked.

"OIC Leningrad District when I was at Viborg. Experiencing acute pain in his backside now."

"Captain, it's Galich. Five hundred meters to wheel over, sir."

"Coming up. Tell them down below."

In the greater darkness of the command position Kolkasrags was a bright green hook pointing the way home. Galich had the broadcast mike. "*Attention. Attention. Altering course to port.*"

"Hold it for another two hundred," said Yanov. "Course 250. . . . Keep to starboard of the channel. I've marked the mine limits on the plotting head. Stand by, stand by. . . . *Now!*"

The deck fell away.

A parallel ruler hurtled off the chart table, slamming into the starboard bulkhead. A pair of dividers stabbed the deck. I grabbed for support. The white sweep of the bow wave looked underfoot.

Then the forces changed, the deck leveled, the bottom dropped out on the other side, and we were steady on the new course.

"Ten degrees of rudder, Comrade," said Galich through the bush.

"Christ Jesus! What happens with full helm?"

"You'll see," said Yanov. "Right, Bosun, the channel's clear of traffic."

A single light away to the north on Veiserahu Bank was the only break in the blackness. The thought, not allowed to breathe, tried to stir.

"Captain sir, we're getting a bit of set to port."

"Steer two five three."

"Two five three."

I made the adjustment on the chart. Checked the time—0350. The lowest part of the night. I couldn't remember what the bunk in *Sailfin* looked like. Yanov yawned.

Intuition got him over to the radar.

"Galich. *Action stations!* I'll man the missile director."

On the Ops Room console for the Sam 4 the echo was closing fast. Yanov wrenched up the volume control, but any speech on the Air Net was still drowned out by the clamor of the Action gong. An empty gesture; where were the hands to man the stations? The clanging died away.

"Warship *Storozhevoy*, this is Saaremaa Reconnaissance One One. Take your way off and illuminate. Over."

"One, One, this is *Storozhevoy*. Negative. Report authority. Authenticate."

"This is One One. Authority Saaremaa Field Command. Authentication Three K Seven. Take off your way."

"This is *Storozhevoy*. Negative. Hold your position and obtain Fleet Command authority. Over."

Nothing.

"One One, this is *Storozhevoy*. I say again, wait for higher authority. If you penetrate my danger zone I shall fire. I say again, I shall fire. Over."

The air net crackled. Range down to eighteen miles, still closing. Speed, five hundred knots. Yanov pointed to a small box at my right. "Radar ID, set it to Friendly Forces. Let's see what type of idiot we're up against."

One wide-arcing splash of echo, three narrow and another wide, swept the face of the display with every rotation of the antenna. Yanov glanced at it. "Il-28!"

Ilyushin light jet bomber of the naval air force, out for blood and glory. Range now twelve miles and turning away slightly.

"Taking up his launch posture," said Yanov.

"Can we evade?"

"Too restricted. It only helps the odds by five percent. Fire Control—are you there, Gunner?"

"Aye sir."

"Take starboard arcs under local control from your position. I'll take port from remote."

"Aye sir. What authority to fire?"

"If he closes to eight thousand. It might scare the bastard into going around the ring once more."

The aircraft, designated on the blue face of the tube by a half moon, was circling us like a wolf with a snow-trapped deer, each circle inexorably spiraling closer. Two other blue half moons, controlled by the Gunner and Yanov, circled with the plane but inside it, at the firing range of four miles. The computer waited patiently for a full moon.

"Nine thousand—stand by."

The moons collided.

"Firing now!"

The ship gave a slight lurch to port. The moon slid off the target. "He's evading, Gunner—range opening."

The aircraft drew back to seven miles and resumed his circling, looking for another chance at the hamstrings.

"He'll come in flat on the deck next time, Gunner. If he starts to close again, depress the height finder and go into horizontal search."

The teletype clattered. "Probably Ledvidev," I said, "to tell us he's stuck under the bridge."

"No." Yanov was pointing a finger at the typewriter. "Further east."

From: Defense Headquarters. Time 0410 . . .
To: S. . . .

The characters rambled crazily. The machine went into an electronic equivalent of "the quick brown fox" to search for signal failure.

We waited. For an old man sitting in the dark on the edge of his bed in his dacha on the island of Serebryanyi Bor in the Moskva. An old man becoming an admiral, making decisions, squashing the hysterics of the regional commander, Mikhalin; placing the call to the leader of the workers and peasants, heir to Lenin's dreams: Leonid Brezhnev.

Calling his Kremlin apartment? The dacha at Usova?

"Where will Brezhnev be?"

"What?" Yanov was surprised. "Duck hunting, I imagine, at his lodge at Zavidovo."

Why not? Each according to his need. Somewhere to drive the Eldorados and the Rolls.

Two words to toss the bomb into the naval lap. And now a journey by an admiral with his thoughts through the dark night and the deserted streets of Moscow. Asking himself in the empty four-lane width of the Novo Khoroshevskaye Shossey, *will Yanov launch?*

Turning into 1905 Ulitza. Answering, *no.* Comforted by the assessment, passing the sleeping zoo, crossing the black wet desert of the Vostaniya Ploschad. Jarred by the white sleeves of the traffic police: A spectral intimation of death . . . *but he might.*

Into the first big ring of the web, Chaikovskaya Ulitza. *Of all men, why Yanov?* On to the next, the Suvorovskiy Boulevard, the line of the second city wall, now gardens between the ribbons of road. *What possible reason for such risks?*

The woman!

Past the Vladimir Mayakovskova Theatre and the Chaikovskiy Concert Hall and into the Prospekt Marxa as on every day of every week of every one of the twenty years.

Beside the old tsarist Riding Academy. *Desperate, then. A man in love. Insane—but God in heaven, how much better a ship on a darkened sea, flat out, than a slow unwinding into age and decay in a state home for old warriors.*

The final turn, the Manytzaanaya Ulitza, the last and inner wall. Past the southwest gate of Dravin's father, through which, tomorrow—today—the postmortems would begin.

Stopped.

Outside the glass doors on the Frunze Ulitza beside the paper windows, and a car door slamming on a godfather—thirty years an admiral—forceful, ruthless. But, stumping slowly, heavily, up the steps, mortal. Like Yanov. And like Yanov, the decision must be reached, held to. *And if twelve arms are severed, or a hundred, or a thousand. . . .*

The attendant would be saluting, hobbling to the doors to let the master in. When he let him out, where would the sleeping world, or Peter Dravin, or Alexey Yanov and his children, be?

"Captain sir"—from Galich. "He's illuminating."

The bridge as bright as the aircraft cabin over Moscow. Harsh sodium yellow jaundiced our faces. *"The sun was shining on the sea"* .... A sensation of running naked across a football stadium.

"The whoremonger's fired, sir."

"I see that, Gunner. I'm going to the bridge. Stand by!"

I stayed alone with the machines; it was a machine's war after all. The plane's radar echo was slipping rapidly past us, already outside his effective range. But a smaller blip, questing like one of the hunting dogs on the estate at Zavidovo, sniffed left, sniffed right. Zigged and zagged.

"Echo's merged, sir!"

My fingernails tried to dig through the aluminum sides of the console.

"Thank you, Gunner." Yanov's voice was calm, appreciative.

"God help the engineer!" I said to the machines.

"A *miss!* The bastard *missed!*" Maximov's voice was ecstatic.

The teletype, given a new life as well, beside me, now printed swiftly, eager to make amends.

From: Defense Headquarters. Time: 0415

To: Saaremaa Station.

Break off all engagements. Station Commander report personally on land line to C in C.

[Signed] Gorshkov.

Gorshkov!

From my silver tea-glass holder, the circle of the seance now complete.

"He's launched another one, sir, from three miles. I'm firing now." Again the gentle push to port.

But this time I knew, too late except for revenge. Sniff, turn. Sniff, turn—the incoming blip inexorable. Sniff, sniff, sniff, sniff.

Yanov on the bridge, through the door. "Galich, he has lock on! *Hard a-starboard!*"

"Aye sir," rock solid.

Holding full strength to the console handles. Books and charts and pencils flying through the air like missiles. And the missile flying straight—no sniff, no turn. Straight as a poisoned arrow down the starboard after funnel.

God could no longer help the engineer.

Tired of sniffing, the nose exploded into the engine room in a million fragments. One for Harijs who had got us to sea, and one for the blades of each of his turbines—numbers One, Three, and Five. The excitement when those lights had changed to green so long ago.

And now all red.

"Captain!"—jubilation in Galich's voice—"we got the son of a bitch!"

But of course too late.

The identification pattern on the scope went first, the blips of the transponder fading from the trace like the wings of a falling angel. And then the main echo melting and dropping with a gung-ho pilot trying so hard for his crew.

On the bridge, the smell of smoke was already coming from the ventilator. "Gunner, get aft and check the damage in the vicinity of the SSN mounting."

"Das!"

The buzzer was ringing from Damage Control. For no reason I remembered the doctor on the night my father died.

"Captain speaking."

"Sinyavsky here. Fire in the funnel and in the forward engine room—we've flooded the space with CO_2 and it'll be out shortly. The engineer is dead and two men seriously injured. Radio Two was damaged, and the secondary HF transmitter has gone. We don't know yet what damage has been sustained by the four forward engines."

"We do. We've lost three of them."

Only a groan from the intercom.

"We can still make good fifteen knots, Vasily Georgeyvich. Our lead should be sufficient. I'll give a situation report to the troops."

Yanov released the switch, slumped into a seat beside the chart table, drained himself by the reaction to the attack. "Bosun, can you find us some more coffee—perhaps a bite to eat?"

"Yes sir. Are you all right?"

"Just a little middle-watch depression. I'll be fine."

I showed him the message. "From the Red Knight's former master."

"So he's on the board. Good." He squared his shoulders and stood up. "Good. At least no more moves without a purpose."

CHAPTER

THIRTY-THREE

Once again the eye was calm: The dead plane replaced by two Bear reconnaissance aircraft circling at thirty miles. No more dives under the belly. The Bears, like vultures, wanted signs of certain death before approaching the carcass. Yanov watched the computer readouts showing their predicted movement. "Well, Navigator, when's first light and where do we make our rendezvous?"

With the light at Ovisi already flashing from the mouth of the Straits, the red line marking *Sailfin*'s limitation was so close that it was painful to look at the chart. I stepped off distances with the dividers. "If they don't use the aircraft, gun range at 0800. Thirty miles east of Gotland and halfway down."

"Gun range." He moved the acquisition hooks on the Director Console in a random pattern with the joystick. "Petya, if some of the eggs get smashed—"

"Crap, Alyosha. We'll all go together. Arm in arm down the plank."

"I know. You hide these things. But I just want to say that if it couldn't be myself—all these years, for Nicolasha and the children—" He held out his hand. "Well, no other man in this world for them, Petya. I mean that."

I looked away. Turned pages in the almanac, scribbled calculations. "First light's at 0710," I said.

"I mean it, Petya!"

Sinyavsky's voice came on the intercom. "I've brought your coffee."

"Thanks. Enter."

"The door's locked."

We grinned ruefully at each other. "Time for more fresh air," I said. "I'll let him in."

If we were feeling a little worn, Sinyavsky was a gray study in exhaustion. Yanov tried to keep morale on an even keel by being hearty. "How's life below decks, Vasily Georgeyvich?"

"Nearly normal. The starboard flats are sealed off around the damage. The sprinklers activated in Three Magazine, but that's under control." His thoughts were with his flock. "Our people?"

"Nothing yet. The rendezvous will be at eight."

"You'll call me when you have word?"

"Of course." Yanov's eyes flicked again at the clock.

"Six-thirty," I said. "He'll be enjoying breakfast."

"He hates it. On bad days he tries a little oatmeal."

"Doubles today, then."

Yanov smiled briefly and went back to his brooding. Sinyavsky left. I imagined the face at the desk pecking at the porridge, eyes blinking slowly, weighing consequences much the same whether or not the stray was caught.

Tribunals, transfers of command, demotions, premature retirements. Dispatch of tugs and coastguard vessels. Dispersal of infected crews and communications staffs—allocation of repair facilities. Rules for executions.

Funerals.

The atheist state that paid such homage to the life everlasting. If he was standing at the window now, the relief contingent for the guard at the tomb would be goose-stepping along beside the wall below him. Black prints in the snow behind, black shadows from the spotlights on the mausoleum ahead. Shades of a cat-face watching the slogans in the square. The lights would still be dominant, but by now a fraction faded, as eastward, across the river, a pale gray line brought daybreak to Moscow. And morning twilight at sea.

* * *

Now eleven vultures circled, flicking electronic glances to confirm our condition. "Airforce Bisons," said Yanov. Jackson's interservice rivalry.

On surface radar, *Dostoyny* and her trio of patrol craft had closed to fifteen miles. Another echo showed intermittently at 158 degrees, thirty miles.

"The OSA's?"

He nodded. "You can hear them chattering on the net. They've had a breakdown—as usual."

"Captain"—Galich confirmed evidence of life on the Bridge. "First light astern, sir—a real flamer. There'll be a front coming up behind it."

"We'll be ashore by then, Bosun. How are you managing after your night's rest?"

The intercom gave a short laugh. "A daisy, sir."

I went up to see the sunrise. Moscow ablaze. *Or red sky in the morning, sailor take warning....*

Yanov met me as I re-entered the Command position. "Tell Sinyavsky I'm going to raise them now."

The squabbling OSA's were drowned out by our stronger signal. "*Dostoyny*, *Dostoyny*, this is *Storozhevoy*, *Storozhevoy*. Over."

"This is *Storozh*—wait."

"Someone's still suffering," I said.

"*Storozhevoy*, this is *Dostoyny*. Send your message. Over."

"This is *Storozhevoy*. A.I. Yanov speaking. Put civilian Henrijs on this net. Over."

A long pause. "*Dostoyny*, did you receive my last transmission? Over."

Another pause, then a reluctant voice. "This is *Dostoyny*. Affirmative. Wait, out."

Sinyavsky was back at the door. "Well?"

"Waiting," I said. "She's calling home."

The teletype was still rattling.

From: *Dostoyny*
To: Fleet H.Q. Time: 0712
Commander, *Storozhevoy* wishes to speak to dissident, Henrijs,

on voice tactical. Request instructions.

Reaction time all the way up was decreasing.

From: Fleet Headquarters Baltisk. Relay from C in C.
To: *Dostoyny*. Time: 0714
1. Comply.
2. Assemble all dissidents in officers' cabin flats.
3. No, repeat no, weapons systems to be engaged.
                                        [Signed] V.V. Mikhalin
                                                        Admiral

Yanov paid no attention.

"Range, Petya?"

"Twelve miles. She should be visible any minute."

The voice net crackled, "*Storozhevoy*, this is *Dostoyny*. Stand by." Sinyavsky stared like a mouse at a cat. A double click. "Kapitan Yanov." The first voice I'd heard on the beach. "This is Henrijs." *No coercion.* Sinyavsky closed his eyes.

"This is Yanov. How is it with you and your party? Over."

"All are well, sir. One or two a little seasick and the children tired, but nothing more. The authorities have been questioning us at length throughout the night, naturally. Over."

Naturally. Yanov handed the phone to Sinyavsky.

"Jans, this is Valda. Tell the people to be of good heart. All will be done in ninety minutes. Call us every five. Out." The receiver was clutched against his chest as though he could transmit life with speech across the ether.

"Captain, sir"—Galich was excited—"echo on scanner. Dead ahead. Eight thousand meters."

I watched the leading edge of the sound wave travel out on its expanding circle.

Splash. A vivid splash of white light on the amber scope, arc twenty degrees. But no ping.

"It could be fish," I said.

Yanov reached over. "And it could help to turn up the volume."

Another circle. Out to six thousand. Past it. Echo narrowed to ten degrees. *Pinguh!*

"Submarine!"

And a way out.

"Captain, sir, I can see *Dostoyny*."

CHAPTER

THIRTY-FOUR

Clearly, five miles astern, and throwing off a huge bow wave. The tiny dots of the Patrol Craft were farther back, white chips of foam in their teeth. A raw day but calm, the sea nearly flat. I swung the glasses forward, westward. A smudge, like a larger wave, appeared and vanished. I rested my elbows on the ledge to steady the lens.

"Alyosha," I pointed. "*Sweden!* And a clearing sky for luck."

Yanov, pacing the cage of the bridge, scarcely looked. His mind was in Moscow.

Mine was in the submarine. She still showed intermittently on the scanner, but the range had steadied, so she had increased speed to travel with us. Galich searched diligently for a periscope.

"Alexey—" Yanov stopped his pacing. "Where's the underwater telephone?" He crossed to the forward bulkhead and threw a switch. The hollow sound of a sea shell came thinly from a small speaker. I picked up the mike.

"Arrow Root, Arrow Root, this is *Storozhevoy, Storozhevoy*. Over." I watched the echo of the main sonar travel out, taking the call signs with it. The same long interval to return. Nothing. I repeated. Waited.

"Stor...ozhe...voy..." A deep, dragging voice from the depths. "Thiis...iiis...Aaroooow Roooot..."

"Thiis is *Storozhevoy*. Dravin speaking. Good morning. Over."

"This iis Aaroow Rooot Comaander....Coffeee's on....Over."

"*Storozhevoy*. Keep it hot. Out."

Childish. But totally exhilarating. On the bridge Galich was being assisted in his search by the young ensign, Turchin. His cooperation had grown inversely as the shrinking distance to freedom.

It was Turchin who observed the movement on radar.

"Captain sir. One of the aircraft seems to be closing."

Yanov jammed his head in the rubber hood blocking daylight from the console face. He grabbed a mike.

"Gunner, stand by!"

A sudden loud hum as the forward mounting trained to starboard.

"Fire Control. Ready in Local."

"Captain sir," Turchin again. "The echo's swinging away, sir."

I traced small arcs with the glasses, starting on the horizon, working upward at five-degree increments. I had *Dostoyny*. Close enough to read her hull number. Off on her starboard quarter, a speck like dirt on the lens, hanging in apogee, immobile at this distance, then beginning to move. Slowly at first, like a sled on a run, gaining momentum as it came down from the top of the turn. Swooping faster and faster.

"Got him!" said Yanov. "MiG-21. Air Force."

Flat across the deck at head height. A flash from red-starred wings.

"He's firing, sir! Rockets."

"The bastard must be mad."

"A complete miss, sir!" The line of white splashes was unmistakable.

"What's happening?" Sinyavsky, unbearably strained, had arrived at my elbow.

"A cowboy shooting up the water for excitement. He's got the wrong ship."

The plane swept up in a bank to port and disappeared into the low cloud.

"Aircraft out of sight, sir."

"Watch him on radar. Call the range."

"Ten miles, sir. Ten point one. Point eight, point eight. Range decreasing. Ten . . ."

Galich: "Got him, sir. Dropping down at thirty degrees on the port quarter."

I caught him again in the glasses. The same firing run as before, but from the opposite side.

"He's still on the wrong target!"

Another ripple of white splashes. "Mother of God!" from the bosun. A flash of yellow flame. Three flashes. "The bastard's hit her. On the fo'c'sle, sir, just forward of the launcher."

Sinyavsky, distraught: "Why doesn't Ledvidev blast the son of a bitch?"

"He can't," Yanov said tersely. "Fleet H.Q.'s last message—no return fire—"

"Captain sir"—Turchin emerged at the head of the Ops Room steps, a blinking mole. "A signal from the Fleet Admiral himself, sir."

Yanov held out a hand.

"Captain sir, submarine on the surface. Dead ahead, three miles."

"Captain sir, aircraft coming around again."

Yanov, watching, ignoring the message burning his palm. "Gunner, if that contact closes inside eight thousand, engage."

"Aye sir."

"Yanov," Sinyavsky's voice stretched high. *"The message?"*

Yanov thrust it at me. "Read it aloud."

From: Defense Headquarters, Time: 0733
To: *Storozhevoy.*
Information to: *Dostoyny:* MP Squadron Riga:

MP Squadron Ventspils:

Fleet Headquarters Baltisk—"

The list of addressees lengthened, giving notice, exemplary. Indelible in print.

"Unless you halt, the next firing run will be at *Dostoyny*'s forward superstructure.

[Signed] Gorshkov."

And the pressure building on Yanov.

"Captain sir, the submarine is closing."

"Petya. *Why?* Why the superstructure? Why the wrong ship?"

"Submarine stopped, sir."

"I see it." His head turned automatically. "Why, Petya?"

But he knew. As Jackson had known.

"It's not wrong, Alyosha." There was activity on *Sailfin*'s bridge.

"The civilians—" His impassive face, his face for the dead. "Of course."

"In the cabin flat—" Sinyavsky was falling apart. *"God protect them!"*

"And *Dostoyny*," I said. "Gorshkov can't limit the damage to the cabin flat. And doesn't mean to. That's why he's broadcast his intentions."

"Aircraft on his next run, sir."

Standing in the hurricane's eye, we watched as though it were an exercise with practice ammunition at a dummy. Measuring the nicety of the pilot's technique. Out of the bank, correct to starboard—slight wobble—a touch back to port. Red stars catching morning sunrise. Wing dipping, steady, nice approach. On course, no wind. Computer check for ship's speed across the sights. Stand by.

The slight recoil on the wings as the rockets left, the shudder in the destroyers' bridge as they exploded. Not yellow now. White, like a platinum scalpel. Completed firing run. Pull back, smoothly— smoothly. And up we go.

"Three hits!"

Flame around the bridge, smoke pouring out.

"Kapitan Yanov, *This is Jan Kristin Henrijs*..."

Sinyavsky threw up.

Yanov, glued to the binoculars, put a hand out blindly for the receiver.

"Yanov. Over."

"Sir, I am being urged to tell you that we have three dead."

Urged, How urged? A Lubyanka urging? A smell, a stain. *"Regards to your mother."*

Sinyavsky grabbed his sleeve. "Yanov—no more. *No more!*"

Alexey shook him off. "Fire Control, Bridge. Prepare SSN, starboard outer missile. Target Assignment One."

"God of Moses! *Yanov*—" Sinyavsky's face was ashen, his hands imploring claws.

We were at a gate. As clearly as when I saw him standing behind the wicker frame beneath the ravens. But beyond this one lay events and consequences locked away since Hiroshima.

"Alexey, *how close?*"

"Into check," he said. "Turchin, take a message."

The Ensign, goggle-eyed, was watching the SSN launcher rising slowly behind the funnel, training due southeast. To Latvia.

"Turchin!"

Gulping, "Sir."

"From: *Storozhevoy*.
To: Commander in Chief.
SSN will be launched at Ventspils unless attacks halted."

"Time?"

"Zero seven four zero, sir."

"Unless attacks halted 0745. Acknowledge.
[Signed]A. I. Yanov."

"Send it. In the clear."

"Das!"

Red knight check.

"Captain sir," Galich, perfect seaman, attentive to his duty: "The submarine's launching a rubber boat."

"*Stor*...*ozh*...*voy*"—the voice from the sea—"thiis...iiis...Aaroow...Rooot...Coomaander."

"Dravin speaking." The delay in answers was interminable. In the waiting, conversations mixed crazily around me.

"Captain sir. Aircraft making his next run."

"Time 0743, sir."

"Bridge, Ivanov speaking. I have the Captain's tea."

"Captain, sir. The submarine is diving."

The first part of the message was cut off. "...Coomaander ...ordered...detach...Ooveeer."

"Boat on the starboard side, sir."

Hidden from *Dostoyny* and the aircraft; Jacowzki squatted black-suited in the stern.

A second decision from the football team. No room for another ship of fools, another Pueblo. The blast of new explosions came clear and crisp across the water—*crump crump crump*. Death in the Baltic and Nikita's chicken shit elsewhere.

But not in Moscow. The radio again: "I am urged to tell you—" What this time? Fifteen dead?

"Arrow Root Commander, this is Dravin. I understand. Thank you for the boat."

Galich's simple loyalty was out of its depth. His eyebrows, black as Brezhnev's, rose in perplexity. "They're going to sink them, sir? And then us?"

Yanov didn't hear. "Yes, Bosun," I said. "Then us."

From Jaring an underwater wave of farewell. ". . . Soorry . . . goood luck . . . God speed . . ."

God speed.

"Is the message acknowledged, Turchin?"

"Yes sir."

"Alexey. *Close enough!*"

"He'll stop. Time, Turchin?"

"Zero seven four four, sir."

"Fire Control, this is the Captain. Firing sequence less sixty seconds."

"Aye sir."

Armageddon minus sixty.

"Turchin, signal it."

"Captain sir, your tea." Ivanov. Standing with a glass in a silver holder. So they were given out like presidential pens. *"What you call in the West good advertising, eh?"*

Galich and I exchanged glances of sanity. He opened his mouth to say something, but a shadow darted in front of him. "Fire Control!"—Sinyavsky had the mike—"this is the Bridge. Cancel—"

Yanov, standing on the edge of the bridge wing, back to the bow, glassed locked on *Dostoyny*, knocked him to the deck without even turning inboard.

"*Steady, Fire Control!* Time, Turchin?" Picking up the tea glass without thinking.

"Thirty seconds sir," quivering.

"*Alexey! NO!*"

"Sent it, Turchin."

At the gate.

Gorshkov had been wrong. He couldn't hold it shut. Jackson was right. Duty must be done. For wives, kids, admirals. My finger slipped through the trigger guard of the Browning.

"Time, Turchin?"

Time. Having his irrevocably final little joke as Dravin shoots his friend. In the back.

Unless?

Galich had raised a massive hand above the helm control. Was setting the rate of turn switch to maximum. Was looking at me, at Yanov's back, at Jacowzki waving alongside.

Yanov had passed through the gate ahead of us. "Turchin, send 'Firing now.' Fire Control—"

"*Yes, Bosun!*"

The fist swept down across the helm to starboard and the deck was gone beneath us.

An impression of Alexey grabbing at the rail, tea glass dropping from his fingers, *"Gone," said Khrushchev, "just like that,"* and my shoulder smashing with a searing twist to take him with it. And then over the edge and falling down and down, past a bright blue warhead and a yellow dinghy and a churning, red-tipped screw.

Falling with shattered glass and battered silver into the gray November water of the Baltic.

OSTERGARN.

CHAPTER

THIRTY-FIVE

It was unbelievably cold.

Stunned, the brain in crisis locked out consequences, random thoughts. Closed down the branch plants. Dragged blood and vital heat home to the animal center. *"Evening news, old boy."* Smashed shoulders, throbbing chop of threshing screws ignored for air. *Do lungs burst under pressure?* Air. Throbbing of blood, throbbing of screws.... *Die without air, old boy....Yanov could jump like your father. Relax, old boy.* Relax and surface.... *Surface!*

Air! Gasps, heaves, gulps of air. Laughing spitting breathing air.

"Good trip, Comrade?" A joke from a comrade. Jacowzki, Comrade Cox'n. Pipe me aboard, Cox'n. Piping a flopping fish, hilarious.

"Too brief. Yanov—he could have jumped at any time, you know."

"Your buddy?" Jacowzki, under enormous stress, was only half-hearing Dravin's ramblings. Already the throttles hurtled us ahead. "Out like a light. Lucky his life jacket inflated."

I was recovering.

Given endless time for recovery in the trip back around the

circle into the boiled wake, until we stopped with the tossing blue jacket alongside. Inert. Head washed by the waves. No joke.

"Be alive, Yanov; Christ, be alive." Dragging him in, he was dead weight. *Not dead, God!* Tear open the jacket throat to check the heart. Beat. Beat!

Beating.

"Jesus!" Jacowzki tore the throttle cables half out of the engine housings. *Storozhevoy*, whistle jammed and shrieking, a pyramid mass of superstructure still heeled hard over to block the sky, was back upon us. "Ship's side! *Watch the ship's side!*"

Jagged metal curled down to rip our guts out. Desperately I fended off. We began to move. But too fast! *"We'll go under!"* Full power was smashing us down into the troughs of the old wake. The boat half-filled with water.

Yanov's eyes had opened, were looking up.

Up past the anti-submarine mortars, up past the air missiles, up past the giant tubes of the SSN, our extinguished lamp. Up past directors, radars, antennae countless in number, stuck on like barnacles on barnacles. Up—almost to the top. And Sinyavsky. *Spider*. Trapped behind a web of wires.

Yanov's eyes closed.

"Jump!"

My shout was lost in the scream of the siren. Wasted, too; the good shepherd leads his flock, not leaves it. Was his hand saluting? Going down with the ship? One of the old traditions which needs no explanation? I saluted back—and meant it. For the faces in the cellar.

The siren stopped.

A thin crack like a snapped lifeline broke the salute. The gun fell from Sinyavsky's hand; the small blackbird body slumped, toppled over, and slipped down into the arms of an eternal father.

But I was alive. And Yanov was alive. Out of Russia and away from an admiral. I bailed like a madman until the speed and the bow rose, and the outboards were skimming us across the swell like a thirty-knot rock in a game of ducks and drakes.

"Someone get carried away?" Jacowzki pointed back at the ship.

"Too nearly," I said. But he meant the damage.

Storozhevoy's after starboard funnel had been split like a can stuffed with firecrackers from the top down past the weather deck to five feet above the water line. I thought of the engineer. Superstructure, mountings, boats and rafts had been fused into a coffin amalgam of aluminum, steel and plastic.

Astern, under a red star and pouring smoke, smashing from history and memory at forty knots—*Dostoyny*. Savaged by her own masters, avenging by example. Inexorable, invincible. Horrible.

And closing.

"Cross the bow, Cox'n, block her out." Gain five minutes' grace, a mile. Two. Before she emerged on the opposite quarter.

"Bad guys are quitting, Boss."

Walls of water at the bows subsided. Mist and steam dropped in a quilt on the two ships. The *Komars* hurried up and sniffed around the edges.

"If those little buggers see us we're in for a run."

But they were satisfied with the catch and not looking. An aircraft made a single banking pass to the east and then we were alone.

Sweden, eighteen miles.

"Medical kit, Cox'n?"

"Under the seat. With some brandy."

I snapped a vial of smelling salts. Yanov shook his head, dragged himself into a more upright position leaning into the vee of the bow, rubbed both hands over his face and through his hair, shook himself again.

"How do you feel?"

He ignored the stupid question. Just stared behind us at the retreating ghosts from his parade, stared into a thin mist falling and rolling between us and his ship, *Storozhevoy*. A name, a word, which has so many meanings.

Stared until there was nothing left to stare at, but gray sea meeting gray sky, and no gray ship between.

The motor coughed. "First tank dry," said Jacowzki. "Switch valves."

I bent forward. A scrap of blackened wood floated in the slop on the bottom. The piano charm. As I reached for it a shrill high

whistle jerked me upright. Yanov was pointing silently to starboard.

Swans.

Led by a magnificent old male with an eight-foot wing span,
flying in a lopsided vee from the northeast. From Finland.

I passed him the charm. "A second omen, Alyosha."

He held it for a long moment, turning it over in his hand.
"No"—thrusting it impulsively at me. "Fortune enough that I'm
here. Yours now, Petya. Let it work for you."

"Superstitious crap, Yanov." But I took it, and tied a new knot
in the lanyard and hung the damned thing around my neck.

He held up the first-aid brandy, grinned. "Drink to it."

So we did, and sang stupid songs and laughed like hell about
names like Face Hole and Hirohito the prick head until even
Jacowzki smiled and the black band on the Ostergarn light was
clearly visible and it was time to sober up.

A mile and a half more to the main island, Gotland, and our
destination—the village of Herrvik, an old fortress. Now a haven
for fishermen, with a customs post, a tiny harbor behind a breakwater. And if Selbach had drawn his mortgage documents cor-
rectly, Erik Lindahl would be on hand to grant us our asylum.

Yanov had the glasses. "Someone's there, by the boats."

I saw them too. Figures at a distance. Blobs of color.

I suppose I began to know then—because of the colors. Because
of the soft green of a dress on a hillside in San Francisco and the
gold of flowers reflecting a shaft of northern sunlight striking at
the beach. Because of her past behavior in arriving early.

He realized what he was looking at. "You arranged—?"

I shook my head. Five hundred yards. Four. Our departure
from Riga in reverse. The engines died, cut back. The screaming
whine dropped to a murmur as we passed into the lee of the
breakwater, gliding the last hundred feet. Eyes only for the slim
figure walking tentatively down the ramp, pausing, walking.
Shoes wet now, but like us not noticing surroundings. Just a
woman standing with her bouquet of flowers.

Yanov over the side, to his knees, wading ashore. *"I shall
return."* Putting out a first hand diffidently, wearing a tight, tight
grin.

She, watching him. Waiting. Biting her lip.

"Nicolasha."

The flowers were squashed between them.

I helped Jacowzki with the boat on the cobble blocks. I was bushed. Stiff and tired in the aftermath. Senses dulled from overload. A smell of fish from the nets.

On the beach the lid was already off. They were laughing, hugging, waving at me. Yanov shouted, "Petya. Stupid bastard, get up here."

From her, a brilliant smile through tears. "Okay on landfall, Petya. Remember?"

"I remember, Niki." I *remember*.

"Come on, man!" Yanov pounded me generously on the back. "A proper kiss; you're entitled."

I took it.

"Petya—for getting him—"

"Nothing, love." I patted her cheek. "Call it the wedding present. I'm just going to talk with Erik."

To give them another moment before the questions started, I walked on up the slope, shook hands, introduced Jacowzki: "The real hero." Asked Lindahl how she got here.

"It is not my doing. She arrived in Stockholm, quite unannounced, and said she would be at the finale either way. She is a remarkable woman." He looked down the ramp at Yanov. "But then, of course, she must be."

"Yes," I said. And at that moment it came home to me that the loan was due. That I must give her up. I walked on alone, to get a grip, to be able to cope.

I stood at the top of the ridge. In front of me on the landward side was a small lagoon. Shallow, showing mud at low tide. Even now at the flood only a few feet deep and cut off from the wind from the sea so that it was dark, mirror-still. A looking glass reflecting the ruined tower of a castle. And a swan.

In this private place, it looked at me. Looked from childhood on the Neva. From Takanen. From legend.

"Swan song Dravin . . . not a shred of truth. . . ."

But the wind changed. Again a smell of fish. And with it for the first time an absolutely certain Russian premonition of a scene about to happen.

But only the heightened senses of machines—Lindahl's tape and camera—can catch it now. Because the time in which it happened was machine time, computer time: the time of atoms. Time sliced down so small that a second held a million generations or instructions or events. Events which passed too quickly for a man to comprehend, let alone control. Too fast even to be felt until the camera freezes, the tape spills out. The run stops.

> *"O Oysters," said the Carpenter,*
> *"You've had a pleasant run!*
> *Shall we be trotting home again? . . ."*

"Dammit, Selbach!" Marshall bitches in the Briefing Room. "Bird's caught *something* all right. Just *look* at it!"

Look, Dravin, because closed eyes and pills won't keep it out; these images on screen are burned in memory forever. Yes, the bird knows now as its head-neck-throat flute outstretched upward in that first long trumpeting call ringing out across the water. Already its wings are beating, half in water, half in air; its black feet running ludicrously late along the surface. Trumpeting, trumpeting.

"Calling their names . . ."

"Names, old boy?"

Careful, Dravin, hold things in, we're nearly there. Nearly there. "Nothing, Marshall. I spotted the bastard here, I think."

Here at this point where the on-screen Dravin spins, jams the glasses to his eyes, points them into the red sun on the sea, sweeping it from side to side. Stops. Frozen like the film. Like the spot coming out of the sun so low that the red stars beneath its wings are salt-spray faded. So low that even the Swedes' one-centimetric radar on the hill above the castle can't tell that a lance hurled by an old Red Knight behind a Moscow wall is in the air.

"MiG 21!" Marshall has to raise his voice for the projector's hum.

But the swan is even louder, clearer, free of the water, scything air.

"Down! *FOR CHRIST'S SAKE DOWN!*"

My voice on the tape screaming. But legend or the wind off the sea blows my words away, and legend or a swan's wings beating above my head ensures that when the faces do turn they must be smiling; that Yanov must be pointing, saying, "Beautiful, Nicolasha. Beautiful."

"For us," she says.

Half a pace forward on the screen, my mouth open, my arms lifting to hold them both. But no sign from the machines that my guts twist in helpless fury against a pilot and his cannons, against his brutal country, against his master—an admiral. *My godfather!* An old man out to smash the looking glass so that it can never turn to let us through. To smash it and have his indelible example reflected in its fragments for all time. Russia and *Rodina*—lest we forget.

Yellow flashes from the aircraft wings. No sounds yet—too quick for that now—but Yanov's head has turned. A puff of sand . . . there! By his foot. By hers.

On tape, Dravin shouts again: this time they hear it. *"Grin, Yanov. GRIN!"*

So stupid.

"So British, Petya," I think she said. . . .

But Yanov's understood at once. A quick look out to sea. Back with a nod for me. His arms tighten around her and when she puts her head up to search his face, she sees a grin that was never broader, never stronger, never warmer. And she gives him back that marvelous smile.

Dravin staggers; is jolted backward by that twenty-millimeter shell that smashed the scrap of wood into the packet of oiled silk above my heart that saved my life. The scrap of wood I hold so closely now.

The on-screen Dravin still tries to get down to the ramp towards them, but he's crawling now and holding only one arm up and his jacket of navy quilting is sodden red. He croaks unclear, unrelated words. "Alyosha . . . hold her . . . landfall . . . hold her."

And an answer like my father's. Just two words.

The last yellow flashes from the wings. A line of rapid splashes cuts the sea, the rubber boat explodes, cobble chips spit. The golden flowers in her hands are ripped away, fall scarlet to ramp, slide down it.

"NIKI!"

Whose shriek was that in the Briefing Room?

"Christ!" From Marshall. "Both bought it." *A curious, tight voice for Marshall.* "Steady, Dravin. Steady, old boy."

The camera is on the aircraft and now there are no faces, only shadows as the fortune teller knew it must be for a union over water.

Something crosses the lens.

"Freeze," says Marshall. "Ah—the bird. Windscreen impact. Go on."

So a white swan shadow must have appeared after all for an atom instant to the pilot.

There is a shattering explosion: Fragments of Plexiglas, titanium alloy, animal matter. A frame at a time, the aircraft disintegrates with a final flare of red stars into the sea.

The noise follows it on tape: the call of the swan; two quick bursts of cannon fire; two last words of Russian. "Petya . . . Storozhevoy." An afterburning roar.

Then silence.

"Be a guardian for our children, Petya . . ."

A man once a chrysalis cries in the Briefing Room.

On film and in memory, a white feather drifts to join the two locked bodies floating with their flowers on the black and crimson waters of the Baltic. Of Tuonela.

POSTSCRIPT

From *The Washington Post,* June 9, 1976, dateline Stockholm:

... In the small hours of last November 9, the *Storozhevoy,* a Soviet destroyer armed with guided missiles, slipped from its berth at Riga and sailed west without orders.

The ship, one of the new *Krivak* class and part of the Baltic fleet, had been in Riga helping celebrate the 58th anniversary of the Bolshevik revolution. Some of its crew of 250 were undoubtedly left on shore, at liberty or sleeping off a binge.

The leaders of the mutiny on the *Storozhevoy*—for nothing less was taking place—probably counted on the festivities to give them extra time to escape. But according to authoritative Swedish military sources who monitored the fantastic episode with radio and radar, the mutineers were cruelly disappointed.

Riga's harbor master turned in an alarm for the missing ship inside the 30 minutes that is standard operating procedure in the Russian navy. Naval headquarters ashore tried to contact the *Storozhevoy* by radio but received only silence. The puzzled commander sent planes out over the Gulf to find the ship. It was located heading for the Irben Sound, the open sea and the Swedish island of Gotland.

Now Moscow had to be brought in. So excited were the Soviet military that they did not communicate in code but in the clear, in easily understandable Russian.

Moscow reacted vigorously. Riga was ordered to send out a

task force and bring back the errant destroyer at any cost.

About ten planes—Swedish sources are deliberately vague about the number their radar screens picked up—half of them Bears from the Maritime Command and half bombers from the Soviet air force set off in pursuit. They were accompanied by a patrol boat and another *Krivak*-class destroyer.

Four hours after the *Storozhevoy* set out, she was caught. She had reached the Irben Sound and the open sea lay in front of her.

From the sea the errant ship was ordered to "lie dead in the water." The vessel was manned by only a fraction of its crew— apart from those still ashore, it is likely that officers and men unwilling to mutiny were locked in their cabins—and there was little it could do.

The ship had been cruising at half speed. It lacked the men and skills to man its missiles. To fire at the pursuers would invite suicide, sure destruction by the bombers overhead.

The *Storozhevoy* chose to plow on. From Moscow came orders to "fire." The bombers probably dropped their load in a circle around the ship to avoid sinking her. The planes did fire less powerful rockets and that, as one naval officer here said, "made believers" of the mutinous crew. In the confusion, however, some of the rockets hit and holed the pursuing *Krivak* destroyer. . . .

. . . So the mutiny ended and the *Storozhevoy* meekly sailed back to Riga. . . . The damaged destroyer was hidden in an inlet outside Riga until it could be repaired and shown to the world again. Altogether perhaps 50 Soviet sailors lost their lives, either at sea or through the workings of military justice.

Not a word of this, so far as is known, has appeared in the Soviet press. But Moscow was not caught completely by surprise. Months before the affair, *Red Star,* the Soviet military journal, had carried articles warning of the sloppy discipline in the Baltic Fleet. One piece even singled out the *Storozhevoy* by name for its poor food, cramped quarters and "lack of ideological consciousness." The article characteristically called for better leadership. . . .

. . . NATO sources treat the incident as a serious indicator of trouble. Russian ships are undoubtedly sophisticated, these officers say, and great in number. But the mutiny shows that the sailors themselves may be an uncertain force whose reliability in combat is not assured.

The Swedish military take a different view. They look at the *Storozhevoy* as a sport or wild card. Having watched and heard the whole affair, Swedes are impressed with the speed and force with which it was resolved.

Those who think this shows military weakness, said one military man, "are a little stupid. There is not a point of weakness. This demonstrates a will and a skill in making decisions. It shows the Russians are strong enough to do what is necessary."

Apart from these differences of interpretation, a deep human mystery remains: What prompted the sailors on the *Storozhevoy* to risk everything on such a wild gamble?...

From *Paris-Match*, May 15, 1976:

...At 0800 hours, on that morning of 8 November, 1975, the Soviet Coast Guard ships boarded the *Storozhevoy*. It was less than 30 nautical miles from the Swedish Coast.

Repression was immediate, in Riga. The leaders were sentenced to death and executed on the spot. The rest were deported. The whole crew was replaced. The ship was put back in record time. Shortly thereafter it took part in a number of official celebrations, colors flying. At present the *Storozhevoy* is on a "prestige" mission in the Red Sea to make its name forgotten on the coasts of the Baltic....

From the *Berlingske Tidende:* Copenhagen, August 11, 1976:

Russian Admiral: "Among us Mutiny is Unthinkable."
"...Mutiny on a Soviet naval ship in the Baltic—unthinkable. It must be a hoax played by organs established for this purpose which pursue their thwarting aims in the West," Vice-Admiral V. Sidorov, deputy commander of the Soviet Baltic Fleet, told *Berlingske Tidende* at a press conference yesterday.

Vice-Admiral Sidorov's comment is the first Soviet pronouncement—even though it was a denial—on the episode.

"Stories of that sort which appear in the Western world can only invite ridicule among us. We do not believe that we even have to comment on that sort of thing," the Vice-Admiral, who is visiting Copenhagen as the commander of two older Soviet ships, a *Kotlin*-class destroyer and a *Mirka* 1-class corvette, added.

The Vice-Admiral did not want to comment on the torpedo episode in the Baltic last June in which an East German naval ship tried to steal a Danish practice torpedo.

"There is no question of any increase of any Soviet naval activity in the Baltic. Sources which speak of things like that have it all wrong," the Vice-Admiral stated.

He could not agree with Western claims that Soviet strategy has shifted from a defensive to an offensive posture, despite the fact that the Soviet Union today is building more and larger naval craft than the Western powers. . . .

Bestsellers from Berkley
The books you've been hearing about—and want to read

___**THE BIDDERS**	04606-4	$2.75
John Baxter		
___**TROIKA**	04662-1	$2.75
David Gurr		
___**ZEBRA**	04635-4	$2.95
Clark Howard		
___**THE FIRST DEADLY SIN**	04692-3	$2.95
Lawrence Sanders		
___ **THE THIRD WORLD WAR:**		
AUGUST 1985	04477-7	$2.95
General Sir John Hackett, et al.		
___**THE PIERCING**	04563-3	$2.50
John Coyne		
___ **THE WINNER'S CIRCLE**	04500-5	$2.50
Charles Paul Conn		
___ **MOMMIE DEAREST**	04444-0	$2.75
Christina Crawford		
___ **NURSE**	04685-0	$2.75
Peggy Anderson		
___ **THE SIXTH COMMANDMENT**	04271-5	$2.75
Lawrence Sanders		
___**SINCERELY, RONALD**		
REAGAN	04885-1	$2.50
Edited by Helene von Damm		
___**A TIME FOR ACTION**	04840-3	$2.75
William E. Simon		

Berkley Book Mailing Service
P.O. Box 690
Rockville Centre, NY 11570

Please send me the above titles. I am enclosing $
(Please add 50¢ per copy to cover postage and handling). Send check or
money order—no cash or C.O.D.'s. Allow six weeks for delivery

NAME

ADDRESS

CITY   STATE/ZIP

71